Gary E. Parker

DEATH STALKS A HOLIDAY

Publishers Since 1798

THOMAS NELSON PUBLISHERS
Nashville • Atlanta • London • Vancouver

I have three women in my house—Melody, my wife, and Andrea and Ashley, my two daughters. Each of them loves to read. So it is primarily for them that I write. To them I dedicate these pages.

Published in Nashville, Tennessee, by Thomas Nelson, Inc., Publishers, and distributed in Canada by Word Communications, Ltd., Richmond, British Columbia, and in the United Kingdom by Word (UK), Ltd., Milton Keynes, England.

Scripture quotations are taken from the HOLY BIBLE, NEW INTERNATIONAL VERSION ®. Copyright © 1973, 1978, 1984 by International Bible Society. Used by permission of Zondervan Bible Publishing House. All rights reserved.

The "NIV" and "New International Version" trademarks are registered in the United States Patent and Trademark Office by International Bible Society. Use of either trademark requires the permission of International Bible Society.

Library of Congress Cataloging-in-Publication Data

Parker, Gary E.
    Death stalks a holiday : sequel to Beyond a reasonable doubt / Gary E. Parker.
      p.   cm.
    ISBN 0-7852-7784-6
    1. Serial murders—Fiction. I. Title.
PS3566.A6784D43 1996
813'.54—dc20   95–31658
                                                    CIP

Printed in the United States of America

1 2 3 4 5 6 7 - 02 01 00 99 98 97 96

Chapter 1

Friday, November 25

Looking around the parking lot to make sure no one saw her, Leslie Staton leaned over and pulled her red high heels off her size-five feet. The new shoes, purchased only six hours ago for this once-in-a-lifetime night, had cost her just over three hundred dollars. Savoring the moment, Leslie stood in her stockings and caressed the soft leather of the heels and thought of what they represented—style, wealth, a different way of life, a life with no more worries about money. Not that she'd grown up poor. The two incomes her parents earned—her father a manager of a supermarket and her mother a fifth grade teacher—had provided well enough. But Leslie had never experienced luxury. Now that would change—for herself and her parents.

With the glee of a five-year-old unwrapping a Barbie doll, Leslie lifted the shoes over her head. Then, not caring who saw her, she jumped her petite body high into the chilly air and clicked her heels together. She couldn't remember the last time she'd felt so totally thrilled.

Twenty stories above her, in the plush offices of the TransSouth Building, temporary headquarters of the Atlanta Braves, her husband, Hal, and his agent were tidying up the details of his first long-term major league contract. After winning nineteen games, making the All-Star team, and finishing third in the Cy Young Award voting, Hal had earned a substantial increase over the major league minimum the Braves had paid him for his first two years in the big leagues. The new contract would pay him 1.3 million dollars per year over the next three years.

Talk about a fantastic day! Yesterday she and Hal had celebrated their impending good fortune by driving up to Atlanta from Cordele. A meal at their favorite eatery—The Black Velvet Inn—complete with prime rib for both and the best jazz ensemble in the South—served as the appetizer for the enchanted evening that followed. They danced until one, and after that, well, Leslie smiled, words couldn't describe what happened after that.

They had slept late Friday morning, eaten a brunch with Hal's mom and dad, and then visited three different malls. Afterward, they left Hal's folks at their condo and rushed to the 4:00 P.M. meeting with the Braves' high brass. It had taken almost two hours to go through the fine print on the contract. But finally, Hal and the Braves completed the transaction. He signed the dotted line and made himself and his ecstatic wife, Leslie, instant millionaires.

With her red heeled shoes still in her hands, Leslie pranced slowly toward her car. She knew she needed to hurry, to hustle back to the condo, pick up Hal's mom and dad, and get to the restaurant before their reservations expired. That's why Hal had sent her ahead. He needed her to pick up his parents while he finished up. But she just couldn't rush herself. Events like this deserved some savoring.

She lifted her hands over her head like a referee signaling a touchdown and stretched luxuriously. A whiff of wood smoke hit her nostrils as she inhaled the cool air of the last Friday of November. Somebody was making use of a fireplace.

Leslie stopped walking and twisted slowly around and around, once, twice, three times. All around her, the lights of downtown Atlanta twinkled. To her left, one of the skyscrapers sported the outline of a golden Christmas tree across its front. Another season of celebration had begun.

Leslie suddenly felt a twinge of guilt. Though not zealously religious, she did believe in God and knew that some being beyond herself had surely blessed her and Hal. To this point, though, she had felt no sense of gratitude for her good fortune.

She swallowed hard and made a decision. She would go to church on Sunday and express her thankfulness in a tangible way. A gush of warmth washed over her, and a bright smile broke out on her cherubic face. She and Hal would certainly celebrate this Christmas.

The lights in the parking lot flickered on and stirred Leslie out of her musings. Hugging herself against the quickly dropping temperature, she glanced at her watch. 5:42—already almost fifteen minutes late for their reservation and she still had to go by the condo.

Rushing now, Leslie padded across the concrete toward section C. Two rows away, she spotted her tan Toyota Camry, a 1988 vintage with 112,000 miles on its odometer and a dent the size of a coffee table on the front left fender. One of their first purchases, she decided, slipping her shoes under her left armpit and thumbing through her purse for her keys, would be a new car—maybe a BMW.

Approaching from the rear, she reached the Camry. A frown crossed her face. A black van on the driver's side of her car was parked only a few inches away.

She saw instantly that she, even at her tiny ninety-nine pounds, couldn't slide through the narrow space between the vehicles. Shrugging, she walked around to the passenger side and pointed her key at the car door. Her eyes glanced down. She couldn't believe her bad luck. The right front tire was as flat as an ironing board.

A flush of red climbed up her neck, and her pulse pounded several notches higher. They would miss their reservation. Worse still, by now Hal's folks would be wondering what had happened to her. Hal's dad hated being late. In fact, if he weren't fifteen minutes early, he usually complained.

Leslie sighed and told herself to calm down. No way she could have avoided this. It wasn't her fault. Don't sweat the small stuff. She and her husband were beautiful and young and wealthy and deliciously in love, and the Christmas season ruled the air. No need to fret.

The red on her neck receded, and her heart rate slowed back down. No reason to let a flat tire ruin this day. She would simply go back into the building, call an auto service, and have them come and fix the flat. She could take a taxi to pick up her in-laws, or she could wait on Hal—no matter how long it took him.

Throwing her keys into her purse, she bent over to slip on her shoes. The headlights of an approaching car crawled across the pavement and lit up her toes. Leslie looked up and saw a white Mercedes pull to a stop beside her. The tinted window on the driver's side of the Mercedes buzzed down, and a man's slender face stared out at her. The sound of a Christmas carol, "O Holy Night," rolled out of the Mercedes. "O holy night, the stars were brightly shining. It was the night of the dear Savior's birth."

Leslie stood and stared through the shadows at the man. Though she couldn't see him clearly, he looked unusual, somehow slightly frail, almost effeminate. Thick gray hair blanketed his head, and his cheekbones sat high on his face, almost directly under his eyes. His teeth gleamed under the lights from the parking lot.

"Is there a problem, miss?" he asked. His voice was flat, soft, and toneless.

"A flat tire," said Leslie.

"They happen at the worst times," said the man.

"Fall on your knees! O hear the angel voices . . ." the music from the radio continued to float through the night air.

"Well, this one certainly did," agreed Leslie.

"Can I help?" he asked.

Leslie paused. It would take five minutes to get to a phone inside the TransSouth Building. Maybe ten to get back upstairs to Hal. More time for Hal's dad to stew.

"I need to use a phone," she said.

"At your command," said the silver-haired stranger. "Here."

He turned and pulled a phone from the console beside him. "At your disposal." He pushed it through his window, and Leslie took a step nearer, grabbed the phone, and punched information. The sound of a coughing engine caught her attention for a second. Four rows over, a pickup truck backed up, shifted gears, and drove away.

An operator answered Leslie's call. "Give me the number of Triple A Auto," she said.

Repeating the number so she wouldn't forget it, Leslie dialed Triple A. A busy signal rewarded her efforts. She ground her teeth together, shook her head at the man in the Mercedes, and tried again. A blue Taurus pulled up behind the Mercedes and beeped its horn. The driver's side window closed and snuffed out the sounds of "O Holy Night." The Mercedes eased into a parking space two spots down from her Toyota, and the driver stepped out.

The Triple A number rang. *Great,* thought Leslie, *at least it's not still busy.* She threw a thumbs-up sign to the gray-haired man as he leaned back against the front fender of his car. The man wasn't very tall, Leslie noted, not more than seven or eight inches taller than her 5'1". His gray hair seemed out of place on his face, and she couldn't tell his age—between thirty-five and forty-five she guessed. She wondered why he had grayed so soon. Maybe a lot of stress. She noted his starched white shirt, gold watch, and fresh black shoes. A man of obvious refinement.

"Triple A, what can we do for you?"

Leslie smiled, exhaled, and turned her attention to the phone. Rushing, she explained her situation and gave her location. Assured by the operator that help would arrive within fifteen minutes, she hung up. Finally, some good luck. Maybe she could get to the condo within the hour.

She turned toward the Mercedes, looking for her gray-haired rescuer. She didn't see him. She stood still for a beat, scanning the parking lot. Had he gotten back into his car?

Confused, Leslie walked toward the Mercedes, trying to see through the darkened glass of the windshield. She needed to give the man his phone, thank him for his help.

She reached the car and leaned over the driver's side window. Cupping her hands around her cheeks to block out the glare of the parking lot lights, she stared inside but saw no one. Where had the man gone? Puzzled, she started to raise up. Something cold touched the back of her throat. It felt like steel. She froze instantly in place.

"Sharp is the knife you feel," said a voice behind her, its tone breathy and small. "Follow my commands, or die where you stand."

Leslie's throat turned a nervous red that rose upward into her face. She tried to think, to focus on the odd words and strange voice behind her. She wondered if her attacker was the man in the Mercedes. She couldn't tell by the tone of the voice.

Getting more panicky by the moment, Leslie's mind jumbled up, and she found herself unable to fight back. She knew what she should do. She should fight, that's what all the experts said—fight, scream, run, yell, do anything but go along with the attacker.

She opened her mouth to scream, to call for Hal, to yell for anyone within the sound of her voice. But when she squeezed her throat together, nothing came out. Her voice died in her chest, and though she choked herself trying, her vocal cords emitted no sound. A sense of numb disbelief washed over her, and she felt like she did the day she had her appendix taken out, when the doctor had put her under anesthesia. Her arms hung limply at her side, and her legs started to quiver. She knew she was about to pass out.

The cold metal of the knife slipped from the back of her throat to the front. "Move to your left," said the breathy voice.

As compliant as a puppet, she obeyed, taking a step to the left. Inside her head, though, the movement jarred her back to reality. She needed to hang on for only a few minutes. The repair truck from Triple A would reach her, or someone would drive through the parking lot and see what was happening. If she could only stay alive until then— until someone saw the tragedy about to occur and stepped in to stop it.

Within ten steps she and her abductor reached the black van beside her Toyota. An arm wrapped in a black jacket reached to the back of the van and swung the door open.

"Get in," said the voice.

For an instant, Leslie hesitated. She sensed she had to do something now if she planned to survive. If she ever crawled inside the van she would never crawl out, would never see Hal again, would never bear his children, would never sit by the fireside and grow old with him.

A surge of anger swept through her. She clutched her hands into a fist. She would not die without a fight.

With a scream that cut through the air like a panther screech, she suddenly twisted around, raised her right foot off the ground, and aimed for the genitals of her attacker. A knee blocked her kick.

She raised her hands, her fingernails bared, reaching for the skin of his face. Her fingers never reached their target.

A quick blow, as forceful as the chop of an ax, struck her across the side of her throat.

With a muffled groan Leslie Staton collapsed onto the pavement. From somewhere far away, she heard a slight grunt and felt a pair of arms wrap around her waist. The arms lifted her up, moved her through the air, then laid her down again. Her face landed softly on what seemed like carpet. A second later, the dark closed in, and she felt nothing else.

Five minutes later, the black van pulled onto Interstate 285 and headed north away from downtown Atlanta. Sliding into the whiz of Friday afternoon traffic, the driver twisted on the radio and dialed through the stations. The sound of Elvis Presley oozed through the speeding vehicle. "I'll have a blue Christmas without you . . ."

Listening to the music, the driver laughed. A blue Christmas indeed.

Chapter 2

Though a spot of sweat the shape of Florida cut through the back of his blue cotton shirt, Hal Staton tried to remain calm as he closed the door and stepped into the outer offices of the general manager of the Atlanta Braves. But he couldn't hold in his excitement forever.

With the general manager of the Braves no longer watching, he let out his pent-up glee. A whoop reminiscent of a Texas cowhand jumped from his lips, and he grabbed his agent, Rex Stamps, in his burly arms, lifted him into the air, and twisted him around and around and around. The air whirled faster and faster, and Hal felt himself getting dizzy.

Not wanting to make himself sick, he gradually slowed down his well-muscled body, easing the merry-go-round gently to a halt. Dropping Rex onto a leather sofa, Hal fell into it beside him. After a couple of moments, the room stopped swirling, and he paused to take a breath. He noticed a grinning brunette secretary sitting behind a desk not more than ten feet away. He laughed out loud at the secretary. She smiled wider. The phone rang. The secretary picked it up, identified herself, listened for a couple of seconds, then raised her eyebrows at Hal.

"It's for you," she said. "Your father."

Hal shrugged at Rex, raised himself from the sofa, and reached for the phone. "Yeah, Pop, what's up?" he asked.

"We've missed our reservations," snorted Mr. Staton.

The blond eyebrows over Hal's blue eyes squeezed together and met over his nose like a golden brush. "How's that, Pop? Leslie left here about an hour ago to pick up you and Mom and take you to the restaurant. I had to stay here a bit longer, make sure Rex didn't foul up anything."

"Well, she's not here," said Mr. Staton, his voice irritated. "Any way she misunderstood you? Went to the restaurant by herself?"

Hal bit his lip and considered the possibilities for a second. "Nope, don't think so. She specifically said she would swing by for you and Mom, that you three would go ahead and get our table."

"Maybe traffic caught her somewhere."

Hal wanted to believe that but knew it wasn't likely. The condo was less than three miles away. Even with heavy Friday traffic, it wouldn't take an hour to reach them. But if not a traffic jam, then what? Car trouble? That would explain it.

He cupped his stubby fingers over the phone and turned to Rex. "Call the restaurant, Rex. Leslie never showed up at the condo."

Rex turned to the secretary. "You got another phone?" he asked.

"Yeah, next office. I'll show you." Rex and the secretary stood and scooted out of the room.

Hal spoke to his dad again. "Look, Pop, I don't know what happened to Leslie. Maybe the Toyota broke down. It's got over 100,000 miles on it. If that's not it, then all I can figure is she got lost somehow, got turned around on the interstate or something. Rex is checking the restaurant just in case she got fouled up and went on over there. I'll leave here right now. If she had car trouble, I'll find her on the way over."

"You want me and Mama to wait here?"

"Yeah, Pop. Nothing else you can do. I'll be there in a few minutes. Don't worry about a thing." He popped the phone into its cradle.

Rex stuck his head back into the office and shook it. "She's not at the restaurant," he said. "Or at least they couldn't find her."

"Doesn't make sense," said Hal. "It's not like Les to run off somewhere without telling me."

Rex laughed. "Listen, Hal. Leslie just watched you sign a million-dollar contract. That kind of thing might have sent her over the edge a bit. I bet she's at Lenox Mall right now, spending a big chunk of the money you just made."

Hal smiled with his buddy, and the gap between his two front teeth made him look like a young Tom Sawyer. Nodding good-bye to the secretary, he marched out of the office and took the elevator to the lobby. Within five minutes he and Rex had passed the security guard at the entrance of the thirty-story building and made their way through the parking lot to Rex's car.

Walking up behind the black Lexus, Hal suddenly stopped. His mouth fell open, and he stuffed his hands into his pants' pockets. Behind Rex's Lexus, under the lights of the parking lot, he saw his own Toyota Camry. He twisted to Rex and tilted his head sideways.

"That's my car," he said, his voice barely a whisper.

Rex nodded and stepped over to it. He tried the door. It was locked. He peered inside for a second, then turned back to Hal.

"What gives, Hal?" he asked. "You think she caught a cab?"

Hal didn't answer. A breeze picked up his blond hair and whipped it into odd strands, making him appear wild and unruly. His blue eyes sat wide and open over his broad face. He gritted his teeth and a vein in his left jaw popped up and turned purple. When he spoke, his voice sounded deep as death.

"Her shoe," he said.

"What?" asked Rex, confusion written on his face.

"Her shoe, over there."

Rex followed the path of Hal's eyes as they stared down at the asphalt parking lot. He saw the shoe. A red high heel. Sitting heel down and top up beside the right back tire of the Toyota. Sitting there naked and alone as if something or someone had lifted Leslie right out of it and whisked her away into the darkness of the chilled November air.

Chapter 3

Monday, November 28

Rasheed Ruoff had worked as a custodian at the capitol building in downtown Atlanta since 1954. Part of his daily assignment called for him to get to the building before anyone else and sweep off the granite steps that led like a concrete wave up to the front of the mammoth structure. Since 1989 he'd used a gas air blower to do the trick.

The job, surprisingly, never bored him. It had never bored him because cleaning these steps was, surprisingly, a job for the curious. And he was a curious man. Always had been, even though he had never graduated from high school. Didn't take formal education to guarantee curiosity.

Rasheed loved to climb out of his maintenance truck just as the first rays of the sun licked down on the earth, strap the gas blower to his sixty-four-year-old shoulders, and walk out to the first step. The feel of the sun's heat climbing onto his back thrilled him. Carrying the heat of that sun, he liked to begin his work—one row of steps at a time across the wide expanse of concrete. When he finished one row, he moved to the next, up and across, up and across, up and across.

Scattered through the years, Rasheed had found the most amazing things on those granite steps. Six months after the fall of Saigon, he had almost tripped and stabbed himself on a Marine's silver sword, broken in half. In 1979, a tractor tire turned up the morning the state senate voted down a farmer's aid bill. He'd found a hundred-dollar bill twice (and scores of smaller denominations not worth mentioning). One Christmas a box full of Bibles, drenched by a December rain, rewarded his efforts. The year Hank Aaron broke Babe Ruth's record for home runs, a picture of The Hammer in a gold-ringed frame sat on the top row of the steps.

Rasheed couldn't even remember most of what he found—coins and bottles and beer cans and pairs of underwear and shoes and hats. Most days he didn't find anything worth remembering. But the occasional reward kept his head down, his eyes focused on the concrete at his feet. He didn't want to miss anything.

It seemed to Rasheed that people came to the capitol and dispensed with their mementos because they wanted to memorialize something, wanted to mark a line of shifting and changing in their lives, wanted to leave an old thing behind so they could get on with something else.

His joy came from finding the old thing and trying to use it to figure out the new. The articles he found served as his clues, and when he found himself getting bored with his job, he forced himself to think of one of these artifacts, to try and imagine the kind of person who tossed it aside.

On Monday morning, Rasheed Ruoff followed his usual routine. He stepped out of the maintenance truck, zipped up his jacket against the frosty air, and slipped on a pair of gloves. Pulling the gas blower from the truck bed, he strapped it over his shoulders and shuffled across the lawn toward the capitol steps. The grass, frozen white as sugar on a doughnut, crunched under his feet.

He hummed as he walked, stretching his back and looking up into the gray slate of the morning sky. It looked like it might rain, maybe even snow a bit. Clouds as thick as shag carpet hung low over the horizon and kept the sun blocked out. Rasheed stopped humming. This wasn't his favorite kind of day. Suddenly, his bones felt stiff, and he thought for a moment of next April when he would reach retirement age.

He reached the bottom step and switched on the blower. A sheaf of brown leaves jumped up as if wakened from a hard sleep and flew away from the blower and off into the frigid air. A candy wrapper followed the leaves as Rasheed slowly aimed the blower at the steps. The dust and trash of the weekend past zipped and whirled and dashed away as he advanced. He finished the bottom step and mounted the second one. After that came the third.

One after another he made his attack, blow the steps across and up, blow the steps across and up, one level following another, up and blow, up and blow, up and blow. He started to hum again as he worked, hoping the humming and the movement would loosen his back and lift his mood. He reached the midpoint of the steps, halfway from the bottom and halfway from the top. He paused to catch his breath.

For the first time that morning, he raised his eyes to the top of the capitol steps. He puckered his lips and lowered the blower. His humming stopped and his brow wrinkled like folds in a blanket. A black bag the length of a bed lay directly beneath the center column that anchored the domed building in the center of the top step.

Rasheed switched off the blower. It looked to him like somebody had deliberately left that black bag in such a conspicuous spot. For a second, he thought it was a carry-on bag—like traveling folks used to carry their suits and shirts on an airplane. But no, it seemed thicker than that. *Like a—well,* he thought, *like a body bag.*

Unhooking the strap that held the blower across his shoulders, Rasheed laid the contraption down and climbed the concrete stair steps. As he drew closer to the black bag, his stride widened, and he took the steps two at a time.

Within a couple of minutes he reached the top step. The bag, about seven feet long he figured, lay at his feet. The bag looked like it was made of plastic or an imitation leather. A metal zipper cut through the heart of it. The bag swelled out wider in the center and narrowed off at the top and bottom.

Rasheed knew something lay inside the bag, and for a second, he wondered what to do. Should he open it?

He twisted around, halfway hoping to see a security man. None in sight. He glanced at his watch. 6:19 A.M. Should he get someone else to open the bag?

Rasheed nudged the black bag with his toe and started humming again. This might be the biggest find of his career. It might be the one to keep him guessing for the rest of his life, all through his retirement and beyond. If he didn't open it, he would never see. Someone else would come and usher him away. Someone else would open the bag, and Rasheed would go to his grave kicking himself for letting this one get away.

He bent over and touched the zipper. It felt cold, like a frozen ice tray. He lifted the zipper and pulled it up ever so slowly from the bottom toward the top. The zipper reached the midpoint of the bag. Rasheed let go the zipper and took both sides of the bag in his hands.

As if peeking through a keyhole at sights he shouldn't see, Rasheed tugged the two sides of the bag apart and peered inside. His fingers trembled.

"Sweet mother of Methuselah," said Rasheed. He dropped the folds of the leather.

But the bag didn't close completely. Instead, the bottom third gaped open and Rasheed stared into it. Inside he saw the find of his life.

A red high heel. A red high heel attached to the left foot of a dead and naked woman.

Chapter 4

"Wake up, Star Trek," said Debbi Anderson as she rolled over on the bed and shook her husband's shoulders. Without opening his eyes, Burke sleepily raised a hand to wave off her admonition.

Though eager to begin the day, Debbi paused for an instant trying to make a decision. Roust out her husband of six weeks or give him a few more minutes to snooze? Deciding to practice charity, she chose the second option.

She had learned in their six weeks of marriage that, unlike herself, Burke liked to slide gradually into consciousness. As he put it, most of the heart attacks men suffer happen between 7:00 and 9:00 A.M. as they get up to start the day. Obviously, climbing out of bed was a tough experience, and he didn't like to rush into it.

Relaxing beside him, Debbi sighed contentedly and threw a leg over his side. For several minutes she lay still, staring at him and enjoying the sound of his rhythmic breathing. A blaze of sun cut through the multihued drapes to the left of the bed and lit up his brown hair. A breeze blew through the open window and fluttered his bangs off his forehead, making his long eyelashes more prominent. The sound of ocean waves washed in behind the breeze.

Debbi squeezed her leg tighter around Burke and smiled. She'd given him the nickname "Star Trek" because his old one didn't fit anymore. In college his friends had called him "Freon"—because of his cool approach to life, especially to women. He'd been shy back then, almost too much so.

Debbi snuggled closer to his back. That cool approach had evaporated after he met her. So she named him "Star Trek"—because marriage was a strange new land, and he was eager to explore it.

She touched Burke's face and traced the line of his strong chin. Leaving his chin, she ran her fingers down to his chest.

Though not tall, just a shadow under six feet, Burke had a strong body. He stayed in shape by running nearly forty miles per week and doing some light weight lifting at a local health club.

Debbi's smile became a grin, and she pinched Burke's right bicep. Whether he liked it or not, she had waited long enough. It was time to wake up.

"Wake up, O mate of mine," she whispered, gently poking him in the ribs. "Time's a-wasting."

"What's the rush?" grumbled Burke, slowly opening his copper-colored eyes. "We're off for the day, the Atlantic Ocean is right outside our door, and we've got nowhere to go and no one rushing us. Relax and enjoy."

"But I don't want to sleep away such a glorious morning."

Scraping his eyelids, Burke raised up, stared at his watch for a skip, then moaned and flopped back onto his pillow. "I don't think there's any chance of that. It's barely seven thirty. Leave me alone until ten." He slammed his eyes shut.

Debbi huffed out a big breath but decided not to push it. Let him put it off a few more minutes. After all, she did enjoy lying beside him, watching him sleep.

She dropped her head onto her pillow and curled up in a fetal position. Goodness, but she did love the guy. Not only was he handsome but he was smart too. A 3.9 average at the University of Georgia. A 4.0 at Wesley Theological Seminary. Practically all A's through his residency at Emory during his doctoral program in psychology. He was working on his dissertation now.

She patted her pillow and breathed a silent prayer of thanksgiving. She had married Burke in October—almost two years after they met. She remembered the night he proposed . . .

⋙

On the last Friday in August, after a year and a half of dating. He had worn his newest suit—a navy blue one with window pane squares. He took her to Johnny B's, an upscale restaurant in Buckhead. After the candlelight dinner, he told her to wait at the table. He needed to get something from the car.

Five minutes later he returned, holding something behind his back. He hauled it out and showed it to her—a rectangular box wrapped in silver and adorned with a red bow.

With a drop of sweat hanging off the end of his nose, he handed her the rectangular box. She took it and placed it on the table. He motioned to her to unwrap it, and she obeyed. Inside the box sat a pair of jogging shoes.

"So we can run together," said Burke, a light sparkle playing in his brown eyes.

"But I don't run," said Debbi.

"Now you can," insisted Burke. "You need to stay in shape. Try them on."

"Here?"

"Sure, no better time than the present."

"I don't think so," said Debbi, shaking her blonde curls. "I didn't wear my sexiest dress to accessorize with Reeboks."

"Do you love me?" asked Burke.

"You know I do," said Debbi.

"Then put on the shoes." The intensity of his voice gave her no choice.

Shrugging, she dropped her black heels to the floor and pulled the right shoe out of the box. Leaning under the table, she shoved her toes into the white canvas.

"What in the world?" She jerked the shoe off and lifted it onto the table. With a quick thump, she bounced its heel on the tablecloth. A shiny round object dropped out of the shoe. A ring. A diamond ring. An engagement ring.

Before she could close her gaping mouth, Burke said, "I think you know what I'm asking, Debbi."

She pouted her lips. "I want to hear you ask it."

Burke exhaled and the candle on the table flickered and almost went out. "Okay, here it is. Will you marry me, Debbi Meyer? Will you marry me and make me the happiest man in the world?"

Debbi smiled. "I will definitely marry you," she said, "but I will not go running with you. . . ."

⁂

Now he lay beside her. The man who made her life complete. A wave of joy rushed through her, and she reached out and touched the side of Burke's face. He had made her life complete in more ways than one. He had led her to God. That brought another kind of completion. The kind that lasted forever.

Debbi took a deep breath. Speaking of forever, if she didn't wake him, he would sleep that long. An impish grin on her face, Debbi raised up, picked up her pillow, and fluffed it out as if about to lie down again. But then, instead of lying down, she suddenly slammed the pillow onto Burke's head. Whap. The sound ricocheted off the walls of the hotel room, and a second whap followed right behind it.

By the time the second blow hit, Burke had jerked himself up and grabbed his pillow too. He swung it over his head and brought it down on Debbi's shoulder. She recoiled backward, but only for a moment.

Dodging his second shot, Debbi stood up on the bed. Her blonde hair, cut just above her shoulders, fanned out and framed her face in the morning sun. Her black nightie hugged the contours of her firm body. She took a better hold on her pillow. Before she could use it though, Burke grabbed her by the ankles and tackled her onto the bed.

"Our first fight," he bellowed, burying his head into her stomach, trying to pin her down. "And never forget—you started it."

"I started it?" huffed Debbi, struggling to break free. "No way! You started it by your refusal to wake up and give me the attention I so richly deserve. And if I ever get loose from this stranglehold, I'm going to make you regret that for the rest of your life."

Burke tightened his grip. Debbi reached for his ribs and started tickling him. He started giggling. His grip loosened. She tickled harder.

"Stop it," he moaned. "You know I can't take that, stop it or—"

The phone rang, interrupting his threat. For a second neither of them paid it any attention. The phone jangled a second time, then a third.

"You going to answer that?" asked Debbi, her sharp fingernails easing off his ribs.

"Will you stop tickling me if I do?"

"Never."

"Will you let me go?"

"Never."

The phone rang again.

"But it might be important."

"Okay, let's declare a truce until I answer the phone."

"Agreed. A truce is declared."

Simultaneously, the two stopped struggling, and Burke leaned across the bed and picked up the phone. "Hello," he said. After a couple of seconds, he bit his lower lip and handed the phone to Debbi. "It's for you."

She took it. "Hello, this is Debbi."

"Yes, Debbi, this is Mimi Stoddard."

Debbi rolled her eyes toward the ceiling. Mimi Stoddard, her new boss at the *Atlanta Independent.*

"This isn't the best time, Mimi," said Debbi. "As you know, I'm on a long weekend. I'm not scheduled back in until tomorrow."

"Yes, I know," said Stoddard. "And I do apologize for calling you. But circumstances here leave me no choice. As you know, we're a bit shorthanded since the new ownership took over and cleaned out the deadwood. We've got fewer reporters than before but just as much news."

A wave of mixed emotions washed over Debbi. Though Mimi Stoddard had been her boss for only three months and Debbi didn't know her too well, she suspected she wouldn't have called unless something extremely newsworthy had happened.

Debbi licked her lips and squeezed the phone tighter. She raised her eyebrows at Burke. Something that newsworthy might mean she needed to go back before tonight. She hated the thought of doing that. But a story important enough for Mimi Stoddard to call her like this must be hot. She sighed and focused her attention on the phone.

"I'm listening," she said.

Burke leaned over and began kissing her back. She rubbed his thick hair with her free hand. On the other end of the line, Stoddard cleared her throat.

"The wife of Hal Staton turned up dead on the steps of the Georgia capitol building this morning. The cops just identified her for the press."

Debbi sucked in her breath, and her body tensed like a tree branch being pulled back in a strong wind. She stopped stroking Burke's hair. He stopped kissing her neck. "The wife of the Braves' pitcher?" she asked.

"None other. She disappeared Friday night. In the parking lot of the TransSouth Building. The Braves have a temporary office there while they're remodeling the stadium complex. Staton filed a missing person's report right after dark. The cops searched all weekend but found no trace of his wife until this morning."

"Who found her?"

"A custodian at the capitol. She was wrapped up in a body bag. Naked and dead."

The breeze from the open window blew across her face, and Debbi suddenly felt cold. She shivered and fingered a strand of her blonde hair, pushing it toward the corner of her mouth.

"How'd she die?" asked Debbi.

"Not exactly sure yet. Police aren't saying much, and we haven't had time yet to dig too deeply. The medical examiner will give a report soon enough. Probably doing his duty right now. That's why I need you here. Somebody's got to get busy on this one, and you're one of the few experienced reporters we have."

Debbi stuck the strand of hair into her mouth and chewed on it for a moment. She knew Stoddard was right. Three months ago a conglomerate from New Zealand had purchased the *Independent* from longtime and legendary owner Nelson Steadman. Wanting to cut costs, the new management had wasted no time issuing pink slips and early retirement packages to more than two-thirds of the old team. Stan Wraps, Debbi's beloved former editor, fell to the ax as did Randy Fontly, Linda Clips, and a whole host of other good people.

The team hired to replace them was primarily younger and less experienced. Younger meant cheaper. That seemed to matter most to the new owners.

That's why Debbi figured she kept her job. Because she was a veteran of only three years herself. Still inexpensive.

She had thought about quitting as a show of support to her friends. But Stan Wraps talked her out of it. "You stick with it," he said. "Do your job. Build your reputation. Within a few years you can make your move. Work for any paper you want. But not yet."

Taking his advice, she had stayed. That made her one of the more experienced reporters on staff. One of the few who could handle this kind of story with any kind of expertise. She pushed her hair out of her mouth. A childish habit, she knew. One she had decided to stop.

"I need to call you back," she said to Stoddard.

"Okay," said Stoddard. "But do it within the half hour. I need you here by this evening. The cops have set a press conference for 7:00 P.M., and I'm counting on you to cover it."

Hearing Stoddard's insistent tone, Debbi frowned, hung up the phone, and turned to Burke.

"What's going on?" he asked, his eyes wide awake.

"A murder in Atlanta. Leslie Staton, Hal Staton's wife. Stoddard wants me back to cover it."

Burke pushed his pillow behind his head and lay back in the bed. "But this is our last day," he said.

Debbi knew Burke was right. Stoddard shouldn't be so insistent. She could return tonight and dig in with the story first thing in the morning. What difference would one day make?

She took a quick, deep breath and tried to calm herself.

No need to get angry at Stoddard though. This thing had two sides to it. Stoddard was handing her the lead on a major story, a story with national implications. Any reporter worth the ink in her pen would jump at that kind of opportunity. How could she not go back and get in on the action from the first day? Fall one day behind and she might never catch up.

Burke raised up, opened his arms, and leaned over close to her. She fell into his arms and felt his warm chest against her body. For several seconds, she closed her eyes, enjoying the quiet moment.

"What are you going to do?" he asked.

She sighed but said nothing. Burke loosened his arms from her, pulled away, and climbed out of bed. In bare feet, he walked to the window and stared out at the ocean waves bouncing along the shore. After a few moments, he turned back to her.

"You want to go back, don't you?" he asked.

She shrugged. "If I wait until tomorrow, Stoddard might decide I'm not her kind of reporter, might decide I'm not willing to pay the price to handle the lead stories. I'd hate for that to happen."

Burke left the window and moved back to the bed. He sat down and put his arms around her again.

"Let's get packed," he said.

"Are you sure?" asked Debbi. "I don't want you to think my work is more important than our time together. If you're going to be mad later, tell me now, and I won't go. We'll stay right here all day, we'll—"

Burke placed a finger over her lips and shushed her. "It's all right, Debbi. I think we should go back. We've had two good days and three fantastic nights. I would love to have the rest of the day with you, but I'm proud of your career, too, glad for what you do. It's what brought us together, remember? Another story you covered."

Debbi nodded. A newspaper story had brought them together. She had almost died covering it. But Burke had saved her life.

He continued his reasoning. "I want you to do what you do best." He smiled and started nuzzling her shoulders again. "Well, what you do second best." Burke lowered his lips to her neck.

"You promise you won't get mad if we go back?" she asked, her voice soft and relaxed.

He raised his eyes. "Let's just say you owe me one," he said.

Debbi laughed and threw her arms around his neck. "Any ideas how I can repay you?"

"I'll work hard to think of something."

Chapter 5

Stuart "Stubs" McVaine hunched his five-foot seven-inch frame over the paper-covered metal table and cleared his throat behind his light blue mask. "Let's get started," he said, pointing a glove-covered finger at the body in front of him. Frieda, his bug-eyed assistant, eased her way into position to comply with the order.

Stubs reached for the zipper on the body bag and slipped it down. Per procedure, so as not to contaminate any evidence, the authorities had kept Staton wrapped in the black container. The sound of the zipper cut through the silence of the room. Stubs stared down at the body slowly being uncovered.

The cops had brought her in early that morning, but two other weekend homicides had prevented him from getting to her first thing. Fortunately, the cold weather of the last few days had kept her body in prime condition.

Seeing her now, Stubs wished he could have put off this autopsy forever. Normally he did his job with a calm emotional detachment. But this body was different. The death of Leslie Staton disturbed him more than he dared to admit. Not just because he was a devout Atlanta Braves fan either. No, even though Stubs had attended Braves games back when it wasn't cool, back when they lost far more than they won, the death of Leslie Staton bothered him because he had a daughter about her age. In fact, his girl, Sharon, looked a bit like the picture he had already seen of Leslie Staton. Unfortunately, Staton didn't look much like her picture anymore.

The body was fully exposed now. Stubs forced himself to focus on it. He began his visual scan at her feet. Little feet, size five to five and one-half, he guessed. No injuries to her feet.

His eyes moved upward to her ankles, calves, knees, thighs, chest. A petite woman. Not much more than one hundred pounds, if that. Just like his Sharon.

McVaine grunted and stared at Frieda for a second but said nothing. He looked back at Leslie Staton. Her chest. White as typing paper.

Stubs turned his attention to her hands. Long fingers for such a small woman, he noted. The nails were polished in red, but none of them was broken. Apparently she hadn't put up a struggle. Maybe her abductor had surprised her, given her no chance to fight.

His breath coming in short gasps, Stubs wished he could smoke a cigarette. If he had his way, he would cut a hole through the blue fabric that covered his lips and shove a Salem menthol right through it. But a city ordinance made smoking in city buildings illegal. Stubbs smiled grimly. Other than in the autopsy room, he usually ignored the ordinance.

His eyes moved from Staton's fingers to her wrists. Contusions evident there. Bruises, to say it in layman's terms. Obviously, someone had tied her up, and she had struggled against the binding. Rope maybe. Or some type of wire. Later tests may or may not tell him which one.

Stubs nodded. The bruises hadn't killed her. No, Stubs knew what had killed her. He had seen it the moment he unzipped the body. But he hesitated to look at it again. No one should have to see sights like that. But someone had to do it. As the chief medical examiner for Atlanta for the past seventeen years, that job fell to him.

He took a deep hacking breath, wished for a cigarette again, and turned his attention to Leslie Staton's face. There he saw the evidence of death. A mass of injuries he didn't even care to describe. Injuries that left her face unrecognizable. Injuries caused by the crushing power of some deadly instrument wielded by a maniacal killer. Injuries no one should see, much less inflict.

Stubs shook his head, and the folds of flesh under his chin moved side to side. "Steady," he said, as if talking to Frieda but in reality trying to calm himself. "We've seen worse, we've seen worse."

Frieda nodded at him. Her watery gray eyes bugged out like a frog's over her mask. Stubs stared down at the deceased. Yes, he'd seen worse, but he didn't know if he'd ever seen anything sadder. He knew Leslie Staton had been a beautiful young woman. A woman like Sharon, his daughter. But she would never be beautiful again. Not even the most skilled mortician could do that miracle.

Chapter 6

A sense of foreboding settled on Burke as the highway stripes from Charleston to Atlanta clicked away beneath the wheels of Debbi's old Volvo. He tried to shake off the feeling but couldn't. He kept thinking back to October 31, twenty-five months ago, to the last murder case Debbi had covered. The case that had brought him and Debbi together.

He had shot a man that Halloween night. To protect Debbi and to stay alive himself, he had shot the man and killed him. From time to time, he still dreamed about that dead man. In his dreams, he saw the man's eyes, the bangs of his hair hanging like broom straw on his forehead, his mouth opening as the bullet hit him, opening as if he wanted to catch the bullet in his teeth. The bullet hit him in the head. Stopped him in his tracks and splashed him stone dead into a muddy driveway.

Burke shivered in his seat and glanced over at Debbi. She had dozed off. He shook himself and changed positions behind the wheel.

The experience of two years ago had changed his life. In the year following it, he had shifted career tracks—leaving the pastorate of a rural Methodist church and entering the doctoral program at Emory. Though he felt good about his vocational change, he didn't feel good about the situation that led him to do it. And he certainly didn't want to get mixed up in another murder case. It was too dangerous for him and Debbi.

Sighing, he rubbed his free hand on the pocket of his pants and forced himself to examine his fears. He had no rational reason to think Debbi would face any danger as she covered this story. It wouldn't unfold like last time. She would write the information as she received it, not investigate it herself.

Forcing himself to see the bright side of the situation, Burke pressed the accelerator harder. The miles clicked past. One after another, mile by mile by mile.

He was just depressed, he told himself, depressed over having to end his weekend early. Upset because he had to end the idyllic day before he had planned.

He should feel good for Debbi. This murder would set Atlanta on its ear, and she had the lead for the *Independent*. This gave her another chance to prove herself, another chance to advance her career. The story would unfold safely, he told himself. Debbi would do well. And he would cheer from the sidelines for her as she did.

With that thought in mind, he watched the miles gradually pass. Burke turned the corner of the last intersection and spotted their new home.

Within seconds, he pulled into the driveway and smiled. They had leased the house but kept an option to buy. He loved the place—an older, three-bedroom brick and stucco Tudor style that needed a lot of fixing up. A magnolia tree as tall as a telephone pole sat in the front right of the yard, and a dogwood that bloomed pink in the spring decorated the left. A hedge of azaleas bordered the sidewalk that ran from the concrete drive to the front porch. A swing and two rockers made the porch a comfortable place.

Burke glanced at his watch. Almost 4:00 P.M. The trip from Charleston had taken them just under six hours. He nudged Debbi awake. "We're home," he said quietly. "If you're going downtown, you need to get shaking."

Wiping her eyes, she nodded and sat upright in the seat, instantly awake. A gift she had that Burke envied.

Parking the car, he grabbed the luggage out of the back and headed to the bedroom to unload it. Debbi hustled to the kitchen. Burke heard her rustling about, obviously fixing something to eat. They hadn't stopped for lunch. He liked the sound of her activity in the house. Marriage agreed with him.

Within fifteen minutes they sat down at their almost-new dinette set and began to shove mouthfuls of salad into their mouths. Between bites of lettuce and sliced turkey, the two talked through their plans for the afternoon.

"I'll go by the newspaper office first," said Debbi. "That'll give me a chance to check in with Stoddard and get some background. After that, I'll head to the press conference."

"What about Hal Staton? Will you see him?" asked Burke.

Debbi swallowed a drink of cola. "I don't think so. Stoddard didn't mention him this morning when I called her back."

Burke sighed and thought of the dead woman's husband. For a brief moment, an image of Debbi in a casket flashed into his head. He jerked himself away from the thought.

"He's got to be devastated," he said. "I can't imagine anything worse than what's happened to him. They're practically newlyweds, I think. I read about their wedding two or three years ago, right after he came up to the Braves from Richmond."

Debbi nodded. "Yeah, it was on the sports page. TV too."

"You remember all that?"

Debbi tilted her head. "Of course I do. I'm interested in sports just like you are."

Burke hung his head, momentarily shamed. It was true. Though only 5'4", Debbi had played point guard for her high school basketball team. She stayed active now, too, participating in a gymnastics class three times a week at their health club.

"Sorry," he said. "I forgot you're one of the new breed."

"Don't you love that about me?"

"No doubt about it."

She brushed a strand of her golden hair from her forehead. He reached over, caressed her cheek, and stared into her green eyes. Eyes the color of an old Coke bottle. He could lose himself in those eyes. Burke sighed, grateful for Debbi's presence in his life. Before her, he had felt awkward around women—all thumbs and stumblings. But she had transformed him. Gave him a confidence he had never before known. Not that he was arrogant or anything. Just more comfortable with himself. He didn't know if he would survive if anything happened to her.

"Don't you die before me," he said, half seriously.

For a second, Debbi paused and stared at him. He kept his gaze fastened on her but said nothing else. She looked down at her plate.

"I promise I won't," she said.

He dropped his hand from her face, then smiled. "Okay, just make sure you keep that promise. I just married you, and I don't want to go through that courting thing again."

Debbi changed the subject. "What will you do this afternoon?"

He shrugged and thought for a few moments. He could get in his running. But somehow, he didn't feel like it right now. "Maybe I'll go by the clinic," he said.

"But you won't have any appointments, will you?"

He shook his head. "Nope. They're not expecting me until tomorrow." He thought for a moment about his part-time work as a counselor at the Personal Care Clinic. The clinic was part of a corporation that had sixteen counseling centers scattered across Atlanta, and almost sixty more located in other major cities in the South. The corporation typically set up three- or four-person operations—two or three therapists and one secretary—in high visibility areas. They made counseling part of the neighborhood scenery.

Right now Burke put in about twenty hours per week. After he finished his doctorate, he would probably go full-time. He liked the work, believed he genuinely ministered to people through it.

"Why don't you go with me?" asked Debbi, interrupting his thoughts.

His eyes clouded over. "I don't know about that," he said.

"What's to stop you?" Debbi countered. "Stoddard won't care."

Burke shrugged, weighing whether to say anything about his misgivings, about his desire to stay out of this. One murder case per lifetime was plenty enough for him.

He stared at his beautiful bride and started to speak. But then he saw the eagerness on her face. Not wanting to dampen her enthusiasm, he changed what he planned to say. "Won't the cops mind?"

"If you stay quiet, they won't know that you're not with the *Independent* like me. If they say anything, you can wait outside."

"What about Staton? What if you get to see him?"

Debbi laid her fork down and propped her elbows on the table. "If I get a chance to talk with Staton, I definitely want you along. I don't know how to talk to a guy who's just lost his wife. You've got more experience in that sort of thing than me."

Burke sighed. Debbi was right. During his time as a minister and now as a counselor, he had worked with a number of grief situations. He didn't see how he could refute her logic. Besides, her desire to have him around pleased him. In spite of his fears, he couldn't turn her down.

"If you think it'll help, I'll be glad to come," he said.

Debbi grabbed her fork and wadded a clump of salad into her cheek. "Then it's settled. Let's eat up and get going."

Burke agreed and turned his attention to his food. It didn't take him long to finish. Within fifteen minutes he and Debbi had chugged down the rest of their meal, pulled out of the driveway, and were headed toward downtown Atlanta. Slipping into the flow of the surging traffic, Burke twisted to stare at his new wife. He still couldn't believe it. He was married to the most incredible woman on the face of the earth. If anything happened to her, he would die. He just knew he would.

Chapter 7

At about three o'clock Stubs McVaine finished his initial assessment of his autopsy of Leslie Staton. Sitting down in a squeaky chair behind a metal desk, he puffed a drag off a menthol cigarette and stared across it at Frieda. She stared back, her froggy gray eyes never leaving his face.

Frieda lifted a dictaphone off her lap and set it on the desk. A haze of bluish smoke floated through the air. Stubs flicked the ashes of the cigarette in the general direction of the tray on the desk but missed by about five inches. He knew the cleaning service would find the ashes later. They might even report him. But he didn't care. At times like this, city ordinances against smoking didn't matter much.

He nodded to Frieda. She flipped on the dictaphone. He cleared his throat and began. "Leslie Ann Staton, 26, of 222 Forest Drive, Cordele, Georgia, died, as best I can tell at this point, sometime between 8:00 P.M. and midnight on Sunday, November 27. Staton suffered from two different patterns of wounds prior to death:

1. A pattern of welts and bruises to her wrists and ankles. The pattern indicates she remained tied up with a rope-type binding and injured herself as she tried to twist out of it. These wounds, though painful, played no part in her eventual demise.

2. A series of blows to her head, neck, and throat. These blows, by a heavy instrument of undetermined type, crushed the skull, causing brain hemorrhaging and death."

For a second, Stubs paused and took another pull on his cigarette. He knew the nasty weed could kill him. But the cigarettes covered some of the smell of his work. He worried more about the smell killing him than he did about the cigarettes. Years at this business definitely took their toll. An untimely death like Leslie's took the worst toll of all.

Certainly Stubs hated to see anyone die. But his usual assortment— gunshot wounds, stabbings, car wrecks, etc.—seemed a regular part of the natural order. Society always suffered from some measure of mayhem.

He accepted the necessity of that process. It kept the herd thinned out. In an imperfect world, death was as necessary as birth. But, Stubs sighed, Leslie Staton's murder demonstrated a different type of death. A totally unnecessary death. A death attributed not to any natural order of beasts or normal humans. No, something worse than normal snuffed out her life. A different kind of human. An evil, deliberate, calculating human. A human of shrewd mind and black heart. Or, Stubs grunted, no heart at all.

Visualizing what Staton had endured, he shuddered. The kind of evil that killed Staton was beyond his capacity to understand. He blew out a mouthful of smoke, and it curled up around the top of his bald head like a gray cloud looking for a place to land. Murder. He couldn't understand it, and he couldn't fix it. All he could do was examine the remains, reach his conclusions, and hand them over to the police. Leave the rest of it to someone else. He flicked his ashes and continued his dictation.

"My conclusions suggest this as a potential scenario. We know an abductor grabbed her between 5:45 and 6:00 on Friday evening from the parking lot of the TransSouth Building. Through the day Saturday and much of the day Sunday, she remained tied up in some indeterminate location. The beating took place Sunday night. The killer used a heavy object as the instrument of death. From all the evidence I've noted on this report, I estimate she died sometime between 8:00 P.M. and midnight. Following her death, the killer moved her to the capitol and left her there for someone to find on Monday morning. All indications say she stayed outside for several hours after her death, probably from about two in the morning until she was found."

Sighing heavily, Stubs stopped and stared at Frieda. Her buggy gray eyes glared back, but she stayed quiet. She wasn't one to say much until Stubs spoke to her. "It's not much to go on, is it?" he said.

She shook her head. "No, not much."

"This guy's smart," said Stubbs. "Smarter than normal. No sloppy murder here. No loose details. Nothing that connects to anything else. No skin under fingernails, no hair fibers, no blood except for hers, no sexual violation to leave behind any body fluids, nothing . . ."

Frieda's eyes widened. "It's hard to believe it's not sexual."

He nodded. "Sure is. But I think staying undetected is more important to this guy than anything else. Sexual contact brings too many variables into it, makes it too hard to clean up."

"So you think the motive for the murder wasn't sexual?"

Stubbs puffed his cigarette, once, twice. "Hard to determine right now. But there's nothing to suggest it is—no evidence anyway. We won't know for sure until we ask whoever killed her."

He leaned forward. "Type up the report," he said. "Pass it to the police. Give me a copy. . . . You know the routine."

Frieda nodded and left the room. Stubs leaned back and sucked on his cigarette. In three more years he would punt this gruesome job. After he got in his twenty.

Chapter 8

It took Burke and Debbi longer at the *Independent* than they had anticipated. When they arrived, Mimi Stoddard immediately pulled Debbi into her office, leaving Burke waiting outside the glass-encased cubicle. Stoddard closed the door. Burke eased away and found a water fountain. After a couple of sips he walked back to the hallway outside Stoddard's office and propped himself up against the wall to wait.

Inside, Debbi sat on a square-backed chair while Stoddard towered over her. *Stoddard is at least five ten*, decided Burke, watching through the glass. With her spiked heels, she looked even taller. Auburn hair cupped around her chin, framing her angular cheekbones. As she talked, she pointed a sharp index finger at Debbi.

Debbi shifted side to side in her seat as if wanting to dodge the finger's aim. She flipped a strand of hair into the corner of her mouth and began to chew on it.

In the hallway, Burke gritted his teeth. The hair in the mouth told him Debbi felt upset. It was a habit she was trying to give up. Obviously, she didn't like what she was hearing.

For a split second he thought about knocking on the door to rescue her, but he knew he couldn't do that. Not in this day and age. Fighting off his protective instincts, he shoved his hands into his pockets and swallowed hard.

Okay. Debbi was one of the new breed. She could handle herself.

He pivoted away and walked to the bathroom. A couple of minutes later when he came out, he saw Debbi walking out of Stoddard's office. Stoddard stayed close behind her.

Stoddard's voice sounded like a high-speed drill bit burrowing into a metal can. "Now, don't forget. I want hourly reports. Whatever you know, I need to know. Don't blow this. It's a sizzler. The Braves Best and a Beauty Queen." She lifted her index finger and aimed it at Debbi. "Don't forget, reports on the hour."

Almost running, Debbi hustled over to Burke. "Let's shake it," she said, her voice a whisper. "That finger of hers is liable to go off."

"Where to?" asked Burke.

"To Peachtree Precinct. There's a news conference at seven."

Five minutes later, they sped out of the parking lot, and Burke directed the car to the police station. Debbi laid her head against the seat and closed her eyes.

"I think my boss lady is bad news."

"She does seem a bit pushy."

Debbi grunted but didn't answer. Burke didn't press her. For almost a minute they drove in silence. Burke stared out the windshield, trying to see past the frosted glass. The temperature outside hovered around twenty-five degrees. A clear sky full of stars blinked down on them.

"So what did Stoddard tell you?" he asked.

Debbi opened her eyes. "Oh, two things. One, she gave me Hal Staton's Atlanta address and phone number. He's a Cordele boy originally, but he keeps a condo here in town."

"Is he still in Atlanta?"

"I don't know yet. I'll need to call and find out."

"What else did Stoddard say?"

"She gave me some background on the detective heading up the murder investigation. He's a guy named Derrick Role. He transferred in from Atlanta Buckhead about five months ago. Comes in with a reputation as a rising star. Seems he bagged a city council member last year for taking a million bucks in construction kickbacks.

"The mayor loves Role. He's in his mid-forties, a University of Georgia graduate with a degree in criminal justice. They've just made him head of the homicide division, and he's on a track to become chief of police within the next few years if the political ball bounces right."

For an instant, Burke thought of the former chief, Frank Conners. Conners had been chief during his ordeal with the Atlanta cops. "Conners retired, didn't he?"

"Yeah, took the job of head of security for Senator Steele."

"Role must be pretty competent," said Burke.

"Stoddard seems to think so."

Debbi glanced at her watch. "We need to hustle, sweet cakes. It's getting close to seven."

"I'm on my way." Without another word, Burke pressed the accelerator and the speedometer jumped upward. Paying close attention to the road, he whipped through the after-work traffic, weaving past slower vehicles, changing lanes often. Beside him Debbi closed her eyes. He took her hand in his and squeezed it. She smiled but stayed quiet.

Burke's mind swirled as he drove. It seemed incredible to him that within a few minutes he would find himself back at Peachtree Precinct Police Station, back at the scene where his worst nightmare had almost come to pass. For a second, it all came back to him. But he wouldn't let it linger.

Focusing on his driving, he fought off the awful memories. Within fifteen minutes, he turned off the interstate loop and made the final turn into Peachtree Precinct where Role had set up shop to oversee the investigation.

Quickly parking, Burke took a deep breath and followed Debbi up the sidewalk. He could handle this, he told himself, trying to slow his galloping heartbeat. He didn't need to feel so afraid. So why did he?

At the doors Burke suddenly stopped. Debbi paused, too, her face wrinkling up in confusion. He wiped his hands on his pants. "Burke?" she asked.

"Just a second," he said. "This is a little traumatic for me."

Debbi nodded her understanding. "Two years ago you walked through this same door, didn't you?" she asked.

"The very same." Burke sighed and rubbed his temples, unable to push the memories completely away. A couple of detectives named Avery Mays and Jackie Broadus had investigated that case.

Burke wondered if he would see Mays and Broadus inside. He hoped so. Two years ago they had shown themselves friendly, helpful even. Especially Broadus, a tall, dark-headed divorcée. He had talked with her three times since the ordeal was over.

The first time at the police station the day he finally wrapped things up. The second time on the phone almost a year later when she called out of the blue and asked him for the names of a couple of books dealing with depression. The third conversation occurred only a month ago—right after he began his counseling job at the Personal Care Clinic.

Jackie had called and asked to come by his office. Said she needed to talk with someone in his line of work. He agreed to meet her, but not at the office. Because he thought of her as a friend, he didn't want to make it an official visit. . . .

❧

They met at an ice cream shop near Peachtree Precinct. Each of them ordered a cone with two scoops of butter pecan. Ice cream in hand, they took a seat and talked. In that conversation, Jackie revealed a deep-seated guilt over her failed marriage. Felt she had caused it by her insistence upon a career. Felt that if she had settled down and had kids like her ex-husband had suggested, she might have held the marriage together. But she couldn't do that, she said. Not yet. Her career meant too much to her. And she didn't want to end up like her mother—a depressed, unfulfilled woman talking to the walls after her seven children moved away and her husband died.

Sure, Jackie told Burke, she wanted a family. But a different kind of family from her mother's.

Her ex-husband had rushed her though, tried to force her to give up her work. Jackie balked, asked him to wait a while. He did what she asked for seven years. Then he walked out. Divorce followed.

Burke listened carefully to Jackie, suspecting that her inner disquiet came from more than a failed marriage.

Licking his ice cream, he asked, "What do you want out of life, Jackie?"

She took a sip of water and shrugged. "What everyone wants, I guess. The normal stuff. A home and family. Good friends. A million bucks."

He smiled with her. "What will that bring you? If you get all that. The million bucks, the home and family, the friends?"

"Oh, I don't know. Happiness, I suppose. Contentment."

"Do you think that's what it takes?"

"It would be a start."

Burke nodded. "Can't argue with you there. But I suspect even all that wouldn't do it in the long run for you, Jackie. I suspect it'll take something else, something more abiding than what you've mentioned. I mean, think about it. You've had all that to some extent. You've had a husband, and before that a family with your parents and brothers and sisters. I know you have friends, or at least you do if you want them. But none of that made you happy."

"It must be the million bucks, then," she said, a smile playing on her curved lips.

Burke grinned with her. "Don't you wish it were that easy? No, I don't think you'll find happiness even with a million bucks."

"Then where do I find it?"

He smiled. "Obviously, not where you've been looking."

"And where have I been looking?"

"Where most people look. To your career. Before that, to your marriage. But neither of those worked."

"Not so far," she agreed.

Burke paused, lifted a napkin, and wiped a dribble of butter pecan off his thumb. When he looked up, he stared into Jackie's dark eyes. "You ready to search somewhere else?" he asked.

She dropped her shoulders, then turned away and gazed out the window. "You know somewhere else to look?"

He leaned forward, placing his elbows on the table. "I'm willing to suggest a place to start," he said.

She faced him again. "God?" asked Jackie.

"It's worth a try," urged Burke. "God wants you to find happiness. Offers it to you, in fact. Offers you forgiveness for your failed marriage, purpose for the work you do. You know, normal stuff we all need."

"You make God sound appealing," said Jackie.

"To me, God is appealing," he said, his voice speeding up with enthusiasm. "Just think about it. God loves us and wants us to love him in return. That makes all the difference in the world if you ask me. After all, if God doesn't exist, then life makes no sense at all, has absolutely no meaning. We just wander and stumble around here for seventy to eighty years and then we die. We die and disappear like a log rotting in the middle of a forest somewhere.

"But if God is real, well, then our lives have purpose and reason. We have value, eternal value, value to the God who made us and to the people around us."

Jackie stared down at her hands. For several long seconds, the room fell silent. As if understanding the importance of the moment, the customers behind them also stopped talking. Burke waited for Jackie to respond, praying silently that she would nod an assent to his suggestion, that she would open the door that would give her a fresh view of what made life meaningful. Finally, she placed her hands back on the table. "You've given me a lot to think about," she said. "And I promise I will think about it."

For an instant Burke started to press his case but then decided against it. He couldn't push Jackie into anything. If he tried, he suspected she would bolt like a skittish deer. He rocked back in his seat and nodded. "Okay, good. I'll help you in any way you want."

That ended that conversation. Since that day, he hadn't seen her again. . . .

⋙

Now, standing in the hallway leading into Peachtree Station, Burke wondered if he would get another chance to talk with Jackie Broadus about faith. Maybe not. Maybe he should have taken more initiative the last time.

He felt Debbi touch his elbow. "You okay?" she asked.

"Huh? Oh yeah, just a rush of memories there for a moment."

"I'm not surprised," said Debbi.

He shrugged. "It seems so long ago sometimes. At others, like only yesterday."

"And here we are again," said Debbi.

"Yeah, again."

"You don't want to be here, do you?"

Burke cleared his throat. "No, not really. This place scares me. Even though it turned out all right, I keep seeing Sonny Flake's face, keep seeing his eyes. They opened up real big, as if he suddenly saw the bullet heading toward him and knew it would kill him."

"You don't have to come inside," said Debbi. "I'll understand."

Burke shrugged and considered her offer. On the one hand, it looked attractive. Stay away from the memories, run from them. Leave them alone—ignored and unexamined. He had tried that for over two years. But the memories wouldn't go away. They kept pushing themselves back into his consciousness, insistent, demanding that he consider them.

"I know I don't have to go inside," he said. "But maybe I've been trying to do this the wrong way. Maybe the only way past all this is not around it but through it. I've tried to push it all down inside, but it won't stay. It keeps forcing its way back up. Maybe it's time I faced the past, stared it in the eye, made it blink."

Debbi smiled, her pleasure notched on her face, and grabbed his hand. "At least nobody's chasing you this time," she said.

Burke laughed lightly and took a step forward. "Thank the good Lord for small favors," he said, his mood lightened by her good humor. "Let's get going."

Together they pushed open the doors and checked in with the duty sergeant. He pointed them to the crowd gathering in a glassed-in room to their left.

Burke checked his watch. "Press conference in ten minutes," he said.

Debbi nodded and cut her way through the room, taking a spot near the rear of the group waiting for Derrick Role. Burke followed her, scanning the crowd as he moved, hoping to get a glimpse of Mays or Broadus. He didn't see them.

A murmur from the group cut short his search. A man of medium height but desk-broad shoulders entered the room from the right front. The coterie of reporters opened up as if welcoming a king.

A neatly trimmed black beard covered the man's face. A double-breasted suit the color of a green olive fit snugly to his back. His hair, combed straight back from his heavy eyebrows, was as dark as an iron skillet.

Taking his place on a raised podium in front of the media, the man smiled, and his white teeth glistened under the glare of the camera lights. With practiced ease, he adjusted the height of the microphone on the lectern.

He raised his right hand to quiet the crowd. They obeyed almost instantly. He cleared his throat.

"My name is Derrick Role," he began. "As you know by now, I'm personally heading the homicide team investigating the murder of Leslie Staton. I will have overall control. Assisting me and handling most of the footwork will be Detective Jackie Broadus. She's not here tonight because she's busy conducting interviews. Two other detectives will be named to the team before tomorrow."

He reached inside his coat pocket and pulled out a white sheet of paper. "I want to read a short statement," he said, opening the paper and spreading it out on the lectern. "Then I'll take a few questions." He coughed into his hand, then began again.

"As most of you are already aware, at 7:14 P.M. on Friday, Mr. Hal Staton, a prominent member of our community, filed a missing person's report regarding his wife, Leslie Staton. She had disappeared in the parking lot of the TransSouth Building.

"The officers who investigated that report discovered these facts. Mrs. Staton called Triple A Auto just before six o'clock. According to their dispatcher, Triple A arrived at the scene about 6:15, saw no one there, and left—assuming the call was a false alarm. At about 7:00, Hal Staton came down to the parking lot from a meeting with the Atlanta Braves and found the car. His right front tire was flat—courtesy of an apparently deliberate puncture. Mr. Staton found a red high heel behind the car. The shoe belonged to Mrs. Staton. That's when he called us."

Role paused for a moment and jutted out his prominent jaw. Though he couldn't tell for certain, Burke thought the pause was intentional, like an actor waiting for suspense to build. He stared at Role more intently. The detective continued.

"Given these facts, the officers on the scene immediately treated this as an abduction. They called in our missing persons team. That team went to work—issuing an APB on Mrs. Staton, wiring Mr. Staton's phone in case of a ransom call, searching police files for the names of any known sports fanatics who might be stalkers.

"Through Saturday and Sunday, nothing much happened. No response to the APBs; no ransom calls. We did get one call from a woman who says she saw a white Mercedes in the parking lot at the same time she saw Mrs. Staton. We've talked to the woman and are pursuing the information on that car."

Role shook his head slightly and tugged at the sleeves of his suit. Gold cuff links sparkled from the buttonholes of his starched white shirt. Burke definitely believed the hesitations were planned, maybe even practiced.

Role moved ahead. "Now, tragically, we know why no one made any ransom calls. This morning, a custodian working at the capitol building found the unclothed body of Mrs. Leslie Staton. She was wrapped in a military-style body bag.

"Our preliminary autopsy tells us she died from a brain hemorrhage caused by at least two blows to the head with a heavy instrument of an undetermined type."

Folding the paper, Role stuck it back into his pocket and pushed out his chin again—as if trying to free his neck from his shirt collar. He rubbed his hands through his hair.

"You need to know a couple of other data points," he said. "One, I'm giving you all this information so I won't have to worry about leaks from law enforcement people. If I don't give it to you, you'll pay somebody for it, and I want to save everyone a little time and money." He paused briefly and Burke thought he noticed a bit of a smile crack his lips. "Second, Mr. Hal Staton has offered a $250,000 reward for information leading to the arrest and conviction of the person or persons who abducted and killed his wife. Now, I'll take questions."

Scores of hands jumped into the air. Role recognized a dumpy guy off to his left. The man asked, "Detective Role, you said the custodian found Mrs. Staton in a military-style body bag. Is there a possibility the killer is a former soldier?"

Role shrugged. "Sure, it's a possibility but not necessarily so. A person can buy these bags at army surplus stores or through a host of military equipment magazines. Our forensics people are checking the bag for clues to the place and date of purchase and possibility of prior use."

The hands reached for the ceiling again. Role pointed to Burke's left, to a slender man in a blue and red striped bow tie. "That's Reginald Voss," whispered Debbi. "Anchor for the six o'clock news for WATL."

Burke nodded, recognizing the prominent man. "I'm surprised a guy of his stature is here," he said, his voice matching Debbi's.

"No reason for surprise," said Debbi. "He's known as a man of action—likes to mix it up in the trenches. When it's a top story, he rolls up his sleeves and dives right into the middle of it."

"Well, this is definitely a top story," said Burke, tilting his head to hear better.

"Detective Role," asked Voss, his words clipped and precise. "With the Olympics due to start here in the next six months, do you think this is a murder aimed at the athletic community? Do you think someone might do it again, with one of the international athletes as a target the next time?"

Role's eyes widened and he tucked his jaw into his neck.

"That's an extremely imaginative and hypothetical question, Mr. Voss, but I don't see how answering it will gain us anything. Speculation about a killer with a grudge against athletes simply spooks the population without cause and confuses investigators who are doing their best to solve a crime. I'm sure that such a creative notion intrigues you and maybe a few others in this room. After all, a common ordinary murder is so routine. But your suggestion—well, that would really sell. That would swell ratings, make your job more exciting, get you more attention, more air time. But," and here a sliver of a grin creased Role's lips, "my job is different from yours. My job is to catch killers, not make celebrities of them. So, if you please, keep your sensationalistic questions to yourself."

The hands shot up a third time. Burke turned to Debbi. She nodded. "Let's try to call Hal Staton," she said. "I don't think Detective Role plans to reveal anything more than he's already said. If he does and I need to get it, I can play the television tape when I get back to the paper."

Burke followed her as she eased out of the crowded room to a pay phone on the wall by the duty sergeant's desk. She pulled a pad from her purse, checked the number listed on the pad, then dialed. Burke heard it ringing. It rang and rang and rang. After the fourth ring, a computerized message told her the number had been disconnected.

Chapter 9

For the next three days, everywhere Debbi turned, she ran into dead ends. She learned on Wednesday that Hal Staton had fled south to Cordele to stay with his parents and make preparations for the funeral scheduled for Friday. Debbi tried to call him there but had no luck. According to all reports, he planned to give no interviews.

She spent several hours trying to reach Jackie Broadus. Hoping to cash in on her past experience with the dark-haired detective, Debbi left seven messages, two each for Tuesday and Wednesday and three on Thursday. But Broadus didn't return the calls. *She's too busy for me,* Debbi assumed.

Debbi's only consolation came from the fact that no one else seemed to get much information either. Not her rivals in the print media, not the national tabloids, and not the radio or television news jocks.

Scuttlebutt around the break table at the *Independent* said Detective Derrick Role had sent a strong message to his investigation team—anyone who leaks, leaves. So far, no one had leaked anything. Except for the approximate time of death and the time and place of discovery of the body, everything else remained a mystery. Given the paucity of information available in Atlanta, Debbi decided on Thursday night to go to Cordele for Leslie Staton's funeral.

Wearing her green and navy bathrobe, she sat at the kitchen table by the window at home and discussed the trip with Burke.

"The funeral is at two," she said. "If all goes well, that should put me back in here by 6:30."

"You think Staton will say anything, hold a press conference or something?" asked Burke, sitting across the table from her, sipping from a cup of hot cocoa.

Debbi shrugged. "No way to tell. But if he does, I want to be there. I certainly don't want to be the only one not there if he does speak."

"Anybody going with you?"

"Nope, don't think so. Stoddard says I'm on my own with this for now."

"Do the police have any leads?"

Debbi pulled her robe closer to her body. "I hate to say it, but I don't know. The cops have pulled the covers over their heads on this one. They've kept this whole investigation as quiet as anything I've ever seen."

"Have you talked to Jackie Broadus?" asked Burke.

Debbi shook her head and her blonde bangs bounced down and into her eyes. "Nope. I called her, but she didn't call back."

Burke squinted. "That doesn't sound like her," he said. "Not from what I know. I expect she'll call you back eventually, maybe tomorrow."

Debbi leaned forward and touched Burke's cup. He handed it to her, and she slurped a swallow of his chocolate. "I don't know about that," she said. "Cops aren't known to get chummy with reporters unless they think it will make them look good."

"But Jackie's not like that," said Burke, defending her.

"Oh," said Debbi, arching an eyebrow. "You know her that well?"

Burke cleared his throat. "Well, I do know her. She visited with me a month or so ago. Remember, I told you about it. I consider her a friend. Maybe not a close one, but still a friend."

Debbi's eyes brightened as a thought struck her. She sat the cocoa cup down hard on the table. A drop of it sloshed over the side. "Why don't you call her for me?" she asked.

Burke quickly waved off the notion. "No way. Not me. I don't want to get near this investigation. You do your job for yourself. I'll read about it later in the paper."

The light in Debbi's eyes died and her shoulders slumped. Disappointment gripped her whole posture. For several beats, no one said anything.

Burke took her hand. She watched him carefully. His brown eyes were tense, as if something behind them were stretching, pulling, tugging at him.

He began to talk—slowly at first, hesitant and unsure. "Look, sweetheart, I don't . . . don't want to—to hurt your feelings. I know you live . . . for this kind of thing. But . . . I don't know about all this." His words picked up pace as he continued to speak.

"You know what it does to me—it dredges up a ton of bad memories. I shot a man two years ago. I still see his face in my dreams sometimes. I still see the blood that spurted out from the side of his head. I still see his eyes as they dimmed out, as the life in them vanished. I just don't want to relive all of that, and the idea of getting mixed up in another murder investigation makes me nervous, makes me, I don't know, scared that somehow I'll have to do something like that again. Or worse yet, it makes me afraid that something will happen to you like almost happened the last time, that somehow you'll end up in danger."

His pace slowed as his voice wound down. "I don't want any part of that. Can you understand my feelings, Debbi?" he asked, his voice soft. "Can you?"

Debbi nodded and placed her other hand over his. She knew all this was hard for him. Burke was a quiet man of gentle compassion, and he had not yet gotten over the emotional trauma of having killed another human being—even though it was in self-defense.

She did understand. If he didn't want to do it, she certainly wouldn't pressure him. "I understand, Burke," she said. "It's not fair for me to ask you to do this. I'll get Broadus sooner or later. I expect you're right; she will call back." She took her hands from his and stood up.

He held to her, not letting her go. For almost a minute, they held their poses, she standing beside him as he sat at the table, he squeezing her hands, staring up into her eyes. She could see the wheels spinning in his head. She knew he wanted to please her, to do what she asked. Just like she wanted to please him and do what made him happy.

Burke sighed and stood up. He wrapped his arms around her head, placing her in a hammerlock. Knocking on her skull, he growled playfully, "One phone call is all?"

"One phone call is all."

"I don't guess one phone call can hurt anything," he said, pretending to twist her neck.

"Are you sure?" she asked, not fighting his playful wrestling.

He let her go and shook his head. "Yeah, I'm sure. Besides," and here he puffed out his chest, "I'm certain she'll talk to me."

Debbi cut her eyes up at him. "Don't flirt with her, Mr. Burke Anderson. You're a married man. And she's a beautiful divorcée."

"You're the one who wants me to call her."

"But for business purposes only."

"I assure you I'll keep it strictly professional. So relax and let me handle it."

"So long as you remember the ring on your finger."

He leaned over and kissed her on the cheek. "I don't think you'll let me forget it."

"You can bet I won't," Debbi said.

Chapter 10 ❦

Friday, December 2

Behind the wheel of her Volvo, Debbi stared out at the fresh day. Only a few clouds dotted the sky. The sun, though bright, seemed farther off than usual, smaller and insignificant. The weather channel said to expect a high of forty. Debbi took a breath. The air felt thin, as if a giant had inhaled and sucked most of the oxygen away.

Pulling past a milk truck, Debbi imagined what she would find when she arrived at the funeral home in Cordele. A sad-faced widower in a black suit with dark circles under his eyes. A long line of cars with their headlights burning, passing through red lights on the way to a cemetery. A quiet burial spot, probably under a tall Georgia pine and carpeted by brown pine straw. A minister with a melodious voice, reminding the congregation of the promise of eternal life with Jesus Christ.

Weaving her way through traffic, Debbi wondered about Leslie Staton's spirituality, about her relationship to God. A believer herself for only twenty months, Debbi hoped that Leslie Staton hadn't died alone. She hoped that Leslie had felt the touch of Jesus as she felt the blows of the killer, that Leslie had seen the light of eternal life even as the darkness of physical death wrapped its arms around her.

For a brief second, a sob swept through Debbi's body and the highway blurred on her. What a tragedy if Leslie died without the hand of God leading her through her agony!

Debbi remembered her own conversion to Christian faith and the comfort it had given her. As the only child of divorced parents, she had felt lonely all through her childhood. Even though other people seemed to like her, she still felt somehow isolated, as if cut off from some basic anchor—surrounded by an ocean of humanity but stranded like an island. The bottom line was that her parents' divorce had robbed her of the one thing she most wanted—security.

When she met Burke, he introduced her to the One who would never desert her. He introduced her to God, to faith in Jesus Christ.

A cat darted across the road and Debbi swerved to the right to miss it. Jarred out of her ruminations, she thought of Hal Staton. She wondered how he felt right now. His young wife snatched from him during the prime of their lives. Was he afraid? Angry?

Breathing deeply to get control of her emotions, Debbi focused her eyes again. She wouldn't think about Hal Staton's grief right now. She had a job to do. Too much emotion might prevent her from doing it well.

The white stripes of the highway whizzed by, and she concentrated on them. One by one, one by one, one by one. The first hour passed and then a second. The white stripes continued to zip by—stripe after stripe after stripe. Before the third hour ended, she saw the sign to Cordele. Turning off the highway, she pulled her notepad from her purse and glanced down at the directions to the funeral home she had scribbled there. Four miles and then a right. A half mile and then a left. Four houses, then a gas station, then the Duckworth Funeral Home.

Debbi pulled into the parking lot. A man in a black suit pointed her to the left, to one of the few remaining empty spaces. Switching off the engine, she stepped out. The sun peered down at her, but its warmth seemed halfhearted. A whipping wind jerked at her hair, pulling it back off her forehead and ears. She pulled her camel-colored sports coat closer to her shoulders and eased her way up the sidewalk.

Inside, an usher directed her to a seat on the back row. All the rest were filled. The pews in front of her were jammed shoulder to shoulder with people. An organist played a hymn she vaguely recognized. A baby squalled out from somewhere ahead, and Debbi heard a mother shush the child. A mahogany-colored casket sat in the center of the aisle at the front of the chapel. Flowers of every imaginable color surrounded it.

For several moments, Debbi wondered about her new faith and its teaching about life eternal. Was it possible? Possible that God re-created the deceased believer? Re-created them in a spiritual dimension in a form unknown to the human mind?

Debbi sighed. It really did come down to faith. Faith that just as an azalea bush bloomed, then died, then bloomed again, so also did a person. If azaleas did, then why not people?

Smoothing down her skirt, Debbi shook off her question and scanned the crowd, hoping to catch a glimpse of Hal Staton. She didn't see him. Probably in a family room off to the side where prying eyes couldn't see, she decided.

She examined the people in the pews again. Her gaze came to a stop when she spotted Detective Derrick Role in the second row from the front. The detective wore a crisp white shirt under a navy suit. His black hair touched the top of his collar in the back. Even from behind, Debbi could see his immaculate grooming. *Probably wearing his cuff links*, she thought.

The organist stopped playing for a second. Everyone shifted in their seats. The baby in the front cried once, then stopped as if suddenly aware of the gravity of the moment. A gray-haired minister swept into the room in a flowing black robe. He stepped to the podium and began to speak. "Jesus said, 'I am the resurrection and the life. He who believes in me will live, even though he dies.'"

Listening to the minister, Debbi leaned back, closed her eyes and waited. Waited for the service to end. Waited for the burial to end. Waited for the real pain of Hal Staton to begin.

Chapter 11

About 155 miles away, Burke escorted the woman, a housewife with an alcoholic husband, out the door, then returned to his desk. He scribbled a few notes about the session onto a yellow legal pad and placed them in a folder. His secretary Molly would enter them into the computer.

Finished with the notes, he buzzed Molly. "What's next?" he asked her.

"Hold it a skip. I'll check."

Waiting, Burke slipped open his top drawer and lifted out a Nerf ball. He tossed the ball into the air. He liked his counseling job. It fit his personality. Quiet without being shy. A listener. At his best one-on-one rather than in a crowd.

His eyes scanned his office. It was comfortable, clean, and neat, a lot like a dentist's office. Green ferns in the corners. Brown leather chairs. Soft lighting. Subdued colors in the wallpaper. Only a couple of differences from the dentist's office—a couch instead of a dentist's chair. And no drill.

"Burke?"

"Yeah," he answered, turning his thoughts back to the issue at hand.

"You've got a thirty-minute break before your next appointment."

"Thanks, that'll give me time to make a couple of phone calls."

Burke tossed the ball toward a trash can in the corner to his left. It fell short. He sighed and tilted his leather chair back against the wall. Picking up the phone book, he flipped through it for a moment, then punched in the number of Peachtree Precinct Police Station.

He plopped his feet onto the edge of his desk while he waited. A dispatcher answered, and he asked for Jackie Broadus. The dispatcher put him on hold. He opened a drawer on his desk and pulled out a Baby Ruth bar. He chewed open the wrapper and took a bite off the end of the bar.

"Jackie Broadus here," said a familiar voice.

Burke swallowed the bite of candy and sat up in his chair. "Yeah, Jackie, this is Burke Anderson. You got a minute?"

Broadus laughed, a deep and throaty sound. "For you, Burke, anytime. What's going on with you these days?"

"Well, as you know, I'm married now," said Burke.

"You two taking care of each other?"

"Well, I'm happy. Just hope she is."

"I'm sure she is," said Broadus.

For a brief instant, the line fell silent. Burke took a deep breath, then moved to the reason for his call. "Look, Jackie, I know I probably shouldn't do this, but I'm calling you for a specific reason. I don't quite know how to ask you this, but—" he hesitated.

Jackie bailed him out. "But your wife wants me to tell her what I know about the Staton homicide, right?"

Burke cleared his throat. "Yeah, Jackie, you got it. Debbi's working the story for the *Independent*, and she obviously wants all she can get. She's in Cordele today with the Staton funeral. We decided I should call you."

"After I didn't call her back."

"Yeah, after you didn't call her back."

"Is she forgetting that detectives should solve cases, and the media should simply report it when they do?"

"Well, you know Debbi. She gets nosy about things like this. Of course, I'm glad she does. Her nosiness saved my bacon a couple of years ago."

"Her nosiness can also get her in trouble."

"Yeah, I know, but it can get her a headline too. That's what she likes. Besides, the media occasionally helps an investigation every now and again, uncovers information the police haven't found."

"Yeah, every once in a while," agreed Jackie. "But not that often."

For a second, neither of them said anything else. Burke decided he wouldn't take it any further. If Jackie wanted to say anything more, she would do it without his insistence. No use alienating her.

Jackie cleared her throat. "Look, Burke, I'd like to help Debbi, but I don't know if I can. Derrick Role has clamped down on this with the threat of death over everybody here. Any leaks and he says he'll track down the sieve and plug it up with his foot down somebody's throat."

Burke remembered the self-confident detective. For an instant, he wondered about Broadus and Role. Any chance of romance there? Is that why Broadus didn't call Debbi back?

"He sounds like a tough guy," said Burke.

Jackie grunted. "He goes out of his way to make it seem so."

Burke thought he heard a note of resentment in her voice. "He's new, isn't he?"

"Pretty much so."

"And he jumped over a lot of good people to reach his present spot in the pyramid."

Jackie didn't respond.

Playing a hunch, Burke said, "People like Avery Mays."

The line stayed silent. Burke stayed quiet too. He twisted his chair until it faced the window and thought of Jackie's former partner, a rumpled man in his mid-fifties who treated words and news media like social diseases. Mays was a detective who had faithfully put in his years and made his contribution over and over again. "Mays deserved a shot at homicide chief, didn't he?"

"Maybe so," said Jackie. "Not that he would have taken it. Avery doesn't like the spotlight."

"But he deserved the chance to turn it down."

"No question about that."

"What's Mays doing now?"

Jackie hesitated, then said, "Oh, he turned in his badge. Doing a bit of private investigation."

"I guess you miss him."

"I guess I do."

Burke heard the reluctance in her voice. She didn't plan to say anything else about Avery. He changed the subject.

"So Role's threats have zipped all the mouths," he said.

Jackie laughed. "You're slick, Burke," she said. "Trying to see if I resent Role because he leapfrogged my best friend to get his job."

"Well, do you?"

She laughed again but without much enthusiasm. "No comment."

"So you're not going to tell me anything?"

She sighed. "Tell me this. Why should I tell you something that I don't tell the rest of the media?"

Burke leaned forward. "I really don't know how to answer that, Jackie. Except to say you can't give it to all of them and keep it a secret that you're the source of the leak. Plus," and here Burke took a calculated gamble, "Debbi won't print anything you tell her unless you give her permission to do so."

For a brief beat, Jackie said nothing. Burke knew she was considering his offer. He listened to her soft breathing over the phone.

"Well, the first part of what you say makes sense," she said. "But

I'm not sure about the second. You want me to give her information, but she won't print it?"

"That's right. Not if you don't tell her she can."

"If she's not going to print it, then what'll she do with it?"

"She'll use it to see if it leads her to something else. It's been known to happen, you know. A smart reporter finds a loose string the cops missed. She follows that string. It ends at the truth. That becomes her story. She helps the cops and herself at the same time."

Burke heard Broadus sigh as she thought it over. He and Debbi had helped Jackie two years ago. Had gathered information she and Mays hadn't found. Had solved a crime for the two detectives. If she thought they might assist her again, she might give him what he wanted.

Broadus said. "You two did pretty well the last time I worked with you."

"We survived."

"And didn't you tell me your studies had something to do with criminal behavior?"

"Well, I'm working on a dissertation that deals with the role of the conscience in the development of the sociopath."

"And you did some clinical work at the Atlanta Correctional Institute, didn't you?"

Her memory surprised him. He had briefly mentioned his time at ACI during their visit a month ago. "Yeah, a summer ago, as part of my therapy hours. I saw everything there—petty criminals to death row inmates. Not a pleasant place."

"But an educational one?"

"I definitely learned a few things."

Burke heard her take a deep breath. She said, "Look, I don't have a full-time partner here at Peachtree. Since Mays left in September, they keep giving me special assignments like this one. That's fine by me, but it leaves me sorting through tons of details that Mays usually handled. I'm better with the big picture than the bits and pieces. Avery always remembered the facts. I threaded them together until they made some sense. "But now I don't have anyone like him around. Role stays pretty much in the office overseeing it all, dealing with the politics and publicity of the situation. The guys he put with me are pretty green. So I need somebody to talk through this stuff with me. I operate better that way. Keeps me from losing the forest in the trees."

"Sounds like you need somebody to make sure you don't miss anything."

Jackie cleared her throat. "You could be right. Here's what I'll do. I have to come near your office in a couple of hours. I'll drop by a copy of what we have so far. That'll include an autopsy report. See what it tells you. You're a smart guy, and your wife seems to have a bright head on her shoulders too. It *is* possible you two might get something out of this I don't see. After you read it and chew on it a bit, call me back at home, tell me what you think. Here's the number."

Burke wrote it down on a pad on his desk. Jackie continued to talk. Her tone hardened. "Now listen to me, Burke. Tell Debbi she cannot print this. If she does, know this for a fact: Debbi Anderson will never, and I mean never, ever, receive anything else from me or from any cop who likes me, in Atlanta or anywhere else in Georgia. You understand me on that?"

Burke grunted. "You've made it very plain," he said. "But rest assured, I repeat, rest assured, she won't print anything you give to us. You have my word on that."

"Then look for the report by the time you leave today. And, Burke?"

"Yes?"

"Tell your lovely bride hello for me."

"I'll do it."

Placing the phone down, Burke steepled his hands and lifted them over his mouth. Whether he liked it or not, he was now involved. He shuddered. Somehow, he suspected, before it all ended, he wouldn't like it at all.

⤜

On the other side of the phone, Jackie Broadus leaned back in her chair and stared at the ceiling. For a second, she craved a California Lady, the expensive cigarettes she had smoked since she was seventeen. She linked her hands behind her head, remembering she had given them up in September.

She thought for a moment about Burke Anderson. She liked him. Considered him a friend. Smarter than anybody she knew except Avery Mays. Two years ago, he had demonstrated an unexpected resourcefulness.

She trusted Burke's integrity. If he said Debbi wouldn't print the information, she could count on it.

Smiling, Jackie kicked up from her chair. A guy with Burke Anderson's rare combination—honesty, intellect, and common sense—might serve her purposes well.

Chapter 12

The minister said, "Let us pray," and Debbi bowed her head. "Almighty God, who walks with us through the dark valleys, we ask you today to reveal your loving presence to this grieving family. We implore you to wrap your arms of care and comfort around their shoulders and hug them to yourself. We ask you to remind them ever and again of your promise of eternal life for those who live by faith in your Son Jesus. We . . ."

Listening to the prayer, a sharp pang of guilt hit Debbi. She suddenly realized she had driven to Cordele out of a less than pure motive. She had wanted only to advance her story—to take advantage of a grieving man. How callous of her. How unbelievably cold and calculating. How un-Christlike.

The minster concluded his prayer. "And we ask this in the name of the Father and of the Son and of the Holy Ghost. Amen."

For a brief second, Debbi kept her head bowed and considered fleeing back to Atlanta the moment the service ended. Nothing else she could do here.

But then another thought occurred to her. True, she couldn't talk to Staton today and she shouldn't. But she could communicate with him. No, not in an effort to ask for anything for herself. That would be wrong and she knew that. But she could offer him something he might need.

The organist touched her fingers to the keys, and the strains of "How Great Thou Art" swept into the quiet room. The minister walked to the front of the casket. Two funeral attendants in black suits appeared from the back and nodded to the pallbearers. The pallbearers stood. The minister led the group down the aisle.

As the pallbearers passed, the congregation stood and began to file out also, row by row. Everyone remained silent as the pews emptied.

Debbi waited until the room cleared, then stood and trudged outside. She watched as the people from the congregation slipped into their cars. The wind had stopped blowing, and the air hung limp, like an exhausted runner, unable to move another step. The lights on the cars flipped on, and a police escort led the funeral procession from the funeral home and onto the highway. Debbi waited as the cars drove slowly away.

As the last car pulled off, she climbed into her Volvo and headed in the opposite direction. At a red light she opened her purse, lifted out her notepad, and checked her directions. Go two miles, then take a left turn at the light. Drive six miles outside the city limit sign, and turn right past a one-lane bridge.

It took her about fifteen minutes to get there. She spotted the mailbox on the left side of the blacktopped road. The name was painted on it in big white letters. STATON.

At the mailbox, Debbi turned onto a gravel driveway that snaked through a pasturelike field. About a hundred yards down the drive, she spotted a white frame house. A porch wrapped around the house on three sides. A grove of green pines bracketed the house on the back and the right, and a rusted green pickup marked the end of the gravel path that served as the driveway.

As Debbi braked the car, a yellow dog the size of a small pony appeared from behind the pickup. With a casual lope, the mixed-breed animal covered the distance that separated it from Debbi. She flipped off the engine. The dog sniffed at the car tires. Rolling down her window, Debbi paused for a couple of moments to see what the dog would do. He sat down beside her door and stared up at her.

Slowly, so as not to startle the beast, she eased the door open. The dog laid back his ears and growled softly. Debbi quickly closed the door. *Okay, think of another way to do this.*

She picked her notepad and pen off the car seat. She would write the note from inside the car, then figure out a way past the dog.

She started scribbling, keeping one eye on her canine companion.

Dear Mr. Staton,

First, please accept my heartfelt condolences for you and your family in your tragic loss. I don't know how you're going to get through this. But please know that people like me, people who don't know you except by reputation, will offer their prayers to God for you to have strength to endure.

I want you to know I am a reporter for the Atlanta Independent. *To be honest, I came to the funeral today hoping to get you to speak, to tell me and everyone else about your grief, to get you to share with us what you know about the circumstances of your wife's death. But at the funeral service, I came to understand how wrong that was. It was selfish of me to even think of it. I ask your forgiveness.*

What I want to say to you now is simply this. My husband is Reverend Burke Anderson. I am going to leave a card of his with this note. He is a counselor with the Personal Care Clinic in Atlanta.

I'm sure you have tons of people who can and will give you plenty of support as you deal with your pain. I'm equally certain you can find adequate professional care from a number of sources.

But if you should ever find yourself wanting somebody to talk to, please feel free to call him. I can't guarantee he can help you, but I can guarantee he will listen to you. Listening is his best thing. Anyway, again I ask you to forgive my intrusion today. It was self-serving and crude. May the God who loves all of us forgive me for it as well. I'm praying for you.

Debbi Meyer Anderson

Finished with the note, Debbi reached into the glove compartment and pulled out one of Burke's business cards. She laid it on the note, then carefully folded the paper. She checked out the dog again. He had moved from the side of the car and planted himself by the front door of the house. He looked like a guard at Buckingham Palace.

Taking a deep breath, Debbi opened the car door. The mutt stiffened and raised slightly up on his haunches. But he didn't leave the front stoop.

Gently, Debbi placed her feet on the gravel driveway. The rocks crunched under her feet as she walked toward the house. The yellow dog laid back his ears and whined. At the steps of the porch, she stopped walking and held out her hand. The dog sniffed her fingers. She waited. The animal opened its mouth and bared its teeth.

For a brief instant, Debbi thought of running, then realized the beast would drag her down before she ever reached the car. She stayed still. The dog's tongue flicked out and licked her hand.

Debbi started breathing again, and she gratefully scratched the animal behind the ears for several seconds. Then, not trusting her good fortune to last, she edged up the steps, slowly opened the screen door and wedged the folded note behind it. Hoping nothing would happen to the note, she backed off the porch, away from the dog, and into her car.

She started the engine and backed out of the driveway. The dog on the steps opened his mouth and licked his lips but never moved.

Chapter 13

S itting behind his desk, a standard-issue rectangular oak, Burke flipped through his Day-Timer. Seeing nothing listed for the five o'clock slot, he buzzed his secretary. "Molly, anything else scheduled for me today?"

"I'll check."

Burke picked up his Nerf ball and squeezed it, hoping the day was over. He had a chapter of his dissertation almost finished, and he wanted the rest of the afternoon to work on it.

The phone buzzed. Molly said, "I don't find anything here, Burke."

"Then we're done for the day?"

"With patients we are. But paperwork never ends."

"Don't remind me," said Burke, squeezing the ball. "How bad is it?"

"Hold on a sec, I'll check."

Burke twisted his chair around until he could see outside. He wondered how Debbi was doing, if she had talked to Hal Staton. He wondered about Staton. What kind of man was he? How would he handle this tragedy?

For a second, Burke asked himself the same question. How would he handle it? Would it make him bitter? Would it turn him against God? He didn't know. Hopefully, he would never have to find out.

Molly interrupted his musings. "You've got a couple of things you might want to check. A manilla envelope for one. A pretty lady cop brought it by twenty minutes ago. You had a patient, and she said she couldn't wait. I'll bring it in."

Burke dropped his Nerf ball and leaned forward. Molly opened the door, handed him the envelope, and marched out. He stared after her for a second. Molly had come with the job. He shared her with Tom Cato, his boss at the clinic.

She was about sixty, he figured. Liked to mother him. As a single man until a few weeks ago, Burke had discovered the mothering had come in handy more than once. Molly made a mean lasagna.

He turned to the brown envelope, focused on it. The initials J. B. were handwritten in the upper left-hand corner. Burke bit his lip and fingered the envelope for several seconds, feeling conflicting emotions. Inside this folder lay the details about the murder of a vivacious young woman. He wanted to read those details. But the idea of doing so scared him.

He felt that once he read it, he would close the last door of escape from this course of action. The information would trap him, make him a prisoner to whatever flow of events that followed. He didn't like that feeling, the sense of losing control to fate, the sense of giving up his self-determination.

Confused by his feelings, he shoved the envelope into his briefcase and buzzed Molly. "I'm heading out," he said.

"Don't forget the paperwork," she said. "Insurance forms pay the bills."

"I'll come in early Monday," he said.

"Okay, but don't blame me when Tom blasts you out for leaving it undone."

Grinning, Burke hustled out the door and left the clinic. The laid-back Tom Cato never blasted anyone out.

Whizzing in and out of traffic, he kept glancing at the folder in the seat beside him, almost wishing it would disappear so he wouldn't have to read it. It seemed alien to him, a snake lying in wait to sink its fangs into his flesh and poison him to the point of death. He hoped Debbi was home when he got there. He could give the envelope to her and wash his hands of the whole affair. He had done his part—called Broadus, delivered the police report.

Feeling spooked, he opened the window of the car, sucked in a deep breath of cold air, and forced the thoughts of the envelope out of his head.

It took him about thirty minutes to drive home. In the driveway he braked quickly behind Debbi's Volvo. Great. She *was* home. She would open the envelope. He might not even read the report.

Feeling better, he tucked the envelope under his arm and scooted inside. "I'm home," he yelled, throwing off his jacket.

"In here," Debbi called, "in the bedroom. Just got back from the funeral."

He found her sitting in front of the small desk they kept across from their bed. She had the computer on. A mound of paper was stacked high beside the terminal. She looked up from the screen as he entered.

"You got anything from Jackie?" she asked.

He tossed it to her. "A full report. Right here."

She caught it and held it up to the light. "You read it yet?" she asked, excitement spicing her voice.

"Nope, I didn't open it."

"I'm surprised," she said. "Surprised your curious little mind could wait so long."

"I didn't want to open it without you," he said, not telling her he didn't want to open it at all.

"You knew I'd make you pay for it if you did."

"That's a good point," said Burke.

Debbi nodded. "Let's see what we've got," she said, ripping the top off the manilla folder. "See what the cops know that we don't."

She pulled a sheaf of folded computer paper from the envelope and laid it flat on the desk. She looked up at Burke. "Don't you want to read it with me?" she asked.

He shrugged. "Like I said before, it's your job, not mine."

Her brow furrowed and she reached for a strand of hair. For a second, she fingered it as if about to say something, but then she dropped it back into place. Her eyes left Burke and flickered back to the pages of the police report.

Burke watched her as she read. She flipped from the first page to the second, then to the third. As she read the third page, her green eyes watered, and she pulled a tissue from a box by the computer. Through her sniffles, she plowed on with her reading.

Burke stayed still as long as he could. But then he couldn't take it any longer. Anything that made his wife cry also affected him. He couldn't let her deal with this alone.

He dragged a chair from the corner over to the desk and wrapped his arms around Debbi's shoulders. She had made such an incredible difference in his life. He couldn't desert her now, not when she needed him.

As he held her, Debbi finished her reading, laid her head against him, and closed her eyes.

Burke picked up the report and took a deep breath. For Debbi he would ignore his fears. He started to read.

The basic information came first. Name, age, address, height, weight, etc. of Leslie Staton. Next came the date and approximate time of death, the state of the body, the place of discovery, the last person to see her alive, the name of the man who found her—all the information he already knew.

Burke flipped the page and read the autopsy report. It cataloged the known facts of Staton's death. In forensic terms it cataloged the extent of the injuries, the width and depth and length of each bruise and cut and contusion. Though not grasping each of the technical terms, Burke gathered enough to know the basic facts.

"Not your typical method," said Debbi.

"It's worse than most," agreed Burke.

"She must have suffered terribly."

For almost a minute, both of them fell silent. The hum of the computer drive whirred through the room. Burke sighed, stood up, walked to the window behind their bed, and stared out at the pine trees in the backyard. A black crow swooped in for a landing in the top branches of the dogwood by the garage.

"I think whoever did this will kill again," he said.

Debbi froze in her seat. "What makes you say that?"

Burke turned and faced her. "I don't have a logical reason for saying it, not really. But in every case I've ever read about, something this brutal, this premeditated, always leads to another murder. It's not like a Saturday-night stabbing or shooting like we usually see—between people who know each other, people in the same circle of friends or family. No, something this far out of the norm means we're dealing with a different type of situation, a different type of person."

Debbi stood, crossed the room, and placed her hands on his hips. "You're suggesting a serial killer," she whispered.

He felt her fingers shaking. He wrapped his arms around her and pulled her close. "I'm afraid I am."

"But you heard what Role said at the news conference. He said that suggestion was out of place, premature, even dangerous."

Burke took a deep breath. "What else could he say? It's his worst nightmare. A serial killer on the loose in Atlanta just months before the Olympics. Thousands of people from across the world are already here, getting ready. Atlanta has a chance to change its image, make a huge international splash. Now this happens. A public-relations disaster. Role will deny it's a serial killer as long as he possibly can."

"At least until another person dies."

"And long past that if he can find a way to do it."

Leaving the thought hanging in the air, Burke walked back to the desk, picked up the report, and turned to the final page. He held it out to Debbi, inviting her to read along with him. But this time, she was the one not interested. Her green eyes had gone vacant, distant, seeing something he knew he would also see if he gave himself permission to look.

He blinked, then stared back down at the report, trying to comprehend the medical examiner's summation—the conjecture about the time of the injuries, the type of rope used on her wrists to keep her prisoner, the sequence of events that led to her death. His mind, though, kept drifting on him, drifting toward Debbi and what she was seeing. The words on the page drifted too—up and away from him, and he found his concentration confused, mixed up, and chaotic.

He felt Debbi touch his elbow. He turned and laid the report on the bed. He wrapped his arms around Debbi and began to rock back and forth, back and forth, hoping as he did that his rocking could somehow help both of them forget the evil that walked about loose in the town of Atlanta, the town they both called home.

Chapter 14

Saturday, December 3

Choking back a stomach surge, Rosey Anita Benton pushed her bony bottom off the cold concrete pad that served as a seat at the Dixie Land Motor Speedway and stood up. "I don't feel so good," she said, as if talking to herself.

Her best friend, Janice, a redhead wearing a teal scarf around her neck, looked up for a second, waved as if dismissing her, and turned her attention back to the track.

Rosey's stomach rumbled under the black belt she wore around the waist of her faded jeans. She hugged her skinny arms around her waist and shivered. The night air chipped at her nose, and a stiff and steady breeze kicked up the paper cups at her feet and blew them away from the bleachers. Rosey squinted her pale blue eyes and stared down and across the twenty rows of seats and steel girders that separated her and the rest of the spectators from the racetrack.

On the other side of the girders, she spotted Bobby Bartholomew Benton, better known throughout Atlanta and the surrounding suburbs as Triple B. Bobby tucked his crash helmet under his right arm, saluted to her as he always did before a race, and headed to his modified 1993 canary yellow Thunderbird. In spite of her stomach distress, Rosey waved down to her man. She truly loved Triple B, her husband of seven years. And not just because he had rescued her from a waitress job on the midnight to eight shift at Paul's Motor Stop off I-85. No, she loved him for more reasons than that. She loved him because he was witty and sincere and romantic and generous and intelligent and industrious.

She knew that years before she met him, Triple B had built and maintained his race cars himself. Ran in the Bomber car class back in those days. Now, though, what with his wealth and all, he paid someone else to do the mechanic work. He just drove.

He had moved up in class too. Sometimes ran Late Model Class, every now and again the Sprint. He owned six different cars now. But someone else built and maintained them.

These days, Bobby stayed busy selling cars, not fixing them. And he was a master at that.

His advertising people, acting under his supervision, had plastered his pudgy, puppylike face on billboards all over Cobb County. They had dreamed up a series of attention-grabbing television commercials that made Bobby more famous than he had ever imagined possible.

The ad that first made him famous showed his 295-pound frame wearing a bikini bathing suit standing in front of his car lot holding a baseball bat over his shoulder. His stomach, round as a giant marshmallow on steroids, slopped over the edges of the swimsuit. Behind him, a string of flapping orange banners popped in the breeze.

Staring into the camera, Bobby waved the baseball bat above his bald head and shouted at his audience, "When I say TRIPLE B, I'm not thinking what you're thinking. I'm not thinking, 'He's a bald blimp with a baseball bat.' No, it wouldn't be nice to think that.

"When I say TRIPLE B, I mean best price, best service, and best trade-in. So get yourself down to TRIPLE B AUTO SALES on 3000 Gable Avenue, and let us fit you up with a top-of-the-line, pre-owned automobile. Our cars get you where you're going and lift your spirits on the way. Plus, they cost less than anyone else's you'll find. So, remember, TRIPLE B. Not bald, blimp, and baseball bat. But best price, best service, best trade-in."

Rosey smiled at the memory. She'd seen the ad almost two years before she met Bobby. Liked him on the spot. What a crazy, happy-go-lucky guy.

She had almost dropped her order pad the morning he walked into the truck stop and sat down at one of her booths. He had flirted with her the whole time she served him. She flirted back. All part of the job. Harmless fun.

Before he left, he asked for her phone number. She refused to give it to him. "I'm not that kind of girl," she told him, pushing her button of a nose into the air.

The next night he came back and asked for her number again. She refused a second time. A third try followed. Same result.

On the fourth night he said, "Honey, eating here is costing me a fortune. If you don't give me your number, please know that you're going to be responsible for Bobby Triple B Benton going into bankruptcy. Do you want that on your precious little conscience?"

Rosey gave in. She had played hard to get long enough. He wooed her for three more months before he popped the question. They got married a week later in the parking lot of one of his four car lots. Under a banner that proclaimed "Bobby B's Best Deal Yet. He Sold Himself to Rosey."

Now Rosey loved everything about Bobby. Especially the Saturday-night races at the Dixie Land Motor Speedway. She knew the name sounded pretentious. It sounded like a major raceway for Nascar. But it wasn't.

Thick red clay covered the three-quarter-mile oval, and no big-name drivers ever raced there. But Rosey and her friends didn't care. They gathered faithfully every time the gate opened.

They sat through the dust clouds that choked them in summer and the nipping wind that reddened their noses and cheeks in the fall and early winter. Except for the last three weeks of December and all the months of January and February, a crowd of 800 to 1000 people gathered religiously every week to watch their boys do their thing.

That's why Rosey came. To watch her boy Triple B do his favorite thing—race his late model and sprint cars against all competitors. This was the last race of the season.

Her stomach growled and shifted her back to the present. "Gotta go to the ladies' room," she said, doubling over with the pain. "I'm suffering some major-league nausea here."

Janice looked up at her. "You just went thirty minutes ago," she said.

"Yeah, I know," said Rosey. "But it's time again. Seems like my stomach gets weaker as my hair gets grayer. A couple more years and I'll need a port-a-potty with me everywhere I go."

"Hurry back," said Janice.

"I got about thirty minutes," said Rosey. "They don't start until 7:30. If I don't feel better after my bathroom break, I may go rest in the car for a while."

"You want me to go with you?"

Rosey hesitated. She had some Maalox in her car. She would try that after the bathroom. "No, Jan, I think I'll survive. Just give me a few minutes."

Janice nodded her head. Rosey turned to walk away. Her stomach growled, and she doubled over with a sharp cramp. After a few seconds, she turned back to Janice. "Look, Jan, I'm hurting more by the minute here. I'm going to try some Maalox. If that don't work, I may punt it and go home."

"I'll go with you," said Janice, standing up.

Rosey put a hand on her friend's shoulder. "Nope, no cause for that.

Nothing you can do. You stay here. I'll be fine. I'll get better in a few minutes, or I'll head home."

Janice shrugged. "Okay, Rosey, you're a big girl. Let me know if you need me."

Rosie nodded and hustled up the concrete steps. At the top, she squeezed through a stack of men. In unison, the men tilted their heads and watched as she walked past.

A minute later, Rosey stepped behind the concession stand and headed toward the ladies' room in the back. A string of yellow light bulbs, bouncing back and forth in the wind, hung bare on thin electrical lines and bathed her face with their squashlike color. She tried the door to the bathroom. It was locked.

Frustrated, she knocked on the door. "Hold your water," yelled a voice from inside.

Rosey hopped up and down a few times, both from the cold and the impending bathroom crisis. "How long you gonna be?" she called.

"Don't know, some things you can't rush."

Biting her lower lip, Rosey looked around. She didn't see anyone else. She left the women's room, made a quick left, and stepped to the men's room door. She rapped on the door, hoping no one would answer. No one did. She grabbed the handle and took a step to go in.

"Excuse me," said a voice directly behind her.

Momentarily forgetting her stomach problems, Rosey gulped and turned around, preparing herself to make apologies for violating the separation between male and female. The man's appearance cut her short.

He stood not more than five feet away under the yellow lights. A pair of dirty jeans and a short-sleeved knit shirt clothed his slightly frail body. Gold-rimmed sunglasses completely obscured his eyes, and he held a long cane in his right hand. His head bobbed back to front, front to back, back to front. Several days' growth of scraggly beard blotched his face, and a green and white baseball cap fit snugly over his head.

"Excuse me," said the man again.

For several seconds, a furrow of puzzlement crawled onto Rosey's face. This guy seemed strange. In the wind, his voice sounded thin, wispy. He wasn't real big. The cane in his hand seemed half as tall as he was. And his eyes. Why would he wear sunglasses at night? Weird.

The man tilted his head forward, as if trying to hold himself up against the wind. At that moment, Rosey figured it out. The man was blind.

Rosey cleared her throat. "I'm here," she said, feeling the need to point to herself so he could locate her.

The man's head stopped bobbing, and he tilted it to the right and held it still. "You're a woman?" he said, apparently surprised.

"Uh, yeah, and somebody's in the ladies' room. I don't feel so good, so I'm improvising. My intestines don't know the difference."

The man chuckled. "I expect not." He tapped his cane on the ground. Rosey noticed that the end of it looked new, as if it hadn't been tapped on the ground too often. A stab of pain pushed suddenly against her abdomen.

"I guess you want the rest room, huh?" she asked, her voice high with distress.

He shook his head. "Nope, not at all, that's not why I stopped you. I'm about to freeze to death out here, my jacket's in my van, and the friend who brought me is down on the track. I thought I could find my way myself, but as it turns out, I was too optimistic. So I need someone to take me to my van. I heard you knock on the door, thought you might help."

Rosey nodded her head, and the curls of her dyed red hair flipped up in the wind. "Sure, man, no problem, be glad to help you as soon as—"

A tall man in a black leather jacket rounded the corner and made a beeline for the bathroom. Rosey started to hold up her hand to protest that she had gotten there first, but then she decided the man wouldn't understand. He paused for a second as he spotted her and the blind man, but then he zipped past them and through the bathroom door.

"I'm sure he'll only be a minute," said the blind man, a slight smirk playing on his lips.

Rosey sighed. "Come on, mister, let's find your van. That's better than standing here waiting. What color is it, and what kind?"

"Navy blue," he said. "A 1992 Aerostar. It's on the fourth row, in section K."

Taking him by the hand, Rosey forced a bit of bile back down. As fast as she could—without bumping the blind man into anything—she pulled him away from the yellow lights by the bathroom, away from the concession stand, through the chain-link fence at the entrance of the raceway and onto the dirt parking lot outside.

Within minutes she spotted row four, section K. She saw the blue Aerostar. It was the last car on the row. The row was the one nearest the tall pine trees that surrounded the parking lot. A black shadow fell over them as they reached the fifth car nearest the blue van. Rosey looked up. The lights on the overhead poles on both sides of the van were out.

Rosey pulled her sweater closer to her skinny arms. The wind blew her hair into her eyes. She pushed the hair away. The blind man stayed silent.

"We're here," she said.

"Here are my keys," he said, his soft voice almost lost in the stirring wind. "You can unlock it much easier than I can."

She nodded. Of course. Tough for him to find a keyhole. She stepped to the side of the van and, hoping to catch a bit of light from the moon, held the keys up. At that instant, the moon disappeared behind a bank of swirling clouds.

"It's the biggest one," he said.

She found it and leaned over, searching for the lock on the door. She felt the blind man moving behind her. She pushed the key toward the lock, inserted it, and twisted. She opened the door to the van. The wind almost pushed it closed again in her hands. A hot flash of pain shoved into her stomach. She started to turn, to run back to the bathroom.

A whacking blow from the side cut her short. She slumped for a second against the van, then tried to push herself up. The cane, she realized. The blind man had hit her with his cane. She felt a whoosh of air. The man had raised the cane again, over his head. She started to raise her left arm to ward off the blow. But she moved too late. The second blow of the cane knocked her out.

As she sagged to the ground, the blind man grabbed her under her armpits and lifted her into the vehicle. Climbing in behind her, he slammed the door shut. A wide smile cutting across his face, he crawled quickly over the seat and into the driver's side. Switching on the engine, he barreled away from the racetrack. Only when the wheels of the van hit the pavement of Highway 285 almost four miles away did he pull off his sunglasses.

Chapter 15

Holding her silk housecoat tightly to her chest, Jackie Broadus eased out of her recliner and padded barefoot to the window. Outside she saw the lengthening shadows of the afternoon sun bathing the ground. A row of magnolia trees led from the front of her condominium to the sidewalk a hundred feet away. Jackie spotted a man and woman holding hands walking past the trees. She sighed, walked away from the window, and trudged to her bedroom down the hall.

The weekend had been lonely. Not scheduled to work for the first time since Staton's body turned up, she had arranged a date with a high school basketball coach for Saturday. But his team lost on Friday night, and he called afterward to say he needed to stay in and study film. She let him off the hook without too much strain. After all, she had only dated the guy once, and that wasn't the most exciting night she'd ever experienced.

Jackie checked her watch. Almost four. The day had passed like a kidney stone—slowly and with a lot of discomfort. Frustration over the lack of progress on Staton's case and her ever-growing feeling of personal isolation made her miserable.

Hoping it would lift her spirits, she had actually attended church that morning. Talking to Burke Anderson had tipped her toward the decision. Somewhere, somehow she had to find something to make some sense out of her life. But the church service seemed foreign. Stuffy and cold. No one spoke to her as she entered the sanctuary, and she left the building feeling as lonely as when she entered.

Slipping off her housecoat and dropping it on the bed, she licked her lips and thought about a cigarette. Other than getting a divorce, giving them up had been the hardest thing she'd ever done. She stepped to her dresser and shuffled through the drawers, checking to see if she'd left any behind when she cleaned them out in September.

Not finding any, she groaned and stomped her feet. Nothing

seemed to go her way these days. Without Avery Mays around, her work brought little pleasure. She had no close relationships—either male or female. Her mother lay in a nursing home in Albany. And she couldn't find a cigarette.

Her full lips shaped into a pout, Jackie looked around the room as if searching for an answer to her frustration. Her eyes stopped when they reached the floor-length mirror on the wall leading to the bathroom. She appraised herself in the glass.

Almost 5'8". Dark black hair, shoulder length. Body still firm, legs lean and strong, stomach relatively flat for a thirty-four-year-old. Well-developed chest, high cheekbones, and clean white teeth. Most people found her attractive. Some used the word "gorgeous" to refer to her. She sighed. Then why did she so feel so lousy about herself?

She stared at the mirror for almost another minute. But it gave her no answer to her question.

Jackie licked her lips and twisted away. Okay, nothing there. Nothing in the condo. Nothing but four walls, walls staring back at her on a glorious day when all the world seemed content. All but her.

She shrugged and decided to get out of the condo. She would drive down to Peachtree Precinct. See what treasures the weekend had delivered. At least at the station she would find some warm bodies. The four walls of an empty apartment made for pretty poor company on a sunny Sunday afternoon.

Moving quickly now that she had made a decision, she slipped into a pair of khaki pants and a navy blouse. Her gun, a police issue Glock 17, rested in its holster hanging on the bottom post of her bed. She lifted the weapon and strapped it around her shoulder. A bulky beige sweater that concealed the gun completed her outfit.

It didn't take her long to reach the station. She lived only ten minutes away. On a quiet Sunday like today she made it in seven. Jackie liked living so near her work. Less muss and bother with traffic.

Avery Mays always told her she should get farther away. Her proximity made it too easy to go in when she shouldn't, he said.

She argued that was precisely why she liked her location. She lived for her work. She loved the rhythm of an investigation, the movement toward culmination that cases inevitably took. One slow step after another, a process like building a house, one block on top of another block. If she hadn't ended up a detective, she would probably have become an architect. She loved the symmetry of putting the bits and pieces of a case together, putting them together until the form became apparent and led to an arrest.

As one of the youngest females in Atlanta to ever make detective, she felt it her duty to uphold the standards for every woman who would follow her. Her work gave her life meaning.

At least at one time it had. The last couple of years, though, she had found the work less and less satisfying. She knew now she needed more.

Parking her car, Jackie hopped out and sucked in a deep breath. *Goodness, what a beautiful day. Chilly but not a cloud in the sky.* People out walking their dogs. Birds chirping. Couples holding hands. And her feeling so completely alone.

Nodding to the duty officer at the entryway, Jackie checked in and headed for her cubicle on the right side of the narrow hall, four offices down from Derrick Role. His office door was partially open. Jackie started to knock and go in, then thought better of it. No use bothering the boss.

She stepped to her desk, a city-issue metal job. Since Avery Mays's retirement last summer, she had really felt at loose ends. Not given to making friends easily, Jackie had no intimates at Peachtree now, no one in whom to confide. *Oh well,* she sighed, *it will get better eventually.* She had to believe it would. The alternative was too bleak not to believe it.

Flipping on her computer, Jackie scanned through Saturday's crime reports. She saw nothing remarkable. Just the usual weekend mayhem. She leaned back from the computer and stood up. A knock sounded on her door.

"Come in," she said.

Derrick Role, fresh in his starched white shirt and cuff links, pushed into her space.

"I thought I saw you walk by," he said.

"Yep, too quiet at home."

"You checking through the file?"

"Thought I'd get an update. See if anything interesting happened yesterday."

"See anything?"

"No, not really. The usual assortment."

Role grunted and looked down at his feet. "We had a call a few minutes ago you might find intriguing."

She waited for him to continue.

"A missing person's report," he said.

Jackie shrugged. "So? We get them every weekend. Teenagers, angry husbands, roommates who split up at bars and don't check in the next morning."

"This one is the wife of Bobby Benton."

"Triple B?"

"None other."

Jackie paused and eased back into the chair behind her desk. Role remained standing. Jackie asked, "When did she disappear?"

"Mr. Benton's not sure. He was driving in a race at the Dixie Land Speedway. It's a little dirt track about twenty miles out. Mrs. Benton left the stands at about seven. Told her friend she wasn't feeling well and needed to go to the rest room. Told her friend that if she didn't feel better, she would go on home. That's the last anyone saw of her."

Jackie picked a paper clip off her desk. "So why didn't Mr. Benton call us last night when he got home, when he first found her missing?"

Role fingered his right cuff link. "Mr. Benton didn't go home. He left the racetrack with a couple of buddies. They had a morning of hunting planned. He made it home about 1:00 P.M. today."

"So Mrs. Benton could have gone home last night? Then left to go somewhere else this morning. Maybe she just hasn't come home yet."

"That's possible," said Role. "And Mr. Benton thought of it. So he checked around. Called her closest friends. None of them have seen her. And she has no family in Atlanta to visit."

"So Mr. Benton called us."

"Yep, about an hour ago. He said this wasn't like her. Said she never went anywhere without telling him, leaving him a note or something."

"But we really don't know if she's missing or not," countered Jackie. "She might be out Christmas shopping."

Role moved closer and perched on the edge of her desk. "That was my first reaction too. But with Mr. Benton being such a prominent man and with the death of Leslie Staton last weekend, I decided to handle this cautiously. I dispatched a blue team to drive by the racetrack. See if they saw anything."

"And did they?"

Role sighed. "They found Mrs. Bobby Benton's car."

For several beats Jackie said nothing. She felt her heart pounding under her blouse. The gun strapped to her side seemed to move in rhythm to her heartbeat. A spot of sweat the size of a butter plate welled up under each of her arms.

"So we can assume someone abducted her."

"Unless she was so sick she took a cab to a hospital or something. Or she met someone she doesn't want Mr. Benton or anyone else to know about."

Jackie stood and walked around Role to the one square window that graced the right side of her office. The sun had almost disappeared. The wonderful Sunday was about over. She wrapped her arms around her waist and hugged herself. For a moment she felt cold.

What if she had disappeared over the weekend? Who would even know? No one. Absolutely no one. She could vanish overnight and not a single soul would ever know. To make it worse, other than an ailing mother in Albany and a former partner she hardly ever saw, she couldn't think of too many who would truly care.

Sighing, she turned back to Role. "You want me to get the process started?"

He nodded and raised off her desk. "Yeah, but discreetly. Until we know more, we can't do much. All we have is a missing person. So check it out, but go slowly. We're walking a tightrope here. We can't panic over a missing person who might turn up any minute. But neither can we sit on our hands when the wife of a man as well-known as Bobby Benton disappears."

Jackie nodded. Role certainly understood the politics of it all.

Chapter 16

Monday, December 5

Monday morning dawned bright and sunny, but Stubs McVaine hardly noticed as he stepped out of his car at 7:18 A.M. He never noticed the weather on Monday mornings. For Stubs McVaine, Monday mornings were as welcome as acne to a seventeen-year-old on the night of the prom.

He disliked Monday mornings because they always produced the grisly harvest of an Atlanta weekend. And seventeen years of experience told Stubs that an Atlanta weekend never produced a crop worth harvesting. But harvest them they did.

The ambulances delivered them from the funeral homes, from the hospitals, and from the nursing homes. They delivered the toe-tagged, chilled-down, bullet-filled, and disease-riddled remains of big-city violence and death.

Stubs knew how essential his work was. Autopsies provided road maps to police investigators. They suggested the cause of death, the time of death, the weapon of death, the direction from which the death injury came. Anything and everything you wanted to know about death, death, death. Not a pretty business. But a necessary and usually helpful one.

At times he became a full-fledged partner in the process of solving crimes. Because he recognized the value of his work, Stubs usually remained reasonably content, if not exactly ecstatic. But he was still a merchant in the wares of death. And, goodness, Monday mornings were a test of a strong man's fortitude.

Walking through the parking lot toward his office, Stubs lifted a cup of steaming coffee to his lips. Though the temperature hovered at about 45 degrees, he wore a short-sleeved blue dress shirt but no jacket. The black hair that lay like a fur rug on his arms stood to attention against the chill.

Sucking on his coffee, he checked in with the security desk, slipped on his white lab coat, and clicked on the computer in his office. Propping his feet on his desk, he scanned the screen, reading through the list detailing the weekend's body count.

Stubs didn't do all the examinations himself. No way one person could handle all the Atlanta traffic. A team of more than twenty doctors and lab technicians worked with him to keep the bodies moving across the metal examination tables and out the door to their eventual burial places.

Stubs worked exclusively with the police department now, though that's not how he started out seventeen years ago. But as forensics became more specialized, the doctors did too. For the last nine years he had served as the principal medical examiner for the Atlanta Police Department. He liked his work, but not enough for him to look forward to Mondays.

He heard a knock on his door. He glanced up from the computer. Frieda stuck her head into his office.

"You checking out the list?" she asked.

"Checking it twice," he said. "And it looks like Atlanta's been naughty and not nice."

"You see the one we got a few minutes ago?"

Stubs raced his eyes over the list again. He saw one marked 6:12 A.M. A woman. Not yet identified. No list of injuries listed on the sheet yet. Too early for that.

"Police have any idea who she is?"

"Not yet, but one of the guys who brought her in said they'd had three missing person's reports since Saturday that fit her general description. I'm sure they're checking it now."

Stubs opened his drawer and pulled out a cigarette. "Who found her?" he asked, lighting his smoke.

"A jogger," she said. "In Curry Park. Lying on a bench. Wrapped up in a sheet. It's all there, soon as you get a chance to read it."

"You see her yet?"

"Nope, just got here thirty minutes ago. No one has done anything except bring her in. Per procedure, she's still in the sheet so we don't lose anything."

Stubs nodded and punched the computer keyboard, drawing up the directory that listed the known details for each of the bodies in his care. "Pull her out, Frieda," he said to the redhead. "We need to take a look at her."

Frieda twisted and marched off. Stubs focused on the computer screen. Hit the print key. Waited for the paper to spool out. Lifted the paper from the printer. Stood to go to the examination room.

Within minutes, he had slipped into his gown, donned his rubber gloves and mask, and stepped to the side of the metal table that supported the body of the dead woman. With a nod, he gave Frieda the go-ahead. She unwrapped the folds of the sheet covering the body.

A woman in faded blue jeans and a sweater the color of a Christmas tree lay in front of him. Early to mid-forties, he guessed. He saw a wedding ring on her left hand. Subtract robbery as a motive.

Her face was clean, unmarked. So clean, she looked almost alive. The cold weather over the weekend had preserved her well. Her hair, copper colored, was slightly mussed as if she had slept on it the wrong way.

Stubs raised his eyebrows and scanned her face and throat more carefully. "Don't see much here," he said, as if to himself. "Typical signs of exposure. It did get cold this weekend."

"Under thirty Saturday and Sunday nights," said Frieda.

Stubs saw a discoloration on the woman's neck. "A contusion on the left side of the neck," he said. "Running from the middle of the throat to the back of the head. Someone whacked her one from behind and slightly to the left side, I'd say."

After a few more moments of study, he nodded and took a breath. "Okay," he said. "Let's flip her."

Grabbing the body by the ankles and under the back of the shoulders, he and Frieda gently rolled it over. Stubs grunted and Frieda gasped. Dried black blood caked the body from the base of the neck all the way down past the buttocks, all the way to the knees.

Through the blood, Stubs saw that the back of the sweater and jeans was missing. The back of both garments had been cut out—as if someone had taken scissors to them and sliced away the material. From the top of the shoulder to the knees, bare and bloody skin stared up at them.

The deceased had been beaten. No, *whipped* described it better. For several seconds Stubs didn't move. He desperately wanted a cigarette. He sucked the air, trying to pull it down into his lungs. *Man, what a mess.*

The wounds cut deeply into the flesh. Deeper than a normal belt would do. And there weren't really any welts visible either. Swelling yes, but welts no. More like lashes. Lashes biting into the tissue and digging out the skin.

Careful not to touch the skin, Stubs lifted his right hand into the air and moved his fingers in a tracer pattern over the wounds. He tried to imagine the killer as he carried out the whipping.

What angle did he take? What kind of whip did he use? Was the woman standing or lying down as she received the blows?

Stubs stopped his tracing for a moment. His bald head leaned closer to the body. The bright lights overhead glistened off his hairless dome.

He picked up a pair of surgical tweezers from the instruments lying by the table and reached toward the upper right shoulder of the remains of the woman. He touched one of the gashes in her shoulder. Probed into it for a long second. Pinched his thumb and forefinger together. Lifted out a quarter-of-an-inch sliver of an off-white, unidentified material. Held the sliver up to the light. Squinted as he studied it.

"What do you think it is?" asked Frieda.

"Well," said Stubs, still staring at the object, "you know I'm not one to make conjectures. But, if I'm guessing, I would say this is a piece of bone of some kind."

"Bone?"

"Yep, bone—as in knee bone connected to shin bone and so on and so forth."

"Is it hers?"

"Nope, don't think so. The cuts in this area don't go deep enough for that."

"Then what would bone be doing—?"

Stubs shook his head vigorously. The flesh under his chin rocked back and forth. "Now, there you go again. Don't ask what we can't answer yet. Until we test it, we don't talk about it. Got that?"

Frieda nodded her agreement. Stubs cleared his throat and handed the sliver of material to her. "Bag it," he said.

He stared back at the woman's body. *Such a shame,* he thought. *So sad.* It looked like a tough Monday lay ahead of him.

Chapter 17

"So I'll see you again next Monday," said Burke, standing to follow the man and woman out the door of his interview room. The couple nodded and stopped by Molly's desk to make the appointment.

Burke walked back to his office, sat down, and called Debbi. He did this every day at 12:30 sharp. He didn't reach her every day, but he called anyway. The doting of a newlywed, Debbi called it. "Give it about a year," she said, "and you won't even return my calls, much less make one yourself."

Burke smiled. Right now he certainly didn't feel like it would end. Right now, he loved her more than he did the day he married her. He heard her answer.

"Yes, sweet lady," he said. "It's me. Aren't you surprised?"

Debbi laughed. "Overwhelmed with shock," she said. "How's your day going?"

"Oh, you know, the usual, an alcoholic at 8:30, an anorexic at 10:00, and a husband and wife who have forgotten they need to talk to each other at 11:30."

Debbi sighed. "Not an easy job you have there."

"Well, they never promised me a rose garden. What about you? Anything exciting today?" He swiveled his chair so he could look out the window. The couple he'd just seen climbed into a blue pickup truck and drove off.

"Nothing much so far. I didn't get here until about eleven. Since then I've made a couple of calls, tried to reach Hal Staton again, but no luck. I don't know if he's ever going to make a statement to the press."

"What about the woman who said she saw Leslie Staton in the parking lot before her abduction? And the Triple A repairman? Any contact with them today?"

For a second, the line fell silent. Burke wondered if he had upset Debbi. He knew she had not talked to these people yet. But Reginald

Voss had. The witnesses had come to him to offer their accounts. For a price, of course.

It was one of the drawbacks of print journalism. Television offered more glamour and more money. With a high-profile case like this, print reporters without cash to offer usually fell far behind the tube in the race for exclusive headlines.

Mimi Stoddard had jumped all over Debbi for not getting to the people first. No matter that Debbi had no way to even know who they were. Stoddard had called her at home on Sunday—the moment she saw the television interviews. Told Debbi the *Independent* paid her to ferret out these people, to get their stories before anyone else.

"No, nothing from them," reported Debbi. "I tried to call, but they're not available. Apparently, they've said all they have to say."

"Until somebody offers to slip them another check," suggested Burke.

"Yeah, probably so."

"What else you working on?"

She cleared her throat. "Well, unfortunately, we've got three women reported missing over the weekend. A teenager last seen at a high school basketball game Friday night, a great-grandmother who disappeared from a nursing home on Saturday about 6:00 P.M. and the wife of Bobby Bartholomew Benton who went to the bathroom at a racetrack and never came back."

"Triple B Benton?"

"That's the guy. The man who does all the wacky used car commercials."

"I know," interrupted Burke. "His face is everywhere—billboards, television, you name it. He's one of the best-known personalities in Atlanta. Rich as a country club Republican but no pedigree to match. Any word on the—"

"Hold it a second, Burke," said Debbi. He heard her drop the phone. An indistinct voice chattered with Debbi on the other end. Burke pressed his ear to the phone, trying to hear the conversation. It sounded like Mimi Stoddard, but he couldn't be sure.

Holding the phone to his ear with his shoulder, he pulled a manilla file from his top left desk drawer and flipped through the notes on his next appointment. A teenage boy whose grades had suddenly started dropping. Parents suspected drugs. "Burke?"

"Yeah, still here."

"Look, I gotta go. We just got word that the medical examiner's office has the body of one of the missing women. A jogger found her this morning in Curry Park. Stoddard wants me to get over there, see what I can find out, then head to the police station. Detective Role has a news conference scheduled for six. Can you meet me there? At Peachtree?"

Burke leaned back in his chair and took a deep breath. Here came the choice again. He wished Debbi would stop asking him these things. He had already fulfilled his part of the bargain when he called Jackie Broadus. That was enough.

"I don't need to be there, Debbi," he said, trying to keep his voice even. "As I've said, this is your baby, not mine."

"But aren't you interested in this?"

"Of course I'm interested. But it's not something for me to stick my nose in. You go ahead. I'll see you at home later. You can tell me all about it then."

He heard Debbi clear her throat. He imagined her chewing on her hair. Her sign of concern.

"If that's the way you want it," she said.

"I think it's best."

"Okay, see you tonight. Love you."

"You too, precious." Burke cradled the phone into its base and leaned back in his seat. He knew he'd have a hard time concentrating this afternoon. He sensed, without exactly understanding why, that the dead woman was the missing wife of Triple B Benton.

Chapter 18

B acked up by a traffic jam on the north loop, Debbi arrived at Peachtree Station about twenty minutes past six. Most of her competitors were already in place, and Detective Derrick Role had already made his opening statement. Spotting Mimi Stoddard in the second row of the bustling mob, she began to squeeze through the camera gear and portable lights and production technicians and media personalities. Though a few people seemed reluctant to let her pass, within a couple of minutes she tapped Stoddard on the shoulder.

"Where have you been?" Stoddard hissed, keeping her voice low.

"Behind a zillion cars on the loop. A cattle truck wrecked and the highway was covered with Holsteins. Nothing I could do about it. What did I miss?"

"A bunch. Detective Role started fifteen minutes ago. Said a jogger found a body in Curry Park at about five this morning. They've identified the woman as Rosaline, or Rosey Anita Benton, wife of Bobby Bartholomew Benton. Died sometime Sunday they think. Just like with Leslie Staton. Tests are continuing now."

Debbi nodded and considered the ramifications. Two women abducted—one on Friday, one on Saturday. Killed on consecutive Sundays. Advent Sundays.

Debbi swallowed hard and turned her attention to Role. The detective seemed as calm as quiet water, impervious to the frenzy of scribbling pencils and whirring tape recorders and moving cameras. Role's voice oozed through the shuffling room.

"Though I cannot and will not divulge the manner of this woman's death, let me say one thing and make it as clear as I possibly can make it. I say this to preempt the first question I expect you to ask. The demise of Rosaline Benton occurred in a manner totally incongruent with the manner of death for Leslie Staton. It in no way, I repeat, no way, matches that, or even approximates that of Leslie Staton. Both these women apparently died on a Sunday, but except for that fact, they have nothing in common. So we have no reason to suspect anything but two separate killers. Anyone who speculates otherwise does so without benefit of any known fact to support that conclusion. Now, I'll take a few questions."

Hands shot into the air all over the room. Role smiled and pointed to a skinny reporter to his left. "Yeah, can you tell us why we didn't get word about the disappearance of Mrs. Benton over the weekend?"

Role shrugged. "That's easy. Mr. Benton didn't report it until Sunday afternoon about three. He had no reason to do so until then. Mrs. Benton felt sick Saturday night at the track. Told her friend she was going to the bathroom; if she didn't feel better, she would go home. When she didn't come back, no one suspected a thing.

"After the race, Mr. Benton went out for the night with some buddies. He arrived back home about one Sunday afternoon. When he didn't find his wife there, he called around. He couldn't find her. So he called us.

"At that point, we started the process for a missing person search. But we get those on a regular basis. It wasn't a murder until this morning. That's when the body was discovered. So that's when we informed the media."

He stopped and fingered his left cuff link. Hands shot into the sky again. Role pointed to Reginald Voss. The popular anchor nodded. His voice matched Role's for calm richness. "Detective, you've made it clear from your opening statement that you don't believe these two deaths connect. Yet what are the chances that the wives of two fairly well-known personalities would disappear and then turn up dead on consecutive weekends? Doesn't that seem a bit odd to you?"

Role shrugged and hitched at his pants with his elbows. "Not necessarily. Hundreds of so-called personalities live in and around Atlanta. Ball players, politicians, actors, and actresses—you name it and we have it. Even used car salesmen and media people. Anyone can get famous here. And, as we all know far better than we want, about 375 people a year, almost eight a weekend, get killed in Atlanta. So for this to happen would fall well within the bounds of possibility. In fact, it's probably a wonder it doesn't happen any more than it does. We—"

"So you're completely ruling out the possibility of a connection between these two deaths?" interrupted Voss.

Role grunted and scowled for an instant. Then he smiled again. "You press your case, Mr. Voss. Let's give someone else a chance."

The hands reached for the sky. Role nodded to Debbi. She cleared her throat. "Would Detective Broadus concur with your conclusion?"

she asked, nodding toward the tall female detective standing to Role's left, on the floor level below the raised platform.

A murmur rose from the crowd. Role wouldn't take kindly to that question. It took attention away from him.

Role stepped back from the microphone and grinned. His wide teeth seemed to brighten the room. "I'll let Detective Broadus answer for herself."

Stepping up and over to the mike, Jackie flipped her long dark hair off her shoulders. When she spoke the room fell silent. Her voice rose from her throat without effort, a voice slightly husky and a bit mysterious.

"From what we know right now," she began, "I would concur with the conclusion reached by Detective Role. The methods of death differ completely. That doesn't fit with a typical serial killer. Everything Mrs. Staton had with her was taken—right down to the clothes on her back. So robbery could have been the motive with her. Not so with Mrs. Benton. The descriptions of the last people seen with the two women also differ dramatically. So given these facts, we cannot, at this point, operate on any theory other than two different perpetrators. But, as I'm sure Detective Role would agree, we remain open to the evidence. As we receive other information, we will consider it. And upon receiving that information, if we decide that the possibility of a serial killer exists, we will immediately notify the media and the public."

Role held up his hand as Jackie broke off her answer. Role said, "Let me assure you that the safety of the people of Atlanta remains our primary consideration. If, and that's a big 'if', if we get anything that indicates a connection between these deaths, we will warn people without delay. You have my word on that." Mimi Stoddard shot her hand into the air.

"Detective Role, when do you expect to receive the autopsy report?"

A softball question, thought Debbi. One that allowed Role to switch the focus.

"Well, we've already received preliminary information from the medical examiner. That's why I'm here with you. More comprehensive tests, fiber, blood, gastrointestinal, etc. will obviously take more time."

A squatty guy beside Stoddard shouted, "Do you know how she died?"

"Yes, we do think we know what killed her."

"Do you know the weapon used?"

"I have no comment on that at this time."

"Was it a gun?" shouted the squatty man. "Or a knife?" yelled someone else from the front. "What about strangulation? I heard the first woman got strangled."

The questions poured from everywhere now, one shouted out after another. The air filled with questions like arrows raining down from the heavens. The crowd seemed to have lost its sanity.

"Let's get out of here," yelled Debbi, trying to get Stoddard to hear her over the crowd. "I think the mob has taken over."

Stoddard shook her head. "You go ahead with what you've got. I'll hang in until he's finished. If he says something off the cuff that might help us, I'll call you."

Nodding her understanding, Debbi said, "I'll see you at the paper."

A couple of moments later, she pushed her way out the door of the station house and into the silence of the front walk. Hugging her sweater to her shoulders, she walked out to the street. Traffic moved by as the light changed. She stopped and took a deep breath. Off to the left, at the front of a mall, she saw an artificial Christmas tree the height of a telephone pole. Feeling a need to clear her head, she forgot about going back to the paper and headed toward the tree.

The lights on the tree—red and green and yellow and white—blinked on and off, on and off, on and off. A car passed, and the sounds of a carol whipped out the window and through the air. She reached the door of the mall and opened it. The smell of peppermint hit her nostrils.

But she didn't feel much like celebrating. The first two Sundays of Advent. Two women dead. What a horrible time to die.

Chapter 19

On Tuesday morning at 7:15, Burke took Debbi by the hand and walked her briskly toward the front door of Danny's Doughnut Shop, a ramshackle but extremely successful breakfast spot favored by truckers, construction workers, and environmentally conscious yuppie types who wanted to mingle with people with mud on their boots. Burke and Debbi liked it because Danny baked the doughnuts himself—fresh every morning.

The smell of coffee hung in the air, and its warm aroma softened the edge of the morning's damp chill. A cloud of fog wrapped around the earth, hiding the sun and making the orange roof over Danny's ghostlike, like some kind of Chinese pagoda rising out of the mist. Burke opened the door for Debbi as they pushed inside. The sound of a Randy Travis song poured out of the jukebox. Burke quickly scanned the room. He spotted Jackie Broadus in a booth in the back.

Without waiting for a waitress, he steered Debbi toward Jackie. They exchanged pleasantries as he and Debbi sat down.

"You ordered yet?" asked Burke.

Jackie nodded. "Yeah, for all of us. Grits, eggs, and toast. You said on the phone you had to make this fast."

"Yeah, I do. I have an 8:30 appointment."

A waitress in a yellow uniform appeared at Burke's shoulder. Burke stared at her for a moment but didn't recognize her. She was new at Danny's.

"You want something to drink?" she asked, staring at Burke and Debbi.

"Yeah, root beer," said Burke. The waitress stared at him for a skip as if he were crazy, then nodded and turned to Debbi.

"Orange juice for me," said Debbi. The waitress scooted off.

Jackie jumped right in. "You didn't seem too eager about this meeting," she said, facing Burke.

Burke's mind skipped back to the previous evening. Debbi had come home late. Talked to him for two hours, giving him all the gory details of another murder. He didn't particularly want to hear it. He felt like a moth getting pulled into the dancing flames of a major fire, and he knew what happened to moths when they flew too close to heat.

Jackie had called right after sunup. Her insistent voice instantly jarred him awake. She needed to talk to him she said. He considered for a moment how he could refuse her request. But then he realized he couldn't. She hadn't refused him when he asked for help for Debbi. Seeing no way to avoid the meeting, he set up the place and time.

"You just surprised me, that's all," he said, staring across at her. "I didn't expect to hear from you."

Jackie shrugged. "I need somebody I can trust to think through this with me. I'm not comfortable with anyone at Peachtree right now."

"That's honest enough."

"It's the situation as I see it."

Debbi leaned forward. "We're glad you called, Jackie. If we can help, we want to do it."

Jackie nodded. "You won't believe the latest one," she said. "A really bizarre situation. That's why I wanted you to read this. Whoever did this is wound differently from anyone I've ever seen. It gives me the heebie-jeebies."

She picked up a manilla envelope from the seat beside her and slipped it over to them. Burke opened it, and Debbi leaned over his shoulder to read along.

Basic information about Rosaline Anita Benton on the first page. An up-to-date account of the investigation on the second. Details about the death on the third and beyond.

Burke's brown eyes widened as he slowed his pace and read the autopsy.

"Lashes extend from just above the back of the knee to the top of the shoulders. On average, these lashes cut a good two inches into the flesh. At certain places, especially above the buttocks in the back of the abdominal area, the cuts gouged even deeper. The gashes caused massive loss of blood and internal shock. From the interwoven nature of the cuts, it is impossible to determine the exact number of the blows. My best estimate says that the abductor whipped her between thirty-five and forty-five times.

"Other than the lashes, the wounds on Mrs. Benton's body were minimal. Abrasions around the wrists. And a laceration on the back of the skull, as if from a stout stick."

Sweat broke out on Burke's forehead. The yellow-clad waitress popped a root beer and an orange juice onto the table. Burke jumped, startled by the movement. He stopped reading and looked up at Jackie. She shrugged her shoulders and stared down at the top of the linoleum-covered table as if trying to escape. "What do you make of this?" he asked, his voice soft.

She sighed and shook her head. "It's beyond me. I was hoping you'd tell me something."

Burke turned to Debbi. She pushed a strand of blonde hair into the corner of her mouth and chewed on it. "She was whipped," she said.

Burke lifted his root beer and sucked down a drink. He looked at Jackie. "I don't see anything about sexual violation."

"That's because there wasn't any."

He twirled his glass around. "And there wasn't any with Staton either?"

"Nope. But that doesn't mean there's any connection between the two."

"I know that. The method of death is too different."

"And Staton was robbed," interjected Debbi. "Nothing left on her. Absolutely nothing, except that one red shoe."

Burke twirled his glass again. "But the same kind of anger that killed Leslie Staton also killed Rosaline Benton. A hideous, monstrous anger."

"You think the same person killed both of these women?" asked Jackie.

He shook his head. "No, I can't say that, don't have any basis to say that. All I'm saying is the same *kind* of person killed these women. Somebody so tortured inside, so emotionally scarred, so fouled up from some terrible trauma in their past that now they're acting out their anger, paying someone back."

"Sounds like a lot of psychological mumbo jumbo to me," said Jackie. "Whatever happened to plain old meanness? What you would call 'evil'?"

Burke nodded. "No doubt these killers are evil, Jackie, more evil than we can imagine. So evil they've lost the ability to feel their conscience. So evil life means nothing to them and death means everything."

Jackie turned for a second and stared out the window. The vague outline of a cedar tree was silhouetted against the fog. She turned back to Burke and Debbi. "I don't understand that, Burke."

He glanced at Debbi, then leaned toward Jackie. "What don't you understand, Jackie?"

"I don't understand why such evil exists. If God exists like you say, and if God loves us like you insist, then why does God allow this kind of evil?"

"That's a question theologians have tried to solve for centuries. There's no easy answer."

"Then give me the hard one."

Burke took a sip from his glass. "Okay, try this. Imagine you're God. You want to create a world. You want to create human beings. You want those human beings to love you, to worship you. But how do you get them to do that?

"Love, if it's genuine, has to be chosen. You can't make someone love you; you can't force someone to worship you.

"So God created us and gave us choices. He wants us to choose love, love for God and for other people. But not everyone does. Some choose evil, they choose to reject God, they choose to hurt other people." He paused and shrugged. "That's the way I understand it."

"So we do it to each other."

"Yes, we bring evil into the world through our sin."

Jackie bit her lower lip. "And you say Jesus gives us a way out of it?"

"No, Jesus doesn't give us a way out of the world. So long as we're alive, we'll struggle with sin and evil. Not everyone will choose faith. And even those who do will still foul it up from time to time. But Jesus gives us the way out of our sin. Jesus gives us grace, and grace is a way out of our evil; it gives us forgiveness."

"All we have to do is ask for it?"

Burke smiled. "That's what I believe, Jackie. It's a free gift. We open our hands and receive what God offers to us."

Jackie opened her hands, palms up, and studied them for several long moments. She closed her hands into fists. "It's too easy," she said. "Some of us don't deserve that gift."

Debbi, silent so far through the exchange, covered Jackie's hands with hers. "Hey, Jackie, none of us deserve it. That's the wonder of it all. God gives us what we don't deserve. If we had to earn it, no one could receive forgiveness. We all come to God with empty—"

The waitress slapped three platters onto the table and interrupted Debbi. "You need anything else?" she asked.

"Nope, we're fine," said Burke, hoping the intrusion wouldn't derail their conversation. "We'll let you know if we need anything."

He focused on Jackie again but saw instantly that the moment had passed. She sipped from her coffee a couple of times, then changed the subject. "Well, look, I appreciate what you've both been saying, and I'll think about it some more I'm sure, but right now I've got a couple of other things on my mind. Like the possibility of not one but two sociopaths running around in Atlanta at the same time. Burke, what's the probability of that?"

Burke smiled a grim smile and decided not to press her back to the subject of faith. Pressure wouldn't work with someone like Jackie. He stayed with her train of thought. "Oh, from what I've seen, the chances are very good. In fact, I think it's a miracle we don't have more of this than we do."

He stared down at the autopsy report again. His eyes squinted as he glanced over the page. Something about the report jarred a dim memory, poked at a forgotten fact, but he couldn't put his finger on it. He took a bite of eggs. Still confused, he said. "They *don't* seem to connect, do they?"

"Apparently not," said Jackie. "Except for the day they died, they have nothing else in common that I can see."

"Don't forget they're both the wives of well-known Atlanta personalities," said Debbi.

"But that's not necessarily a connection," said Jackie.

"Unless there's a connection between them," said Burke. "Maybe the husbands are members of the same health club, participated in the same Rotary, attended the same church or something."

"We're checking that," said Jackie. "But so far nothing we've found indicates any relationship. I've spent most of my time talking to the people who saw Staton and Benton right before their abductions. A woman in a Taurus saw Staton in the parking lot right before she disappeared. Said she saw a white Mercedes. The woman described a gray-haired man there."

"And Benton?"

"One man saw her outside the rest room talking to another guy. But the witness said he didn't notice much—he was in a bad way, bladder-wise. The only thing he remembered was the guy had on dark glasses and looked kind of shabby."

"Not the Mercedes type?" asked Debbi.

"Not at all.'"

Burke took a bite of his eggs. "What about the wives?" he asked.

"What about them?" asked Jackie.

"Anything tie them together?"

"That's another unknown. We're not that far down the line yet." said Jackie. "Remember, no one is proposing the theory that the same killer did both women. In fact, Role says point blank that a different person did them. So no need to delve too far into finding a common thread. As long as we reject a serial killer, we're investigating two different cases."

Burke nodded. "Nothing else you can do then, is there?"

"Nope, except keep our eyes and ears open. See if anything turns up to connect the two."

Leaning back in his seat, Burke twisted and looked out the window. The fog still lay over the ground. He couldn't see a thing past the edge of the building. The traffic zipping by on the street forty feet away was ghostlike, practically invisible. It seemed so odd to him. Here it was, right in the middle of the Christmas season, the season when God proclaimed good news to the world, the season when God came to cleanse the world of sin and evil and make all things right, and a monster or monsters stalked the streets of Atlanta killing women for no apparent reason. Staring out the window, he nodded at Jackie, then whispered, "Oh, you can mark my word, Jackie—something will turn up."

Chapter 20 ♦

A white cat wearing a rhinestone-studded collar eased into the ten-by-twelve closet and rubbed up against a set of slender but well-muscled legs. From above, a pair of eyes as black as fresh asphalt stared down at the cat.

"In a moment, Snow," said the figure in the closet, the voice high and breathy. "In a moment."

Snow blinked and stared up at her owner.

Above the cat, a handful of fingers—as thin as chopsticks and well manicured—trembled slightly as they pulled a leather-encased notebook off the top shelf. Squeezing the notebook in the thin fingers, the figure padded lightly to an eighteenth-century mahogany writing desk and sat down. Snow jumped onto the desk by her owner.

For a second, both of them sat still and stared past the desk and out the open window.

The window always stayed open—even in the dead of winter—as if waiting for someone to enter—or escape.

On the ground below, a pack of brown leaves, the last of the autumn hold-ons, skittered like a pack of frightened gerbils toward the wrought iron gate that surrounded the two-story colonial home. From the gate—the center of a ten-foot tall fence with spikes on the top—a cobblestone driveway snaked to the four columns that guarded the front of the imposing structure. The house, a red-brick colonial, rested in the center of six acres, looming over the grounds like a sentinel watching for anything to step out of place. Tonight nothing did.

Inside the house, Snow's nose wrinkled. Beside her, so also did her owner's nose twitch. "Nothing to smell, Snow," said the breathy voice. "Nothing foul and fetid."

A cold wind popped through the open window momentarily, but no aroma blew in with it. The world seemed empty of smells, as if a vacuum cleaner had sucked them all up and out of the air.

The black eyes shifted back to the notebook, and the thin fingers unsnapped the cover of the diary and flipped open the pages. The black eyes read slowly over the words.

Snow meowed, and a handful of the thin fingers left the pages of the diary and rubbed the cat behind the ears. As if reading along with its owner, the cat sat down and zeroed its green eyes on the notebook.

The black eyes savored the first two pages, rereading the beginning of the entry from Monday, November 28. The writing was precise and neat, though small, as if written by someone from a land of midgets.

The figure at the desk breathed softly while reading the entry, relishing the memories the words brought back.

"It began yesterday, the first Sunday of Advent. The day I turned thirty-three. My Jesus year. The year it all needs to happen. For me to reach my completion. For me to follow my destiny. For me to claim my revenge. . . ."

The words spilled on across the page, words describing the abduction of Leslie Staton, words detailing her murder, words rehashing the publicity created by her death. . . .

The thin fingers pushed a strand of bleached blonde hair off the forehead. In its natural state, the hair matched the pitch-black eyes. But dyes had changed the hair color fourteen times in the last ten years.

Three years ago, surgery had changed the face. Shaved down the nose to make it less sharp, less prominent. Tightened up the skin under the chin and along the ear lines. Made the face seem extremely slender, as if someone had put on a mask that wasn't quite big enough for the frame underneath.

That described the figure at the desk precisely. A mask not quite big enough for the frame underneath. No one knew what lay underneath the mask, the mask worn so convincingly every day, the mask that moved so effortlessly in normal society and seemed so, well, so acceptable and real.

But the mask hid the reality. Hid it underneath a dozen disguises, a hundred facades, a thousand faces. The faces were easy—one disguise after another. Disguises of men aged twenty-five to fifty-five and women from thirty to forty. *Faces, faces everywhere. Faces, faces, masks we wear.*

The lips on the stretched face grinned. But the lips were as thin as the face, and the grin seemed more like a sliver of pain than a smile of joy. But the lips deceived. The heart beneath the grin felt genuine joy tonight, joy at the success of the last two Sundays.

Both episodes had followed the script to a T. The abductions, the trips to the hideaway in the concrete basement under the brick house, the punishment that followed, the death that came next, the return of the bodies. One body to the capitol. One body to Curry Park. One on the brick. One on the bench.

So clever, so cool.

Yes, it had all transpired according to the plan. The plan that had been evolving for years. Evolving as the year of thirty-three approached. The Jesus Year.

The slim lips grinned again, and the fingers left the cat's ears. The cat jumped off the desk and rubbed up against her owner's calves. The fingers turned the page of the diary to the description of the second death, the death of Rosaline Benton.

What a wonderful disguise chosen for that bit of work! A blind man.

A blind man indeed. But they were the blind ones. All those out there who couldn't see, who didn't know the truth. Who didn't know the truth about life and death. The truth about God. Those who didn't know about the weakness of God. The weakness of God who couldn't prevent the suffering of helpless children. The weakness of God who couldn't or wouldn't deliver those children from the hands of adults who preyed on them.

The thin fingers trembled, and the notebook shook as the hideous memories pushed up. The memories of the humiliation suffered, the memories of the prayers asking for the humiliation to end, the memories of the prayers falling like dead leaves on winter grass, the memories of a God who either didn't hear or didn't choose to answer.

The fingers stopped shaking and gradually gripped the diary tighter. Well, now the child had grown up and no longer suffered from humiliation. The child had grown up since the years of weakness.

The child had spent sixteen years training in martial arts. The child had a body honed to a peak of perfection by rigorous daily workouts and strict attention to diet and rest. The child had attended college and graduate school and studied mythology and ancient religions. The child knew about weapons that were centuries old and tortures that only the strongest and most vile could imagine repeating. The child could mix wigs and makeup and masks until no one could tell anymore who lay behind the latest disguises.

Now the child who was no longer a child would show them. Now the child would extract the revenge that a weak God had refused to give.

The slender fingers closed the notebook, and both hands squeezed its leather cover for a moment. Then, laying the diary down, the figure stood, picked up the cat, and walked lightly over to the king-sized, four-poster bed that sat in the center of the cavernous room.

For a second, the black eyes skipped around the expensive furnishings. Then, with deliberate care, the slender fingers tossed the cat onto the bed. The room blurred in front of the black eyes.

As gently as a mother shooing a bee away from a baby's face, the thin fingers flicked away the tears that clogged the vision of both of the black eyes. Snow, sitting in the middle of the huge bed, licked her lips, stared at her owner, and meowed.

Chapter 21

With a diet soda in her left hand and a folder full of papers in her right, Jackie Broadus marched into Derrick Role's office immediately after lunch on Thursday and plopped herself down on the beige leather sofa sitting across from his desk. Role had brought the sofa from his own home. He was redecorating, he said, and didn't need it anymore.

Leaning against it, Jackie thought it looked new. Like the rest of the office. Role had redecorated the whole thing with his own money when he moved over from Buckhead. Not standard procedure, but the powers in administration didn't seem to mind so long as it didn't cost them anything.

Across from her, Role leaned back in his chair and linked his fingers behind his head. His cuff links flashed in the sun that flooded into the room from the window behind him. "So," he began, "tell me what we have."

Jackie readjusted her seat, pushing down the tan skirt she wore. She cleared her throat and thought for a moment about opening the folder that lay in her lap and reading from it. She didn't think she did well in these kinds of interviews.

Her former partner, Avery Mays, had always handled these situations. He kept track of the details, remembered with point-blank recall every word an interviewee spoke. In this kind of setting, he would rattle off exactly what the people had said and what the latest forensic studies showed. He would drown the brass with minutiae and leave them shaking their heads in wonder at his grasp of the case.

Jackie, meanwhile, sorted through the scattered pieces like the assembler of a puzzle. She lived more by instinct, by intuition and imagination. She looked for the big picture, the grand scheme, the feelings that drove a criminal, the motivation that pushed the murderer over the edge. She took the pieces Mays cataloged and began to tie them together—a corner to a corner, a blue piece to a blue piece, a thread to a thread. Gradually, the whole scene came into view. She and Mays had made a perfect team. He would lay the puzzle in front of her, and she would put it together.

She left the folder closed. "Well, we've spent the whole week sorting through everything we know and talking to everyone with any connection to these two families, and right now we have a jumble of information but nothing that leads us anywhere."

"Run me through it."

Jackie took a deep breath. "Well, I won't repeat the obvious. You know the approximate times of death, the days on which the abductions occurred, the actual causes of death, and the information gathered from the last people to see Staton and Benton alive. We know that the body bag around Staton is not army issue. It's like the ones used in morgues and hospitals. It probably came from a medical supply company. But no luck yet in tracing it. Both women were tied up, but we have no way to determine what kind of rope was used. We found no fiber on their wrists, no skin under nails, no signs of sexual involvement, nothing to tie us to a killer."

"So you're saying we're at a dead end?"

"Nope, I try to never say that. We're still interviewing people who work at the Braves' headquarters and at the racetrack. Maybe one of them saw something but hasn't come forward. Plus, we're running through the files we have on our celebrity stalkers to make sure one of those nuts isn't involved in this."

"If they were, then that would mean the two deaths are connected."

Jackie nodded. "Yes, but I think it's reasonable that we check the celebrity hounds. If we don't and it turns out one of them is involved, we'll look negligent if we haven't covered that base."

Role shrugged and waved her to continue. She did. "We're also checking for any enemies Staton or Benton might have had—someone with a grudge, a long-held anger, you know, the normal motivations for murder."

"You have to do that for the husbands too."

"I know. The grudge could be against Hal Staton, so they killed his wife. Same with the Bentons."

"It would seem odd if two celebrities or their wives had someone angry enough at them to kill them."

Jackie patted the folder. "It would, but I've seen odder things."

Nodding, Role rose from his chair and turned to stare out the window. "I'm under a lot of political tonnage here, Jackie. From the mayor. Above him, from the governor. I've gotten calls all week. The powers up the line want this thing wrapped up—and soon. It's a public-relations nightmare, everybody remembering what happened to Florida a few years ago when they had those highway shootings. Tourist traffic nose-dived like a seagull after a dead fish."

He pivoted to face her again. "What about the Mercedes in the parking lot?"

"Not a thing. It's disappeared without a trace. We've run a search on the people who park in that lot every day. Twenty-two Mercedeses, according to the report, but the owners either don't match the description or have alibis."

Role put his hands on his hips. "You have anything tying the two families together?"

Jackie paused for a moment and searched her mind. She and her assistants had found no connection so far. No mutual clubs, friends, or interests. Nothing. Except for the fact that they both lived in Atlanta and enjoyed a certain celebrity status, she knew of nothing else that the Statons and the Bentons shared in common.

"We haven't found a thing."

Role nodded as if she had proved his point. "Then that leaves us with no reason to believe in a serial killer."

Jackie had to agree. Role was right. They had no reason to suspect anything but two isolated deaths. She stared down at the report in her lap. She bit her lower lip and pressed down her skirt. She felt like she was missing something from the reports, some vital fact that she should know, some tidbit of information that would make some sense out of all the scattered pieces. But she couldn't think of anything.

"You're right. If we don't find something that connects them, then we have no basis to suspect a singular killer."

Role stepped back to his desk and took a seat. Looking down, he dismissed Jackie with a toss of his hand. "Keep at it," he said. "And keep me informed."

Without another word, she stood to leave. The folder in her lap slipped onto the floor. The photos taken at the medical examiner's office splashed across the beige carpet. For a second, Jackie stood transfixed over the scattered pieces. There it was, scattered at her feet. The pieces of the puzzle. The tragic evidence that she had to use to find the perpetrators of two horrible crimes.

She bent over and hurriedly picked up the mess, clutching it to her chest as she rushed out. Role never even glanced up.

As she walked into the hallway, her eyes blurred on her. She stopped and leaned against the wall. Her breath came in ragged gulps. Two women dead and she without a clue as to the identity of the killer. She felt as if she were sinking in quicksand, being drawn down and under, down and under into a dark place she didn't want to see.

She closed her eyes to calm herself. The pictures of Staton and Benton rose up behind her eyelids, and she shook her head trying to clear out the images. It didn't help. She opened her eyes.

The images of other murders she had investigated danced into her mind. The murder of a stoop-shouldered old man shot for the $4.26 he carried in his hip pocket; a fifteen-year-old girl killed by a jealous boyfriend; a business executive poisoned by a fellow worker who wanted his job. Murder, murder, murder. Premeditated, senseless, illogical murder.

Murder seemed inescapable, as pervasive as the breath she sucked into her lungs. She felt like she was choking—as if all the evil she had seen had its hands around her neck, choking her, killing her, squeezing the life out of her.

She wrapped her hands around her throat and rubbed up and down, fighting to slow her breathing. She swallowed and took several slow deep breaths.

Murder came with her job. The job that had cost her a husband. The job that seemed right now to bring nothing but bad dreams and broken relationships and lonely weekends.

She tried to think of something else. Something pleasant. Some person she could count on. She thought of Avery Mays. A tiny smile broke onto her face. Avery would understand.

She walked into her office and closed the door. She dialed Avery's number. No one answered. She sat down at her desk and wondered who else she could call. She did want to talk to someone, someone who could help her get some perspective on what she was feeling.

Burke Anderson. She could talk to him. He would listen. Debbi too. Both of them would listen. She would call them.

Chapter 22

On Friday morning, at about nine-thirty, Hal Staton laid his shotgun over the back of his broad shoulders and carefully closed the screen door to his parent's farmhouse. Outside, he paused for a beat and stared up at the sky. As often happened in mid-December, gray clouds covered the sun and bleached out the horizon.

Hal hunkered down in his jacket. Briefly, he wished he had worn a hat. Then he smiled grimly. What difference did a hat make? For that matter, what difference did anything make?

With a whistle, he called Snapper, his mixed-breed watch dog and good buddy, to his side. Together the two stalked away from the gravel driveway and into the tall pines that dotted the two hundred and thirty-two acres of his parents' homeplace.

Walking through the woods, the pine straw rustling softly under his work boots, Hal thought of all the fun he and his two brothers had enjoyed as children playing in these woods and the open fields they surrounded. He had shot squirrels and rabbits and deer in these woods. In the fields, especially the level one behind the bleached-out barn, he and his brothers had first begun to play baseball. There, behind the barn, his father taught him how to focus on a target, how to wind up, how to follow through, how to whip a ball through the air like a fired rocket.

He and Snapper reached the barn. Hal stopped for a moment while Snapper hiked his leg against a dead stump. Turning around, Hal stared at the old building, searching its side for the circular target he had drawn on it like a bull's-eye the year he had turned eight. Not seeing it, he edged closer to the barn. He saw the old target. The years had faded it almost into nonexistence.

Hal leaned his shotgun against the barn and touched the rough planks of the wood. Traced his fingers over the old bull's-eye. He had used this target as a catcher's mitt when his two brothers wouldn't catch for him.

Stepping back, he picked up a dirt clod from beside Snapper's tree stump. Holding the clod, he backed off about sixty paces. He focused on his target, wound up, whipped his talented left arm over his head, and hurled the clod at the circle. The clod popped into the center of the bull's-eye and splattered out, a dry thud sounding as it hit. Hal whistled and Snapper moved away from his stump.

His days of boyhood innocence were over. The days of any kind of innocence were over for that matter. As far as he was concerned, everything was over. With Leslie dead, what difference did anything make?

Hal had lived with two dreams in his head all the way through high school, into two years of college, and then four years of minor league ball. Dream number one—make Leslie Washburn his bride, and dream number two—play baseball for the Atlanta Braves. Both his dreams had come true. But a murderer had snuffed out the first of those dreams. And Hal had discovered in the last two weeks that, with the first dream snuffed out, the second one didn't seem too important anymore.

Grabbing his shotgun, he started walking again, and Snapper followed. Hal knew where he was headed. To the seven-acre pond about a half mile from the house. The pond where he fished as a child. The pond his father had stocked with bass and bluegill. A covey of doves darted up from the field in front of them. For about ten strides Snapper gave chase. Then, obviously seeing the futility of it, the yellow dog slowed, stopped, and padded back to Hal. Hal leaned down and patted the animal on the back.

None of it made sense to Hal Staton. Why Leslie? Leslie, who never hurt anyone. Leslie, voted "Most Friendly" in their senior class at Cordele High. Leslie, who worked as a volunteer every Tuesday morning at the nursing home two miles from their condo in Atlanta. Leslie, who didn't swear or drink or talk badly about other people.

No, Hal thought, shaking his head at the thought, she wasn't perfect. She ran chronically late, she spent a bit too much on clothing for his tastes—like those red high heels two Saturdays ago—and she occasionally became impatient with his constant focus on sports. But as far as he could see, she came as close to perfect as anyone he'd ever known.

He breathed deeply and watched his breath crystalize in the December air. Amazing how lonely a person could feel. Even a popular person like himself.

He had called his agent, Rex Stamps, almost every day since the funeral. But the last couple of calls, Rex had tried to talk about baseball. Obviously, he wanted to get Hal's mind off the tragedy. Trouble was, Hal wasn't ready yet to move on.

Hal's parents didn't know what to do with him either. They were gone today, over to Macon to visit his mother's ill sister. Wouldn't get home for about a week. So no one around today.

Hal coughed. Christmas would arrive soon. But he wouldn't find any joy in it.

He had already given his parents their gifts, though they didn't know it yet. He had visited an attorney on Tuesday. Signed over all his recent signing bonus to them. About $600,000. He wouldn't need it anymore after today.

The lawyer had questioned him about his decision. But Hal had assured him he was doing it for tax purposes.

Cresting a hill, Hal spotted the pond in the bottom of the meadow. A couple of mallard ducks sat like decoys on top of the still water. Though not frozen, the water looked like glass, the reflection of the clouds above and the stalky reeds on the sides shining through it.

For a moment Hal paused and took it all in. As if sensing his mood, Snapper rubbed up against his leg. After patting the animal, Hal started walking again. Within minutes he reached the side of the pond.

Laying his gun beside him, he sat down on the grass. A touch of cold moisture permeated his faded jeans and crawled up against his skin. Hal paid the cold little attention. He didn't feel cold at all now. Just the opposite. Sweat had started to seep into his clothes. In fact, he noticed with a tinge of surprise, his shirt felt wet with perspiration.

Scrunching down into the wet earth, he pulled Snapper to his chest and hugged him roughly. The big dog licked his face as if trying to comfort him. Hal held him for several moments, inhaling the warm breath of the animal into his own lungs. Then he let him go. Snapper popped his haunches into the ground beside him.

Hal reached for his gun. He snapped open the twin barrels. Nodded his head. It was empty.

For a second he paused. The shells were in his shirt pocket. Two shells. One for each barrel of his twelve-gauge shotgun. He almost grinned. How silly of him. He wouldn't need two shells. One would do the job nicely. Quickly and decisively.

He took a deep breath and gazed up into the sky. He wanted his last memory to be of Leslie. She had sat with him by this pond. Here he had kissed her for the first time. After a high school baseball game. He had pitched a no-hitter and stroked out three hits, one of them a home run.

"I'm coming to be with you Leslie," he whispered. "We'll be together forever."

Staring into the sky, he wondered if that were true. Would he be with Leslie forever? The thought that he might not scared him for a minute. What guarantee did he have? He shrugged his shoulders. He didn't have a guarantee. But he did know one thing for sure. He wouldn't be with her on this earth. A murderer had made that a certainty.

Ready now, he took off his jacket, folded it, and laid it beside his feet. He closed his eyes. Time to do the deed. He heard a bell toll. Bongggg.

He almost smiled. The bell of the Mt. Olivet Baptist Church. Almost a mile away. But you could hear that bell all over the county on a still day like today. It tolled again. Bongggg.

When the bell ended, he would do it.

Bongggg.

He had seven more bongs to go. The Mt. Olivet Baptist Church. He had attended there every Sunday as a boy and through his teenage years.

Bongggg.

He had claimed Christian faith there. Experienced what the Baptists and others called salvation. Came to that belief they talked about, that belief in Jesus.

Bongggg.

Had even drawn a paycheck there the summer of his freshman year in college as he worked as a fill-in youth minister.

In the middle of his sophomore year, he had lost his faith. Too many parties and too much success had made him cold to Jesus. No need for God when you could do it all yourself.

Bongggg.

The Braves drafted him, paid him more money than he'd ever seen. He'd married Leslie. All the world was a mountain, and he stood on the peak of it. Triumphant.

Bongggg.

Yeah, maybe he should have been grateful. Maybe if he had been, Leslie might still be alive. But Jesus had never seemed real to him. Not even when he claimed to be a believer.

Bongggg.

Jesus always seemed more like a fairy tale than a real man. If he were real, why not make it plainer? Plain enough for everyone to see. Plain enough for him to see.

Bongggg.

Plain through some sign, some signal.

Bongggg.

That was it. The last bong had sounded, and no sign had come.

Time to do the deed.

Hal opened his eyes and reached into his shirt pocket. Grabbed a shell. Started to shove it into his shotgun. Stopped and squinted his eyes.

Something was stuck to the side of the shell. A piece of paper. A card of some kind. Crinkled at the edges and slightly faded.

Hal picked the card from the shell. Held it up so he could read it. Though the letters were faint, he could still read them.

"Personal Care Clinic. Burke Anderson, Christian psychologist."

His hands began to shake as he read the phone number. He could hardly hold the card. He had read Debbi Anderson's note the day of Leslie's funeral. Had shoved it into his shirt pocket and forgotten it.

His mom washed the shirt later that week. Handed him the note again. He threw it away. Apparently though, the card stayed in the pocket through the washing.

Hal shook his head several times, then twisted and stared in the direction of the church.

Snapper whined. Hal shrugged at the dog. "What you think, boy? Is this sign enough?"

The dog woofed. Hal started to laugh. Snapper leaped into his arms. Holding the animal to his chest, Hal stood up, threw back his head, and thundered toward Mt. Olivet Baptist. "Okay, okay, we'll see what you want to say. If you're really there, then show me more. One step at a time, show me more."

At the sound of his voice, the two ducks on the lake jumped off the water and soared away. Snapper just squiggled harder in Hal's arms.

Chapter 23

Burke climbed onto a stepladder and draped a string of lights over the front stoop of the house. This string, attached by an extension cord to five other strings, gave him complete front coverage. White lights outlined the two dormer windows that popped out like owl eyes from the second story, and white lights framed the porch than ran full across the front. The lights blinked off and on, off and on, just like the lights his daddy strung every year on his home in Alabama. White lights on the house at Christmastime—a sure sign of being domesticated.

He and Debbi didn't have the inside decorated yet. That would happen next week. But they had finished the outside. Lights on the bare dogwood by the front porch. Wreaths on the mailbox and above the two round-top windows that framed the front door.

Finishing his job, he glanced at his watch as he stepped off the ladder. 12:15 A.M. Debbi, home from the *Independent* since 11:30, greeted him with a kiss as he dismounted. Marriage sure agreed with him so far.

For several seconds they stood and stared up at their home, appraising their work. Burke nodded, satisfied with the work. Debbi winked at him. Everything okay.

Thirty minutes later, after a cup of hot chocolate by the fireplace in the den, he and Debbi crawled into bed. Both of them were tired, and within another thirty minutes, they fell asleep.

Outside, a dog barked. The wind rustled a few loose leaves up against the side of the house. The hours ticked by. The Christmas lights blinked. A bank of clouds played tag with the moon, and the night brightened and darkened in conjunction with their movement.

Burke tossed and turned in his sleep. He dreamed. He dreamed in color. He saw Debbi in his dream. Debbi in a white dress. Debbi on her wedding day. Debbi walking to him down the aisle.

But it wasn't Debbi's face anymore. It was his sister Sarah's. His sister Sarah who died when she was barely two years old. She choked to death on a hot dog. While he took care of her. She died, and he had always blamed himself for her death.

The face changed again. This time it became the face of Sonny Flake, the surprised face of a man shot to death by a gun held in Burke's own hand. Once more, the face shifted. Now, it was Leslie Staton. The face the paper had printed the day after the discovery of her body. The beautiful face of a smiling woman. A woman full of life. A woman now dead.

The face metamorphosed a fourth time. Metamorphosed into the battered face of Leslie Staton after her death. A tragic face. Damaged beyond recognition. A sad, suffering face.

Suffering. Everyone suffered. Suffering a part of life. Suffering for everyone. Even God suffered.

The face became Jesus. Jesus suffered too. He suffered at human hands. The soldiers abused Jesus. Beat him. He was beaten and bruised for our iniquities. Beaten and bruised for our sins. Beaten and bruised like Leslie Staton. Beaten on the head and body by those who hated him. By the sinners and evildoers of the world.

The sinners and evildoers. Everyone. Everyone sins and does evil.

Especially him. Especially Burke. He had sinned. He had failed, failed the night his sister died. He had suffered from an epileptic attack and passed out. And his little sister, Sarah, had died while he was unconscious. Tragic. Horrible. Suffering. Death.

The face of Death. No one wanted to see that face. But everyone would. Everyone would see the face of—

The face of Death reached out for Burke in his sleep. He saw the face, the black eyes and twitching nose and long white fingers reaching out like talons to sink into his flesh.

Burke woke with a start and jerked up in the bed. Sweat poured down his face but he didn't feel warm. He felt chilled. He looked down at his arms. Goose bumps rose up on them. He shuddered and checked the clock. 6:15. He started to lie down again. He turned over to face Debbi.

She wasn't there. He called out for her, but she didn't answer. He lay still for a moment, listening for her moving around in the house. He heard no sound of her.

Feeling slightly panicky, Burke threw off the covers and padded barefoot in his gym shorts out of the bedroom. On the kitchen table, he found a note. "Gone for a walk, back by seven." Clutching the note in his hand, he walked back to the bed and climbed under the covers. But he didn't go to sleep. The feeling of the empty bed, the bed without Debbi, kept him awake.

Chapter 24

Angelica Drexler lifted a spoon of hot chicken soup to her lips. Sick with the flu for three days now, she had shoved her two boys out the door with her mother to spend the night at her house. No use the boys coming down with this misery.

Besides, she needed the quiet. Her head felt like someone with a jackhammer was working inside it, and red veins cracked through the pupils of her normally clear brown eyes. Her nose was swollen and red from constant blowing. She had gone through four boxes of Kleenex in three days.

Chilled, she wrapped her flannel nightgown tighter to her throat and coughed. Her chest rattled from deep inside as if a part of her lungs was loose. She reached to an end table beside her recliner, flicked a dab of Vicks vapor rub onto her fingers, and dabbed it under her nose.

Mercy, she hoped she felt better tomorrow. She had a ton of Christmas shopping left to do, and she hadn't even started her holiday baking.

Grabbing a Kleenex from a box beside the Vicks, she blew her nose and glanced at her watch. Almost 8:00 P.M. Probably four to five hours before her husband, Karl, the senior pastor of the Spirit of Love Church of Atlanta, would get home. As the presiding minister of the concluding session of the annual meeting of the independent, charismatic churches of Georgia, he would most assuredly stay out late.

Angelica knew the routine. The conference itself, consisting of a succession of passionate sermons, would go past ten. Leather-lunged preachers trying to outdo each other made for lengthy messages. Afterward the men would wipe the sweat off their brows, pack up their Bibles, and go out to eat.

Imagining her lanky-framed man standing tall to deliver the closing address, Angelica smiled and momentarily felt a bit better. Goodness, how she did wish she could be there when he delivered his message. With a voice that sounded like it originated in the bottom of the Mississippi River and a vocabulary that combined hip-hop street talk with seminary finery, Karl could outpreach them all. He could outthink them all too. And he worked as hard as his great-great-grandfather—a slave who picked cotton for more than fifty years in the boiling sun of south Georgia.

Angelica tossed her used-up tissue toward a trash can in the corner. God willing, her Karl would soon outrank them all as well.

His church had more than nine thousand members already. After only seven years. Two television stations covered the morning services—one live and one tape delayed.

Angelica patted her hair. She would wash it tomorrow even if it killed her. Mercy, how the church house did rock each Sunday. With contemporary music, a drama group that rivaled the best in Atlanta, and her husband's expressive preaching, how could it not succeed? People of all races flocked into the pews each week. It didn't seem to matter to most of them that Karl was black. Who would have imagined it? In the heart of Atlanta, a black preacher building a church to rival even the biggest of the white ones. That notion did lift a body's spirits.

Placing her soup spoon into the bowl, Angelica leaned forward in her reclining chair. Might as well go on to bed. A long night's rest might just knock this wicked mess out of her chest. She lifted her tray from her lap, clumped in her fluffy bedroom slippers into the kitchen, and set the tray on the table. Snapping off the light over the stove, she walked to the door to lock up.

Finished with the back door, she turned, crossed the den, and checked the front. Already locked. Breathing heavily and coughing as she moved, Angelica flipped out the last of the downstairs lights and climbed up the stairs. A draft of cold air hit her as she stepped into her bedroom. She hugged her arms around her full chest. Lord, where was that wind coming from? A shutter flapped against the bedroom wall, and she saw the problem. Someone had opened a window.

She squinted her eyes in the darkness of the room. Who opened that window? Roger, her ten-year-old, or Karl, Jr., the second grader? But she'd been in that bedroom since they left.

The shutter slammed again. The wind whistled through the room. Angelica reached behind to flip on a light. Nothing happened. The room stayed dark. She twitched the switch again. Huh? What was wrong with the power?

For several seconds, she stood still against the wall. Okay. A window open, the light burned out. She stepped into the hall and flipped the switch. The light flickered, then died. Okay, a fuse had blown. But she didn't feel like going down to the kitchen to the fuse box to fix it. Besides, she didn't even know where a new fuse was or even if she had one.

She stood and thought a moment. Call her mother. She lived only ten minutes away. She could call her mother to come get her. She could spend the night with her mom.

Angelica stepped to the waterbed in the center of the bedroom, leaned across it, and grabbed for the phone. She dialed a number then realized she had heard no dial tone. She punched the hook switch to get a tone. Nothing.

Okay, a dead phone. And the power out. What next? She heard a sound. A muffled footstep. From the direction of the stairs. Somebody there. She called out. "Karl?" No sound. "Mama?" No one answered.

Jerking herself off the bed, Angelica felt a wave of dizziness. She stumbled against the wall, then struggled to get to the closet.

Karl kept a gun in the closet. On the second shelf in a metal box. If she could just reach it in time.

Falling against the closet door, she knocked it open and stretched frantically on tip-toes, reaching for the second shelf, searching for the box that held the gun. She heard the door to the bedroom swing open, but she didn't pause to look around. Her long fingers pushed away a stack of sweaters. There, she felt the box.

A voice called out from the bedroom. "Mrs. Angelica Drexler, I've come for you. No need to run, no place to hide."

For a second she waited, hoping the intruder would give up, go away. She tried to figure out the voice, wondered if she knew the person behind it. It was strange, a voice that seemed disconnected, a voice with no depth, a voice as thin as a fingernail.

She shook her head. No, she didn't recognize the voice.

Her hands trembling, she eased the box down and opened it.

Thank God. A black pistol—she didn't know what kind—lay in the box. She pulled the pistol out and dropped the box to the floor. Footsteps sounded on the carpet, moving toward the closet.

"Mrs. Angelica Drexler, I've come for you. I've come for you and all those others like you, those who see but close their eyes, who know but deny the knowing."

Angelica cocked the pistol. The door to the closet swung open. Angelica blinked, and her bloodshot eyes widened.

"Angelica, I've come for you."

"I'll shoot," she said, her voice shaky.

"I'm sure you will, but you cannot kill." Long slender fingers reached for the gun.

Angelica squeezed the trigger. The hammer snapped shut, but the gun didn't fire.

For a second, Angelica stared at the pistol. It hadn't fired. She pulled the trigger again, then a third time and a fourth.

"No bullets, Angelica Drexler, no bullets. You can shoot, but you cannot kill."

With a scream that tore through the darkness of the closet like a wounded cat, Angelica Drexler attacked. She leaped forward, her fingernails poised to strike and her wide white teeth bared.

But she never reached her target. The intruder moved quickly to the left and grabbed her around the throat. The fingers gripped her windpipe and squeezed. Angelica reached up with her hands to pry away the fingers, but they were tighter than a vise, and she felt herself losing consciousness. Her eyes rolled up in her head, and she fell forward onto the floor.

Standing over Angelica, her assailant smiled wickedly. So perfect, so dark. Here in the closet where no one could see.

Chapter 25

Monday, December 12

Derrick Role's appearance surprised Jackie. Unlike herself, he looked as fresh as a newly hatched egg. His eyes danced brightly, open and eager, and his hair lay in soft waves down to his collar. As usual, a set of golden cuff links held the sleeves of his white shirt together.

She sighed, thinking of her own unkempt outfit. Khaki pants as wrinkled as a bulldog's face, a white cotton blouse with a ring around the collar, and a navy jacket without a button on the left sleeve.

Role stood by the front door of a military recruiter's office. Behind him, the smiling faces of two soldiers—a young man and woman in army green—beamed out with a glossy sheen. Underneath the soldiers the words "Be All You Can Be" beckoned to anxious young recruits.

The recruiting officer, a square-jawed man with a crew cut that would have made John Wayne proud, stood beside Role.

Jackie had received the call only fifty minutes ago. Four hours after she had finally fallen into bed after almost two and a half days without sleep.

The officer had found the body of Angelica Drexler. The body that Jackie and Role and a significant part of the Atlanta Police Department had been searching for over most of the weekend. The recruiting officer found her sitting upright beside the dumpster where he parked his car every day.

Jackie's search had begun early Saturday morning. Angelica Drexler's husband, Karl, had called 911 at almost 2:00 A.M. After coming home from a preaching conference, he found the door to his house open and his wife missing.

The abductor had robbed the house, taking a television, a box of jewelry, and a computer from Karl Drexler's study.

The investigation began immediately. But so far they were shooting blanks—no fingerprints and no signs of struggle.

Karl Drexler told them about the gun he kept in the closet. They checked for it. It was there in a box on the second shelf. Apparently Mrs. Drexler either couldn't get to it or knew the person who abducted her.

Jackie and Role had spent all day Saturday and Sunday overseeing the search. With no body at the time, they couldn't call it a homicide. Officially, it went into the books as a missing person's report. But they put on the full-court press anyway. Interviews with all her friends. A house to house canvass in her neighborhood. Anybody see anything? Hear anything? Suspect anything?

Nothing. Nada. Zip.

The only thing they didn't do was alert the media. Karl Drexler had agreed with them about this. They could do their work better without community hysteria. Without wasting the time it would take to hold press conferences and answer unnecessary questions. Without worrying about the hundreds of crank calls these kinds of cases always created.

Not wanting to concede anything, Role had carefully pointed out to Drexler the differences between this case and those of Staton and Benton. The intruder came into her home, rather than taking her from a public area. The missing items showed robbery as a motive—like Staton, but unlike Benton. Maybe it didn't connect with the previous murders.

Through Saturday and Sunday, Jackie didn't know what to believe. On the one hand, two murders and one disappearance on three consecutive weekends sure did look like a pattern to her. But on the other hand, each one seemed different enough to create doubt about a singular killer. But maybe that's the way the killer wanted it.

One thing for sure. If Angelica Drexler turned up dead, then the possibility of a singular killer definitely stepped to the top of the charts in her book.

Now, walking briskly to Role, Jackie made that mental shift. To her way of thinking, one plus one plus one, in spite of the differences in the deaths, added up to one serial killer.

The military officer glanced at her as she stopped beside Role, but he didn't stop talking. "I drove in about 7:15. We open here at 8:00 sharp. I pulled my vehicle to my regular spot. Over there, behind the building." He pointed with a precise finger.

Jackie and Role stared past his finger at the dumpster at the end of his point. The officer cleared his throat, then continued. "I left my vehicle. I spotted something by the side of the dumpster. Thought it was a blanket of some kind. I decided I better inspect it. I didn't know that it wasn't a bomb or something. Besides, it didn't fit there. Out of order. I didn't like that. I walked to it. Within a couple of steps, I saw it was a body. A woman's body. In her bathrobe. An aqua green bathrobe. I knew she was dead. I've seen a few bodies in my day. They have this look, you know what I mean?"

Role nodded. The recruiter continued. "Anyway, I didn't touch a thing. I knew that wouldn't help you guys. I called 911. They sent an ambulance. Called you in." The officer stopped. For a second, Jackie thought he might salute to conclude his report. He stood ramrod straight as if waiting for a command.

Role asked, "You inspect the ground around the body?"

"Nope, in fact, I walked immediately out of the area. Didn't want to violate the scene."

Role fingered a cuff link. "You did well. Thank you for your help. We will need you to make an official statement later, but for now I think you can go about your regular duties."

The man nodded. "Just let me know. I'll do the right thing." He walked away.

Role turned to Jackie and licked his lips. "You won't believe this one," he said.

She wrinkled her brow. "What do you mean?"

"The body. You haven't seen it?"

"No, I haven't."

"You won't believe it."

"Show me."

He tossed his head to the left. "Okay, but you won't believe it."

She followed him around the side of the building, away from the recruiting office and toward the dumpster. Around the corner, she ducked under the yellow tape marking the sealed off area. She said hello to a couple of EMTs. She blinked her eyes against the glare of red and blue that flashed from the tops of the police cars and ambulances gathered like a circled herd around the body. She eased to the enshrouded form laying on a gurney in the middle of the circle.

Bending over, she took a deep breath and lifted the sheet. For a brief second, she stood transfixed. Then she dropped the sheet and pivoted away. Her hand flew to her mouth. Not because she wanted to throw up. But because she wanted to cry.

She looked over at Derrick Role. He nodded, and she shook her head. He was right. She couldn't believe it.

Chapter 26

Still in his pajamas, Burke pulled the cedar Christmas tree off the back porch, through the hallway, and into the den. Anxious about the unsteady tree stand on the bottom, he carefully lifted the tree and set it between the two center windows that framed the back wall of the room. For several seconds, he eyed the seven-foot evergreen to make sure it was straight. Maybe a bit more to the left? He moved it. Okay.

Satisfied, he turned, flipped the switch to the CD player, and selected a Christmas CD. The music poured into the room. "Chestnuts roasting on an open fire. Jack Frost nipping at your nose. . . ."

He pivoted from the tree and tossed another log onto the stack already blazing in the fireplace. The fire crackled, and he rubbed his hands together.

"Debbi, where's that hot chocolate?" he called to the kitchen.

"In a minute. You get the tree in?"

"All ready to decorate. Soon as you get here."

"Hold your water, I'm on the way."

He turned to check the tree again. Seemed to be leaning a bit. Slightly to the left. He grabbed it by the trunk and pushed it to the right. Good, now it looked straight.

He smiled and hummed along with the music. Today he and Debbi would decorate their first tree together. He had taken the day off for the occasion. After the tree, he planned to take her shopping. After shopping, dinner. After dinner—well, after dinner back to the fireplace and beyond. What a wonderful way to get ready for Christmas.

Burke took a deep breath. The smell of the cedar tree filled his lungs. He grinned as he remembered his battle to get the tree on the stand. Almost two hours of hard wrestling. He touched his hair—cedar sap still in it.

But he had succeeded. The tree stood before him, on the stand and steady. And almost straight. Only a bit too far to the right.

"Is that chocolate ready?" he called, easing the tree slightly left.

"Almost."

Burke turned to the box of decorations sitting on the sofa beside the tree. He lifted a white star out of the box and examined it. His mom and dad had given him the star about a month ago as an early Christmas present.

Today he would place the star on the top of his tree, just like his dad had always done in their home. Putting the star on the tree was a job for husbands. Burke smiled. A job for fathers. Hopefully, someday he would know the feeling of being a father.

He heard the telephone ring. "You want me to get it?" he yelled.

"No, I've got it," said Debbi.

He laid the star on the sofa and pulled a box of new lights from a sack and started ripping them out. Debbi walked into the room. "It's Jackie Broadus," she said.

Burke's arms dropped to his sides. The lights dangled to the floor. He knew about the body of Angelica Drexler. It was all over the news. Debbi had been out half the night making sure the *Independent* kept up with all the details. But he hadn't heard from Jackie. Didn't know anything beyond what the media had reported.

"What's up?" he asked.

"She says she has an autopsy. Wants you to take a look at it."

Burke laid the tree lights onto the sofa. "When?"

Debbi shrugged. "Don't know."

Burke stood completely still for a moment. "What if I told you I didn't want to get any more involved with this, that I'd gone as far as I want to go?"

Debbi scowled. "I'd say it wasn't like you."

"How so?"

"Well, you know—Jackie's your friend, isn't she?"

Burke thought about that for a moment. Debbi was right. Besides, the death of a third woman had made him certain that a serial killer was at work. Someone needed to put an end to the carnage. If he could aid Jackie by listening to her, then so be it. It was the least he could do. "I better take it," he said.

Debbi smiled. "You bet."

He walked to the table by the sofa and picked up the phone. "Yeah, Jackie. What's going on?"

She cleared her throat. "I called your office. They said you were home for the day. I didn't think you would mind if I called."

Burke paused, but only for an instant. "You're right, Jackie. I don't mind."

Sounding more confident, Jackie continued. "Good, I wanted to keep you and Debbi up-to-date. If you're going to help me, you need to know the latest."

"I'm afraid we're not doing you much good."

"Well, no one else is either."

"That's true."

"Well, anyway, this thing has gotten stranger by the minute. You know the basics."

"I know a recruiting officer found Angelica Drexler yesterday morning. Found her in front of a dumpster as he came to work. She was still dressed in her robe and bedroom slippers. That's about all."

"That's the public information. But we've gotten an autopsy report now. It's the craziest thing. Drexler shows no signs of being tied up like the first two. She has bruises around her neck indicating a degree of strangulation. But she didn't die of strangulation.

"In addition to the strangulation, she had another pattern of wounds, and I've never seen anything like it. She's got a series of cuts in her skull. They're spaced about one every two inches, and they wrap completely around her head—on her forehead, over the tops of her eyes, above the ears, and across the back of the skull."

Burke's eyebrows arched as Jackie continued. "The serrations are uniform in depth and width. About an eighth of an inch wide and the same deep.

"The cuts, however, didn't kill her." Jackie paused as if to give him a chance to soak all this into his system. He rubbed his forehead.

"What did?"

Jackie's voice took on a flat tone, as if she had memorized what she was about to say so she could repeat it without feeling anything. "Angelica Drexler died sometime between noon and six o'clock on Sunday, December 11, as the result of a puncture wound that entered through the back of the skull and traumatized the brain. The instrument of death is as yet unknown. But it had to be a sharp object made of some metallic substance."

Burke squeezed the phone for several moments but didn't speak. Neither did Jackie. The sound of Christmas music oozed through the silence. "Hark the herald angels sing, glory to the newborn king."

He didn't want to hear what Jackie had to say.

"Peace on earth and mercy mild."

Didn't want Jackie Broadus to tell him this.

"God and sinners reconciled."

Didn't want to hear of death anymore.

"Joyful all ye nations rise, join the triumph of the skies."

Didn't want death dogging him at Christmas time.

"With angelic hosts proclaim."

Didn't want death dogging him ever again.

"Christ is born in Bethlehem."

But he couldn't avoid it. Jackie was a friend. He couldn't say no to a friend who needed him.

"Burke?"

"Yeah, Jackie, I'm here. Just thinking."

"I know what you mean. It's a mess, isn't it?"

"Yeah, you could describe it that way."

Jackie sighed. "Look, Burke I gotta go. It's busy around here—as you can imagine. But I wanted you and Debbi to think about this. A third one—and all of them on Sunday—makes it seem more and more like a serial killer. Even Role is considering the possibility. Not officially yet, still enough differences between the cases for him to publicly deny it. But between you and me, I've reached the conclusion we're dealing with one person."

"But you don't have any evidence for that."

"Not any I can stand on."

"Then you've got to find some."

"I'm doing my best."

"We need to help you."

"I'm open to all ideas. Call me later today. I'll tell the dispatcher to put you straight through."

Burke hung up and opened his arms to Debbi. She stepped into them, wrapping her arms around his shoulders. He held her closely and stared at his Christmas tree. Today he would decorate his first tree with his wonderful wife. But he didn't think he would feel much joy in it.

Chapter 27

Thirty-four miles away from Burke, behind a set of double mahogany doors that led into a 24-by-26 dining room, a pair of black eyes danced across the article on the front page of the *Independent*. Below the eyes, thin lips sipped southern mocha coffee from a china cup first used in England over a hundred years ago.

Finished with the coffee, a set of slender fingers eased the cup into a saucer and perched it on a cherry dining table. A white candle as tall as a broom handle sat in the center of the table, its flame dancing merrily across the wall even though it was daylight. Beside the candle sat Snow, her tongue licking up and down on a front paw.

A blaze of sun cut through the double windows behind the table, and an erratic breeze puffed in and out past the cream-colored lace curtains that bordered the windows. The sun illuminated a head of thick brown hair.

The lips curled into a jack-o'-lantern smile. Another dye job to prepare for another die job. *Oh, how clever you are. Three are dead and more to come. More to come. More to come. Three are dead with more to come.*

The 5'9½" frame stood up from the high-backed wooden chair and walked over to the window and stared out at the expansive yard. Rows and rows of neatly clipped yews and hollies lined the cobblestoned sidewalk that led away from the doors of the ivy-covered house toward the gate by the street outside. What a majestic mansion.

A mansion left by the last of the foster parents, the best of the rest of them combined. The killer's mind scattered and, for a moment, recalled the unfortunate tragedies of the past.

A succession of eight different foster homes, one after another, from the age of six until the age of eighteen. One bad dream on top of a previous bad dream. Rigid disciplinarians, some of them, others lax and inattentive. Most of the foster parents living near the poverty line and taking in children primarily to receive the money the state gave for their support.

Only the last ones were different. The last ones were the best ones. In fact, the only decent ones.

The last ones were wealthy beyond anything imaginable. Wealthy and unable to have children of their own. So they took in a scared and angry child.

For a moment, the black eyes softened at the memory. The last of the foster parents almost made up for the worst of the others. They had adopted the scared and angry child. For a season, the child lived happily with them. And not simply because of their money. Sure, the money made a difference. But it didn't guarantee anything. It didn't buy what counted most—a sense of acceptance, a foothold in a genuine family, a connection to someone else. No money could buy that.

The last of the foster parents gave more than money. They also lavished the child with love. The love they gave almost made up for the pain caused by the worst of the others.

The black eyes hardened again. But not quite. Nothing could make up for that.

The eyes peered out into the driveway beyond the window. Two vehicles sat there. No, not the Mercedes and the black van. Those were only disposables. Bought with cash in Miami and registered in a false name. Driven up to Atlanta for their once-and-only purposes. Afterward, parked in the worst section of the slums of Atlanta for the locals to enjoy.

Staring at the Jeep Cherokee and U-Haul, the black eyes crinkled at the edges. The thin lips smiled again, and the killer turned to Snow. "What do you think, Snow?" asked a high and breathy voice, the words as clipped as the hedges bordering the sidewalk outside. "You think the police will find the vehicles?"

Snow tilted her head.

"No, they won't. It would be a major miracle, wouldn't it. Almost enough to cause one to believe in God again."

The lips snarled downward. God. What a joke. No way to believe in God anymore. Not after all that happened in the past. The black eyes rolled up toward the cathedral ceiling of the dining room as the memories floated back. Memories of the foster homes—one after another, each one seemingly getting worse, a downward spiral toward the cesspool of the worst of all, the home of the tall preacher who spoke with such pretty words. . . .

A home near Brevard, North Carolina. A beautiful, white-framed house perched on a ridge beside a church made of white stone. A rim of towering green trees framed the white house. The trees turned orange as a pumpkin in the fall. Snow fell in the winter and blanketed the house, and cool mountain breezes surged through the open windows in the spring.

What a wonderful place at first. Tables laden with garden vegetables and fresh meat every Sunday after church. People in the church oohing and ahhing over the black eyes and the smiling face of the preacher's new foster child.

Three other children lived in the preacher's home. All of them adopted. The preacher's wife, a young thing barely more than a child herself, couldn't have children. So sad, said the members of the white-stoned church. So hard on a young preacher not to have children of his own.

But how good of him to take in other children. Children who had no other place to go. Children like the black-eyed child who always seemed sad and quiet. And no wonder. The parents of the child murdered on their tenth anniversary. Murdered in their sleep. The child had been asleep, too, three rooms away. But the killer had not touched the child.

Five years had passed since the murders when the child walked through the front door of the preacher's house. No one had ever been arrested for the killing of the parents. What a shame. But how good for the preacher to take in the child. The child who had no other place to go.

Now that the preacher had the child with the black eyes, the preacher and his wife had four children. The black-eyed child was the oldest—just past eleven. The rest of them were under six.

Too young.

Too young to endure the agony.

It didn't take long for the agony to begin. Two months after the child with the black eyes arrived. The third Tuesday in July, on a night when the heat soaked into the house like a hot fog, soaking the family in the white-stoned house with heavy sweat and a southern summer smell. That night the agony began.

The agony.

A child's worst nightmare and a human being's worst evil. An evil that slaughters innocence with the sharp-edged knife of lust.

An evil that gives birth to hatred.

That night the hatred came to life in the child. The hatred came to life—a force as black as the child's eyes—a force that grew and grew in the awful nights that followed, nights when a sweltering mountain breeze flushed through the open window and a tall preacher crept in through the open door.

The preacher had to duck as he tiptoed through the door, and he whispered quietly as he pursued his ungodly aims. The child heard the words as they hissed from his lips, and the words fueled the blazing anger. They stoked the anger higher and higher and burned away whatever hope the child had ever possessed. The child learned from the words, learned that much of what appeared so pretty and so clean often covered putrid sin underneath.

The church members failed to notice. Blinded by the flowery words of the tall preacher, they fawned over him. Fawned over him and blinded themselves to his intimate pats on small children, girls and boys.

The eleven-year-old foster child living in the preacher's home stared out the open window as the preacher pursued his evil desires. The child stared out through black eyes and prayed that the God who should see and stop such things would sweep into the room and strike the man dead. Strike him dead with a divine vengeance. Strike him dead with a dagger of righteousness and a club of judgment.

But God did nothing. God said nothing. God was nothing.

The hatred in the heart of the child burned away the child's belief in God. A belief the child took into the preacher's home. A sweet, simple trusting belief. A belief born of hope and nurtured by necessity. If God didn't care for the homeless children of murdered parents, then who would?

The child had loved God in the early days of the time in the preacher's house. But the love for God died in the preacher's arms.

Four weeks after it started, the child ran out of the lovely house of the tall preacher of pretty words and his shy young wife with the small birthmark on her chin. The child ran away from the man who did it and the wife who knew but did nothing to stop him.

Yes, the wife knew. Her eyes made it plain she knew. The wife wore haunted eyes, eyes that never quite looked at anyone, eyes that seemed eternally riveted to the floor, eyes that glistened but never smiled.

Once the child tried to tell the wife. But the wife grabbed a wooden spoon from the cabinet of the lovely house and whacked the child with the spoon. Whacked and whacked the child with the spoon until it broke in her hand. During the beating, the eleven-year-old kept screaming the truth, kept screaming it and screaming it, screaming it until the wife with the furtive eyes covered her ears and ran out of the room, the broken pieces of the wooden spoon clattering to the floor as she fled.

That hurt the child most of all. The wife of the preacher knew but did nothing. She saw but refused to see; heard but refused to hear. . . .

Standing by the window, the child nodded toward the morning sun. At thirty-three, the child had grown up.

The child smiled, picked Snow from the dining table, and rubbed her behind the ears. "The blind shall see, Snow," muttered the child. "The blind shall see."

Chapter 28

At 7:30 P.M. Burke and Debbi sat in a corner of Ming Li's and finished their last bites of dinner. Burke forked up the remains of his cashew chicken, and Debbi sipped on hot herbal tea. His eyes checked her out and liked what they saw. A kelly green sweater and skirt suit he had bought her for the holidays made her eyes even more conspicuous.

Staring at Debbi, however, Burke found himself becoming more and more melancholy. The phone call from Jackie Broadus had shaken both of them. How could anyone concentrate on the joys of Christmas when a murderer of the worst kind floated around unseen and uncaught in Atlanta?

To make it worse, Jackie had dropped by and left Drexler's autopsy report, complete with photos, in their mailbox. They found the information when they came in from shopping to dress for dinner. The photos shocked them both.

Burke swallowed a bite of rice and shook his head. He didn't even like to think about them.

"A dollar for your thoughts?" said Debbi.

He laughed lightly. "I thought it was a penny."

"Inflation, my dear, you can't get anything for a penny anymore."

He appreciated her efforts at humor. She had tried all day to keep his spirits up. "I expect you can guess my thoughts and save yourself the money."

She nodded. "Angelica Drexler?"

"And Leslie Staton and Rosaline Benton."

"I'm the same way. I can't get them off my mind."

"Me either. But I didn't want to ruin the day dredging it up again."

"But don't you tell your patients to talk about their feelings?"

"Sure I do."

"Then take some of your own prescription. If you don't, it'll only get worse."

He paused for a beat, trying to get a handle on his feelings. Then he leaned forward, thankful Debbi had broached the subject so he could talk it over with someone. "I keep thinking it has to be one person," he said.

"Killing a woman every Sunday," said Debbi, her face downcast.

Burke sighed. "Something has to tie it all together, some scheme, some pattern. But I can't get a handle on what the connection might be."

He leaned backward, momentarily spent by the effort of his words. Debbi nodded and took up the challenge.

"They're wives of celebrities," she said. "They're abducted on the weekend, Friday or Saturday. Killed on Sunday, discovered on Monday, in a variety of places."

Burke chewed his lip for a second. "Yeah, that's been churning around in my mind a lot. The locations of the bodies. Anything to connect those?"

"The capitol building, Curry Park, and a military recruiting station. Nothing in common that I can see."

"Wait a second," said Burke. "Think of the locations. One on the west end, one on the south, now this third one also on the south." He took a napkin from the table and pulled out a pen. He marked an x on the spots where the bodies were discovered. One on the middle left of the napkin. The second one on the lower third of the napkin on the right. The third one just to the right of it and a bit more south.

"Nothing there," he said. He dropped the pen on the table.

"What about the locations of the abductions?"

He shrugged and flipped over the napkin. The TransSouth Building. Bottom left in southwest Atlanta. The racetrack in top center—north Atlanta. Angelica Drexler's house, middle right. More northeast than anything else. No obvious connection.

"Go back to the celebrity angle," said Debbi. "Has Jackie found anything to tie the husbands?"

"Not that she's told me."

"And the wives?"

"Nothing that I know about."

Debbi sipped her tea. "Well, I'm like you. I don't think this is happening at random. The killer, if it is one person, is picking these particular people for a reason. The planning is too precise, too carefully orchestrated."

"If he's picking them out, then he has to have a rationale for choosing these three."

"Exactly."

"So why did he pick them?" asked Burke.

"It has to go back to the celebrity angle."

"But why these celebrities?"

"That's what we have to find out. If we can answer that, then we can predict the next one."

"Can predict it and get there first. Set a trap for his coming."

Burke closed his eyes for a moment. He thought through the autopsies and the police reports that Jackie had shown them. What was it he was missing? Somewhere, something had to stand out; something had to offer a bit of light, shed a clue to the direction they should take. He thought of Staton, Benton, Drexler. Blows to the head. Whipped. Cuts along the forehead and a puncture through the skull. What odd ways of killing people.

No instruments of death found. Nothing found at all. Nothing. As if the killer had vanished with no trace left behind. If only they had a trace, a tidbit of information, even the tiniest sliver of—

Wait a minute. He opened his eyes and stared at Debbi. "Do you remember Benton's autopsy?" he asked.

She shrugged. "Yeah, I remember it."

"Do you remember what the medical examiner said they found in one of the gashes?"

Debbi's reached for a strand of hair, then dropped it. Her eyes squinted at him. "Something about a piece of bone, if I recall."

"Bingo. That's the only thing this killer has left behind. The one piece of evidence that the police haven't explained."

"But what does it mean?" She stared at Burke, expecting him to make it all clear to her.

He threw his hands up in the air. "I don't have the foggiest idea what it means. But I think we need to find out."

Chapter 29

Wednesday, December 14

All through the day, Burke found it difficult to concentrate on his clients. Unfortunately, the first one came at 7:30 A.M. and a steady stream followed. Rushed by the schedule, he skipped lunch and took no coffee breaks. He held his bladder, too, not going to the bathroom even once.

He hadn't experienced many days like this since he started at the clinic. But when he had, he enjoyed them. Except for today. Today he found the rigor taxing.

He knew the problem, and it wasn't his work. It was his preoccupation with the murdered women. He couldn't get himself free of them. They distracted him, scattered his energies, tore his thoughts away from his patients.

All day long, he tried to shut out the pressure building up in his chest, tried to wipe away the images of the murdered women.

But he found that he couldn't. He had seen too much, and the more he tried to forget Staton, Benton, and Drexler, the more their faces pushed into his mind. He hoped his clients didn't feel or see the chaos swirling around inside him.

At 4:20, just when he thought he would burst, the last client stood from her seat to leave. The woman, a recent divorcée in her mid-thirties learning to deal with feelings of guilt and failure, shook his hand and walked out of the office.

Burke followed her out, then skipped back inside. Within five minutes, he had scribbled a few notes to himself about the session, said good-bye to Molly, and checked out of the clinic. By four-forty-five he had sped home, slipped into his jogging shoes and shorts, and started his run. Today he desperately needed the sweat the run would bring.

The last of the leaves had already fallen from the trees, but Burke still enjoyed the scenery of the last days of fall. The air held a crispness to it, and the smell of fireplaces danced in the breeze in front of him as he ran.

118   GARY E. PARKER

He crossed the street two miles down from his house and headed past a school building. As his legs loosened, he began to relax. He ran with his arms at his sides for a few blocks, letting his shoulders droop. His breathing slowed, and he let his mind drift.

He ran past the school and into a small park. A squirrel darted across the path in front of him.

Burke's feet pulled him through the park and back onto a paved street, an oak-lined avenue about four miles from home. He listened to the pounding of his running shoes on the asphalt. Man, he loved that sound. The rhythm of it. The strength it conveyed.

He breathed easier and easier, settling into his stride. He felt himself moving into the zone that he enjoyed so much, the zone where his body moved on autopilot, and his mind expanded beyond the norm of the daily grind. Most people called it the runner's high.

Burke saw it as a time of spiritual release. He did his best thinking and praying when he ran. Running gave him time to focus on his spirit, to center that part of himself that truly loved God, that part that adored the Lord.

Burke knew about whole-brain thinking—the notion that the left brain directs the analytical, logical side of the personality and the right brain the intuitive, emotional side. When he ran, the right side often kicked in, and he found himself able not only to believe intellectually in God but also to love God with his emotions. Burke loved the pounding of the pavement and felt spiritually diminished when his days became too busy to get in his miles.

He sucked in a deep draught of air and tried to push away his anxieties about the murders. He feared he was losing his perspective. The murders weren't his problem. He didn't even want to stay involved. If not for Debbi's work, this would never have fallen to him.

He lifted his hands over his head and flexed his fingers. The last of the day's sun beamed down on his back, and his body heated up. He directed his thoughts away from the deaths. He focused his mind on the spiritual. He sensed God's presence.

A light breeze touched his forehead. A leaf fell a few strides in front of his feet. The leaf hung in the air for a moment as if suspended by an unseen hand, then settled on the path.

Burke began to think about the class he was teaching on Wednesday nights at his church. A six-week seminar on the life and death of Jesus. His pastor and he had agreed that the Christmas season was the perfect time to offer this course about the incarnation of the Lord.

The road ahead of Burke turned left and began a slow incline up a lengthy hill. He bowed his neck and pushed harder to keep up his six-minute-per-mile pace. His breath came more heavily.

Tonight he and his class would consider the arrest and trial of Jesus. The betrayal of Judas, the arrest in the Garden of Gethsemane, the appearances before Pilate and Herod, the beating by the soldiers, the mockery of the purple robe and the crown of thorns, the walk up the hill to Calvary, the crucifixion.

Burke knew the story so well. He had grown up on it in his home outside of Birmingham, Alabama. Tom and Thelma, his mom and dad, gave him daily doses of the story in the family's morning devotionals and in the weekly trips to their tiny, red-bricked Methodist church.

Burke grinned as he ran, remembering those days. Not always exciting but certainly consistent. The life of Jesus. The death of Jesus. The resurrection of Jesus. Over and over, over and over, he heard the teachings.

All of it had fascinated him. Given his reflective personality, he had brooded on it often. In his room at night, after everyone else had gone to bed. At school when class became boring. On his daily runs with the cross-country team he anchored in high school. The person of Jesus fascinated him. Still did.

Especially the suffering, the death, the atonement. What love it showed. So sacrificial to undergo such humiliation. For one with the power of the universe at his disposal to allow grubby human hands to hit him, to allow puny soldiers to whip him, shove a mocking crown onto his head, tie him—

Burke's mind jolted to a stop, and his pace staggered for a moment. He started running faster. His breathing pace quickened. Was it possible? Was that the connection?

He crested the hill, and the road made a left turn past a live oak as thick as a trash barrel and headed down an incline. A mixed-breed dog rushed up behind him and barked, then stopped and ran back into its yard.

Burke breathed out a washtub of air. Could it be? He nodded to himself. Sure, it was possible, but who would believe him?

He wiped a rim of sweat out of his eyes and glanced at his watch. He'd finished about five miles. He would shorten his route. Get home immediately, try to reach Debbi before going on to church. See what she thought of his theory. If Debbi thought it made sense, he would call Jackie Broadus.

Speeding up, he pushed to the bottom of the hill and made a left turn at the intersection. Within seven minutes he reached his front porch. Sitting on the steps, he pulled off his running shoes and took several deep breaths. The last of the day's light streaked into his front yard and peeped through the four pine trees lining his driveway and threw long shadows across the brown grass. He thumped the dirt off his shoes and stood up to go inside.

Suddenly, a shudder climbed across his shoulders. If his theory was right, a fourth woman would die on Sunday. Her wounds would not be pretty.

Chapter 30

Five minutes after Burke slipped off his running shoes, Debbi sat down at her desk at the *Independent* and checked through her messages. She found nothing pressing and turned to her Rolodex to look up a number. A shadow fell across her shoulder. She glanced up and saw Mimi Stoddard standing over her, a slender grin playing on her cheeks.

Debbi took a second and appraised her boss. A five-feet ten-inch, auburn-haired henchwoman who had fired Linda Clips and Randy Fontly and forced Stan Wraps to retire. A navy, pin-striped suit, rigid posture, and teal eyeglasses made her appear every inch the yuppie professional woman.

Debbi knew she shouldn't resent Stoddard for the personnel purge at the *Independent*. After all, someone else gave her the orders to do the firings. But she sensed that Stoddard had enjoyed the job, the power that allowed her to terminate people.

"What's up, Mimi?" she asked, pushing her thoughts away for the moment.

Stoddard leaned over and waved a manilla folder at Debbi. Her smile widened. "A little present for you," she beamed. "One I think you'll enjoy." She popped the folder onto the desk. "Open it," she ordered, easing herself into a half-sitting position on the edge of Debbi's desk.

Debbi obeyed, sliding the folder open and pulling out the pages inside. She recognized immediately what it was—three autopsy reports. One for Leslie Staton, one for Rosey Benton, and one for Angelica Drexler.

Arching her eyebrows, she stared at Stoddard. "Where did you get these?" she asked, genuinely surprised.

Stoddard played it nonchalant. "Oh, a woman has her ways. You're not the only one who's ambitious around here."

"You're not going to tell me?"

"Of course, I'm not. You know the first rule of journalism—'never reveal your sources.'"

Seeing Stoddard wasn't going to divulge anything, Debbi focused again on the autopsies. She pretended to read them, taking her time as if to absorb the information. She hoped her body language registered shock, that Stoddard wouldn't guess she had already seen these. If Stoddard found out she had this information but had not used it, she would blow her stack.

After a few minutes, Debbi closed the file, placed the folder on her desk, and raised her eyes to Stoddard. "Strange stuff, don't you think?"

"Extremely strange," said Stoddard. "And extremely hot. This will make the morning edition a sizzler."

Debbi saw a glint in Stoddard's eyes, the glint of an animal that has brought down a kill.

"You plan to print this?" she asked.

Stoddard's brow furrowed in confusion. "Are you kidding me? Absolutely, I plan to print it. How could you even question that? Any editor worth her weight in newspaper would use this. We've got the autopsy reports for the three most sensational cases in Atlanta in several years. I'd be crazy not to use it. I want the best story you can write."

Debbi thought for a moment. She knew she was treading on thin ice. If she published this under her byline, Jackie Broadus would surely go ballistic. But if she refused, Stoddard had the power to do something even worse. Stoddard had the power to dismiss her from the story. For that matter, Stoddard had the power to dismiss her from the paper.

Swallowing hard to buy a moment of time, an idea struck her. "Shouldn't we respect the right of privacy for the deceased?" she asked, hopefully.

Stoddard rolled her eyes. "I'm not that sentimental," she said, dismissing the thought.

Debbi tried another tactic.

"What about the police investigation? If we run with this, won't it jeopardize their work? Tell the killer what the cops know, what clues they have?"

Stoddard shrugged. "Yeah, that's possible. But, hey, if we don't print it, someone else will. You know the authorities don't keep this kind of stuff under wraps for long. I'm surprised some of this hasn't gotten out already."

Debbi nodded. Stoddard was right. Every police precinct in the city had enough leaks to sink an aircraft carrier. If the *Independent* didn't use this today, WATL would probably broadcast it tomorrow.

But that didn't solve her problem. She had promised Broadus she wouldn't publish anything from the police reports. She threw Stoddard a suggestion.

"Okay, Mimi, you're right. We should print the salient points from these reports. But you're the one who should do it. You brought in the material. You deserve the byline."

Stoddard stood up and picked a paper clip off Debbi's desk. She bent the paper clip out straight and paced across the front of the glass-encased cubicle that housed Debbi's desk and computer. Debbi watched her as she considered her suggestion. Stoddard tossed the paper clip into the waste basket in the corner.

"Nope, can't do that," she said. "I'm the managing editor, not a writer. My job is to make assignments, not take them."

"But managing editors write sometimes," urged Debbi.

Stoddard stopped pacing. For a second she hesitated, her eyes squinting. "What's your problem?" she asked. "You've never seemed shy about headlines. I thought you would die to get your hands on this, get your name over it in a byline. Now you turn frigid on me. Clue me in to the problem here." She paused and waited for a reply.

Debbi didn't know what to say. She couldn't tell Stoddard about her promise to Jackie Broadus. Reporters shouldn't make decisions like that without editorial approval. But if the information came out under her name, Jackie would never believe that Stoddard had forced her to do it.

Debbi grabbed a strand of hair, then dropped it. She didn't have a choice. She had to write the piece. If she didn't, Stoddard would simply take her off the story and get someone else to do it.

Resigned, Debbi nodded. "You're right, Mimi. We have to use this, and I'm the one to do it. I'll get started immediately."

"You might be a bit more pleased about it," said Stoddard, pouting at Debbi's reluctance.

Debbi forced a smile. "You're right again, Mimi. I suppose I'm just out of sorts today. But I'll get on it right now. Thanks for your help."

Stoddard grunted and stalked out. Debbi sighed and leaned back in her chair. She didn't know how she would explain this to Jackie.

Chapter 31

B urke called Jackie Broadus as soon as he walked into his house. Without giving her any details, he asked her to meet him after church. She agreed—they would meet as soon as possible after 7:30 P.M. at Danny's. Hanging up, he buzzed Debbi, but the receptionist at the *Independent* said she wasn't in the office.

Anxious to talk to her but unable to do anything else about it for the moment, he jumped into the shower and cleaned up. By the time he climbed out, complete darkness had fallen outside. He flipped on the lights in the bedroom and slipped hurriedly into a pair of gray slacks and a blue button-down shirt. A navy and red tie made him almost ready for church.

With a towel hanging over his shoulders, he called the newspaper again. This time he reached Debbi.

"You coming to church tonight?" he asked immediately, not pausing for small talk.

"No, can't make it. I've got a 6:00 P.M. appointment with the guy who saw Rosey Benton before she disappeared from the track."

Burke checked his watch. Five-forty. "You better get going then," he said.

"Yeah, pretty soon. What's up?"

Speaking rapidly, Burke began to pace as he poured out his theory. He told her about his running, the concentration on the life and death of Jesus, the leap from those thoughts to musings about the murders. As he talked, he wondered what Debbi was thinking. Verbalizing his belief made it seem improbable, silly even. But, even still, he couldn't help but think it possible.

He stopped pacing as he finished and plopped down at the desk across from the bed. Debbi said nothing for at least ten seconds. He rubbed the towel over his hair and cleared his throat.

"You're mighty quiet," he said.

"I'm considering what you've told me," she said. "It has a horrible logic to it. But it leaves a couple of major questions."

"Such as?"

"Such as why, for one thing. Why would anyone do what you've suggested? It's so bizarre, so, I don't know—so totally, completely, absolutely beyond the pale of anything that a normal person would do."

"But this is no normal person," argued Burke, his voice edging up a notch. "Whoever we're dealing with here has gone far beyond the line of anything we call normal. This guy is bad, evil to the core."

"You're assuming it's a he?"

"No reason not to."

"Why's that?"

"Because a woman serial killer is almost unheard of."

Debbi paused for a moment before continuing. "But isn't it possible it's a woman?"

Burke thought a moment. "Yeah, I suppose it's possible. A woman killing women. But to what purpose? That's what keeps bugging me. Somewhere, we have to find a motive in this."

"If it's a woman, maybe it's jealousy. She's jealous of the position and wealth these celebrity wives have."

"Or she's avenging some slight, some pain they've visited upon her."

"If it's a man, it's the same possibility," said Debbi. "A woman abused him during his childhood, and now he's striking back. You know the scenario."

"It could be the other way, too, though. The anger might be directed at the men."

"How so?" asked Debbi.

"Well, think about it. What better way to hurt a man than to take away his wife?"

Leaning against the wall, Burke thought of the agony he would suffer if someone abducted Debbi. For the first time really, he found himself sensing what Hal Staton must be feeling.

"I see what you mean," Debbi said. "Kill a man's wife, and kill a man."

"If he loves her, I can't think of a better way."

"It's certainly a possibility," agreed Debbi. "The killer murders women to get to the husbands. Or it could be a combination of motives. Obviously the killer wants to hurt both of them, the men and the women."

"But we still have the same question," said Burke. "Why? Why would anyone do this?"

Debbi paused. "I don't think I'm the one to answer that," she said. "Motivation is your department. But your theory makes as much sense as anything else I've heard."

Burke grunted, not at all sure that he had convinced her. For that matter, he hadn't convinced himself. He rubbed the towel over his head. His hair was about dry. He knew Debbi needed to go. So did he. His class started in thirty minutes. "We'll talk more about it when you get home," he said, deciding to drop the subject so they could both get moving.

"Probably about midnight," said Debbi.

He hung up the phone and slipped on a pair of loafers. He could just make his class on time if he rushed.

Chapter 32

Flashing pinpoints of white light blinked on and off, on and off, in the black eyes as they stared out the open window of the bedroom on the backside of the colonial home. The flashing lights, reflections of the strings of lights that hung in even rows across the top and down the sides of the house, made it seem as if the eyes were being turned on and off by an internal finger flipping a lamp switch. On and off, light and darkness, life and death, on and off.

The black eyes blinked on and brightened as they saw the red and green bulbs brightening the branches of the evergreens and the hedges that dotted the yard and bordered the cobblestoned sidewalk.

Oh, what a lovely time of the year, mused the figure behind the black eyes. The time of Advent. The time to prepare for the birth of the baby Jesus. The time of arrival. The time for lights and love.

The black eyes dimmed as the lights blinked off. Not everyone could have love.

The black eyes flipped on. But everyone could have lights. Even if you preferred the darkness.

The darkness had always seemed so much more the place. The darkness covered, provided a place to hide; a place to work without anyone knowing; a place where bad things could happen without anyone able to see.

No eyes had seen back then—back then in the dark when the preacher came. Back then in the dark when evil ducked under the door and tiptoed to the bed. Evil walked out to play in the darkness. It stalked about on silent feet in the darkness and wore the cloak of secrecy.

The black eyes darted away from the lights outside the window and scanned the bedroom. "Snow?" called a breathy voice.

The white cat slithered from under the bed and jumped into the air. Slender fingers caught her and pulled her close, rubbing her behind her ears. The cat purred. Her owner padded away from the window in bare feet and nestled into the leather seat behind the writing desk.

So be it. Now the darkness was an ally. Everything was happening according to plan. No one suspected a thing. The news media made it plain. No one closing in, no one the wiser. No wise men out there to find their way to the light-draped house. No angels to proclaim the truth and bring the people running.

A smile creased the angular face below the black eyes. Slender fingers loosed the cat, dropped it to the floor, and lifted a silver pen from the desk. The fingers opened the leather-encased notebook lying on the desk and wrote.

"I am nearly there. I am almost finished. I have chosen well and executed to perfection. I find no sin in me. I do what I choose to do, and soon I will have finished the work I commissioned myself to do. The work of uncovering. The work of revealing. The work that no one else would do. The work I waited to see done for me. But no one else can do the works that I must do. I alone am able. I alone am able to reveal for all to see. For all to see. For all to see. For all to see on Christmas Eve."

The slender fingers laid down the silver pen and picked up a copy of *Atlanta Life*, a monthly magazine read by more than two million subscribers.

The black eyes crinkled at the edges as the slender fingers flipped the pages to the middle section of the magazine. The eyes scanned the headline of the feature article—"Atlanta's Famous Faces: Keys to Their Success."

What a wonderful article. All about the fifty most famous faces in the capital city. Thirty-eight men and twelve women. The faces almost everyone knew. The faces people saw in advertisements in the malls, making speeches on the television screens, and grabbing headlines in the newspapers.

It had taken almost a year to interview the people and write the story. One hundred and eight people in all. One hundred and eight interviewed to find the right four, the four that fit the pattern.

The black eyes twinkled. Four had been found. Four had been found and the fifth was always there. And four plus one made five. And Christmas was coming, and none would be left alive.

Chapter 33

Burke spotted Jackie the instant he walked through the door of Danny's Doughnut Shop. She rose up from her seat to greet him as he approached her booth.

"We've got to stop meeting like this," said Burke, extending his hand.

"Only if your wife finds out," said Jackie, laughing with him and sitting back down.

"Believe me, I've already told her," said Burke, taking his seat across from her.

"I knew you would," said Jackie. "The good ones are always honest."

Burke nodded. "And taken."

The waitress who had served them eight days earlier appeared at his shoulder. "A root beer?" she asked. Burke smiled and nodded. Jackie took coffee.

Turning back to Jackie, Burke leaned in closer. "I'm glad you could meet me," he started. "Even though I wish it could be under better circumstances. Since I first called you at Debbi's request, I've tried to stay away from all this. I didn't want to get mixed up with another murder case, but it looks like I have. I'm more and more pulled toward it, like I'm being sucked into a whirlpool or something. Even though I don't want to think about it, I do, almost constantly. I'm having trouble focusing at work, keeping it—"

"It can become an obsession," said Jackie, interrupting him.

"Tell me about it. Everywhere I turn, everything I do reminds me of the killings. That's why I called you, asked you to meet me. I can't get the wounds out of my mind. They're so unusual, so disconnected. That's what bugs me. They're so bizarre, they seem alike. They—"

Jackie held up a hand to stop him. "You're saying you think they have something in common. That something ties them together." Her face registered caution.

Burke sighed. "I know it seems crazy. But, listen, this afternoon I went running. I was thinking about a seminar I'm teaching at church—a study of Jesus. I started rolling these murders over and over in my mind. Leslie Staton beaten in the head and face. Rosey Benton whipped. Angelica Drexler with wounds on her forehead, around her ears, and across the back of her skull. All of them dying on a Sunday—beginning with the first Sunday of the Advent season.

"As I ran, the two streams of thought jumbled up on me—the life of Jesus and these murders—they merged. I started seeing the death of Jesus, the whipping by the Roman soldiers, the mockery of Herod and Pilate, the crown of thorns they shoved onto his head, the spikes driven into his hands and feet, the walk to Calvary, the—"

The waitress interrupted him. She set his root beer and Jackie's coffee on the table. "Anything else?" she asked. Burke shook his head. She eased away.

Jackie took a sip of her coffee. "I appreciate the lessons you're teaching, Burke," she said, a bemused look on her face, "but I don't see what you're driving at. A beating, a whipping, a puncture wound on three separate Sundays—the first three Sundays of Advent. I see the parallels, but I'm not sure I see where it takes you."

Burke nodded. "I'm not sure it takes you anywhere," he said. "I may just be getting my religion all mixed in with something that doesn't match at all, but the thing that tied it all together for me was the one thing the killer left behind. The piece of bone reported in Rosaline Benton's back—"

"We're running tests on that," interrupted Jackie. "We don't have anything conclusive yet."

Burke chewed on his lip. His voice dropped a notch. "The Romans sometimes used whips with bone slivers on the tips," he said.

Jackie's face blanched. "How gruesome."

"Exactly, gruesome but effective." Burke paused and reached into his jacket. He pulled out a palm-sized Bible. "Here, I want you to read something."

He flipped the Bible open to Matthew 27 and pointed to verse 26. "Here, read to verse 31."

Jackie took the Bible and began to read aloud.

"'But he had Jesus flogged, and handed him over to be crucified. Then the governor's soldiers took Jesus into the Praetorium and gathered the whole company of soldiers around him. They stripped him and put a scarlet robe on him, and then twisted together a crown of thorns and set it on his head. They put a staff in his right hand and knelt in front of him and mocked him. "Hail, king of the Jews!" they said. They spit on him, and took the staff and struck him on the head again and again. After they had mocked him, they took off the robe and put his own clothes on him. Then they led him away to crucify him.'"

Finished, Jackie dropped the Bible onto the table and stared at Burke.

"Think about it," he said. "The wounds of Jesus. The beating with the sticks, the lashing, the crown of thorns. Isn't that what the autopsy reports describe?"

Jackie sipped from her coffee. Placed her cup on the table. Steepled her fingers in front of her mouth.

"That's an interesting jump," she said. "From three dead women with no conclusive connection to three dead women killed by one person using the wounds of Jesus as a pattern for murder. Given your religious background, I can see how you would think of it."

She paused, picked up the Bible again, and stared at it. "Serial killers usually mark their work with an identifiable trademark. They repeat their method, it becomes something akin to a signature, like they're boasting of their exploits."

"I'm aware of that," said Burke. "And I think that's exactly what this killer is doing. He's leaving a signature. Killing on each Sunday of Advent is part of it. But the rest is not so clear. He's using a pattern the typical cop would never see. That's part of the game. To murder in a pattern without anyone discerning the pattern. To perform with such brilliance that no one can decipher the code." He stopped and sucked down a swallow of root beer.

"If this is true," said Jackie, "and for the sake of argument for the moment, let's suppose it is, then tell me why he chose these women? Were they picked at random, or are they part of a pattern? Except for the last one, they don't seem to have anything to do with religion."

"They have the commonality of being the wives of prominent personalities."

"Yes, but what does that tell us?"

"Somebody angry at the rich and famous perhaps?"

Jackie pursed her lips. "That's possible. Someone slighted at some point by the high and mighty. So they're random celebrities, famous but not connected in any other way."

Wrapping his fingers around his root beer glass, Burke pondered the conclusion. "I don't have a way to determine that yet. Maybe they do tie together in some way known only to the killer. Maybe there's a pattern there, too, if we could only figure it out."

"If we could, then we could determine who the next victim might be. If there is another victim."

A sigh swept through Burke. "Oh, I don't doubt there'll be another victim. Unless something totally unforeseen happens, we'll have another victim."

"But why this pattern?" asked Jackie. "This pattern that imitates the wounds of Jesus?"

Burke shifted in his seat. "I've been trying to figure that out. If my theory is true, then it shows someone with a deep-seated anger, a deep-seated religious rage. Whoever killed these women is mad at someone, I don't know who—mad at God maybe. He blames God for something, wants revenge for something he believes God did to him."

"Or didn't do for him."

"Yeah, that's possible too. Either way, the motive becomes the same. Strike back at God, hurt God, kill God."

"Kill God?"

"Yeah, you know what I mean, like the Jews and Romans killed Jesus. It's a progression, one step at a time, from the arrest in the garden to the crucifixion. At the end Jesus dies. God in the flesh dies at the hands of the human race."

"So God dies."

"In a sense, yes. He's killing God."

"So he's an Advent killer?"

Burke swallowed hard. "That's one way of saying it."

"But he's not killing God. He's killing women."

Burke rubbed his hands on his pants, then took a sip of root beer. "Yeah, that confuses me too. I don't know why his anger is directed toward women."

Jackie picked up the Bible a third time. She clicked her teeth together as she scanned the words. She stared at Burke. "You really believe this, don't you?"

Burke thought for a couple of beats. Did he really believe this? To say yes tied him to the case no matter what happened from this point. It meant he had to go all the way in the effort to help Jackie stop the killings. It became his case as well as hers, and he would have to follow it to the end regardless of the consequences.

He sighed heavily, then stepped over the edge, away from his hesitance. "Yes, I really do believe this."

Jackie paused for several long moments, staring at Burke. Finally, she said, "Then I'll tell Derrick Role about it. See what he says."

Burke shook his head. "He'll laugh you out of the office. He's bound by his previous statements to say the deaths aren't connected."

"I know," said Jackie. "But he's living by the politics of it all. He can't very easily admit to the whole world that we've got a crazed serial killer on the loose in Atlanta. We've moved beyond all that, didn't you know? We're a new Atlanta now, queen city of a new South. Even if Role wanted to believe you, he can't publicly say so. He can't adopt a theory proposed by a Christian psychologist unconnected in any official way to the case."

"But you'll offer it to him anyway?"

Jackie grinned. "I'll offer it to him anyway. As my idea at first. See what he says. If he shows any interest at all, I'll tell him where the theory originated. See if he'll talk to you."

Leaning back in his seat, Burke sipped from his glass again. A quiver passed through his hands. "Come Sunday it won't matter what he thinks. We'll know one way or another by Sunday night."

Jackie's eyes widened. "So you think another woman will die on Sunday?"

"If my theory is right, it's guaranteed. One woman per Sunday."

"Then I pray to God that your theory is wrong."

"But I thought you weren't religious."

"Usually, I'm not," said Jackie. "At least not officially. But lately I've begun to wonder. And in this case I'll definitely make an exception."

Chapter 34

Thursday, December 15

Jackie Broadus popped through the front doors of Peachtree Station and headed straight to her desk. Several people spoke to her as she passed, but she paid them no attention. She felt foul. She'd been up almost all night, unable to sleep after her visit with Burke Anderson.

Leaving Danny's Doughnut Shop, she'd headed straight to the station house. There she called the people who had seen Staton and Benton the nights of their abductions. Armed with the new theory from Burke, she wanted to reinterview everyone who'd given a statement, go back through everything she knew, see if any of it tied together.

The calls had yielded nothing fresh. Frustrated, Jackie had pulled up the computer files on the murders and searched through them again. It took her almost two hours to restudy the information compiled there. Again, though, nothing jumped out at her.

At a dead end, Jackie had shut down her monitor and left Peachtree. Driving toward her condominium, she got stalled in a traffic backup caused by a six-car wreck and didn't get home until almost 12:30.

At her condominium, she headed straight for the kitchen and fixed herself some herbal tea. From the kitchen she walked into the bedroom, dropped a Garth Brooks CD into her player, and fell onto the bed to stew on what she knew so far.

The two men seen at the abduction sites fit the same general description in terms of height and weight. But that didn't go far in connecting the two murders. One man could see and drove a Mercedes. Looked like a business executive. The other guy was blind and dressed like a redneck.

No one had been seen with Drexler. How did her abduction fit the pattern? If it fit at all. With the questions jumping through her mind like sheep over a fence, Jackie had finally fallen asleep just after two.

Now, sitting down at her desk, she knew she looked like death warmed over. Her head throbbed like the twin engines of a small plane. Black circles lay under her normally clear eyes, and her dark hair sat pinned up in a bun in the back. She always did that when she didn't have time to wash it. Maybe she could wash it tonight.

Rolling her neck around on her shoulders to loosen it up, she pushed her chair closer to her desk. Time to check the evening's reports, see if anything new had surfaced overnight. Her eyes fell on a copy of the *Atlanta Independent* that someone had left for her. The circles under her eyes widened and stretched as she read the headline story. She slammed her fist down on the newspaper and jumped out of her swivel chair.

She couldn't believe what she had just read. Surely, Burke and Debbi wouldn't sabotage her this way. But there it was. As plain as the nose on a clown's face.

That's what she felt like. An ignorant clown. Duped by a guy she thought she could trust.

Her eyes riveted back to the headline and she sat back down, scanning the article again, almost as if to make sure she hadn't imagined it.

CELEBRITY DEATHS CALLED "BIZARRE"

The story underneath quoted a high-ranking but unidentified police department source. It detailed the deaths of Staton, Benton, and Drexler, repeating the information already given to the public.

Jackie skipped quickly through this part, but her eyes slowed as she read the next paragraphs.

> According to autopsy reports given to this reporter by our high-ranking source, the method of murder in each death can only be described as "bizarre." That's the word used by the police authorities.
>
> Leslie Staton died from a brain hemorrhage caused by a series of vicious blows to the head. Rosaline Benton died from blood loss that resulted from what police call a "flogging." And Angelica Drexler's demise occurred due to a puncture wound that pierced her skull cavity.
>
> So far, police investigators cling to their claim that the deaths are unrelated. As our source said:
>
> "Though we admit the weekend abductions and Sunday deaths form a pattern of time and the fact that these are semicelebrities in Atlanta form a pattern of choice, the methods of death are so diametrically different that we can't, with any assurance, establish a connection between the murders."

Jackie stopped reading. The conclusion of the story carried nothing breathtaking. She shook her head and sighed deeply. Role would tear the precinct apart searching for the leak. She would stand as one of his prime suspects.

Jackie picked up a pencil and twirled it in her fingers. How best to approach this? Go ahead and admit her connection to Burke and Debbi Anderson?

Another thought came to her. How could she tell Role about Burke's theory and not connect herself to this story? If she told him about the theory and who originated it, Role would certainly find out that Burke's wife worked with the *Independent*. That would tie her directly to the leak.

But if she didn't tell Role about Burke's theory, would that hold up the investigation? If Role thought it had any merit at all, he would investigate it. She knew he would. No matter what she thought of the man's political ambitions, she recognized a good cop when she saw one.

Role was a good cop. He wouldn't let politics keep him from doing his job, would he? She didn't think he would.

So if she kept Burke Anderson's suggestion to herself, she might impede an investigation. That might give a serial killer more time to kill another woman. She couldn't do that.

She would tell Role about Anderson's theory. She would confess that she'd given him the autopsy reports. She would resign from the case, take her medicine like she should. And if she managed to keep her rank as a detective, she would never trust anyone again.

Folding the paper and placing it under her arm, Jackie gritted her teeth. For reasons far beyond this case, she had wanted to trust Burke. He had seemed genuine to her, not superficial and dishonest. Her time with him in the last year had given her some hope, had caused her to start thinking about the possibility of the God he trusted. But if he, as this situation seemed to indicate, had so little integrity that he would lie to her, then how could she dare believe in the God he followed?

Still pondering the problem, Jackie stalked away from her desk and down the hallway to Role's office. It wouldn't do to buzz him over the phone. No, for this she needed to talk with him face-to-face. Dreading the encounter, Jackie's shoulders sagged, and she felt terribly sad.

Chapter 35

Burke Anderson sat in his leather wing back chair and concentrated on the face of the sixteen-year-old boy slouching on the sofa across from him. The boy, referred to the clinic by the guidance counselor at North Park High School, was going through a tough time. His girlfriend had moved away in August when her father took a new job in St. Louis. Worse still, his parents had divorced in September, and a favorite uncle had died of cancer the weekend before Thanksgiving.

All of it had piled up on the teenager, and he had fallen into a bleak depression. He started skipping school, and his grades dropped. He quit the football team and started staying out until the wee hours of the night.

His mother, with whom he lived while she and his father fought for custody, found a matchbox half-full of cocaine in his shirt pocket last Saturday while doing his laundry. She had called the guidance counselor and the counselor had called the clinic. Burke had seen the boy twice before this and had made some progress in getting the kid to trust him.

Now the teenager drew his gangly legs up close to his body and hugged his arms around his humped shoulders.

"So you're feeling confused by all that's happened to you in the last year," offered Burke.

"Yeah, confused and, I don't know, helpless, you know, pushed around, like I don't have anything to say about what happens to me, like what I want doesn't count. I mean, like, nothing is happening like I want it. And I can't do a thing about it."

"Things happen that we can't prevent," agreed Burke. "It makes us feel pretty helpless."

Burke saw the boy's lower lip quivering. "I don't like feeling helpless," he said, his voice shaky.

Burke waited for him to continue. He sensed they were at a point of breakthrough. If the boy would let go of his anger, he might begin to move forward with his life.

"It feels lonely," said the boy. "Like a child all by himself, weak and, and . . ." He started to cry softly, the tears puddling up under his eyes and clinging to his cheeks.

Burke stayed still for several long seconds, letting the kid pour out his grief. Then, sensing the right moment, he stood and stepped to the sofa. Leaning over, he put his hand on the boy's back and patted his shoulders.

"It's okay to cry," said Burke. "It helps us, helps us wash away some of the pain we feel. It won't solve your problems, won't bring your uncle or girlfriend back. But it will release some of the tension, free you from some of the anger."

The boy continued to cry for another minute. His nose began to sniffle. He wiped his face with the sleeve of his shirt. His sniffles filled the room, and Burke grabbed a Kleenex from a box on his desk. "Here, try this," Burke said. "I keep them here for just this reason. They're softer than a shirt sleeve and won't feel crusty later on."

The teenager laughed, took a Kleenex, and swabbed his nose. For another couple of minutes, he sat still and quiet. Burke didn't rush him. The boy's red face brightened. "Talking with you has helped me a lot," he said.

"I'm glad," said Burke. "I like talking to you. We all get down some-time and need someone who'll listen to us."

"I'm going to see you again next week," said the kid.

"I know," said Burke. "I'll look forward to it."

The kid blew his nose.

"I think that about finishes us for the day," said Burke. "That okay with you?"

The boy nodded and stood up.

"Why don't you step into the rest room and wash up for a mo-ment?" Burke suggested, wanting to give the boy a dignified way to wipe away his tears before he walked out.

The teenager smiled and Burke pointed him to the private rest room adjacent to his office. The boy walked to the rest room. Burke sat down and began to jot out his notes. The phone buzzed. Burke picked up.

"There's a man named Hal Staton on line one for you," said Molly.

Instantly Burke's adrenalin surged. Hal Staton! "Put him on," he said quickly, leaning forward in his seat.

"Hello, is this Burke Anderson?" The voice sounded shaky, a bit weary maybe.

"Yes, is this Hal Staton?"

"Yes, it is. I'm calling you from Cordele, wondered if I could make an appointment to see you."

The teenage boy stepped out of the rest room. "Hang on a minute," Burke said to Staton. "I'll be right back."

Punching the hold button, Burke stood and walked the kid to the door. "I'll see you again next Thursday at three," he said, talking as fast as possible without being rude. "My secretary will give you an appointment card. Call me if you need me between now and then."

The boy shook his hand and moved into the reception area. Hurrying, Burke closed the door and hustled back to the phone. He picked it up without sitting down. "Hello, Hal," he said.

No one answered. He punched the line for Molly. "What happened to Hal Staton?" he asked.

"Don't know. Did he hang up?"

"Apparently so. Look, call information in Georgia for me, see if you can get a number for him."

Slamming the phone down, Burke twisted around and faced the window. He knew Staton had called him for something important, maybe something urgent. The few words Staton had spoken sounded like a warning. No, that wasn't it exactly. Not a warning. More like a plea.

His phone buzzed. "Yes?"

"The number for Hal Staton is unlisted," said Molly. "No way to reach him."

His legs quivery, Burke stepped behind his desk and checked his calendar. He had two appointments listed for the afternoon. The last one ended at 2:00 P.M. He buzzed Molly again. "Cancel my afternoon sessions," he said. "I've got an emergency on my hands."

Five minutes later, after calling Debbi, he sprinted into the parking lot and climbed into his car. Debbi had agreed to meet him at an Exxon station at I-75. From there they would go to Cordele.

Speeding out of the parking lot, he breathed a short prayer. A prayer that he would not arrive in Cordele too late.

Chapter 36

Jackie peered in through the glass-encased office and saw Derrick Role sitting at his desk, his feet propped up, his left ear jammed into a telephone. His white, cuff-linked shirt looked freshly starched, and she wondered how he managed to look so immaculate all the time. She could put on a blouse in the morning, and it would resemble crinkled aluminum foil by lunchtime.

She knocked on Role's door. He glanced up at her. His brow furrowed, then he waved her to come in. She obeyed, opening the door softly and taking a seat on the sofa across from his desk.

"I'm doing all I can," said Role, dropping his feet to the floor. "I'll call your office just as soon as I know something." He hung up and nodded at Jackie.

"The governor," he said nonchalantly. "Wants to know the status of our investigation. Seems these murders are dampening the holiday spirit for the folks in the top of the political tree. Making the voters somewhat restless."

"But the governor just got elected. Not up again for four years. What's his beef?"

Role fingered a cuff link. "Oh, you know politicians. He got elected on a crack-down-on-crime and cut-taxes platform. Expects us to slam dunk every case that dribbles through here—from spitting on the floor at the mall to multiple murders. No pleasing these guys."

Jackie tried to imagine the pressure hanging over Role. To have the governor calling him. From what she'd seen of the governor, you didn't want him on your neck. A man in his late forties. High energy. Dynamic. By common consent the best orator in Georgia politics in a century. Married to a beautiful woman. Expecting his first child after over twenty years of marriage. Due sometime this month from what the paper had reported on the society page.

"So the governor's not taking well to Atlanta's latest killing spree," she said, her sarcasm unmistakable.

Role grunted. "Not a bit, and I'm suffering the consequences." He leaned back in his seat. "Speaking of which, what's the status of it all?"

Jackie stared at him for an instant, wondering if he had seen the morning's paper. Nothing in his expression indicated one way or the other. She took a deep breath and decided to get it over as quickly as possible.

"Have you read the *Independent* this morning?" she asked.

Role rocked forward in his chair and leaned over his desk toward her. "Let's assume for the moment I haven't," he said. "Is there something in there I should've seen?"

Not sure of his ploy, Jackie plowed ahead. "I suppose you could say that. Debbi Anderson, their lead reporter on these murders, printed some information known only to us and the medical examiner's office." Jackie hesitated but only for half a second. "You need to know I'm the one who gave her the information."

She stopped and waited for Role to respond. He didn't say anything at first. Instead, he stood up, walked around and perched himself on the corner of his desk. Jackie could smell his cologne. Brut, if she correctly remembered her fragrances.

Role kicked his right leg out from the desk like a boy swinging his feet off the edge of a log over a stream. He rubbed his hands through his hair. Jackie waited for him to swear, to scream, to lash into her for breaking department policy and jeopardizing the investigation.

But he didn't. Instead, he suddenly stood up and smiled. "You gave Debbi Anderson the reports?" he asked.

"Well, actually I gave them to her husband."

"Why him? What's the connection?"

As quickly as possible, Jackie reminded Role of the case Burke was involved in two years ago. She told him she was one of two detectives who headed that investigation.

Role nodded as he listened. Of course, he said, he remembered now. He recalled a few of the specifics. Broadus and Avery Mays worked the case. A preacher involved in the mess.

Jackie told Role that during the case, Burke Anderson met and fell in love with Debbi Meyer, the young reporter assigned to the story, and recently they had married.

That's how the reports turned up in Debbi Anderson's hands, Jackie explained. She gave them to Burke, and Burke passed them to his wife. "He made me a promise," said Jackie. "But I guess he couldn't keep it."

Role nodded, then hopped down from his desk. He opened a

drawer, picked out a rubber band and, still standing over her, began to twist it around and around on his index finger.

Watching him, Jackie couldn't get a handle on his feelings. He seemed strangely calm for one who had made such dire threats against leaks.

"Why did you give him the reports?" asked Role.

Jackie smoothed down her khaki skirt. Maybe she could make Role understand. "For one thing, Burke promised me that Debbi wouldn't print what I gave her."

"Why did she want the information if she didn't plan to use it?"

"Remember, Burke made the promise, not Debbi. He either lied from the start or he couldn't get Debbi to keep the promise."

"I don't understand your gain," said Role. "What was in this for you?"

Jackie paused for a moment and bit her lower lip. Here's where it could get tricky.

"Burke Anderson is brilliant," she said, explaining it to herself as much as to Role. "When Avery and I worked with him two years ago, he stayed more than one step ahead of us all the way. He's almost through with a Ph.D. in psychology from Emory. He's now a psychologist with a clinic here in town. He—"

Role held up his hand. "I know a dozen psychologists in Atlanta. For a hundred and twenty bucks an hour, I can get any one of them to read your autopsy reports. What can Anderson do that they can't?"

Jackie shrugged. "I don't know, not for sure. But, like I said, he's one of the sharpest people I've ever met. He's spent a major part of his doctoral work studying abnormal psychology. These murders were so strange, so beyond what we normally see, I thought a guy with that kind of background might be able to tell me something, see something I was overlooking."

She stopped and stared down at her hands. Surprisingly, they weren't shaking. Getting this off her chest felt good.

"So—did he?" asked Role.

Momentarily confused, Jackie's brow furrowed. "Excuse me?"

"Did he tell you anything, see anything you had overlooked?"

She rubbed her hands together and desperately wanted to stand. But Role had the floor and didn't seem inclined to stop his pacing and give it up.

"He has a theory."

"I'm listening."

"I need to warn you it's highly unusual."

"These are unusual cases."

Jackie smoothed her skirt and sucked in a deep breath. "Okay. Here's what he thinks. He believes the deaths are connected, that one person did them. That—"

"But the descriptions of the last people seen with the women don't match."

"I know, and Burke hasn't really addressed that problem. Disguises are possible. It's also possible that the people seen with the deceased had nothing to do with their abduction."

Role nodded and Jackie continued. "Burke believes there's a pattern to the murders. A pattern a cop wouldn't easily see. A pattern that only a religious person would see." Jackie paused and breathed deeply again.

"I'm waiting," said Role.

"Well, it's like this," said Jackie, spewing out the words. "Burke believes the wounds of the dead women follow the pattern of wounds suffered by Jesus as recorded in the Bible—the blows to the head, the whipping, the crown of thorns. The women were killed on the first three Sundays of Advent, the time when Christian people prepare for the birth of Jesus. He thinks someone is killing these women from some intense religious rage, rage against God for something he perceives God did or didn't do at some point in the killer's past. Burke believes that another woman will die this Sunday if we don't catch the killer before that happens."

Jackie stopped to give Role a chance to respond. He stood dead still in the middle of the room, his hands at this side, the rubber band dangling from his right thumb. She heard a clock ticking overhead. She glanced up at it. Almost nine o'clock. The second hand moved five seconds.

Role said, "You buying any of it?"

Jackie shrugged. "I don't know yet. But I think it deserves consideration."

"It has lots of holes."

"I know that. And I know we can't really operate on something that's so flimsy. But that's what he thinks."

Role moved back to his desk and took his seat. He twirled his rubber band on his thumb. "We can't let anyone know we're considering this," he said. "And I mean no one. You tell Burke Anderson that I said it was hogwash. That I immediately dismissed his screwy idea. Make sure that he buys what you say. In fact, tell him that I'm interested in knowing where he was on the nights these women were killed. The threat of having to answer a few questions should quiet him down for a few days. No matter how ironclad his alibi."

Role reached for the telephone. Jackie, feeling fortunate that Role hadn't blasted her for giving up the reports, saw her chance to escape. She stood and moved toward the door, a sigh of relief climbing from her toes into her lungs. She touched the doorknob.

Role's voice nailed her dead in her tracks. "Oh, Jackie, don't think I've forgotten what you did. You will face the music about the leak. But I'm not sure yet which tune I'll play. See you soon."

Opening the door, she trudged out. For now, she stayed on the case. For that, she felt thankful.

Chapter 37

On the way to Cordele, Debbi reached Jackie Broadus on the car phone. She'd tried several times already that morning, but her efforts had proved unsuccessful. She didn't know if Broadus had ignored her calls or hadn't had a chance to return them. Debbi figured the former seemed more likely. She couldn't blame her. Even if the story weren't her fault, it sure appeared as if it were.

When the dispatcher at Peachtree connected her to Jackie, Debbi gripped Burke by the arm, took a deep breath, and plunged right into her apology.

"Look, Jackie, I know you don't want to talk to me and Burke right now—and I can understand why you wouldn't—but I'm asking you to give me one minute of your time. Can you do that—give me one minute to explain?"

She paused for an answer. "I'm here," Jackie said coolly.

"Good, I appreciate it that you'll hear me out. You need to know two things. First off, I want you to know that neither I nor Burke told anyone about the reports you gave us. I know you'll find that hard to believe. But it's the truth. Mimi Stoddard brought me a copy of the medical examiner's report late yesterday and demanded that I use it in my story. Stoddard didn't know that I already had the reports."

Burke dodged the car to the left to avoid a piece of metal in the road. Debbi waited for Jackie to speak. She didn't. Debbi said, "Jackie, you there?"

Jackie answered. "Yeah, I'm here. Do you really expect me to believe you?"

Debbi nodded to Burke. He took the phone and his voice took on a pleading tone. "Jackie, this is Burke. You've got to believe us. Debbi's telling you the truth. Mimi Stoddard had the same reports we did. Where she got them, we don't know—maybe from the medical examiner's office, maybe from someone else close to the investigation in the police department. Stoddard told Debbi to use the stuff; Debbi tried to get Stoddard to write the story herself, but she refused. She insisted that Debbi do it. Debbi never told Stoddard that she had the material. She pretended she didn't know a thing.

"We tried to call you last night and this morning to warn you. You'll hear us the next time you go through your answering machine."

"You could fake that," said Jackie. "Pretend to warn me, even as you go ahead with your little schemes."

Burke shook his head and handed the phone back to Debbi. She spoke again. "Look, Jackie, I would never lie to you. You're more than a cop to us; you're also our friend. I care about you—Burke cares about you. We wouldn't do anything to jeopardize your career. You've got to trust us on this. Can you do that, trust us?"

She heard Jackie exhale into the phone. Debbi imagined her thinking through what she and Burke had said, trying to reach a conclusion about their integrity, about the depth of their friendship.

"Listen Debbi," said Jackie. "I'm not sure what I believe right now. Role seemed awfully calm when I told him about this. Almost like he expected it, like he knew about it before I did.

"I don't know who gave what to whom. But I do know the damage is done. No matter who did it. So for now, until I can figure out who's lying and who's not, I'll withhold judgment.

"In the meantime, don't expect any more information from me. I need to watch my back on this one. Role is tough to read. I don't want to cross him."

"We understand," said Debbi.

"You said you wanted me to know two things," said Jackie. "What's the second?"

Glad to change the subject, Debbi quickly shifted gears. "Yes, this is important. We're on the way to Cordele right now. Hal Staton called Burke about an hour ago. Said he wanted to see him. Burke had to put Staton on hold for a second. When he came back on line, Staton had hung up."

"Hung up?"

"Yeah, and when Burke tried to call back, information said he had an unlisted number."

"Why did Staton call?"

"We don't know for sure, but when I went down for the funeral, I left him a note with Burke's card in it. Told him to call Burke if he ever needed anything, if he ever wanted to talk."

Jackie's voice edged up a notch. "How far out are you?"

"About sixty miles."

"How fast you going?"

"About seventy-five, but don't call the highway patrol."

Jackie laughed. It sounded good to Debbi. "No, I won't do that. You get to Staton as fast as you can. He might have thought of something since we interviewed him, might know something we need to check out. I'll see what I can find out about these leaks."

Listening to Jackie, Debbi felt a surge of hope. Maybe she believed them. "So you trust me again?" she asked.

Jackie grunted. "Don't count your chickens. Right now I'm not going to trust anyone. You bring me something from Staton, and I might consider it. Until then, the jury is still out. I'll talk to you later."

Debbi laid the phone into the console. If all went well, she and Burke would reach Cordele in just under two hours. If all went well, Jackie Broadus would soon believe in them again. If all went well, she and Burke would soon sit down with Hal Staton and see what he had on his mind.

Chapter 38

When Mimi Stoddard walked out of the ladies' room at St. Sebastian's Restaurant and crossed under the twenty-foot-wide chandelier that hung like a shining moon over the center of the dance floor in the ballroom, she found Derrick Role waiting for her. He smiled warmly and extended his hand in a gallant gesture.

"I wish we had music," he said, twirling her around as she took his arm.

"We could make our own," suggested Mimi, a smile equal to his playing on her face.

"Indeed we could. And we shall," agreed Role, wrapping his arm around her waist and leading her out of the ballroom. "But let us not forget—business comes before pleasure."

"I wonder who said that first," said Mimi.

"I don't know, but at times like this I would like to strangle him," said Role.

"For a homicide detective, that sounds extremely violent," said Mimi.

"To be a homicide detective you have to be violent," said Role.

Mimi arched her eyebrows. "Indeed."

They reached their table and slid into their seats. A tuxedoed waiter appeared and handed them a wine list. Both abstained, asked for water, and a quick menu. The waiter bowed and hustled off.

Role reached for Mimi's hand and kissed it. "You're a beautiful woman, Mimi Stoddard. I'm so glad we met."

Mimi licked her lips, remembering that occasion. . . .

➤

At the country club she had joined when she moved to Atlanta to take over as managing editor at the paper. The *Independent* paid her entry fee. After all, she needed to become part of the Atlanta mix if she wanted to make the paper successful.

She saw Role on the diving board one Sunday afternoon in late August. Right after her arrival in Atlanta. He was doing a variety of Olympic-style dives. Wowing the women who had gathered there with their brood of children to bake in the summer sun.

When he finished his exhibition, he moved to the bar and ordered an iced tea. Mimi moved from her lounge chair and joined him. "You dive well," she said. "On a college team?"

Toweling off, he nodded. She noticed the firm biceps, the dark tan, and flat abdomen. No wedding ring that she could see. "At Georgia," he said. "My first two years. Then I quit. No future in it. I wasn't quite good enough for the Olympics, so I had no way to commercialize my skills. So I took up golf."

"You good at that too?"

Role smiled and his teeth brightened the shadows under the umbrella that covered the bar. "I'm good at everything I do," he said. "If I'm not, I don't do it."

She nodded. "I'll bet you are at that."

From there the relationship began. And, Mimi had discovered, Derrick Role hadn't lied to her when he boasted about himself. In fact, he almost seemed modest. He wasn't just good at everything he did. From what she knew, he was great. And she liked that. . . .

"Not as glad as I am," she said, coming back to the present. "You've made Atlanta bearable for this California girl."

"Glad to be of service."

The waiter appeared again and handed them their menus. Role ordered lamb chops. Mimi chose grilled salmon. The waiter noted their salad and vegetable choices and moved off.

Role lifted a fork off the table and began to twirl it between his fingers. "So let's get the business part out of the way," he said. "Tell me about Debbi Anderson, the reporter you've got on these murders."

Mimi shrugged and filled him in. "I don't know that there's much to tell. She's bright, capable, a South Carolina Journalism School grad. Been with the paper for almost three years now. One of the few holdovers from the old regime. She was too good to let go. About the only one, from what I can see." Mimi stopped and took a sip of water.

Role binged his fork against his glass. "What about her husband?"

Mimi paused for a second, considering the question. Why did Derrick want to know about Burke Anderson? "I know less about him than I do his wife, as you might imagine. I've only seen him a couple of times when he's come into the offices to see Debbi. I think he's a counselor, a psychologist. Used to be a preacher, I hear. That's about the extent of what I know. What's your interest?"

Role laid his fork on the table and leaned forward. "Wasn't he involved in a murder case a couple of years ago?"

Mimi shrugged. "I don't know," she said. "I was in Sacramento at the time."

Role nodded. "Well, I can tell you he was. I can also tell you he's about to finish a Ph.D. with a specialty in abnormal psychology. He spent a summer working as an intern at a prison. Has done a lot of study of the criminal mind. Knows a good bit about what makes killers kill, what makes—"

"Whoa, take a breather here," said Mimi, raising her hands into a time-out signal. "I'm impressed with your interest in my employees and their families and with your knowledge of what they do, but I must say, I don't see the relevance. You see him as a suspect? Or as someone you want to consult on the case?"

The waiter popped a bread plate down and folded back the white cloth that covered the muffins inside. "We have five different kinds of butter tonight," he said. "Strawberry, honey—"

"Thank you," said Role, cutting him off. "We don't need you to label them for us. Let it be a surprise."

The waiter nodded and eased away. Role took Mimi's hand. "No, I don't see him as a suspect. Not now anyway. Though I am checking his whereabouts on the nights of the abductions. Neither am I bringing him in as a consultant. Though I may make a mistake if I don't."

"A mistake?"

"Yes, a mistake. It seems that our good Mr. Anderson holds some definite theories about these murders. Believes they're connected by some strange biblical pattern."

Restating what Jackie Broadus had told him, Role filled Mimi in on the details. She listened with intent curiosity and probed with sharp questions when she didn't follow a particular point.

The waiter brought their food while Role talked, but both of them ignored it. Only when Role finished the outline of the theory did they turn to their plates.

Mimi pinched off a bite of bread and pushed it into her mouth. "That's quite a tale," she said. "You think there's any merit to it?"

"I'm not sure yet," said Role, biting into his salad. "But it bears some thought. That's why I'm telling you about it. I want you to roll it around, study it, think about it."

Mimi chewed her bread. She buttered a piece and handed it to Role. "How does it help you if it's true?" she asked.

"It tells us how the next woman will die, for one thing. Or at least what her wounds will be."

"And those are?"

Role reached into his jacket and pulled out a small Bible. Mimi smiled. "You're taking this seriously, aren't you?" she asked.

He opened the Bible and handed it to her. "You should know by now that I take any possibility seriously. If it turns out that Anderson is right, I want to be the guy who proves it. If not, I haven't lost a thing. Either way, I win. And if I win, we win. Here, read this." He pointed her to John 19. "I've highlighted the key verses."

Mimi read through the highlighted text.

> Then Pilate took Jesus and had him flogged. The soldiers twisted together a crown of thorns and put it on his head. They clothed him in a purple robe and went up to him again and again, saying "Hail, king of the Jews!" And they struck him in the face.

Finished with that section, she scanned the page to the next passage Role had underlined.

> So the soldiers took charge of Jesus. Carrying his own cross, he went out to the place of the skull (which in Aramaic is called Golgotha). Here they crucified him.

"One more place," said Role. He pointed to the last of the highlighted words.

> But when they came to Jesus and found that he was already dead, they did not break his legs. Instead, one of the soldiers pierced Jesus' side with a spear, bringing a sudden flow of blood and water.

Laying the Bible down, Mimi pushed her hair back from her eyes. "Rather violent stuff, isn't it?"

"It wasn't a garden party, that's for sure. If you read the Gospels you see the whole sordid mess. Through the night and into the morning, a group of soldiers beat Jesus in the head and face; they stripped him and whipped him, dressed him in a purple robe to make fun of him, shoved a crown of thorns onto his head.

"Then, to top off the torture, they made him carry his own cross to the executioner's hill. There they drove wooden spikes into his hands and feet and left him to die. To make sure he was dead, they added one final insult. A spear through his side.

"Even if you don't call yourself a Christian, the cruelty of the priests and soldiers makes you want to puke."

Mimi sipped from her water glass, surprised by the depth of feeling coming from Role. She'd always seen him as tough, almost untouchable emotionally. A parallel to the persona that she exuded. "So what do we do now?" she asked.

Role picked up his fork and tapped it against the table. "That's the hard part. We don't know if this theory holds any water. If there's some connection between the women this killer has chosen, we haven't found it yet. The celebrity angle helps a bit, but you can only take that so far. We can't tell all the famous people in Atlanta to keep their heads down. At this point, all we can do is wait until the weekend and see if another woman disappears."

"Nothing else unless you believe in prayer."

"Even if you don't believe, it's worth a try."

"That works for me."

Role picked up a piece of bread and spread some honey butter on it. "If another woman dies on Sunday, we'd better all learn how to pray."

Chapter 39

Pulling the Volvo to the end of the long gravel driveway, Burke squinted through the headlights searching for some sign of life, but he didn't see any. No light glittered from the windows of the white-framed house directly ahead, and no sound poured out of it. Burke braked the car and stared out at the one-story farmhouse. It sat about one hundred yards off the main road, in the middle of a grove of pine trees. In the glare of the moon, Burke saw a rusted-out pickup truck at the end of the drive.

"There's the dog," whispered Debbi, pointing to the yellowish animal as he darted from behind the truck. "He greeted me when I came by after the funeral."

The Volvo eased further up the dark drive, and the dog fell into step beside the wheels. So far, it hadn't barked.

Reaching the house, Burke killed the engine but left the headlights burning. "It looks like they're not home," he said.

"Let's go to the door anyway," said Debbi. "We drove a long way not to make sure."

Burke nodded, pushed off the lights of the car, and slowly opened the door. The dog barked at him. He froze, the door half open and half closed. "What now?" he asked Debbi.

Debbi grabbed her purse off the seat. "I thought of this," she said. "So I grabbed something from a vending machine as I left the paper. Maybe it'll distract him." She held up a pack of peanut butter crackers.

Burke felt like laughing, but somehow that seemed inappropriate. "You think those will do it?"

"It's worth a try."

He lifted the crackers from Debbi's hand, pulled open the package, and threw one onto the ground in the direction of the dog. The animal sniffed the ground for a second, then gobbled up the cracker. Burke tossed him a second one, and he quickly ate it. He flipped the rest of the package to the dog and followed them out the door. The dog, busy crunching the tasty meal, didn't protest.

Debbi climbed out on the passenger side. Together, she and Burke walked to the house. A couple of seconds later, the yellow dog contentedly trailed up the driveway behind them.

Reaching the porch, Burke rapped on the door. The dog barked, but not with anger. They waited a moment and Burke knocked again. Burke heard something thump inside. He leaned over and peeked through the window. Inside, he spotted a bulky figure approaching them through the shadows.

Burke stepped back from the door. Debbi did too. The figure inside the house flipped on a porch light and opened the door. A square-jawed, husky man wearing a red and green flannel shirt, blue jeans, and a pair of tan work boots stood before them. Burke instantly recognized the man from the pictures he'd seen of him over the years in newspapers and on television screens. Hal Staton.

Hal said, "Can I help you?"

Burke held out his hand. "I'm Burke Anderson, and this is my wife, Debbi. After you called today, I decided to come see you. I hope you don't mind. And though I hope to get your autograph before we leave here, that's not the reason we came. We came—"

"You came because I called you. Because I need help."

For a second, no one spoke. The dog whined. Burke said softly, "We all need help, Hal."

Hal nodded and stepped back. "Come on in," he said. They stepped through the door and to the back of the house, the dog tagging along. In a rustic den, Hal switched on a light. "I've been sitting here in the dark," he said, pointing to a large, round-top bay window that overlooked the backyard. "I used to do that when I was a boy. Sit in the dark and watch the moon. Lots of times I could see deer moving in that meadow out there." He indicated a moon-splashed pasture beyond the window.

Burke and Debbi stepped to the window and stared out for a moment. "This must have been a great place to grow up," said Debbi.

"It was," he said, staring wistfully out the window with them. "Nothing like it. Roomy, beautiful. If I had a thousand lifetimes, I'd want to grow up right here every time." He paused and shook his head as if suddenly coming to his senses. "Excuse me, you two, have a seat. I completely forgot my manners. Would you like something to drink?"

Sitting down on a sofa, both shook their heads. Hal pulled up a rocker, sagged into it, and pushed off. The dog lay down at his feet.

The rocker squeaked and the sound filled the room. A silence fell again. Debbi cleared her throat. Staton coughed and reached down to scratch his dog. "It's been a tough two and a half weeks," he said.

"I can't even begin to imagine it," said Burke.

"No way you could. Hell could be no worse." He rocked hard in the chair. The squeak cut through the room.

"Tell me about it," said Burke.

"I don't know that I can," said Hal. "I don't know that I can tell anybody. I'm afraid if I tell it, it'll become real to me."

"It is real," said Burke. "Telling it might start you on the road to dealing with the reality."

A hint of a smile played on Hal's face. "I don't know if I want to deal with the reality."

Burke nodded. "I'm sure you don't. No one would."

Hal slowed his rocking and rose up. "But I have to eventually, don't I?"

Burke nodded. "If you want to get through it, I expect you do."

"I'm not sure I want to get through it."

"Tell me about that."

Hal leaned back again. His dog whined. "Quiet, Snapper," he said. He rocked once, twice, three times. "I'm not sure I want to get through it, that's all. Might be better for me if I didn't, if I ended it all, if I just checked out, you know what I mean."

"I know. Is that why you called me today? Because you almost checked out?"

Hal nodded and stared down at his feet. He rubbed Snapper's head. "Yeah, that's it. I almost checked out. Last Friday. Down by the pond."

"Why didn't you do it? What stopped you?"

Hal grinned. "You won't believe it."

Burke shrugged. "Try me."

Hal nodded, then poured out the whole episode from the afternoon. The walk past the barn, the visit to the pond, the shotgun, the tolling of the bell of the church, the memories of his youth, of going to the church, of working there, the demand for a sign, the reaching for the shells, the card stuck to the shell, the call to Atlanta.

"So, that's why I didn't check out, Mr. Anderson. Your business card was stuck to a shotgun shell, and I took that as a sign from God. Can you believe that? Isn't it the craziest thing you ever heard? Since Friday I've been trying to figure out what it meant, if it meant anything. But nothing has come to me. So today I decided to call you. I didn't know what else to do. But then, when I got you on the phone it seemed silly. Ever since I called you, I've been half mad at myself and half tickled.

"I still don't know what to think about it. That's what I've been doing all evening—sitting here by the window, staring into the pasture, trying to figure it all out, trying to decide if it was a sign or a silly coincidence that I grabbed to keep from killing myself." He paused, scratched Snapper, and chuckled. "So what do you think?" he asked.

Burke steepled his fingers in front of his chin and grinned with Hal. "The Bible says 'God works in mysterious ways his wonders to perform.' This would certainly qualify as a mysterious way."

"So you think this really was a sign?"

Burke leaned forward. "Did it keep you from harming yourself?"

"Well, yes, it did do that."

"Then I definitely see it as a sign. You see, Hal, I think God works in exactly this kind of way. In small, seemingly insignificant gestures, gestures most people don't recognize because they're not looking for them or because they're deliberately ignoring them. I believe God gives us signs all the time in very natural ways. But because they're not grand works, not words written in the sky, not miraculous healings of all our diseases, then most people reject them." He leaned back again. "I'm glad you didn't reject this one."

Hal nodded. "I guess I was looking for it. Or at least definitely open to it."

"Yes, you were open to it, looking for it. The tolling of the church bell reminded you of your youth. Of a simpler time. Of a time of faith, of commitment. Of a time when you believed in God. The same God you now believe has deserted you. That bell served as a sign far more than the card did. It called you back, didn't it? Made you open up to the possibility of God again?"

For an instant, Hal didn't answer. The squeak of the rocker echoed through the room again. Snapper whined. When Hal spoke, his voice was a whisper. "You could say that. The fact that I called you indicates that something is different, that I don't really want to give up on life, that I at least want to give it a try again."

"It won't be easy," said Burke softly.

"I'm sure of that," agreed Hal.

"But we're here," said Burke, grabbing Debbi's hand. "We're here to help you if we can, if you want us to help."

Hal lowered his eyes and stared at his boots. The rocker stopped squeaking. The room became silent. Snapper thumped his tail on the floor. Burke squeezed Debbi's hand. Hal's voice cracked as he spoke. "We all need help, don't we?"

Chapter 40 🕯

At 11:14 P.M. the phone in the sixteen-by-eighteen-foot bedroom of Derrick Role buzzed him awake from the doze into which he had only recently fallen. Scratching his eyes, he bumped the intercom button and raised up in bed. "Yeah, Role here, what's going on?"

"Derrick, it's Jackie. I'm at Peachtree. You need to get down here. About an hour ago, a guy name Lewis Delaney walked up to a patrol officer on Tenth Street and announced that he had killed Leslie Staton, Rosey Benton, and Angelica Drexler and wanted to make a confession."

Role's heart jumped thirty notches. He felt it bump through his rib cage. "Why wasn't I called sooner?" he asked, fully awake now and standing by the closet, grabbing a pair of pants off a hanger.

Jackie cleared her throat. "Because the last time we called you after ten o'clock, it turned out to be nothing, and you told us all in rather impolite terms that you were not to be disturbed at that time of night unless we had something worth reporting. We've been trying to follow your dictates."

"Is the guy clean?" he asked, deciding he better change the subject.

"Nope, he's doped up on something—we're not sure what yet. He's pretty whacked out. We're trying to flush him out, get him a bit more coherent."

"Does he fit the description of the guys seen with the victims?"

"To some extent. He's Caucasian, five ten, medium build. But he doesn't have gray hair. In fact, he's got no hair at all."

"He could have shaved it. Or he could have been wearing a wig."

"Or he could have nothing to do with these murders and only wants some attention."

"He would really be crazy to want this kind of attention, don't you think?" asked Role, slipping socks onto his feet.

"Yeah, but I've seen it happen."

Role sighed. "Yeah, me, too, but let's not look a gift horse in the mouth. We've got a guy who fits the description who wants to confess. That's worth considering, isn't it?"

He heard Jackie pause, then say, "Yes, Derrick, it's worth considering."

"You running his license?" he asked.

"Yeah, right now. His address is listed as 2124 Marshall Road."

"Ten to one, he'll have some priors," he suggested, his voice hopeful.

"Maybe—druggies usually do."

Role slipped a T-shirt over his hairy chest. "How old is he?"

"Thirty-nine, according to the license."

"That fits too," he said. "What about a car? Was he driving one?"

"Yeah, a white van. Registered to a Wilson Delaney."

"A father maybe?"

"Yeah, or a brother."

"You're checking that, I'm sure."

"Already on it."

Role cleared his throat. "Anything of an evidentiary nature in the van?"

"Don't know yet. We've started the process to check it for prints, fibers, blood, you know the routine."

Role nodded and yanked a starched shirt from a closet rack. Yes, he knew the routine.

"Jackie, stay with this guy until I get there. Make sure the van is handled properly. I'll be there in thirty minutes."

He punched off the phone and put on his shoes. Wrapping a tie around his neck, he started to whistle. He had a suspect in custody who said he wanted to confess to three murders. That would certainly read well in the morning's paper and get the governor off his back. Not only that, it would keep him on track to become chief of the whole shooting match. On the way to the station, he would call Mimi. Make sure *The Independent* had the story. She would appreciate his thoughtfulness.

Chapter 41

Ten minutes before Derrick Role walked into Peachtree, Debbi Anderson bolted upright in bed and fumbled to find the phone that rang on the table beside her. On the third ring, she grabbed it and mumbled out a sleepy greeting. She heard Mimi Stoddard's voice ranting on the other end.

"Debbi, this is Mimi, wake up and listen carefully. You need to get down to Peachtree Station. They've got some guy who's confessing to our murders."

Worn out from the trip to Cordele and back, Debbi didn't comprehend at first. "What?" she asked, lying back down.

"At Peachtree, Debbi. A guy's confessing to the killings at Peachtree."

This time it sank in. She propped herself up and reached over to Burke and shook his shoulders. He rolled over and patted her on the arm but didn't open his eyes.

"How long's he been there?" asked Debbi.

"I don't know all the details, Debbi," said Mimi. "And I don't need to know them right now. What I need is for you to get your bones shaking. I think we're the only ones with this news so far, and I want to keep it that way as long as possible. We can get an insert ready for the late edition if we hustle."

A sudden question popped into Debbi's mind. "How'd you get this information?" she asked Mimi. Silence fell over the line for an instant, then Mimi said, "Like I told you before, I'm in the news business, too, Debbi. I cultivate my sources just like you do. And," she spoke with emphasis, "I also protect them just like you do."

Debbi nodded. "Okay, I understand. I'm moving now. You going to Peachtree?"

"Nope, I'm getting what we know right now ready for the paper. You call me the second you get there."

"Hold the presses."

"You do your part, I'll do mine."

Debbi hung up and rolled over, throwing her leg over Burke's waist. She bent forward, giving him a long, hard kiss. For once, he opened his eyes almost instantly.

"What time is it?" he asked.

"Time to wake up," said Debbi.

"Gladly," he said, his eyes dancing.

"But no time for that," she said, jerking her leg up and jumping out of bed.

He frowned. "Then why'd you wake me?"

She told him. He sat up, too, his brown eyes wide with surprise. He threw off the covers and dropped his feet to the floor. "I don't want you out by yourself this late," he said. "I'm going with you."

"I appreciate your loving protection, kind sir, but you're going to be worn out tomorrow."

"I was already worn out. A few more hours won't make much difference."

Debbi didn't argue. She didn't have the time.

Five minutes later, they snapped off the lights in the house and climbed into the Volvo. Debbi drove. Burke sat silently against the door. For several minutes neither spoke. Debbi whirled the car in and out of the night traffic. The glow of the lights from outside bathed their faces. Debbi glanced over at Burke and saw him staring out the window.

"What's on your mind, O husband of mine?"

He sighed and faced her. "Oh, that's easy enough to figure out. I'm wondering about this confession. Wondering if this guy did it, and if he did, did he do it like I imagined? Is he evil enough to have thought of that?"

"I hope not," said Debbi. "I hope no one is that evil."

Burke put his hand on her arm. "But *I* thought of it."

She raised her eyebrows. "I guess you did."

"So if I did, someone else could have. And they could have acted on what they thought."

"Are we that evil, Burke?"

"I'm afraid we are," he said. "We're that evil and worse." He paused for a second, then continued, "We're warped. In every era, no matter where you turn, you see the infection of the sin that corrupts us all. It's like a stain we can't wash out."

Debbi nodded. "It's hard to accept," she said.

Burke squeezed her arm. "Then don't. Don't accept it. I hope we never accept it. If we accept it, give in to it, then we're hopeless, down the tubes. I hope we fight it tooth and nail, fight it with all our strength and all the strength of God, fight it until we defeat it, defeat it and kill it before it kills us. That's our only hope. To kill it before it kills us."

Debbi nodded and pulled onto the interstate loop. She passed a slow moving truck. The night hours crept onward.

Chapter 42

Jackie met Role as he hustled into the front doors of Peachtree. She marveled at his appearance at this hour. His hair was neatly slicked back and his beige suit set off his dark skin. Cuff links glinted in the sleeves of a freshly pressed shirt. He was wrinkle-free, fit for television.

"We're holding Delaney in interrogation," she told him as he stepped to his office.

"He say anything else?"

"Nope, and we haven't asked. Wanted to wait on you."

Role nodded his approval. "Thanks, Jackie. He ask for a lawyer?"

"Negative on that too. We asked him if he wanted one. Gave him his rights, the whole bit. But he didn't want any of it."

"You got everything on tape?"

"Yep, videoed it every step of the way."

Role opened his desk drawer, pulled out a file folder, then looked up. "Great, let's go talk to Delaney."

Jackie followed him down the narrow hallway toward the interrogation room, a square, bare space in the back of the precinct offices. Outside the room, they paused for a moment. Role opened the folder in his hands and studied it. Jackie peered through the glass pane that separated the hallway from the prisoner.

She had stood here many times. A four-by-four table surrounded by three chairs sat in the center of the room. The light inside was bright but not brutal.

She spotted Delaney, guarded by a uniformed patrol officer, slouching in the chair closest to the door, his chin nestled against his chest. Delaney wore navy sweatpants and a faded blue jean jacket over a thick gray sweatshirt. Dirty black tennis shoes covered his feet. His face seemed smoother than most junkies she had seen, as if he had only recently started his habit and hadn't had time yet for his skin to turn pasty and wrinkled and old.

Role closed his folder and pushed open the door. Jackie followed him. They took the unoccupied chairs opposite Delaney. Role initiated the interview, introducing himself. Delaney nodded and Role began.

"Now, Mr. Delaney, as I understand it, Detective Broadus here has already told you about your rights, has already asked you if you want a lawyer, is that right?"

"Yes, sir, that's right." Delaney's words came out slowly, as if he had a hard time thinking of them. Jackie focused on his face, wondering about his motivation for confessing. If he did kill the girls, why come forward? Didn't he want to continue his death spree? If he didn't kill them, then why the confession?

Role moved ahead. "You said you didn't want a lawyer. Right?"

"That's right."

Role grunted. "Okay, Mr. Delaney. Good. Now, here's what I want you to do. I want you to tell us—in your own words—what you know about the deaths of Mrs. Leslie Staton, Mrs. Rosaline Benton, and Mrs. Angelica Drexler. Just tell us the truth, tell us about your involvement with these ladies. Tell us everything."

Delaney blinked his eyes several times and swallowed hard. "I killed those ladies," he said, his words slipping out slowly in the quiet room. "I, I, well I clubbed that first one, whipped the second one, and the third one, what was her name? Drexler? Yeah, that was it, Drexler, I did her too. I . . ."

Delaney continued to pour out his story, to tell how he had taken Staton from the parking lot and Benton from the race track and Drexler from her home, how he had held them in the basement of his house and killed them each on a Sunday. How he delivered them on Mondays to the spots where they were discovered.

As he talked, Jackie found herself tuning out his confession. She was confused. The media had published everything Delaney was telling them. Every stitch of the information coming from his lips was a matter of public knowledge. She squeezed the sides of the wooden chair she sat on and wondered again whether Burke and Debbi had betrayed her confidence. She wanted to believe they hadn't. But Delaney's words made her uncertain.

Trying not to think about Debbi and Burke, Jackie wondered again about Delaney's motive. Would he say he did something he didn't do? She knew it wasn't the first time someone had confessed to crimes he didn't commit.

The motives for false confessions were varied. Guilt for another crime that the confessor had committed without detection. A sick desire for attention, for public notoriety. An effort to get off the streets, to deliberately get jailed and let the government provide food, clothing, and shelter. Jackie had seen it all—and more. But she couldn't tell with Delaney. Was his a false confession or not?

Jackie glanced at Role for a moment, then focused directly on her fellow detective for several seconds. He seemed intent on Delaney's words. Occasionally, he jotted a note on the pad from his folder or asked a leading question.

He wants this bad, thought Jackie. *Wants to wrap this up, declare a victory and move on to the next case. Wants to get his name splashed in the media, get his reputation stroked by another successful collar, get his career moved another step up the ladder.*

Nothing wrong with ambition, she thought. She had some herself and didn't feel guilty about it. Nothing wrong with it so long as it didn't blind a person to the truth.

Delaney's voice edged lower. He was nearing the end of his story. "So, I did those ladies. All three of them. I did them." He leaned back in his chair, apparently pleased with himself.

Role nodded. "So why did you come forward to confess?"

Delaney rubbed his bald head with both hands. "Well, I don't exactly know. It just seemed the thing to do. I mean, I didn't want to do it no more. And if I didn't come to confess now, why—I think I might have hurt me another woman."

Jackie placed her hands on the table. If Role wouldn't ask any hard questions, she would give it a try. "If you were so concerned about hurting someone else, why didn't you come forward after you killed Staton? Why did you wait?"

Delaney chewed on his lower lip. "Well, because I didn't think I would do it again. But it just happened, you know. A couple more times. So then I saw I might keep on doing it, that is, if I didn't turn myself in."

"Why'd you do it the first time? Why did you kill Leslie Staton?"

As if caught in a cross fire and searching for help, Delaney turned to Role. The detective said, "Answer the question, Mr. Delaney. Why did you kill the first time?"

A long pause fell over the room. Delaney rubbed his head. Chewed on his lip. Stared at Jackie. Said, "I wanted to be somebody."

Jackie slumped against her chair. None of it made sense. His motivation to "be somebody" was also motive enough to confess to something he didn't do. Unfortunately, though, if Delaney insisted on his confession as the truth, she knew that Role and a host of other people would more than gladly accept his explanation.

Chapter 43

At twenty-five minutes until noon, Burke laced up his jogging shoes and slipped into a slow pace beside Debbi on the indoor running track at the Stretch It Fitness Club. Though he hated to run indoors, he did so from time to time so he could spend a few extra minutes with Debbi. Though she had sworn the night he proposed that she wouldn't run with him, the comfort of an indoor track and the need to stay in shape had eventually changed her mind.

A gleam of sunlight washed over the track as they passed by a glass wall on the north side of the rectangular building. To Burke's pleasure, only a couple of other people were on the track. By noon the lunchtime joggers would have it covered.

Debbi didn't pay him any attention as he fell into the lane beside her. She had her eyes glued to one of the wide-screen televisions that the health club had positioned at four different spots around the track.

Dragging his feet on the spongy track, Burke made a pledge to himself to get to bed early tonight. The late nights and full days of the past week or so were about to kill him.

Debbi glanced over at him. "You look like dead meat on a stick," she said, wiping a bead of sweat off her brow.

"Thanks for the encouraging words, O sweet wife of mine," he said. "But don't forget—my chivalrous concern for my bride is what caused the destruction of my body."

They turned a corner and headed around the end of the oval track.

"And that concern is greatly appreciated," said Debbi. "Even if it is a bit too protective." She looked up at the television in front of them.

Burke took a deep breath and tried to settle into a rhythm. Running inside seemed artificial to him, and he never quite felt comfortable doing it. The monotony of a track bored him, and the confines caused by other runners crimped his ability to run at his own pace. He constantly found himself having to dodge the other joggers, and they always ran too slowly for his taste.

"How's your morning been?" he said, hoping to break the boredom of the running. "Anything new with—"

Debbi held up her hand to shush him. "Hold on a second, I've been waiting on this." She stared up at the television screen. Burke turned his attention to the TV too. The handsome face of Reginald Voss stared out at them. Debbi's pace edged up. Voss's smooth-toned voice filtered out through the speakers in the roof overhead and filled the air.

"As we reported at 8:00 A.M. this morning, the police have taken into custody a Mr. Lewis Delaney in connection with the deaths of Leslie Staton, Rosaline Benton, and Angelica Drexler. According to Detective Derrick Role, the chief investigator of these cases, Mr. Delaney has confessed to all three of these killings."

Voss paused to take a breath. Debbi and Burke reached the end of the straightaway and turned the far corner of the oval. Their eyes picked up the television on that side of the track.

"We're the ones who reported it first," said Debbi, huffing as she ran. "We scooped the TV guys this time."

Voss continued to speak, his face multiplied in size by the huge screen on the wall. "Since our earlier report, we've learned more about Mr. Delaney." He glanced down at a notepad in his hand. "He is a thirty-nine-year-old high school dropout who works in the produce department for his older brother, Walter Delaney, at the Easy Shop Supermarket on Ludwig Boulevard. He is a regular attender at Atlanta Braves and Atlanta Hawks games. He's well-known as an avid autograph seeker and often waits on the players of both these teams outside their dressing rooms.

"One other word worth mentioning—and this comes from his brother, Walter—Lewis was arrested about four years ago on an attempted rape charge but was not convicted. According to authorities, he is expected to be arraigned . . ."

Voss kept talking but Burke had stopped listening. Voss had said nothing about Delaney's motives, nothing about his reasons for killing these particular women, nothing about what made them candidates for murder, and nothing about the strange methods of death. Didn't Voss care about that? Had the police not asked about that?

Probably not, thought Burke, at least not like he would have. His theory was only that—a theory, and one as bizarre as the deaths themselves. No one even knew about his theory. No one but him and Debbi and Jackie Broadus. He'd not even told Hal Staton.

Burke wondered if Jackie had told Role about his suggestion. Probably not. After the foul-up with the autopsy reports, Jackie had probably decided to have nothing else to do with him. He couldn't blame her.

Two women, both of them dressed in pink sweatpants and sky blue tops, stepped onto the track in front of them, and Burke swerved to the side to miss them.

"This guy sounds like a real possibility," said Debbi, easing up behind him as she, too, passed the women.

Burke huffed out a mouth of air but said nothing.

"A Braves fan and all," suggested Debbi. "If he hung around—hung around after the games—then he, he probably saw Leslie Staton there. Plus the rape charge. Pretty tidy."

"None of the women were raped," said Burke, his voice flat, his feet pounding harder on the track as he almost involuntarily sped up his pace.

"That's true," Debbi said, shifting into a higher gear to keep up with him. "You don't think he did it?"

"I don't have any way of knowing. But I would sure like to talk with this guy. "

"No way that will happen."

"I know."

"So all—all we can do is leave it with the police." Sweat poured faster off her face.

Burke nodded and moved into the left lane to pass the two women again. Ahead of him, a group of three men pounded out the door leading from the men's dressing room. They eased onto the running track and began to walk briskly. Burke breathed deeply and reminded himself that the time spent with Debbi made up for the inconveniences of running with so many people in his way.

Chapter 44 🕯

The slender fingers held an expensive black wig up to the mirror. The glass in the mirror reflected the deep luster of the wavy, shoulder-length hairpiece back into the black eyes that appraised it. Snow sat on the marble countertop of the bathroom vanity beside her owner and stared into the mirror too. The black wig stood out in deep contrast to Snow's pure white fur.

"What do you think, Snow?"

The cat curled her tail up around her neck but said nothing. "Won't it look smashing with a royal blue dress? Accessorized with a pearl necklace and matching earrings? You like that?"

Snow dropped her tail to the countertop, swished it back and forth three times, and then, quite unconcerned about the evening's clothing choice, jumped to the floor.

"Well, you don't know anything anyway," said her owner, obviously perturbed by the cat's lack of interest.

The fingers, trembling gently, laid down the wig, and the killer stared into the mirror. The black eyes squinted with concern.

Delaney's confession had upset the well-orchestrated agenda. That silly newspaper, the *Independent*, had made it easy for him. That reporter, Debbi Anderson, had taken Delaney so seriously. Gave him front page headlines. "Advent Killer in Custody?" read the bold black print.

All the rest of the media followed suit. But they were all so terribly mistaken. So—well—so naive. So ignorant and so gullible.

At first the reports about Lewis Delaney's confession had caused a rush of anger. How dare someone else try to take credit for the splendid work so far accomplished?

So angered, the slender fingers had picked up a Waterford crystal bowl and smashed it against the marble floor in the bathroom, and the black eyes had turned almost red with heated resentment.

Then the anger subsided. It wasn't Delaney's fault. He was obviously a simpleton, a misguided idiot seeking a few moments of public acclaim.

But the media—they should know better. They should investigate before they print. They should check their truths before they proclaim them.

Perhaps they needed a bit of assistance—a reminder that Delaney knew nothing, that Delaney did nothing, that Delaney was nothing.

The black eyes stared down at Snow. How to do that? How to give them a reminder? Ah, that was it. Mrs. Debbi Anderson.

Mrs. Anderson would get a message. It would add some spice to the game that so far had gone so easily. Too easily, really. Too easily for much enjoyment.

Yes, Anderson would get a message. Nothing too obvious. Just enough to make an intelligent person wonder. Enough to make an intelligent person less than certain as the zero hour approached.

Until then, what did it matter? They would know soon enough. The idiocy of this Delaney's confession. The arrogance of such a man to claim such deeds. Only the one who did them deserved to accept the honor for it.

Soon enough all of them would know.

In the meantime? Well, in the meantime, Delaney's stupid confession, for whatever reason he chose to make it, meant the police would slack up with their investigation. Even if they didn't completely believe him, they would act with a tad less energy, do their work with a touch less urgency.

To make it even better, rude husbands and their acquiescent wives would fall back into their normal patterns—patterns that lacked caution and proper attention to security. How delightful! Delaney's confession made it easier.

The slender fingers picked up a rich red lipstick and pressed it to the waiting lips. The lipstick smoothed out evenly. A long tongue slithered over the lips, enjoying the taste, anticipating the preparation, the getting ready, the slipping on of the luxurious dress and shoes, the combing of the hair.

A full-length black mink lay on the bed in the next room. A pair of black, silk stockings draped over the mink. Exquisite black heels rested on the floor. A purse bought in Europe last spring would complete the outfit. Such pretty clothes. Such pretty clothes for such a pretty person.

Everyone agreed on that. No one denied it. Not even twenty-two years ago. Not even during the suffering season.

The slender fingers trembled again at the memories.

During the suffering season, the resolve was born, the resolve to strike back. To hurt the men who did their evil deeds and their equally evil wives who did nothing to stop it.

Not that Hal Staton or Bobby Benton or Karl Drexler or their wives had ever specifically done any monstrous evil. Just that they represented the ones who had. The one who had violated the innocence of the child, and the one who knew of the violation but refused to stop it.

Those who watched and did nothing were the worst of them all—the worst of all evils—to know the good to do and not to do it. To see the evil performed and to let it happen.

The fingers lifted a mascara brush from the bathroom counter. A light touch over the eyebrows would make them darker, make them match the hair.

Oh, but you do look pretty. You've always looked pretty. No wonder the preacher couldn't keep his hands off you.

A grandfather clock in the bedroom gonged the hour. Five times it rang. Another two and one half hours—then the Rossario Theater for the annual performance of Charles Dickens's *A Christmas Carol.* There the next to last of the Advent abductions would occur.

The slender fingers opened and closed, opened and closed as if squeezing a ball over and over again. In a few hours they would grasp a fourth woman's throat and toss her into the back of the U-Haul truck outside. They would hold the instruments of her death and wield them with precision and power. They would prove to all of Atlanta that Delaney knew nothing, that Delaney did nothing, that Delaney was nothing.

The annual Charles Dickens's *A Christmas Carol.* Oh, what a delight it would be this year. The Jesus Year.

Chapter 45

Every year for the past sixteen, Lisa Voss, elegant wife of television news anchor Reginald Voss, attended the Rossario Theater's production of Dickens's *A Christmas Carol,* a highbrow charity production staged to raise money for the St. Theresa's Children's Hospital. Tonight, in spite of the fact that she had recently visited a lawyer and started discussions about the possibility of a divorce from her husband, she climbed into their black Cadillac to do it again.

Reginald's public position made certain appearances with the Atlanta elite mandatory, and until she actually filed the papers and left him the note she'd already written and placed in her bureau drawer, she would fulfill her wifely obligations.

Reginald drove while Lisa fluffed with her hair. She couldn't seem to get the bangs to fall correctly over her patrician nose. She didn't say much. Neither did he.

They never did these days. They had discovered almost eight years ago, the year that the last of their three daughters left home to go to college, that they didn't really have much to talk about anymore. When they did try to converse, it almost always ended up in an argument. So they communicated verbally now only when absolutely necessary. Tonight it wasn't necessary.

A valet opened the door for Lisa at the front of the theater and drove the Cadillac away. Reginald touched her lightly on the elbow, and the two of them stepped up the sidewalk. She wrapped her mink coat tighter around her shoulders and sniffed the air. The aroma of a mixture of perfumes and colognes drifted across the night and reminded her again of the aristocratic crowd that would join them at the theater.

At the door, she reached into her purse, pulled out her ticket, and handed it to the attendant. Reginald touched her elbow again.

"Do you have my ticket?" he asked.

She shrugged. "No, why should I have yours?"

Several other couples stacked up behind them. "Because I brought them both home in an envelope and laid them on your dressing table. They were both in the envelope."

"Well, I got mine out of the envelope, assumed you would get yours, and left it in the envelope."

"So you don't have my ticket?" People behind them started to murmur. Reginald turned and flashed them his biggest smile.

"Let's step out of the way," he said. "Let these people pass." He turned to the attendant. "Excuse me a moment, we'll be right back," he said, grabbing Lisa by the wrist and pulling her out of line.

"Tell me what I'm supposed to do now?" he asked. "Go back home, get my ticket, and miss the first half of the show?"

"I don't know what else you can do."

He sighed and ran his hands through his well-styled hair. "I should make you go back. You're the one who deliberately left my ticket."

Lisa ground her teeth. "You can try to send me back," she said firmly. "If you're ready for me to make the nastiest public scene ever to unfold in the polite circles of Atlanta socialites."

Reginald fell silent for a moment. Lisa watched him, knowing that he was considering his options. He had a knack for that—working his way out of jams with reasoned ingenuity.

"Maybe they have our names on a seating list," he said, confirming her thoughts. "We reserved the middle two seats, four rows from the front. If they don't, we can try one other thing—ask to see the manager of the theater. I know him, not well, but maybe well enough to get inside without the ticket actually in hand."

Several people passed them. Reginald cleared his throat and stepped back into line. Lisa followed him. The line moved forward until they stood before the attendant again.

Reginald said, "Excuse me, sir, my name is Reginald Voss, and it seems that we left my ticket at home. So we have a bit of a dilemma. But I'm sure you have my name on a list of reserved seats. Could I possibly ask you to check that for me?" He smiled hugely. Lisa knew he wanted the ticket checker to recognize him from television.

"Let me check," said the man. He walked off. A dark-headed woman in pearl earrings standing to their left mumbled under her breath.

Reginald whispered harshly to Lisa. "I hope you're satisfied," he muttered. "You're holding up the whole line, and the curtain's supposed to go up in five minutes."

The dark-headed woman disapprovingly shook her head. Her pearl earrings dangled. Lisa didn't say anything. The ticket checker, holding a white sheet of paper, approached them.

The man smiled, then said, "We're in luck, Mr. Voss, we do have your name here. Let me apologize for not recognizing you immediately. I was watching tickets you know, not paying attention to faces. We're honored to have you with us again. Here you go, one ticket, row four, seat ten. Go right in."

Smiling widely, Reginald bowed at the waist and reached for Lisa's elbow. She pulled away from his hand. Side by side, but not touching, they stalked away.

The woman with the pearl earrings stepped to the attendant. "It looks like Mr. Voss and his Mrs. aren't too happy with each other." The attendant nodded his agreement and took her ticket.

In his seat in the theater, Reginald leaned over to Lisa. "You just better be glad I am who I am. If that ticket checker hadn't recognized my name, we'd still be standing in that line. And believe me, if it had become necessary for me to go home, it would absolutely have ruined the evening for me."

Lisa laughed but there was mockery and not humor in it. "Yes, Reginald, your notoriety saved the day for me. If I weren't sitting down, I would bow to your excellence. And let me assure you of this—the evening was ruined for me precisely because you didn't go home!"

For an instant, Voss seemed stunned by her assertiveness. But he quickly regained his composure. "If you feel that way, why don't you leave!" he asked.

She decided she had put up with enough. If Reginald wanted a scene, she would surely give him one.

"You don't have to tell me twice," she said, pushing up from her seat. "I'll take a cab."

She stepped into the aisle and rushed away from him before he could respond. For a moment, tears blurred her vision. She hated times like this, despised them, would do anything to make them stop. She stumbled at the end of the aisle and almost fell. The crowd around them began to mumble.

Behind her, she saw Reginald move. She knew he felt a tinge of guilt. He always did after one of their tiffs. She knew he did love her, though in a rather selfish sort of way.

She also knew he didn't want her to leave and that he would try and make up with her before she left the theater.

But she had suffered enough embarrassment for one night. She wouldn't give him a chance to talk her into staying.

Her decision made, she sprinted up the aisle. In the vestibule, she paused to catch her breath. Her nose dripped with sniffles, but she had no tissue in her purse. From her left, a tall, black-haired woman— the woman with pearl earrings—walked up and handed her a Kleenex. Lisa mumbled her thanks.

Behind her, the doors to the theater bounced open, and Reginald appeared, his hands in his pockets, his head staring at the floor. *Repentant,* she thought. As usual.

The black-haired woman moved away and disappeared down the hall. Lisa wiped her nose with the tissue. Reginald slowed his stride and cautiously approached. "Lisa, dear—" he started.

"Don't try it," she said. "I don't want to hear your half-baked apologies. I've heard them all—time and time again."

"Okay," he said. "But can we go back inside, watch the play, try to enjoy ourselves? I know I shouldn't have blamed you. But I didn't think of the tickets and I assumed you would. I . . . I should have taken care of it myself. I know that now. Come on, my dear. Let's go back. The curtain's going up. I don't want to do this alone."

Lisa blew into the tissue and nodded her head. She didn't really want to go home alone and leave him this way. "You go back to the seats, Reginald, I need to wash my face. I'm sure it's all splotchy. Give me a few minutes, then I'll join you. But we've got to do something about our relationship. It can't go on like this."

Hanging his head, he nodded. "Okay, Lisa. You're right. We'll go to a counselor. I promise we will."

She waved the tissue at him, and he pivoted and marched away. Lisa raised her eyes and moved toward the stairs leading down to the women's room. She'd walked those stairs scores of times in the last sixteen years. Two tiers of fourteen each, down into the basement of Rossario's Theater.

The marble steps were worn down in the middle where shoes had chipped away at them. A row of antique golden sconces cast a yellowish tinge across her mink stole. The light grew dimmer as she descended. She noticed that several of the sconces were burned out. She needed to report that before she left tonight.

No one else was on the steps or in the hallway at the bottom where they ended. Everyone was in the theater.

Feeling suddenly shivery, Lisa wrapped her stole tighter around her shoulders. It shouldn't be so drafty down here, should it?

Four steps from the bathroom, she saw the emergency exit door. It was half open. *That explains the draft,* she thought.

She moved to the door to close it. She heard footsteps behind her. Reginald?

She turned back, but it wasn't him. She spotted the black-haired woman from upstairs—the woman who gave her the tissue.

"You okay, dear?" asked the woman. Her voice sounded breathy, thin.

Lisa squinted her eyes, trying to see better in the dark hallway. The woman's heels clicked on the tile as she drew closer. Lisa nodded. "Yes, just wanted to close this door."

"No need for that, dear," said the woman, standing by her now, reaching into her purse.

"But it's—"

"It's time to go, dear." The woman lifted a curved knife out of her purse and pushed it toward Lisa's neck. "It's definitely time to go."

Lisa reacted instantly, dropping her purse to the floor and jerking her hands up toward her attacker. Her right hand grabbed the wrist holding the knife and twisted it away from her throat. The black-haired woman let go of the knife, and it clattered to the floor.

Lisa lunged for it, throwing her body onto the tile. The sharp toe of her attacker's foot popped into the side of her head and knocked her against the wall, preventing her from reaching the knife. Before she could move again, a second kick knocked Lisa unconscious.

Thirty minutes after the black-haired woman dragged Lisa out the emergency exit door, Reginald Voss left his seat and angrily descended the dark stairs leading to the rest rooms. Outside the women's room, he banged on the door and called out for his wife. She didn't answer. He banged on the door again. No response came from the other side.

Momentarily confused, he twisted around in the hallway, wondering where she had gone. He spotted a wadded up ball of Kleenex on the floor to the left of the women's room. Bending over, he picked up the Kleenex and sniffed. Lisa's perfume.

He slowly shook his head. She had walked out on him and left him high and dry to make the explanations.

Totally disgusted, he swore under his breath and headed back upstairs. He wondered how many days she would stay gone this time. Two, three, maybe four. That was her record. Four days away from him before she came back.

Oh well, it was still ten days until Christmas. Just so she came back in time to get things ready for the girls to arrive.

Shoving his hands into his pockets, Voss headed back upstairs. He might as well watch the rest of the play.

Chapter 46 🕯

Walter Delaney, a squatty man with a brown mustache as thick as a Brillo pad, proved himself an excellent host when Jackie knocked on his door at 8:13 on Saturday morning. After spending most of the day Friday in the interrogation room with Lewis, she welcomed the chance to get back on the street. This was her first shot at Walter Delaney. He'd been out of town Friday, and the authorities hadn't found him until that evening. Jackie hoped he could shed some light on his brother's behavior and background.

Delaney stepped back to let her enter. Inside the house, a small, red-bricked rancher, he offered her a cup of coffee. Jackie declined. Maybe a bit later, she said. Delaney nodded nervously and led her into a den the size of a boxing ring. A ring of yellow bookshelves that looked like they'd been purchased off the back of a truck ran around three walls of the room, and two worn sofas sat opposite each other on the floor.

"I'm here to talk with you about your brother," said Jackie. "We've spent most of the last thirty-six hours with him. He's in a lot of trouble if what he says is true."

Delaney nodded. "You want a seat?"

She accepted his offer, sitting lightly on the sofa nearest the door. Delaney took a seat on the other divan. "Tell me about Lewis," Jackie said, smoothing down her khaki pants.

He shrugged. "Not much to tell. We live here together. He never married. I did, but she died. Cancer, three years ago. Anyway, Lewis lived in the garage apartment behind the house until my wife died. After that he moved in with me. He's quiet for the most part. Don't cause anyone any trouble."

"He works with you, he told us?"

"Yeah, I own a grocery store. It's not easy, I got to tell you. Independents have it tough."

"I'm sure. Lewis a good worker?"

"Yeah, on time. Does what I tell him."

"You know he does cocaine?"

Walter dropped his eyes. His hands were thick, like round cushions with five stubby fingers. He cracked the knuckles of his left hand. "Not for me to know," he said. "He's a grown man. I can't be responsible for everything he does. If he works and causes me no trouble, then what's the harm?"

Jackie tilted her head. "He ever get violent?"

Walter hesitated for a moment, stared down at his hands again. "Well, he does have that arrest for rape."

"But he wasn't convicted."

"Nope, no conviction. No positive identification, no conviction."

Jackie paused, giving Walter time to settle a bit more. He cracked the knuckles on his right hand. Jackie said, "He was driving your vehicle when he turned himself in to us."

Walter rubbed his hands together. "So he borrowed it. I let him. Nothing wrong with that. He doesn't own a car. I drive a company truck most of the time."

"It's a new van."

"Almost new, just bought it in September. Triple B's brought in a whole fleet of demonstrator models. It was a bargain."

Jackie's ears perked up. "You bought it from Triple B Benton?"

Walter paused and glanced both ways as if searching for a trap. "Yeah, I did."

"Lewis with you when you bought it?"

"Let me think a second." He fingered his mustache, twirling it with his stubby fingers. "Come to think of it, I think he was. That a problem?"

Jackie wanted to shake the man. "I don't know, Mr. Delaney. But Mrs. Benton, Triple B's wife, is one of the murdered women."

"That don't mean a thing. Thousands of people go through Triple B's every year."

"That's true. It doesn't by itself mean a thing. But your brother has confessed to Mrs. Benton's murder. And we know he attended lots of Braves games—hounded the players for autographs. Hung around outside the dressing room after the games. That ties him, at least superficially, to the first woman killed."

"But none of that proves a thing."

Jackie decided not to press the issue. No reason to argue with Delaney. He wasn't the one a prosecutor would have to convince. "Can I see his room?" she asked, changing the subject.

Delaney didn't hesitate. "Sure, no problem. Follow me." He jumped up and led her through the house, to the last door on the left of the hallway. Pushing open the door, Delaney stepped back so she could enter.

She eased into the bedroom. It was sparsely decorated. A double bed sat centered in the wall opposite from her. One chair, a metal rocker, sat under the one window to the left of the bed. Light brown curtains decorated the single window. A television perched on top of a dresser. No pictures adorned the walls.

"Can I look around?" she asked.

"Knock yourself out. I'll be in the den if you need me." Delaney turned and shuffled off.

Jackie moved further inside the bedroom. She bent to her knees and peered under the bed, but saw nothing—no shoes, no books, nothing but a little dust and a few cobwebs. She checked the dresser next. Men's clothes—shirts in the top drawer, pants in the middle, underwear and socks in the bottom.

Leaving the dresser, she walked to the closet and opened the door. Inside, the clothes, though few, were neatly hung. One navy blazer. One pair of gray slacks. Four shirts of various colors. Three pairs of shoes sitting in a row on the floor. A small, metallic gray toolbox in the back left corner.

Jackie bent down to inspect the box. It wasn't locked. She lifted the lid. Her eyes widened. Newspaper clippings lay stacked in the bottom of the box.

She lifted out the top clipping and stared at the picture on it. A picture of Angelica Drexler. Quickly dropping the clipping to the floor, she thumbed through the stack. All the stories from the *Independent* about the murders were there. Plus other stories, stories from other newspapers.

Jackie dug deeper. Beneath the most recent clippings, she found others. Headline after headline describing a litany of violent murders in Atlanta. The stories stretched back over three years, detailed every murder she could remember. The stories were cataloged in chronological order in a metal box in the closet of a man who had confessed to the three most recent killings.

Chapter 47 🕯

Abank of heavy clouds moved out about 11:00 A.M., and by the time church ended, a bright warm sun washed down on the streets of Atlanta. Leaving Commerce Street Methodist, Burke, Debbi, and Hal Staton drove immediately to a cafeteria four blocks down the street. Within minutes after going through the buffet line, they had taken a seat in a back booth.

"Glad you could meet us for church, Hal," said Burke, taking a long drink of tea.

"No problem. Like I said when I called yesterday, I need to spend some time in Atlanta in the next few weeks, clear up a few things with my agent, try to move back into the world a little."

"I assume you'll go to Cordele for Christmas?"

"Yeah, my mom and dad are there. I'll need them." Hal drank from his water and fell silent.

Noting Hal's reticence, Burke nodded and settled in to eat. For several minutes everyone made small talk as they zeroed in on the food. After a while though, the small talk played itself out, and the table fell quiet except for the tinkle of forks on plates. Burke breathed slowly and wondered if Hal wanted to deal with anything more personal over their meal. If not, he didn't want to push.

Halfway through the meal, Hal suddenly dropped his napkin into his lap and leaned forward at the table. "Tell me about the other men, Burke," he said.

Burke glanced at Debbi for a second. "What men, Hal?"

"You know, Benton and Drexler. Have you met them? How are they handling this?"

"I've not met them," said Burke. "Debbi?"

"Nope," she said. "Neither has been available. I went to both funerals, like I did Leslie's. But neither man said anything."

"I wish I could talk to them," said Hal.

"Have you tried to call?" asked Debbi.

"No, I didn't want to intrude."

"Getting together with them makes a lot of sense," said Burke. "From an emotional point of view, it could help all of you, give you a chance to vent some feelings that no one else but you guys could understand."

"You think I ought to call them?" asked Hal.

Burke buttered a roll and took a bite. "That's a good thought," he said. "I don't know if they'll be ready to talk with you yet, but if they are, it could be beneficial."

"I'd want you with me," said Hal.

Burke arched his eyebrows, his question painted plainly on his face.

"I don't know if I could face them alone," explained Hal.

Burke swallowed. "I would be pleased to go with you," he said. "If the other men will allow it."

"Then I'll call them."

"Good, let me know when you set it up, and I'll clear my calendar."

For several minutes, they turned back to the food. Burke noticed that Hal only nibbled—a few bites of chicken, a touch of salad, a spoonful of potatoes. Then, as if completing an unpleasant chore, he dropped his fork, took a deep breath, and stared at Burke.

"What are the cops doing with Delaney?"

Burke laid down his fork also. "Oh, I'm sure you can imagine the routine. They're interrogating him, visiting his neighbors, trying to determine if his story is legitimate."

"What've you heard since yesterday?" Staton asked.

Burke turned to Debbi. She swallowed a bite of green beans, and wiped her mouth. "Well, not a lot, other than what the media has said. Derrick Role says Delaney looks more believable than first thought. Apparently he had some connection with all three of the women. You probably saw that in the paper."

Hal shook his head. "No, I left early this morning. Haven't read a paper yet. What's it say?"

"Just what I've told you. Delaney followed most of the sports teams here in town, including the Braves. A kind of groupie, they say. He drove a van bought at Triple B's. He kept a file on most of the murders committed here in Atlanta in the last three years. Apparently they fascinated him."

"Sounds like he's a bit crazy," said Hal.

"Certainly that," agreed Burke.

"But whether he's the killer or not, nobody knows yet," said Debbi.

"The cops have enough to charge him?" asked Hal.

"From what I hear, they do. At least Derrick Role thinks they do." Debbi paused, and Hal took a tiny bite out of his chicken.

"I want to see the guy," said Hal.

Burke tossed a glance at Debbi. "You mean, like go visit him in jail?"

Hal chewed a piece of bread for a moment. "Yeah, go see him in jail."

Burke thought a second. "I don't know if they'll let you do that."

"But I'm a celebrity," said Hal.

"That's true. So are the other men whose wives have been murdered. They might let all of you see him."

"Fine by me," said Staton. "I think they ought to let all of us in, let us tell the scuzbag what we think of him, what we would do with him if it were left up to us, if we could—" Hal suddenly stopped. His wide face turned red and he began to breathe heavily.

Burke reached over the table and patted him on the shoulder. "Easy, my friend. Easy. If Delaney's the guy, Jackie Broadus will find out. She's a good detective. If Delaney's the guy, she'll find out, and he'll pay the price for what he's done to you."

Hal gritted his teeth and his square jaw flexed. "There's no price high enough," he growled.

Burke stared at Debbi in silence. For several moments, Staton sat still, transfixed by his anger, his face red and his eyes dilated. For a moment, Burke thought he might actually snap a tooth so visible was his fury.

A waiter came and refilled their water glasses. A couple at a table beside them stood and walked out. Gradually, the crimson in Hal's face receded. Burke decided it was safe to speak again.

"I can't imagine what you're feeling," he said, giving Hal the opportunity to fill in the blank.

"I just want to know why, Burke, why these terrible things happen."

Burke swallowed hard. "Seems like that's a question everyone's asking these days."

"Whatcha mean?"

"Well, Detective Broadus asked me that a few days ago."

"What'd you tell her?"

Burke wiped his mouth with his napkin. "I told her this. I told her I think God could have set the world up in one of two ways. First, God could have laid it out with everything predetermined, with no choice for any of us, anywhere in life. With each action set up from the beginning—your birthday, your family environment, who you marry, whether you'll believe in God or not, the day you'll die—the whole routine, as determined as a road map with only one highway on it. Lots of people see it this way."

"But you don't?"

"No, I'm a bit freer than that. If God set up every one of our choices from the beginning, then we're nothing more than puppets. If we love God, we do so because we're preconditioned to it. If we reject God, turn against God, then the same thing. Either way, we're not responsible. Whether saint or scumbag, God's the one who made us that way.

"I can't quite accept that view, though I see the strength in it. It protects the sovereignty of God, makes sure that God's in control. But I think God can be in control and still allow some freedom."

"So how do you think God did it?"

"I think God did it this way. God set up the universe with millions of options running through it. People like us come to decisions, forks in the road, times and places where we make up our own minds. We can choose to sin—break the plan of God—or we can choose to do right—follow what God wants."

Hal raised his hand.

"But what sin did Leslie do, Burke? What did she do that caused her to die?"

Burke paused to give himself a moment to consider the question. He knew that moments like this were crucial if Hal was to rediscover his faith. The way he responded could make all the difference in the world in what would happen to Hal Staton in the future—could make the difference in whether or not Hal tried to hurt himself again. Burke privately prayed that he would speak the right words.

"Leslie didn't do anything wrong, Hal," he said, his voice gentle and soothing. "She didn't do any bad thing to cause her to die. But other people's choices affect our lives too. We don't live in a vacuum. People around us act and their actions set off chain reactions and those reactions create other ripples and it all flows through the freedom of the universe."

"So whoever killed Leslie did the sinful thing?"

"Exactly. Given their freedom to choose, they chose evil, they chose sin, they chose murder."

Hal shook his head and gritted his teeth again. "It seems so chaotic, so—I don't know—so senseless," he mumbled.

"It is senseless, chaotic. But how else could it happen? Freedom brings chaos when people choose evil. But when they choose good, when they choose God, then freedom brings genuine love, genuine worship. That's when the chaos ends, when the senselessness stops.

That's when we find ourselves the way God created us—kind and caring, living in a right way with God and everyone else."

Hal picked up his fork and twiddled with it for a moment. "You know I was a believer once," he said.

Burke nodded. "Yes, you told me at your house."

"But I fell away from it."

"You fell away from your belief?"

Hal paused. "Well, certainly from any practice of it. But now, well now, I feel like I'm at a crossroad, as if God is somehow using all this to give me another chance."

"God didn't cause Leslie's death, Hal," cautioned Burke. "Any more than a father would deliberately kill a daughter he loved."

"I'm not saying God caused her death," agreed Hal. "But I do think God is using her death. Or at least I'm using it, using it to rethink what faith is, what I believed in my youth, whether that was real or not. I feel . . . I don't know . . . I feel that this whole awful situation will either make me turn bitter and totally reject the possibility of God, or I'll, I don't know, I'll reclaim something I lost somewhere along the way. Can you understand what I'm trying to say?"

Burke nodded. "Yes, it makes perfect sense. You'll turn bitter or you'll turn back. I don't know that I've ever heard anyone express it better."

Chapter 48

At three o'clock on Sunday afternoon Reginald Voss tossed his newspaper to the floor, leaned over the side of his leather easy chair, and picked up the phone to call Lisa's mother. He hated to do it. Her mother would probably know where she was but would refuse to tell him until he begged. That's the way Lisa's family operated. Thick as thieves. Stuck together like bubble gum to a shoe.

Reginald smiled at his simile. He did have a gift for words. For a second, he hesitated. Why bother with a call? If she wanted to stay gone, let her. No skin off his nose. They were probably going to end up in divorce court anyway.

His face flushed as he thought of all the grief she caused him. Like Friday night—embarrassing him that way—in front of so many people. Crying so everyone could see it, so everyone would think him a jerk for upsetting his wife so. The gall she had.

Reginald yanked up the newspaper again and angrily folded it to the sports page. Lisa's disappearance on Friday night hadn't particularly surprised him. On more than one occasion in the past three years she had disappeared for a night or two. Once she had stayed gone four days, had taken a flight to Miami, spent four days lying on the beach with her older sister. Even that time, though, she had called her mom and given her a number where she could be reached. Said she did it for the girls, not for him. Well, that was probably true.

Reginald laid the paper on his lap. What if one of the girls did call home and want to talk to her mom? It wouldn't do for him to say he didn't know where she was and hadn't tried to find out. Besides, he did want to know. Maybe she would talk to him. Give him a chance to explain. He hated it when she left him all alone like this.

Sighing, he reached for the phone, dialed, listened to it ring, heard someone pick up. "Mrs. Corder, this is Reginald," he said, using her last name as he always did.

"Yes, Reggie, how are you?"

"Um, I'm fine, Mrs. Corder, but I, well, I'm looking for Lisa. Is she there?"

Mrs. Corder grunted. "You don't know where your wife is?"

Reginald rolled his eyes. Man, he despised this. A divorce would do wonders for his disposition. "Right now I don't. Thought she might have come by to see you."

"Well, what if she did? Do you think I would tell you?"

"I think you should, Mrs. Corder. After all, I am her husband."

"But what if she doesn't want to talk to you? What if she doesn't want you to know where she is?"

"Well, if that's the case, I don't know that I can do anything about it. Except say that I do want to talk to her, to see if we can get all this straightened out. Look, I know we've had our problems, but you must believe that I love her. I really do, and I need her too. I don't know what I would do without her."

Reginald paused and waited for an answer. What he said was true. He did love Lisa. If she would only give him the attention he needed, their problems would end.

"Are you going to tell me where she is or not?" he asked, calming himself with his good feelings about his wife.

"When did you see Lisa last?" asked Mrs. Corder.

Reginald hesitated, not wanting to admit she had left him on Friday, and he hadn't called until now. He decided to fudge the day. "Oh, last night, but you know how Lisa is. We had a bit of a tiff, and she left. It's not the first time she's done this—as you well know. But she gets over it. Is she there? Has she called you?"

He heard Mrs. Corder sigh. "No, Reggie, not yet. She hasn't called me. And she's not here. Have you tried her sisters?"

"No, not yet, but I will as soon as I hang up. I'm sure she's with one of them."

"Probably so."

For an instant, he paused, wondering if she was telling him the truth. It wouldn't be beyond her to lie to protect Lisa. Lisa might be standing beside her this very moment, whispering directions to her, telling her what to say. Well, so what? If that's the way she wanted to operate, then so be it. He could live without her.

"Well, if she calls or comes by, will you let me know?" he asked.

"I'll call you if I hear from her."

Knowing that was the best he could get from her and not wanting to beg anymore, Reginald hung up and leaned back in his chair. The sun from outside bathed over his face and upper body. He stared outside the window. A few scattered leaves, brown and crinkled, left over from the fall, blew up against the side of the house. He thought of calling Lisa's sisters. What a chore that would be. They were worse than her mother—if that were possible.

The sun warmed his face. He suddenly felt sleepy. No, he wouldn't call her sisters. Not yet. No reason to ruin a perfectly good Sunday afternoon.

Chapter 49

Lisa Voss opened her heavy eyes and tried to peer through the inky darkness, but she could see absolutely nothing. It was as if someone had jerked every sliver of light out of the air and wrapped it up in a jet black bag. Blinking rapidly, she struggled to focus. She wondered where she was and how long she had been unconscious, but she had no sense of either time or place. She tried to stand up but discovered she couldn't. She was lying flat on a floor—a concrete floor she decided, feeling its cool chill beneath her back. Her hands were tied together, and her feet were attached to something she couldn't see.

For several minutes she lay in the dark pondering a course of action. She licked her lips. They were dry. Her stomach growled. She couldn't recall the last time she had eaten.

She thought of screaming, then decided not. She doubted if anyone could hear her, and it might alert her abductor to the fact that she was awake. She didn't want that. The kicks in the head at the theater had demonstrated a willingness to dispense punishment that Lisa didn't want to test again.

Remembering the blows, Lisa noticed her headache for the first time. It thumped inside her skull like a suction pump, pulling her eyes in closer and closer to each other, squeezing them in to the bridge of her nose. She wondered how badly she was hurt but had no way to tell in the dark.

Forcing herself away from thoughts about her injuries, she concentrated on her predicament. What did this woman want with her? Money? Probably so. Reginald's celebrity status made people think he had more than he actually possessed.

For a second, Lisa wondered if Reginald would pay ransom for her. He might count his blessings that someone else had done him the favor of getting rid of her. This way was much cheaper than a divorce.

Another possibility crossed her mind. Could Reginald have done this himself? Quickly, she dismissed the idea. He hated her sometimes, she knew that. But goodness, she had birthed his three daughters, and she had no doubt that he loved them. And, she admitted to herself, he loved her, too, even in his strange and selfish way. No, he couldn't have done this.

Then who? And why? And how soon would the woman release her and allow her to go home?

Lisa turned onto her side to relieve the numbness in her back. She heard a light footstep from somewhere above. The footstep multiplied into movement, the light taps coming from her left and over her head. A door creaked. A splash of light flooded the room, and Lisa stared quickly into it, hoping to get a look at her abductor. Unfortunately, the glare of the light blinded her, and the door shut before she could see anything.

Though wanting to scream, she stayed quiet, the sound of her heartbeat the only noise in the basement. Lisa felt sure her captor could hear the pounding, pounding of her pulse. It throbbed in her head, a drumbeat of fear. Her eyes blinked, and she almost passed out.

"Are you awake, my pet?"

The question moved out of the blackness, and Lisa recognized the unusual voice of the woman at the theater. The voice yanked her back to alertness. If she had any chance to survive, she had to stay awake, had to face this woman and find out what she wanted.

Willing herself to stay calm, Lisa tried to see the woman's face but couldn't. She decided to close her eyes and concentrate on what she heard. The woman's voice was so different, she couldn't put her finger on it, but it didn't sound normal to her.

"Yes, I'm awake," she said, her voice a touch shaky but still firmer than she expected.

"Excellent, only those who are awake can hear."

Lisa stayed silent. The darkness closed in on her, a blanket smothering her face, shutting out her air, leaving her gasping for breath. Her hands felt cold, as if the blood in her fingers were drawing up into her arms and away from her fingers.

"You sound nervous, my pet. Are you, are you nervous?"

Lisa nodded, then realized her captor couldn't see her. "Yes, I'm nervous. Wouldn't you be?"

Laughter ricocheted off the sides of the walls. "With good reason, you're nervous," cackled her abductor. "Have you figured it out yet?"

"I don't know what you mean."

"Open your eyes, my pet. Open your eyes to see."

Lisa said nothing. She felt a slight stir in the air in front of her face and then the whisper of a finger touching her chin. The finger was cold, like a chilled knife.

"You're to be the fourth," said the breathy voice.

Lisa bit the side of her jaw. "The fourth what?"

"Open your eyes, my pet. Open your eyes to see." The touch dropped away from her face.

The voice, she thought, *the voice doesn't sound right.* It didn't sound—well, she couldn't be sure if it was a woman's or a man's voice. Who was this who had kidnapped her? If this wasn't the woman from the theater, then where was she? And who was this man? If it was a man. Was it a man or a woman?

Her head throbbed, and she tried to swallow but couldn't. She felt herself losing control, about to black out again, about to give up.

She fought out of her panic. "Do you want money?" she yelled, her voice rising with fear. "My husband has money. Name what you want, and I'll get it for you."

She smelled warm breath—coffee, with perhaps a bit of cinnamon clinging to it. She sensed movement again. A hand rose to her face again. The hand caressed her right cheek. Though cold, the hand felt soft, like a woman's hand.

The voice laughed. "I have no need for money. I have money enough for fifty lifetimes."

The hand stroked Lisa's cheek. The voice dropped to a whisper. "The last of the foster parents. The good after all the ugly. Too bad they died, their plane falling from the sky. I received it all—almost three million. Isn't that ironic? The good ones died. The ugly ones lived. That's far too often the story. The good ones die. The ugly ones live." The voice faltered, and quiet fell over the blackness again.

The hand dropped off Lisa's face, and the voice cleared. When it spoke again, the words were firmer, more resolute. "But I'm changing the formula of it all. I'm mending the brokenhearted, rearranging the chaotic, shaping the formless, bringing triumph to the defeated. You're the fourth."

"The fourth what?" asked Lisa, still unaware of her captor's plans.

Laughter cracked through the dark room. "My pet, my pet, don't you listen to the news?"

Like a sledgehammer striking an anvil, Lisa suddenly understood. Three women killed in the last three weeks. Now she was to be the fourth. She gagged on her own spittle as the realization hit her, and she knew, in that instant, that no amount of begging would change the mind of the faceless beast who stood in front of her and breathed sweet cinnamon breath into her face.

Chapter 50

The rain started in the morning as a warm front from the Gulf of Mexico pushed up into Georgia. With no umbrella in the car, Burke ran through the downpour, splashing water as high as his knees as he jerked open the door of the clinic. Molly handed him a cup of hot cider and ushered him into his office. A patient was already waiting, she told him.

All morning the rain fell and the temperature outside climbed higher and higher. Burke saw four clients in the morning, ate a quick lunch, then listened to three more people as they poured out their problems in the afternoon.

The soggy hours passed slowly, clinging to the day like a glob of mud on the bottom of a boot. Though he concentrated on each patient, Burke kept wondering if another body had turned up anywhere, if some nameless killer had snuffed out another woman's life over the weekend.

He dared to think otherwise. With Delaney's confession, the killing might have ended and his theory been proven to be no more than the delusion of an overly imaginative religious psychologist. He hoped that was true, that he was wrong, that the deaths would now cease.

He tried to call Debbi at 12:30 as usual but didn't reach her. He tried again twice more in the afternoon but had the same result. She'd promised to call him if anything turned up. Not hearing from her eased his mind a bit, but the nagging question stayed with him anyway. Would another body show up?

At three o'clock he found himself between patients for fifteen minutes. He called Hal Staton. On the fourth ring, Hal answered.

"Yeah, Hal, this is Burke. Any luck getting Benton and Drexler?"

"I'm hitting .500," said Hal. "I reached Karl Drexler but not Bobby Benton."

"Will Drexler meet with us?"

"He said he would, but he didn't know if he could make it tonight or not. We still on for dinner?"

"Yeah, Debbi's going to meet us at The Salad Bar about ten minutes from here. You know the place?"

"Yeah, I've been there a couple of times."

"So I'll meet you there."

"If we don't drown first."

Burke hung up, grabbed a drink of water, and rushed back to his office. Two more patients to see.

At 5:30 he sent Molly home, locked the door, and headed to The Salad Bar. Popping through the door, he shook the water off his head and spotted Debbi at a table near the entrance. Jackie Broadus sat beside her. Burke took a seat across from them.

"Jackie called me about an hour ago," said Debbi. "I told her we were meeting with Hal Staton. She asked if she could tag along. I figured we owed her one."

Burke raised his eyebrows. "You're not mad at us anymore?" he asked.

Jackie shrugged. "Let's just say that circumstances have toned down my anger for the moment. I've got a confessed killer in custody, and no body turned up today. Derrick Role is pleased and seems disposed to forget the leak, wherever it came from. If he's okay, then I'm okay."

"Then I'm glad you could come," Burke said.

She smiled. "I'm glad you would allow me. Where's Staton?"

"He should be on the way. Karl Drexler may come with him."

"Drexler?"

"Yeah, Hal thought it might be good for the men involved in this to meet, to talk through this thing together. Figured it might help them to spend some time with someone who knows exactly what the other is feeling."

Jackie took a sip of water. "Makes sense to me. You think they'll talk much with me around?"

Burke shrugged. "Don't know. We'll need to assure them you're not still investigating. If they think you are, it might crimp the conversation. Otherwise, they'll probably be okay. It's their first meeting, so I don't expect they'll open up too much anyway. If they ever do, it'll probably come later, when they've developed some trust in each other. We'll just need to wait and—"

A waiter appeared at his elbow and interrupted him. They gave their orders. Chef salads all around. The waiter moved away. The door to the restaurant opened. Hal Staton, umbrella in hand, walked through it. A regal black man a good three inches taller than him followed Staton.

"Must be Drexler," said Debbi.

"It is," said Jackie. "I interviewed him a few days ago."

The two men saw them and eased to their table. The three at the table stood up. Jackie introduced Burke and Debbi to Drexler. Everyone shook hands, then Burke waved them to their seats. "Sit down, sit down, we've already ordered. Weren't sure when you'd get here."

"No problem," said Hal. "I'm sure the waiter will get to us soon enough."

Within seconds, everyone had settled around the table. Drexler wiped a ridge of water off his forehead. "A gully washer out there," he said, his voice deep and melodious. "Water up to my shin bones."

"Warm too," said Burke.

"Hard to believe it's almost Christmas," said Hal.

For a moment, no one said anything else. Drexler coughed. Hal leaned back in his seat. Burke, wanting everyone to find their own space, let the silence linger. He studied Drexler as he waited.

He didn't know much about the man. He was tall—over six two. Fairly thin. Hair slightly graying. He carried himself with a posture of distinction. Everyone who heard him called him a preacher with charisma. Burke had heard bits and pieces of a few sermons over the last two years, and he agreed with the assessment. His voice carried a tone like a bass drum, and he spoke in terms that Burke could only describe as an educated earthiness.

Watching him now, seeing the grim wrinkles etched around his mouth, Burke wondered how Drexler's faith was dealing with the murder of his wife.

The waiter broke the quiet. "So, you've added a couple," he said, appearing from behind a row of potted plants. "Do you need a menu?"

Drexler and Staton shook their heads. "I'll take whatever they ordered," said Hal.

"Me too," said Drexler. "My stomach doesn't beg much for food these days." The waiter stepped back and moved away.

"Glad we could all get together," said Burke, deciding the time had come to move the conversation along. "Though I admit this meeting wasn't my idea. It was Hal's. He hoped to have Mr. Benton here, too, but he wasn't available. But we do have Jackie Broadus. I know you two men have met her."

The two nodded. Burke continued. "Let me assure you she's not here as a cop. She's here because she's a friend of mine and Debbi's. We trust her and hope you will, too, before the night is over."

Hal held up his hand. "It's okay, Burke; I'm glad she's here. She can tell us what's going on." He turned to Jackie. "Anything new today?"

She shook her head. "Nothing that you don't know."

"No body?" Hal asked the question hesitantly, though it was the question on everyone's mind.

"None," said Jackie. "Everything's quiet."

"Perhaps Delaney is the killer," said Drexler.

"We can hope so," said Burke.

"But it's not over for us," said Hal. "Not until they convict him, not until they convict him and punish him for what he did."

Burke stared at Hal. His jaw twitched as he ground his teeth.

"It still won't end for us, my friend," said Drexler. "So long as the light of our memory shines, it won't ever end."

Their waiter interrupted them, placing their salads on the table and refilling their water glasses. Finished, he stepped away.

Burke took a bite of his salad, and the others followed his example. For several minutes, they ate quietly, the tinkling of their forks on the plates the only sound. Burke tried to put himself in Hal's and Drexler's place, to imagine their hurt, to feel their pain. He caught Debbi's eye and sighed. How awful it must be. To lose the one you loved so much.

He laid his fork down. "How long were you married to Angelica, Reverend Drexler?"

Drexler smiled. "Seventeen years, next June. And call me Karl. She was eighteen when we married, an unplucked flower right out of high school. I met her the day I went to proclaim my first message at my first church. She sang a solo that day, had a voice as clear as a morning robin. I sat up straight when she sang that day, let me assure you I did. It didn't take me long to strike up her acquaintance. Six months later I married that honey-voiced girl. Married her right there in my own church. One of the sisters called it 'high chicanery in the name of the Lord.' I kind of had to agree with her. But it was the best thing I ever did. The Lord knows how I did love that woman."

He stopped to take a drink of water. Hal picked up the conversation. "You had fourteen more years than Leslie and me. I married her after my first year in baseball, and during the baseball season, I hardly ever saw her. But that didn't matter. Didn't matter because we knew what we wanted. Then, just as we got it . . ." His voice trailed off for a moment, and his eyes dropped to the table. "I wish I'd had as much time with Leslie as you did with your Angelica," he said, looking up at Drexler.

Drexler held his hands together in front of his mouth. "I wish you did, too, son, but I got to tell you this. It doesn't matter if you had fourteen more years. Shoot, it don't matter if you had a thousand more years. If you loved her, even a thousand years would be too short."

Underneath the table, Burke reached out and grabbed Debbi's hand. Hal and Karl continued to talk, and he was glad. He heard the rain splashing hard against the ceiling. His mind wandered. From all appearances, the murders had ended. Thank God for that. He felt an incredible relief that he wouldn't need to get involved any further in the dark arena of evil that these killings represented.

Now he could go back to his quiet life with Debbi, a life free of dead eyes staring at him, a life where he would never again have to lift a gun and fire it at another human being.

Breathing deeply, Burke squeezed Debbi's hand. He didn't want another woman to die, didn't want another man to lose his wife.

Give me a thousand years with Debbi, he prayed. *Give me a thousand years.*

Chapter 51

At five minutes after four o'clock, Debbi stood at the back of the briefing room at Peachtree Precinct and pulled out her tape recorder. Up front, facing a bank of microphones under the glare of at least a dozen camera lights, stood Detective Derrick Role. To his left and one step behind him, Jackie Broadus watched. Debbi waved to Jackie, but she didn't return the greeting.

Role cleared his throat, and Debbi directed her attention back to him. He tugged for a second at his cuff links, glanced down at a piece of paper in his hand, and began to read.

"On November 28, the first of a series of three bodies was found on the capitol building steps here in Atlanta. On the next two Mondays, December 5 and December 12, two more bodies were discovered. Because of the disparate methods of murder in each case, we did not investigate them as related killings. Subsequent events proved us wrong at that point, and we apologize for our error."

Role paused briefly, as if to make sure that everyone heard his apology. Clearing his throat again, he pushed back his hair and continued. "On December 15, as we continued our investigation into these tragic deaths, a Mr. Lewis Delaney unexpectedly turned himself in and confessed to the slayings. He said that he abducted and murdered Leslie Staton, Rosey Benton, and Angelica Drexler. He made his confession voluntarily—without coercion—and he did so with a full knowledge of the consequences. When questioned about his motive, he said, 'I wanted to be somebody.'"

Role stopped and let the statement settle. Reporters scribbled frantically in their notebooks in spite of the fact that almost all of them carried tape recorders. Role fingered a cuff link, then continued. "When questioned about his reason for confessing, Delaney said, 'I figured three would be enough.'

"It goes without saying that we meticulously followed up on Mr. Delaney's claims. We found that he had been arrested four years ago for rape. We found that he had a fascination with well-publicized murders. We found that he knew the women, at least in a superficial way. We found that he had stalked at least one of them—Leslie Staton. Given our understanding of the disguises he apparently wore, he fits to a tee the description of those who were seen with Staton and Benton.

"As a result of this information and more I cannot disclose, the Atlanta Police Department, Peachtree Precinct, under the direct supervision of Lieutenant Jackie Broadus and myself, have concluded that Mr. Delaney did indeed have motive, opportunity, and acumen to carry out these terrible crimes.

"With his delusions of grandeur, he resented the success of the husbands of these women. In the effort to strike at them, he struck at their wives.

"Since his confession and imprisonment, no other women have disappeared. That, in itself, speaks volumes about the truthfulness of his statement.

"So given his confession and other evidence we have compiled, the district attorney agrees that we should proceed with this case to the grand jury. We feel certain they will find probable cause and hold Mr. Delaney over for trial."

Role stopped and stared out at the reporters. A look of serenity fell over his face. He lifted his chin as if to give the cameras a better angle to shoot his profile.

He smiled slightly, then continued to speak. "I am pleased today to have a joint statement from the mayor and the governor to read for you."

He reached into his suit pocket and pulled out a white envelope. As if unveiling the winner of an Oscar nomination, he flipped out a white sheet of paper. "The note reads: 'Congratulations to the Atlanta Police Department and to Detectives Derrick Role and Jackie Broadus for the successful apprehension of Mr. Lewis Delaney. We realize that the court must now do its work and that the suspect is innocent until guilt is proven. But, at the same time, we rejoice that this series of tragic murders has now ceased. We pray that the wonderful city of Atlanta and the great state of Georgia will never again suffer from this type of serial killing. Again, congratulations and God bless you all.' Signed, Governor Edward Robert Stapleton and Mayor Ron Johnson."

Role nodded as if conferring his approval upon their words. A hand shot up from the back of the room. Role acknowledged it.

"What about the descriptions of the men last seen with Staton and

Benton? Have you found wigs or sunglasses—anything to confirm the use of disguises?"

Role smiled and his white teeth picked up the camera lights. "As you can imagine, we are not at liberty to divulge information like that. All of it will be forthcoming at trial."

A pack of hands popped up. Role pointed to another reporter.

Watching the cool detective, Debbi couldn't help but imagine the immense relief he surely felt. Nothing like an unsolved series of homicides at Christmas time to throw a wrench in an ambitious cop's plans for advancement. But now a man had confessed to those homicides. Now, in spite of the grief the three widowed husbands would feel the rest of their lives, the rest of Atlanta could go back to the season's festivities.

Debbi sighed and her shoulders sagged. She wanted to feel the same kind of relief Role so obviously felt. But she couldn't. She couldn't because right after lunch a phone call had reached her at her desk. The voice on the other end sounded garbled, as if deliberately muffled. The words spoken took her breath away.

"A confession does not a killer make." That was all the caller said before the line clicked dead.

Now she didn't know what to think. Was the caller a kook? A crazy prankster? That's what her mind said, and that's what her heart wanted to believe.

She had tried twice without luck to call Jackie Broadus to tell her about the call. After the second call she gave up. The caller had to be a nut getting his jollies. Why would a murderer call her?

It had to be a cruel hoax. Some kid with a warped sense of humor.

Debbi decided not to call Jackie again. Even if the caller were the killer, she hadn't learned anything in the few short seconds she had him on the line. She had nothing to trace, no evidence to follow up. No, she would keep this to herself. No reason to tell anyone, even Burke. It would only worry him, make him even more protective than he already was.

Standing in the back of the press room at Peachtree Precinct listening to Derrick Role, Debbi tried to convince herself to forget the call. But she couldn't. Somehow, she sensed that Role was wrong, sensed that no one should feel any relief because it wasn't over. As sad as it was to think it, Debbi sensed that it definitely wasn't over.

Chapter 52 🕯

I'm dreaming of a white Christmas, just like the ones I used to know. Where the tree tops glisten and children listen, to hear sleigh bells in the snow. I'm dreaming . . ." The words of the song poured out of the speakers overhead and fell down on the milling crowd that shuffled and hustled and sprinted and surged through the walkways of the Cross Branch Mall. The smell of cedar trees drifted through the air, and a squatty Santa Claus sitting in the crossroads of all the shops hoisted a child onto his lap.

Holding Debbi's hand, Burke pulled her past Santa Claus, away from Amanti's Fashion Boutique and toward Racker's Computers. She dragged her feet the whole way, pretending to resist.

"You don't need to go back to Racker's," she argued. "I'm not getting you any computer equipment for Christmas. That's not romantic enough."

"But it's what I want," pouted Burke. "An upgrade of my 486 to a Pentium chip. It'll run faster."

"Yours runs fast enough," said Debbi. "Let's go back to Amanti's. There's a pair of shoes there I want you to get for me."

"Talk about unromantic. Nothing more lacking in romance than feet."

"I thought you liked my feet," said Debbi, faking hurt.

"I do like your feet," said Burke, patiently pulling her toward the computer store. "I like everything about you, right down to your stubby big toe. What I don't like is a pair of shoes that cost over a hundred bucks."

"But your jogging shoes cost that much."

"Yeah, but I wear them more often than once every four or five months."

In front of the computer store now, he stopped and faced her. "Don't you want to make me happy?" He stuck out his lower lip, like a four-year-old pleading to get his way.

"Don't *you* want to make me happy?" Debbi's pout matched his.

"So what do we do?" he asked. "It appears we're at an impasse."

Debbi's eyes suddenly lit up. "You go to Amanti's," she said. "I'll stay here at Racker's."

"Will that make you happy?"

"If it makes you happy."

"Isn't love wonderful?"

"It is if it means I get shoes for Christmas."

Laughing, Burke threw his arms around her neck, and her perfume drifted up from her neck and intoxicated him. For a second, he felt dizzy, dizzy with love and joy. "If shoes make you happy, then shoes it will be," he said, holding her tightly.

Snuggled into his shoulder, Debbi murmured, "Make sure they're the expensive ones."

"I'll meet you back here in fifteen minutes." He unwrapped himself from her and headed back to Amanti's. Walking through the crowd, he took a deep breath and glanced at his watch. December 21. Four more days until Christmas. What a wonderful time of year. A time to rest and reflect.

The clinic would shut down for the holidays at five tomorrow afternoon. People didn't schedule many counseling appointments during the holidays. Except for emergencies, he would have five days off.

He listened to the mall's Christmas music as he strolled along. "I saw Mama kissing Santa Claus, underneath the mistletoe last night . . ." He thought for an instant of Hal Staton and Karl Drexler and Bobby Benton. They wouldn't have anyone under the mistletoe with them this year. He shook his head, trying to shut them out of his mind, telling himself not to let their sorrow spoil his evening with Debbi. He calmed himself with the knowledge that he planned to see Hal again on December 24 at 11:00 A.M. right before he left for Cordele for Christmas. Drexler might join them.

Burke smiled to himself. Staton and Drexler had hit it off with each other. Had spent almost six hours together in Burke's office since Monday. They had talked and talked about their loneliness, their anger, their shock, their love for their deceased wives.

The two had discovered they had a lot in common. Drexler had played baseball in college for two years. A shortstop. But his light frame made him a good field, no-hit guy and, seeing he had no future in the sport, he gave it up.

Hal told Drexler about his Christian faith, about the summer he worked as a youth minister at Mt. Olivet. He described to him how his faith receded in importance as he became successful in baseball, how the success made faith seem less vital, less needed.

With Leslie gone, Hal told Drexler, he didn't know what he needed, didn't know if faith could help him or not. Didn't know if anything could.

Drexler understood. They could help each other, he told Hal. That's the way God worked most of the time. Through another person who would understand.

Lost in thought about the two men, Burke almost passed Amanti's. But the stunning black evening gown in the window reminded him of his purpose. Debbi wanted shoes. Okay, if that made her happy, he would buy her shoes. Grinning, he turned left into the store. A saleswoman greeted him. "I see you're back," she said, smiling as if she understood the situation.

"Yeah, I'm back. Apparently, my wife will get shoes for Christmas."

"The beige pair she tried on a few minutes ago?"

"Yes, the beige pair."

"I'll need to get them from the back," she said, twisting on her heels and heading to the rear of the store. Burke followed her. A few moments later she emerged with a box in her hands. "Size seven if I remember correctly," she said.

"You've got a good memory."

"You want these wrapped?"

"If you don't wrap them, nobody will."

"You hate wrapping, huh?"

"Doesn't every man?"

The woman smiled and punched the keys on her cash register. Burke leaned against the counter and reached for his wallet. He felt someone grab his hand. He turned to see who it was. He saw Debbi standing behind him. He opened his mouth to protest, to tell her she couldn't see the shoes he was about to buy her, but she raised a finger to her lips and pulled him gently but forcefully away from the sales clerk. He saw a pair of tears under her green eyes.

"What's wrong?" he said, instantly concerned.

She began to sob. He pulled her close. "It's okay," he whispered. "Whatever it is, it's okay."

She raised her chin to him. Her words tumbled out in a torrent of tears. "I just, just saw it on the news—on a television at the computer store. Another body has turned up."

Chapter 53

From across the room in the middle of the king-sized, four-poster bed, a set of slender fingers picked up the control for the television and punched up the volume. The face of Reginald Voss stared out of the screen and reflected in the black eyes that watched him from the center of the bed.

Voss's rich voice poured into the room. "At about 4:00 this afternoon, a Mrs. Barbara Jones, out for a walk with her dog, found a body lying in a shallow ditch near the lake in High Hills, an exclusive area in northeast Atlanta. Mrs. Jones, sixty-six, called police immediately. The police . . ."

A wide smile cracked across the thin face under the black eyes that watched Voss. How dumb Voss was! He didn't even know it was her. Didn't know he was reporting the death of his own wife! What sweet, sweet irony.

Stroking Snow, the figure on the bed breathed a sigh of relief. The pressure had been intense since Sunday night, the night of Lisa Voss's death. After the drop of the body in the dark hours of Monday morning, the rain had started and fouled up the plans. The rain had drenched the ground and kept people inside—kept them from walking down the path by Lake High Hills.

The rain kept people away from the lake, kept them from finding the body, and that was a problem, a torment. From Monday onward a fear arose—a fear that all the plans would tumble and fall under the weight of three days of winter rain that kept the body hidden.

That was the point of all this. They had to find the bodies. Otherwise, how would they know of the revenge? How would they see the completion of it all, the wonderful, brilliant scheme of it all, the finish of the becoming?

But on Monday no one found her. Tuesday came and went too. The fear mounted. Wednesday dawned. Lunch came, but no discovery.

What frustration! What terror! Just like before. When no one knew.

When no one knew of the sexual abuse. No one knew of the preacher's clammy hands. No one knew of the godly man's ungodly appetites.

No one but the godly man's ungodly wife. The wife who knew but did not act.

They had to know. The unmasking had to happen. The day of Advent had to come.

If they found her before Christmas Eve they would know. If not, the unknowing would destroy it all, ruin the unveiling, make the destiny impossible.

The slender fingers dropped the television control and scratched Snow behind the ears. The familiar feel of the cat was soothing. The cat purred her approval.

Good old Mrs. Jones had saved the day. She had walked her dog and passed by the lake and seen the body decomposing in the ditch.

The black eyes closed. Only two more days until Christmas Eve. Until the Holy Night. The night when the beginning would end. And the end would begin.

Chapter 54

Thursday, December 22

The waitress at Danny's Doughnut Shop nodded to Burke and Debbi as they entered the door. "I'll get your root beer," she said to Burke, a tiny grin on her face. He forced himself to smile at her recognition, but his heart wasn't in it. He and Debbi had slept little. They had spent the night running from the *Independent* to the police station and back to the paper.

Finally, at about 1:30, they drove home. But neither fell asleep. They tossed and turned, talked and tossed, wondered and worried.

Burke had rolled over and over, his mind spitting up the questions. Was this murder another in the same series? Or was it something totally different? Who was the woman? The cops hadn't said yet.

And what about the call Debbi had told him about, the frightening words, "A confession does not a killer make." He had started to chastise her for not telling him sooner but then decided against it. She felt distressed enough already. No use making it worse. Besides, her reasoning had been sound. With a confessed killer in custody, why should anyone take a crank call seriously?

Lying in bed, the light from the street outside washing across his dark hair, Burke had felt something shaking loose inside his soul. The call to Debbi was the earthquake doing the shaking.

Up to this point, he'd tried to stay clear of this situation. Even when he had told Jackie about his theory, he had held back his emotional involvement, not wanting to deal with the grim specter of death that her investigation created in his mind. Delaney's confession made it seem like it all had ended. But it hadn't. It had not only not ended, but the call to Debbi had made it personal.

Linking his hands behind his head, Burke stared over at Debbi. Her blonde hair lay like broom straw on her pillow. Her breathing was regular, and he watched her chest rise and fall under the covers.

Soaking in her beauty, Burke sensed a bomb ticking inside his heart. All his life he had tried to remain calm, tried to keep himself in emotional check. That's the way he was brought up—buttoned down and controlled.

Until he met Debbi, that approach seemed reasonable, and he had largely succeeded with it. But Debbi had burned away much of that reticence, had stripped away the heaviest layers of icy detachment that kept his inner feelings concealed. Debbi upped the wattage in his life in a way he had never felt before she came along. To his surprise, he liked the unleashing of feelings that she had fostered. He felt more alive now, more tuned in, more aware of himself and everything else around him.

Burke's hands balled into fists. The thought of some killer threatening Debbi made him furious. Up until that call, these murders had been someone else's problem. But the phone call meant the problem had walked into his backyard.

Burke rolled onto his side and took a huge breath. If need be, he would fight to the death to defend what was his. Whatever it took, he would do it.

Sometime after 3:00 A.M. with this as his last thought, Burke had fallen asleep.

Now, he was back at Danny's. Jackie had agreed to meet him and Debbi here. They had called her last night and agreed to this 8:30 rendezvous.

Walking past the cash register, Burke glanced around for Jackie. He saw her to his left in a corner booth. She waved them over. He nudged Debbi, and they eased through the aisle and took their seats.

"You look tired," said Debbi, dropping her purse onto the vinyl seat.

"Long night," said Jackie, sighing heavily.

"I imagine so. Did you rest at all?"

"About four hours. But it wasn't comfortable, I can tell you that."

The waitress brought Burke his root beer and took their orders. Jackie placed her hands on the table. Debbi laid her hands over the detective's.

"It's a nightmare," said Jackie. "An unbelievable nightmare."

Debbi whispered. "What happened?"

"Well, we know who it is now. And you won't believe it."

Burke moved into the conversation. "Another celebrity's wife?"

Jackie nodded. Burke waited. She would tell them when she was ready.

She dropped her eyes to the table top. "Lisa Voss," she said.

Debbi froze. Burke turned to her. "Who is she?" he asked.

"The wife of Reginald Voss," she answered.

"The television anchor?"

"None other."

"But I saw him on TV last night, reporting the discovery of the body. How—"

"He didn't know," said Jackie. "We didn't get an identification until after midnight."

"But when did she disappear?"

"Last Friday, according to Voss."

"And Voss didn't report it?"

"No, they had an argument at the theater. She left him there. He thought she had gone to a sister's. She's done it before. They've had problems. He didn't think it unusual, so he didn't file a report."

For several long seconds, they all fell silent. Burke sipped from his root beer. Debbi pushed her hair toward her mouth for a moment, then stopped and dropped it against her cheek. The waitress brought their food, but no one ate anything.

"Anybody see her with anyone after she left Voss at the theater?" asked Burke.

"Nope, no one except Voss himself. He said he saw her with a woman at the theater. Apparently Mrs. Voss was crying, and the woman gave her a tissue."

Debbi sipped from her water. "Do you know when she died?"

"Nope, too early to tell. Fact is, we may never know the precise time of her death. The rainy weather, warm temperatures, time between death and discovery. That makes it tough. A body begins to deteriorate pretty quickly. Determining the time of death is an inexact science."

"So you don't know if it was Sunday or not?"

"Nope, not yet and maybe never."

"What's Role saying?"

"He doesn't know what to do," said Jackie. "We've still got Delaney claiming the deaths of the other three women. And we don't know when Lisa Voss was killed."

"So it might be a different killer?" said Debbi.

"It's possible, but we don't know. Don't have any way of knowing. Could be a copycat."

"So Role's sticking with Delaney as the murderer of the others?

Jackie picked up a piece of toast and nibbled at its edges.

"Probably so, at least for now. He doesn't have any choice. As you know, he's pretty far out on the limb with Delaney."

"And the mayor and the governor are on the same limb."

"No doubt about it. Role can't jettison Delaney without losing more than face. He'll lose everything—reputation, political connections, upward mobility, all of it. Until we get something more than the fact that it's another celebrity's wife, it makes sense to stick with Delaney."

"What about Voss?" asked Burke.

"As a suspect?" asked Jackie.

"Yeah. It seems tough to believe he wouldn't report his wife's disappearance."

"We haven't had a chance to question him. When we told him at 2:00 A.M. this morning, he collapsed on us. We had to call a doctor. He's under sedation. When he comes out of it, we plan to question him carefully. But, it's not hard to believe he didn't report her disappearance. If a couple is having marital problems, anything is possible. Take my word for it, two people can do strange things when they're not happy with each other. Since Voss's wife had a history of doing this kind of thing, it's not unreasonable for him to let it go for several days."

"So he's not a suspect?"

Jackie swallowed her toast. "Not officially. But we're not ruling anything out."

Burke took a bite of eggs. Debbi drank some more water.

"I got a phone call," she said, placing her glass on the table.

Jackie furrowed her brow. Debbi continued. "The day of the news conference announcing Delaney's arrest. Someone called me. The voice was muffled." She paused and stared at Jackie.

"Go on," said Jackie.

"The caller said, 'A confession does not a killer make.'"

"A confession does not a killer make," repeated Jackie.

"Yeah, then the line went dead."

"Why didn't you tell me this earlier?"

Debbi shrugged and rubbed her palms together. "I don't know. Didn't seem important at the time. You had a confessed killer in custody. People make crank calls to the paper all the time. I figured that's what it was. Might still be for all we know."

Jackie nodded and leaned back. "You're right. It could be a prank. No way to tell."

"And no way to trace it," said Burke.

"So we're still where we were," said Jackie. "With Delaney in jail, Lisa Voss dead, and nothing to tell us who killed her."

"What about her wounds?" asked Debbi. "How'd she die?"

Burke's eyes widened. He should have thought of that! His theory! If Lisa Voss's wounds followed the pattern, that would prove the deaths of the women were connected. He kicked himself for being too tired to think clearly.

Jackie threw up her hands. "Don't know yet," she said. "I saw the body, much to my chagrin, but really can't tell you anything. Lying out in the rain in 75 degree weather causes all kinds of distortions. We can't tell what killed her until the autopsy is completed. The medical examiner is working on that this morning. As soon as he finishes, we'll know more."

"Can you get us that information?"

Jackie hesitated, took a sip of coffee. "I don't think so. Can't chance it. Fact is, I shouldn't be with you now. Role has made it plain—any leaks here and he'll have our tongues under a Ginsu knife. If something shows up in the press he doesn't like, he's going to blame me for sure."

Burke cleared his throat. "We need to know how she died."

Jackie nodded. "I realize that, but at this point I can't help you. If I find a way later, I'll see what I can do."

Silence fell over the table. Burke shook his head. "We can't wait until later. It's Thursday. The killer has taken these women on Friday or Saturday, killed them on Sunday."

"Then we've got to find him before then."

Burke turned and stared out the window. The rain pelted down on the pavement on the street. "To do that we need to know how Voss died. Where do we get that information?"

Jackie nibbled off her toast for several seconds. "The medical examiner," she said. "He does the autopsies."

"McVaine's the name, right? I remember it from the reports you gave us."

"Yeah, Stubs McVaine."

"We need to talk to him."

"He's not going to talk to you."

"All we can do is try."

"You're convinced it's not Delaney?"

"If it is, then what did he do with the weapons he used?"

"We asked him that. He said he tossed them. Took them to the Clink Road Landfill and buried them. We've got people checking it. But there's a lot of trash out there. Heaven only knows how long it'll take to go through it."

"That's more time we don't have. What about the disguises?"

"Delaney doesn't know anything about any disguise. But that's understandable. No one has definitely connected the people seen with these women to their actual abduction."

"But why haven't they come forward and identified themselves if they didn't have anything to do with it?"

"That's easy. They don't want to get involved. Getting questioned in a murder case is not exactly the best publicity."

"I think it's the same guy," said Burke, gritting his teeth. "Delaney just confuses it all. It's the same killer, and he's moving toward something, some grand finale. It's tied to the Advent Sundays, to the whole Christmas season, to God, to the birth of Jesus, to—I don't know—to some kind of religious hang-up, to some message this lunatic's trying to send, some message we're supposed to see, to figure out."

"Then why this break in the pattern with Voss?" asked Jackie. "Why didn't we find her on Monday?"

Burke shrugged. "I can't answer all the questions, Jackie. If I could, I'd have your job."

Jackie smiled but not enthusiastically. "At times like this, I wish someone else did have my job."

They all dropped their heads in silence. Outside, the rain pelted down, a million hammerings of water against the rooftop. It was less than seventy-two hours until the dawning of Christmas morning. But with another dead woman on their minds, no one at the table in the back booth at Danny's Doughnut Shop felt anything near to a sense of peace.

Chapter 55

At 1:35 on Friday afternoon, Jackie sat on the sofa in Derrick Role's office and watched as he and Reginald Voss sparred with each other. Given Voss's reaction to his wife's death, his demeanor with Role amazed her.

When Jackie had arrived at his house Thursday morning and told him that the body in the city morgue was his wife, Reginald Voss collapsed to the floor where he stood. Not knowing what else to do, Jackie and the two uniforms with her had dragged him to his bed and left him with his daughters who had come home for the holidays.

From the reports she'd heard since then, the daughters had tucked him in and left him alone. They had their own grief to handle.

For the next day and a half, Voss had stayed horizontal. His daughters tried to talk to him, to tell him they loved him, and that they would all get through this together, but he didn't respond.

Knowing his condition, Jackie had advised Role to hold off their interrogation. He agreed but told her to stick close to him. Jackie did, dropping by every four hours or so to see how he was doing.

Lisa's mother set up shop by the phone in the study to handle the details of the funeral. The daughters entertained the friends who dropped by to offer their condolences. They told the curious that Reginald was too distraught to receive visitors.

Jackie had checked on him again Friday morning. His silver gray hair was unwashed, and when he opened his eyes at the sound of her voice, she saw dull gray irises and streaks of red. The daughters told Jackie that their dad had only nibbled on the food they brought him.

His body seemed to have sagged overnight, and circles the size of teabags swelled up under his eyes. *For someone who argued so much with his wife, he sure took her death hard,* thought Jackie.

The family agreed and talked about it as they sat around the television. His daughters wondered aloud to Jackie if he would snap out of it in time for the funeral scheduled for two on Saturday afternoon.

At 1:00 P.M. on Friday, he answered their question. As if emerging from a winter's nap, he popped open the bedroom door and strode into the den where Jackie sat with the family. His hair glistened, his eyes were sharp, and his voice boomed when he spoke. They all looked at him in bewilderment, amazed at the change in his demeanor. But no one questioned it.

"I'm ready to go to the police department," he announced, staring at Jackie. "I want to make sure they're doing all they can to apprehend Lisa's killer."

With that he marched out with Jackie, and she drove him to Peachtree Precinct. There they stepped quickly to Derrick Role's office. Jackie took her place on Role's sofa, a file of papers in her lap. Her eyes widened as she listened to Voss.

He stood ramrod straight and stared down at Role, who remained seated. "I demand to know the situation," said Voss.

Role stayed calm. "We're checking our leads," he said. "When we know something, we'll immediately get in touch with you."

"What leads do you have?"

Role pushed his chair back and stood up. "I'm not free to discuss this with you, Mr. Voss. As you can imagine, it's a ticklish situation. You are, after all, a reporter. We can't make our evidence available to the media."

Voss's face turned purple, and he grabbed his collar as if to loosen it so he could breathe easier. "Do you mean to insinuate, sir, that I would use my position as a grieving husband to obtain information for my broadcast?"

Role shrugged. "I'm not saying that at all, Mr. Voss. But I can't take the chance. What we know has to stay here until we're able to say something definitive. When we get something, we'll inform you and the rest of the media at the same time. Now, if you'll excuse me. . . . I'm supposed to meet the mayor in thirty minutes. Olympic security matters." Role pivoted and walked out of the room.

Watching Role leave, Jackie took a deep breath and stared at Voss. A vein in his forehead seemed about to pop out of his skin.

"Why don't you sit down for a moment?" she asked. "You're under a lot of pressure."

As if in a trance, Voss nodded. He took Role's seat. He dropped his face into his hands and sighed. "What am I going to do?"

"You're going to wait, Mr. Voss. As tough as that is to do, you're going to have to do it. It's all anyone can do."

"Do you know who killed her?"

"No, I honestly don't."

"But I thought this Delaney killed these women."

"We thought so too."

"You're not sure now?"

Jackie sighed and stood. She smoothed down the pleats in her gray slacks. She knew what she was about to do could jeopardize her career if anyone found out. But she couldn't spout the party line if she didn't believe it. To do so mocked the very law she sought to uphold. For her it came down to this—if a grieving husband wanted more than the political coverage talk Role offered to him, she would see that he got it.

She faced Reginald Voss eye to eye. "Officially, I'm sure. You understand that?"

Voss nodded. "But unofficially?"

"And off the record?"

"Off the record," agreed Voss.

"Off the record, I'm not sure at all. In fact, I tend to think otherwise. I tend to think one person did these killings."

"What makes you say that?"

Jackie hesitated. Should she tell him about Burke Anderson's theory? About the phone call to Debbi? She had gone this far. Might as well tell him everything she knew.

Sitting back on the sofa, she began to talk. It took her almost fifteen minutes to explain it all, to go back through the autopsies and police investigations, to sum up what Burke thought and what the Bible said.

Voss fidgeted the whole time she talked. He twisted around and around in Role's chair and squeezed his hands together and fiddled with his tie. She couldn't tell if he was listening or not.

When she finished, he said nothing for several minutes. But he did stop twisting in the chair, and he no longer squeezed his hands or fiddled with his neckwear. When she saw that he apparently didn't plan to respond, Jackie asked, "What will you do now, Mr. Voss?"

He jerked as if awakened. He looked up at the ceiling, then linked his fingers together behind his head. "I think I will call Mr. Burke Anderson," he said firmly. "He sounds as if he's the only one with anything interesting to say to me."

Chapter 56

Two of Burke's afternoon appointments—the 2:00 and 3:15—called at lunch and canceled on him. With only a 4:30 left, he sent Molly home and decided to clean up the stray papers in his "to be filed" folder. That didn't take long. Within thirty minutes, he found himself at loose ends. Not wanting to wait around for two hours, he decided to call his 4:30 appointment and see if he could reschedule it. He had no luck. No one answered the phone.

Frustrated, he punched in the number for Stubs McVaine's office. The secretary who answered gave him the same answer she'd given him three other times already—McVaine wasn't available. Leaving his number again, Burke slammed down the phone.

Stuck for the duration, he pulled a notepad from the desk drawer and began to scratch on it. He drew a rough map of Atlanta, marking the city boundaries with a square around them. Finished with his crude drawing, he placed a dot on it in four places, the dots marking the locations where Staton, Benton, Drexler, and Voss had disappeared. He next dotted the spots where the women had been found.

For several minutes he stared at his dots, searching for a pattern in them. If the killer used a pattern for the wounds, then he might also use a pattern for his abductions and deliveries. The sociopathic mind often worked in such rigid forms. Forms that gave structure to otherwise chaotic lives.

Burke thought about the kind of person who would kill so wantonly. Whoever it was had lost the ability to feel a conscience. Typically, those people grew up in abusive situations.

Amazingly, many of them matured into adults who functioned extremely well in society, sometimes at the highest levels of government, commerce, or industry. Contrary to popular view, sociopaths didn't always exist on the bottom of the socioeconomic scale, underneath the overpasses, and in the sewers. Sometimes they maneuvered themselves right into the upper echelons.

This killer fit the more sophisticated pattern. His victims lived on the high end of the economic hog. If indeed he used disguises, then he had money to purchase the props and to orchestrate the schemes. Even if he didn't, Burke knew that shabby-looking street people didn't haunt Rossario's theater. A person without means would draw instant attention in that well-heeled domain of Atlanta's upper crust.

Like a child playing connect the dots, Burke drew lines from one mark to the other, hoping against hope that something would jump out at him, some clue as to where another woman might disappear.

The phone buzzed. Giving up, he tossed the handmade map onto his desk and grabbed the phone.

"Mr. Burke Anderson?"

"Yes, this is he."

"This is Mr. Reginald Voss. Do you have a minute?"

Burke sat up straighter. "Yes, Mr. Voss. Sure, I have plenty of time. Two of my appointments bailed out on me. What can I do for you?"

"I'll get right to the point. I've been with the police this afternoon, and they don't seem to have any answers to my questions."

Feeling immediate empathy for the man, Burke shifted without thinking into his counselor's mentality. "I'm sure this is a terrible time for you," he said. "It must be difficult to stay patient."

"That's a gracious way of putting it, Mr. Anderson," agreed Voss. "If truth be told, I'm about to go out of my mind thinking about my Lisa dying like she did. It's true we had our problems, but she mothered my lovely daughters and I will always love her for that." He sounded close to tears.

"I am truly sorry for your grief, Mr. Voss," said Burke, his voice gentle.

"Thank you. I appreciate that. But to be honest, I called you for more than your sympathy."

Burke reared back in his seat. "I'm listening," he said.

"I called you because it has come to my attention that you have a thought or two about this murderer. You've suggested a theory that the police are ignoring. I, for one, think they're making a mistake. I believe your idea makes sense."

"Can I ask where you heard about my theory?"

Voss grunted. "I'm afraid not. Sources are confidential, you know."

Burke smiled to himself. Voss's source had to be Jackie. "I understand," he said. "How can I help you?"

Voss paused. Burke remained silent. Voss said, "It's like this. Since I heard your idea, I've been wracking my brain trying to decide what to do. I'm not going to be able to sit idly by this weekend to see if another woman gets killed. I want to do something else, something to, I don't know, something to shake a few trees, see if anything falls out. If the man who killed Lisa is still out there, then I want to do whatever it takes to bring him out of hiding."

"I'm open to suggestions," said Burke, intrigued by Voss's notion.

"Well, I've got one."

"I'm all ears."

"Okay, it may be stupid but here goes." Voss exhaled into the phone. "If your theory is right, then we're dealing with a person who thinks he's smarter than everyone else. If you're right though, it means that you've figured him out. He won't like that.

"What we need to do is let him know what you think. Let him know your theory, see if that'll rock his boat, make him do something foolish, foul up somehow."

Burke paused to consider the idea. It made sense. Sociopaths followed form, ritual, pattern. If something shattered the ritual, it might cause a reaction, might create a chance for a mistake. If he made a mistake, it might lead to another mistake. Once the pattern came apart, anything might happen. The guy might lose it altogether.

Excited by the possibility, Burke asked, "How's he going to know about my theory?"

"Simple," said Voss. "I interview you on the air. We outline your suggestion, describe the type of person you think might be doing this, why you think another death is coming."

"Won't that make the killer more careful?"

"That's possible. Or it might scare him away from trying to kill anyone else."

"Which would be fine by me, but I wouldn't count on it. This kind of person is like a terrorist—will forge ahead no matter how dangerous."

"If so, okay. We still haven't lost anything."

Burke bounced forward in his chair. "I suppose not. But remember—my idea is awfully speculative. I have no proof that I'm anywhere near right."

"I know it's a shot in the dark," said Voss. "But from what I understand from my sources, you could drive a UPS truck through this Delaney's confession. Plus, the call your wife received sounds really ominous to me, like someone wanted to tease her, to make sure that she didn't buy what Delaney was saying."

"You know about that call?"

"Yeah, is that a problem?"

"Not really," said Burke, knowing for certain now that Jackie was the one who had told Voss about his idea.

"Then you're with me on this?"

Burke bit his lip, knowing Voss was right. They didn't have a lot of other options. He thought for a moment about the call Debbi had received and about his determination to protect her. If going on the air with Voss might lead to a mistake by the murderer, then he would do it.

"Will your station let you do this?" he asked.

Voss laughed. "Forgive my immodesty, Mr. Anderson. But I'm the chief cook and bottle washer at WATL. If I want the interview, we do the interview."

"You're taking a gamble, you know. I could be completely off base. Delaney might have done the first three and someone totally different the last one."

"If so, then I've just aired a story with no substance. It won't be the first time, and it won't be the last. Nothing ventured, nothing gained. But if your theory is right . . ."

Burke stared down at the scribbles on his notepad. For a moment he wondered about his own fledgling career. What if it *did* turn out to be a story with no substance? Would his employers at the clinic think him foolish, maybe even unbalanced? And what about the future? Would prospective clients shy away from him because of his involvement in this investigation?

He took a deep breath. He couldn't answer those questions right now. Except for going on the air with Voss, he didn't know what else to do about the murders. Like Voss, he didn't think he could wait around until Christmas and see who turned up dead—no matter what it might do to him personally.

"Okay," he said, conviction in his voice. "Let's give it a shot."

"Okay, come by the station when you finish your last appointment. I'll have everything set up."

Burke laid the phone down, glanced at his watch, and picked up his notepad and pen.

Chapter 57

When Derrick Role and Mimi Stoddard walked into his apartment on Friday evening at 6:15, Role automatically flipped on the television. The habit of a single man, he told Mimi, taking her umbrella. Need the noise of the television for company.

While Mimi dropped ice cubes into two glasses and poured them drinks, Role undid his cuff links and surfed through the channels. His shirt unbuttoned, he dropped onto the sofa across from the television. Mimi handed him his drink, plopped down beside him, and folded her legs under her bottom.

The face of Reginald Voss popped up on the screen. Role stopped flipping channels and rose up straighter in his seat. Voss shouldn't be back at work the day before his wife's funeral.

Role punched the volume button. Voss's smooth voice slipped out of the television speakers. Role jerked back in his seat and stuck against the sofa as if someone had glued him in place.

Voss said, "Just over a week ago, a man named Lewis Delaney confessed to the murders of Leslie Staton, Rosaline Benton, and Angelica Drexler, each the wife of a prominent Atlanta personality. The police department, after an investigation headed by Detective Derrick Role, decided that Delaney's confession provided enough evidence for them to ask the district attorney to present the case to a grand jury.

"Since that time, however, . . ." Voss's voice trailed off for a moment, and he seemed to lose focus. Quickly, though, he gathered himself and continued. "Since that time, another woman, Mrs. Lisa Voss, disappeared. Late Wednesday—December 21—her body was discovered in the High Hill section of Atlanta.

"In spite of this latest murder, Detective Derrick Role continues to accept the Delaney confession and to deny any connection between the first three murders and the death of Mrs. Voss. In public statements both yesterday and today, he assured the Atlanta community and the state authorities that we should fear no more murders."

Voss paused and licked his lips. "This reporter, however, is not so sure. In fact, I have discovered that more than a few people do not agree with Detective Role's assessment of the situation. Those who disagree with Role suggest that this latest slaying fits a pattern consistent with the killings of the first three women."

Licking his lips again, Voss shifted to the left, giving his audience a new camera angle. He continued speaking. "I have one of those people with me here in the studio."

The camera angle widened and brought Burke into view, sitting on Voss's right. Voss gestured to him, then moved ahead. "I have with me Mr. Burke Anderson, a man about to finish a Ph.D. in psychology at Emory and a practicing therapist. Mr. Anderson spent time in his doctoral program studying the sociopathic mind."

He faced Burke directly. "If you would, Mr. Anderson, describe for us in lay terms how a serial killer normally operates."

The camera zoomed in on Burke. He cleared his throat and adjusted his tie. A bead of perspiration glistened on his upper lip. He spoke, his voice a touch shaky. "Well, I don't know that we can label anything about a serial killer 'normal.' But typically, a serial killer uses a particular method of murder. Police identify this as his signature."

Burke paused and tugged at his tie again. "That's what makes these Atlanta murders so difficult. The manner of killing in each case is so different that the police have rejected the singular killer theory."

"Why don't you accept the police conclusions, Mr. Anderson?" Voss set him up perfectly with the question.

Burke gathered himself. The time had come to verbalize his theory to the whole world. His voice firmed up as he began to explain. "I believe if we take the deaths as a group, that they do show a signature. But not one a police officer would recognize. I believe that the murders of Leslie Staton, Rosaline Benton, and Angelica Drexler show at least two discernible patterns."

"Describe those for us, Mr. Anderson."

Nodding his compliance, Burke moved ahead. "First of all, we know that each of these three women died on a Sunday—a Sunday corresponding to the first three weeks of the Christian season of Advent. We don't know yet when Mrs. Voss died, but the suspicion that it happened on Sunday makes good sense. The killings on the same day seem suspicious enough, but it certainly isn't sufficient to prove a pattern. But we have a second commonality also." He stopped and glanced at Voss as if asking permission to continue.

"Tell us about that commonality," said Voss.

"Well, the wounds on the three women also indicate a pattern. When taken as a group, that pattern becomes visible." Burke hesitated again but only for a second. Here it was. Time to spit it out.

"The wounds bear a striking resemblance to the wounds of Jesus as depicted in the Bible. The wounds on the women—facial blows, a flogging, and a series of serrations, or cuts across the brow and over the eyes, fit exactly with those of Jesus as shown in—

Voss interrupted. "So it would take someone with a religious background to see this?"

"Yes, exactly, that's where we see the brilliance of this method."

"Why this pattern, Mr. Anderson?"

"I can't answer that. Except to say that it shows a rage beyond anything most people ever experience. I believe this person hates anything religious. He hates God. It's like he wants to re-create the punishment inflicted upon Jesus by the Roman soldiers, like he wants to kill Jesus again, like he wants to assassinate the Lord."

Voss paused for a moment, letting the words build the drama. When he spoke he almost whispered. "What kind of person would do such a thing?"

Burke didn't hesitate anymore. Bringing his thoughts into the eye of the camera had given them life, made them tangible, believable. He spoke quicker now, firmer. "Generally speaking, a killer like this suffered abuse of some kind early in life. Often it's sexual abuse but not always. Sometimes physical abuse or even emotional trauma can push someone over the edge. But however it happened, a volcano is spewing inside this person, spewing out hot lava, making him want to destroy other people."

"You assume it's a man?"

"Yes, pretty much so. Women serial killers are a rare occurrence."

"You say you told the police your theory a couple of weeks ago, but they refused to accept it?"

"Yes, that's true. Though I can't really blame them. They have to deal with cold hard facts. This is purely speculative. I have no proof of its validity."

"But it is possible?"

Burke nodded vigorously. "I would definitely say it's possible."

"If it's true, what do you expect to happen next?"

Burke paused and rubbed his hands together. "I expect one more death."

"When would that death happen?"

"Probably on Christmas. That's the pattern of this killer. Abduction on Friday or Saturday and death on Sunday."

"And Christmas is on Sunday this year."

"Exactly."

"How will this woman die?"

Burke shifted in his seat and stared down at his lap. When he looked up, his eyes were moist. "It's too terrible to say."

"But the method is in the Bible?"

"Yes, it's there. As plain as day."

Voss turned to face the camera. Tears formed in the corners of his eyes. "I want to say a personal word at this moment. The fourth of these dead women was my wife. I brought this story to you tonight, in the middle of my sorrow, because I don't want any more women to die. I don't know yet if my wife's wounds correspond to this pattern or not. The medical examiner hasn't said. But if they do, then the people of Atlanta need to take care. If they do, it will prove that this Christmas, a demon of death is loose in Atlanta. This is Reginald Voss, for WATL."

On the other end of the television screen, Derrick Role ground his teeth together and squeezed his glass in his hand until his knuckles turned white.

This would never do. What would the mayor think? Worse yet, what about the governor?

They would surely hear about this and probably sooner than later. The whole city would go through the roof. Voss pulled a ton of weight in this city. His wife's death did make Delaney's confession a bit suspicious, and Anderson's theory obviously carried a certain intrigue to it. With people loving conspiracy theories as much as they did and the news media ever vigilant for something rare, this would create chatter in the bars and beauty parlors for days. Even if events proved Anderson's theory completely screwy, Role knew this could still destroy him.

A disturbing thought invaded his deliberations. What if Anderson was right? In that case his career definitely just ended.

Standing up from the sofa, Role raised his glass over his head and held it poised for a moment. Then, with deliberate aim, he threw the glass through the front of the television set. Sitting beside him, Mimi stayed quiet. Neither of them could think of anything to say.

Chapter 58

As Burke walked through the front door of his house after his television appearance with Reginald Voss, he heard the telephone ringing. Wiping his muddy shoes on a carpet strip, he dropped his rain-soaked jacket to the floor and hustled to the den to pick it up.

"Hello," he said.

"Burke Anderson?"

Burke didn't recognize the voice. "Yes," he said.

"I think we need to talk." The voice sounded cautious, edgy. A drop of rain fell off Burke's nose and dripped onto the floor.

"Okay, but maybe you should tell me who you are first."

A couple of seconds ticked by.

"My name is McVaine. Stuart McVaine. My friends call me Stubs."

Momentarily blank, Burke squinted. Who was McVaine? He had heard that name somewhere.

"I'm the medical examiner," said McVaine, answering Burke's question for him. "I saw you on television a couple of hours ago. I think we need to talk."

Burke sucked in his breath and his heart thumped faster. "Name the time and place."

"At midnight tonight. At a place called The Hawk's Nest. It's on Omni Lane, past the stadium."

"I know the area. I'll meet you there. How will I know you?"

"You don't need to know me. I'll know you. I saw you on television, remember?"

The line went dead and Burke hung up. Before he could move away, the phone rang again. Shrugging, he answered. Hal Staton was on the other end. "I saw you on the news," Staton said. "Quite a notion you have there. Why didn't you tell me about it?"

Burke thought for a moment. "Didn't seem any reason to tell you," he said. "It's all very speculative."

"But it makes sense."

"Maybe it makes sense. We don't know anything for sure. I'm not sure I believe it myself."

"I think I know something that makes it even more believable," said Staton, his voice dropping lower as if trying to hide itself over the phone lines.

Burke's fingers tightened on the telephone.

"I finally made contact with Bobby Benton," said Hal. "I think I know what he and I and Drexler have in common." Hal paused and sucked in his breath.

"You're making me tense," said Burke. "Tell me what it is."

Hal chuckled slightly. "Can't do that. Not until we're all together. You, me, Benton, Drexler, and Voss. You think you can get Voss to meet with us early in the morning? Drexler and Benton are set for it. But we need Voss. With what Benton told me, Voss is the key. He'll make or break the pattern."

"You expect me to wait until morning?"

"I don't think you have any choice."

"Then I better call Voss."

"Yeah, I expect you better."

"Where do you want to meet?"

"I don't know. I'd prefer it be somewhere private. With each of us as well-known as we are, it'll be tough to find a spot where someone won't know us. That will make conversation difficult."

Burke considered his options. Not Danny's. No public restaurant would do. He had an idea. "What about my house?" he asked. "It's not far off the interstate coming from Cordele, and Debbi can join us."

"Hey, that sounds good. Out of the public eye. We can talk easier there."

"What time?"

"Is 6:30 too early? Benton said he needs to catch a ten o'clock plane, and I figure we'll need at least a couple of hours."

"Well, for me 6:30 is definitely too early, but for you I'll make an exception."

"Then I'll see you at daybreak."

"Don't expect bells on."

Burke dropped the phone into the cradle and started to unbutton his shirt. A hot shower, a change of clothes, and a bite to eat before he left to meet McVaine would feel so good. He bent over to untie his shoes. The phone rang. Sighing, he picked it up.

"Hello."

"Mr. Anderson, I presume."

"Yes." It was another voice he didn't recognize, a thin tremulous voice.

"Smart, smart, oh, so smart."

"Excuse me?"

"You and your wife—quite a pair."

"Who is this, please?"

"Don't you know?"

"No, how could I know?"

"It shall be made known unto you. You shall know the name. The name shall be called the Way and the Truth and the Death. The name will reveal the Way and speak the Truth and lead to Death. Do you know the name?"

Burke's eyes widened. The hair on the back of his neck stood up, and the rain on his arms instantly dried.

"Who are you?"

Laughter poured through the phone line. "Smart, smart, oh, so smart. But still you see—through a glass dark." The line clicked dead.

Burke lifted the phone and stared at it as if facing down a poised snake. A shudder passed through his arms and shoulders. He knew for certain now that at some point in the next two days, another woman would die. Gritting his teeth, he vowed to himself that he would do anything it took to stop it.

Chapter 59

The Hawk's Nest sat on the corner of one of the busiest night streets of Atlanta. The athletic community—players, management, and fans provided the establishment's primary clientele. A row of other sports bars and late-evening dance clubs squeezed in on all sides around it. A steady stream of casually dressed customers moved crisply to and from their cars and the clubs. A few people staggered as they made their way up or down the street. Loud music seeped through the walls of the buildings and bounced along the concrete sidewalk.

After taking ten minutes to find a parking place, Burke locked his car and hustled down the street to the Nest. The rain that had fallen since Monday had finally stopped, and a biting wind foretelling the arrival of much colder weather cut into his face. He wished he had brought a jacket.

At the door of the Nest, Burke paid twelve bucks for the cover charge and eased inside. A mob of people instantly swallowed him up. Everywhere he looked he saw swarms of people—people standing in the corners, sharing pick-up lines; on stools at the bar, gulping down beer and mixed drinks; on the dance floor, shaking and shimmying to the music.

Burke squinted, wondering if McVaine had arrived, wondering what the man looked like, how McVaine would find him in such a swirl of humanity. A bank of smoke as thick as an afghan wrapped around his head, and he coughed as he swallowed a mouthful of it. A wave of music followed the smoke. He took a deep breath and waded into the crowd, heading toward the bar.

Not more than four steps away from a stool at the corner of the bar, Burke felt someone grab his arm. He turned and saw a short, hairy man at his elbow. The man had eyebrows the color and consistency of Tootsie Rolls crawling over his forehead. Burke thought instantly of a troll. The troll spoke.

"I'm Stubs McVaine," he said. "Keep moving, I've got a table in the corner."

"I'm right behind you," said Burke, more and more intrigued by the mysterious Mr. McVaine.

McVaine steered him by the elbow, and they took their seats at the corner table. McVaine cleared his throat.

"You want a drink?"

"No, I'm okay."

McVaine raised a glass off the table. "Mind if I finish mine?"

"That's up to you."

McVaine sucked down the liquid. His throat bobbed as he swallowed. His Adam's apple was covered with hair as thick as that on his eyebrows. He finished his drink and carefully placed the glass on the table.

Burke spoke. "You said you wanted to talk to me."

McVaine nodded. "That's right, I do. It's about these murders, as you've probably guessed. I've worked with these women from the beginning. I've examined all of them."

The edges of Burke's eyes wrinkled. He thought of telling McVaine he had read all the autopsies except the last one. He decided against it. If McVaine read the *Independent,* he might have surmised that Debbi was his wife. If so, he had probably already guessed that Burke had read the reports. If he didn't know it, no use bringing it up.

"It's all such a tragedy," said Burke.

McVaine nodded and touched the rim of his empty glass. "I constantly deal with this kind of thing."

"Death, you mean?"

"Yes, death. In all its ghoulish forms."

"Has to be a tough job."

"They don't pay me enough."

"Then why do it?"

McVaine lifted his heavy eyebrows. They moved higher, like two fuzzy caterpillars reaching for the sky. "I don't know, exactly. I'm notching the years until retirement on a leg of my bed. But when the time comes, I don't know if I'll retire or not. The job does have its rewards."

"Explain that to me."

"It's simple. I make a difference sometimes. I find a clue the cops need to nail a suspect, something that puts a screwball lowlife behind bars, some explanation that brings a measure of peace to the family of the deceased."

"A worthy purpose," said Burke. "What we all need to make our jobs worthwhile."

McVaine smiled. "Yeah, that's one way to say it. A worthy purpose. That's what keeps me going."

For a moment both men fell silent. McVaine ran his hairy finger around the lip of his glass. Burke leaned forward, placing his elbows on the table. "And what is your purpose in asking me to meet you, Mr. McVaine?"

McVaine's finger left his glass, and he touched his lips as if asking for quiet. His voice dropped lower. "You need to see something," he said.

Burke nodded. His heart rate notched up, and he chewed on the inside of his cheek. McVaine leaned to his right, reached under the table, and pulled out a manilla folder. He laid the folder on the table. "Take a look," he said.

Burke's fingers shook as he picked up the folder and opened it. A stack of pictures lay inside. For a moment, Burke didn't move as he stared at the top picture. His eyes stood still, then widened. A bead of sweat broke out squarely in the center of his forehead. He felt nauseous but forced down the bile that erupted in the back of his throat.

He flipped to the second picture in the stack. This one was taken from a different angle from the first. He studied it for several moments, then checked out the third one. Still another perspective.

The folder contained twenty pictures in all—pictures of the body of Lisa Voss—pictures of the injuries of Lisa Voss.

Burke didn't rush himself. He pored over each picture, one at a time, studying them at all angles, making sure his eyes weren't deceiving him. McVaine stayed completely quiet, fiddling with his glass but saying nothing.

It took Burke almost ten minutes until he felt satisfied. Finally, he finished and laid the pictures on top of the folder. He raised his eyes and stared at McVaine.

"Do the police have these yet?"

"I sent them to Peachtree about two hours ago, right after I called you."

"Has Role seen these?"

"Don't know. Maybe not. From what I hear, he frowns on late night calls."

"Will they call him about these?"

"I would think so."

"Why did you call me?"

McVaine paused for a second before answering. He licked his index finger. "One big reason, I suppose. I'm not sure Role will act on these fast enough to do anything. He'll have to move cautiously, try to find a way off the limb he's climbed. You, on the other hand, can act. I wanted to make sure I gave you the chance. I don't want to do another dead woman this Christmas."

Burke nodded gravely. McVaine was right. Role would have difficulty even after he saw these pictures. If this last murder was to be stopped, he had to find a way other than through the police to do it.

He exhaled slowly, then focused on McVaine. Before he left, he wanted to hear McVaine verify what he saw in the pictures. Until then, he didn't know for sure that he could accept that he had been right, that his theory really was true. He almost whispered the question.

"So what do you see in these pictures?"

"I see what you see," said McVaine.

"Tell me."

McVaine picked up two of the photos—one showing the hands of Lisa Voss and one showing the feet. "I see what you see. The nail-pierced hands and feet."

Burke took the pictures from McVaine and looked at them one more time. A jagged tear—exactly in the center of both palms and straight through the tops of both feet. The puzzle was almost complete. Only one slice of a piece left to snap into place.

Chapter 60

Saturday, December 24

The doorbell rang at 6:20 Saturday morning, and Burke, dressed in gray sweatpants and a red flannel shirt, answered it with a cup of coffee in his hand. On the stoop, he saw Hal Staton and a round-headed man with a girth as wide as a corn silo stamping their feet against the cold. Stepping back, Burke waved them in.

The round-faced man extended a meaty hand. "I'm Bobby Benton," he said.

"Burke Anderson," he said shaking the man's hand. "Let me take your coats."

Hal and Benton complied, pulling off their thick jackets and handing them over. Burke hung them in the closet by the entry and motioned them to follow.

In the den, he threw a log onto the fire he had just started and pointed them to a seat. "We're expecting Voss and Drexler in a few minutes. You guys want coffee—juice?"

Benton said coffee; Hal chose juice. Debbi walked into the room and Burke introduced her to Benton. "I'll get the coffee," she said. She cinched her bathrobe tighter and padded out. The doorbell rang again.

"Back in a second," said Burke. He left the den and opened the door. Voss stood on the porch, and a black Lexus pulled up to the curb. Karl Drexler stepped out. "Come on in," said Burke. "It's cold out here this morning."

"I heard it might snow today," said Voss, quickly stepping past him into the entryway. "Wouldn't that be something?"

With the door still open for Drexler, Burke took Voss's coat and put it away. Drexler, without a coat, stepped to the open door. "Is this the place?" he asked.

"You found it," said Burke. "Have you two met?"

The men shook their heads. "I've seen him on TV," said Drexler, "but never in person." The two men shook hands. Burke led them to the den and introduced them to Staton and Benton.

Standing by the fire, Burke watched as the four men shook hands and said their hellos. None of them small, the four men plus himself and the Christmas tree by the double windows on the back wall filled up the room. Benton especially demanded a large chunk of space. He took a seat on the sofa along the wall opposite the windows and farthest from the fire. *Good thing*, thought Burke, looking at his red face. He seemed overheated already.

Drexler, the thinnest of the group and the tallest, didn't sit. He stayed put near the windows beside the Christmas tree, his hands folded behind his back. The white lights from the tree glittered in his dark eyes, and the star on the top blinked on and off, illuminating his face. *A striking man*, decided Burke.

Burke's eyes moved to Reginald Voss, the silver-haired star of the six o'clock news. Voss chose to sit in the biggest chair in the room, in Burke's recliner, facing the fireplace. For a second, Burke thought he might actually lean back and put his feet up. He certainly seemed relaxed. That fit what Burke knew so far of the man. A bundle of contradictions, Voss preened and postured like a peacock one minute but wept like a schoolboy over his dead wife the next. The crying had occurred over the phone last night when Burke called Voss and asked him to come to this meeting.

"I've got coffee," announced Debbi, moving into the room, clothed in her navy and green bathrobe and bedroom slippers. "Or juice or milk, whichever you prefer." She moved from one man to the other, dispensing her offerings.

Hal, perched on the edge of a straight-backed chair beside the sofa, took his juice. Burke studied him for a moment. A natural athlete with movement as graceful as a young deer. But stronger, more like a mature buck. Hal sipped his juice.

Debbi handed Burke a cup of coffee. Steam rose from the cup and felt good on his face. He took a deep breath and slurped down a sip of the hot liquid. A silence slipped into the room as each of the men stopped talking to down his drink.

The fireplace crackled. Burke sat down on the brick base in front of it. Debbi joined him there, tucking her robe under her legs. Bobby Benton coughed, and Karl Drexler sucked in the sides of his jaws, as if making a fish face.

Burke swallowed and put his coffee down. He looked from one man to the next, studying their faces, trying to determine what made them so powerful. Each so different and yet each charismatic in his own way. Was that what attracted the killer to them? To their wives? The charisma that jumped from each of them like so much lightning bottled up in human flesh?

"I'm glad you could come this morning," he began. "Though I must tell you it wasn't my idea. It was Hal's." He inclined his head toward Hal. Staton shrugged and sipped his juice.

"Hal wanted to get together with you almost from the beginning. At first he wanted to do it because he thought you might be able to help each other through your common grief. Then, as the situation worsened, it became evident that celebrities' wives were the targets.

"Hal and I wondered what attracted the killer to your wives in particular, what commonality bound you together. We believed, and still do, that if we can find that common thread, then we can not only stop the next murder, but we can catch whoever took your wives from you." He stopped and sipped his coffee.

Hal raised his hand, asking permission to speak. Burke nodded to him. Hal smiled slightly and tipped his head to Drexler. "I met Reverend Drexler first. A few days ago. He's been a big help to me. I found out we're a lot alike." Hal stared down at his juice glass. "We talked about six hours one night last week. He used to play baseball. Shortstop and pitcher."

"And you've preached once or twice," added Drexler.

"But not quite as good as you." Hal laughed briefly.

"And your fastball is a bit quicker than mine," said Drexler.

Hal smiled again, then went on. "After talking with Karl, I tried for several days to reach Mr. Benton, but no luck. He had gone to Nashville to see his mama before Christmas. Yesterday, I called one more time. Got him that time, and we agreed to meet for supper. During our meal, we found out we had a few things in common too."

Burke felt the room get quieter. The fire behind him flickered, then almost paused in its dancing movements, as if waiting to hear what Hal would say. Burke glanced at Debbi. For a split second her fingers reached for her hair, but then she dropped her hand and wrapped her arms around her stomach.

"Why don't you tell what we found out, Mr. Benton?" Hal turned expectantly to the round-faced man.

"Naw, you go on, Hal. I, well, it's not too easy for me to rehash all that. I don't like to remember most of it."

"But it's your story, Mr. Benton, not mine. Go on—we're your friends here."

Benton scanned the circle for a moment, then leaned forward and perched on the edge of the sofa. An imprint of his back stayed on the leather for a moment, then disappeared as if in a hurry to escape the burden it had been holding up. Benton rubbed his thick hands together.

"Well, it's like this," he began. "I've been a car salesman for pretty close to twenty years. Done right well with that too. Guess that's what I was cut out for. Move them units on and off the lot. Anyway, about ten years ago, I decided I wanted to upgrade myself, open up a chain of lots here in Atlanta. So about that time I decided I needed to market myself, get myself an advertising agent. So, that's what I did.

"It all worked out pretty well, too, as I suspect you know. I've got the picture of my mama's only son plastered over just about every billboard within twenty miles of Atlanta. If you can see, then you have to see me." He paused, smiled, and rubbed his hands together. His face reddened even more, and Burke thought for a second he might spontaneously combust.

"Anyway, when I started that advertising, I found out what I did best of all. Talk and self-promote. That's my gift, I reckon. The gift of gab, my dear dead daddy used to say. 'Bobby B, your tongue is your greatest tool. It'll take you far if it don't get you in trouble first.' Well," Benton leaned forward and his voice dropped a notch, "my dear dead daddy was right. . . . Look where it has done taken me."

Benton's round head dropped lower and lower toward his lap. The sofa under his heavy legs seemed to slump downward too—pushed down by his heavy body and sagging spirit. Burke could see the top of his head now, and it glowed in the lights from the Christmas tree and the fireplace. He heard a sob, then realized that Benton was crying.

For a moment, Burke didn't move. *Let the grief play out a bit*, he thought. *Let Benton regain his composure himself.* Burke felt movement to his right. Hal stood, stepped to Benton, and put a hand on his back.

"We're here for you, Mr. Benton. We all know what you're going through. Take all the time you want. We're not going anywhere." Drexler shifted his feet, and Voss sat transfixed in the recliner.

Debbi eased up from beside Burke and left the room. For an instant, he thought to stop her, but then realized she must have a good reason for leaving. He focused again on Benton. Hal rubbed the big man's back for another couple of minutes, and the sobs gradually subsided. Hal sighed and moved back to his chair. He leaned it backward, and it danced precariously on two legs.

Benton raised his head. Debbi appeared from the hallway with a box of tissues in her hand. Burke smiled. She handed Benton the box, and he took a tissue and blew his nose. She sat down by Burke again.

"I'm, I'm sorry," Benton sniffled. "But it's all so hurtful. Me and Rosey were so happy. She did please me no end."

"You are most blessed to have had a happy marriage."

Burke jerked his eyes to Reginald Voss. The anchorman stiffly stood from his chair and moved to the window beside Drexler. He was at least half a foot shorter than the reverend, and the Christmas star on the seven-foot tree seemed high above him. "Not everyone enjoys such a pleasurable experience."

"I know them's true words," said Bobby. "You see, Rosey was my second wife. My first wife and me split up after only three years."

"Lisa left me many times," said Voss, staring out the window. "But I always talked her into coming back. I did love her, though I know I didn't express that to her satisfaction. If only I hadn't talked her into coming back that last time. If I hadn't then she'd still be, she'd still be—"

"That blaming yourself won't help none," said Benton. "It won't bring her back, and it'll add guilt onto the burden of your grief."

"But I should feel guilt," said Voss.

"No more than me."

Both men stopped for a second. Burke stared at Voss, then past him and out the window. Through the early morning light, he saw a dribble of snowflakes drift out of the gray sky and fall toward the ground.

"Why should you feel guilty, Mr. Benton?" Drexler asked. Benton placed his round head into his meaty palms and sighed heavily. "'Cause the Lord is punishing me with Rosey's death."

Burke shuddered. In his theology, God didn't work like that—killing one person to punish another. He started to make this point, but Drexler didn't give him a chance.

"How's that, Mr. Benton? Why would the Lord punish you?"

Benton's heavy shoulders shook as he started to sob again. At first, it seemed that he wouldn't answer the question. Everyone tensed, waiting. The fire crackled. Burke saw more snowflakes feather down to the ground.

Bobby began to speak, slowly at first, then more quickly as he unburdened himself. His words spewed out through a succession of sobs, and his breath came in ragged gulps. "The Lord is punishing me 'cause I, 'cause I started out so good, but . . . but I couldn't keep it that way. I turned bad. My easy talk made people too easy, and I . . . I could talk anybody into about anything, and I did it. I talked that woman . . . that woman into that affair after I married my first wife. I had that affair with a woman . . . with a woman in my church, and the church kicked me out, and I lost my marriage and, and I lost my call all at the same time, and I knew . . . I knew that sooner or later I'd suffer for it, for the glib tongue that talked me into so much, so much . . ." His breath gave out and he couldn't talk anymore and his round head fell into his lap and he buried his face in his meaty palms.

For a split instant, it didn't hit Burke. Everything was quiet. Then the fire behind him crackled, and the hair on the back of his neck stood up. The star on the top of the tree blinked. Burke stared at Hal. Staton nodded as if acknowledging something they both understood now. Easing from his seat, Burke knelt down beside the sofa and put his arm on Benton's back.

"Were you a preacher, Mr. Benton?" he whispered.

The quivering back shifted and nodded.

"But you had an affair and left the ministry?"

Another nod.

"He served a Pentecostal church in Dothan," said Hal. "Preached there for three years in his early twenties."

Burke sighed and glanced over to Drexler. Drexler nodded. "That makes three of us who were or who are in the ministry," he said, his deep voice filling the room.

Everyone's eyes shifted to Reginald Voss. He stood still, his face staring out the window, his back to them. When he spoke, his voice cracked.

"I spent a year and a half in an Episcopal seminary. My parents wanted me to follow in my father's footsteps."

The fire crackled. The lights on the tree blinked. The star on top blazed down on their faces. Burke raised up from his knees and moved to the center of the room.

"Gentlemen," he said, nodding slowly, "I think we know what you have in common. Each of you, at one time or another served, or planned to serve, in ministry in the church. Our killer picked you for that reason."

"But how?" asked Hal, instantly moving to the next issue. "That's what we need to answer. Who would know that about us? It's not like any of us advertised it."

"I can't answer that," said Burke. "But somebody knows each of you well enough to have found it out."

"If we can find out who that is, we'll have our killer," said Drexler.

"We don't have time for that," said Burke. "On Christmas another woman will die."

"Another celebrity's wife," said Hal.

"A celebrity with a connection to ministry," said Drexler.

"We have to find out who that is," said Burke.

The room fell silent. Burke glanced from one man to another—Benton a quivering mass on the sofa, Hal standing protectively over him. Drexler—regal and quiet by the window. Voss near the Christmas tree, underneath the star.

Burke stared at the blinking star. The star of Bethlehem. The sign that led the wise men to Jesus. The star that stood over the stable and beckoned all to come and see.

Something clicked against the window, and he stared past Voss to the whitish sky beyond the drapes. Sleet. Sleet was clicking against the window. And Christmas was just a bit over sixteen hours away, and another woman was about to die.

Chapter 61

Clouds the color of an old nickel banked up heavier and heavier through the morning, sporadically spitting out bits and pieces of snow and sleet as they worked their way into position over Georgia. The temperature plummeted as the icy weather advanced, and rows and rows of chilly sparrows lined themselves up on telephone wires as if the wires could somehow heat their feet.

At 2612 Rosewood Lane, a pair of black eyes stared out from a second-floor bedroom window at the sparrows and, above them, at the thick clouds. The figure behind the eyes smiled. The colder and grayer the weather, the better for the work at hand. Fewer cops poked around when the weather turned frigid.

For several long minutes, the sturdy but lean frame by the window stayed completely still. Thoughts of the last evening swirled around behind the black eyes. The black eyes took on a glint of red as the thoughts turned nasty.

Burke Anderson had figured it out. No, not all of it. No one could unwrap all the layers—layers like a seven-layer salad, one move on top of another and that one on top of a third and so on and so on—a riddle wrapped in an enigma covered by a mystery. No one could figure all of it out. But Anderson had done well, decoding the nub of it.

For a moment, the black eyes glazed over, and the unthinkable thought floated up behind them. Could Anderson stop it? What if he tied the first string to the second one and the second to the third?

Like a puzzle, the first part of a mystery was always the hardest. One piece led naturally to the next one, and before long the whole thing took shape.

Anderson had pulled the first piece together. What if another jumped out at him?

A sigh of relief escaped the thin lips. Anderson could not do that. Even if he were smart enough, which he wasn't, he didn't have enough time. Less than sixteen hours away from zero hour. Even if Anderson deduced the second part, door number three remained unopened. Only one person knew what lay behind door number three.

The sparrows on the telephone lines suddenly started chattering. An instant later they swooped down off their perch, landed on the lawn, and began to peck away at the bird feed left there for them. Seeing the sparrows, a squirrel squeaked and scampered off.

Leaving the window and the thoughts of Burke Anderson behind, the slender frame moved to the desk and carefully pulled a folder from the top drawer. Trembling fingers opened the folder and pulled out the pictures—one of each woman—Staton, Benton, Drexler, and Voss.

For a moment the eyes studied the pictures. Each woman was so beautiful in her own way. Beautiful in form and, to all appearances, beautiful in her relationship with her husband.

The eyes studied Lisa Voss an extra second. She, of all of them, seemed ready to consider something different, seemed ready to break away from her loutish husband and claim her own place in the sun. Such a pity she had to die.

But by then the scheme was on automatic pilot. There was no time to choose someone else, no time to pick a doormat, a woman who let her husband dominate her and keep her from doing what she knew was right.

Like the preacher's wife did so long ago. She ignored the wrong and let it happen, ignored the wrong and let a child suffer so horribly.

Yes, she was young—only nineteen. Younger than her husband. But that didn't excuse her. Youth didn't excuse her weakness, a weakness that made her unwilling to resist the evil that slept in her bed and preached pretty words to a naive congregation. She should still have had the courage to take a stand and say "no more." But she didn't. She was a woman without strength.

The slender fingers placed the pictures of the four victims on the desk. Snow jumped up beside the pictures and twirled her white tail in the air.

Snow's owner rubbed her behind the ears. "No way to know these women, Snow. Perhaps they had courage, perhaps not . . . But no bother. They were so perfect for the message. The message I've held within so long, the message that boils in me like molten lava, the message now spewing to the surface."

Snow purred as her owner talked. She liked the sound of the voice. Her owner talked so seldom. Snow tilted her head and pricked her ears at the sound of the words.

"The Bible makes the message so clear, Snow. He who is not for me is against me . . . is against me . . . is against me." The words rico-cheted off the walls, pinging and pinging, playing their song.

The memories of those awful nights surged up like bony fingers from a grave, seeking to pull down another victim. "The women weren't for me, the women were against me. The women weren't for me, the women were against me."

The black eyes closed trying to push aside the awful memories—the memories that had haunted for years—memories that no amount of therapy, no amount of education or self-help, no amount of later love, ever quite scraped away.

A bead of sweat glistened between the black eyes, and the slender fingers moved away from Snow and slowly flicked it away. "Only one way to remove my memories, Snow. Only one way."

Snow's green eyes blazed brighter and brighter.

"Snuff out the memories, Snow. Snuff them out. Tonight, Snow, tonight it will happen. I will snuff out the memories. I will snuff out the memories and free the soul from the stain of what was and what could never be."

As the words stopped, Snow eased away, down the side of the desk onto the hardwood floor. The slender fingers that had stroked Snow's ears placed the folder with the pictures back in the desk drawer. In the drawer beside that folder lay a second one. The fingers picked up the second folder.

"Time to open the last folder, Snow. The one that will tie all the pieces together, the one that will finish my work and insure that the memories will die."

The slender fingers picked up the folder and opened it to the pic-ture of the final woman, the one woman who could have stopped it all, the picture of the wife of the preacher from the white-stoned mountain church.

The black eyes stared at the picture. It showed a woman of obvious distinction. Her full hair, dark except for the slight graying at the temples, was cut sharply along her chin line in a stylish flip, framing her face. She had pouty lips and eyes the shape of pecans, the edges bent slightly upward, giving her an oriental appearance.

The twenty-two years since the suffering season had actually helped the looks of the preacher's wife. She was forty-one now. The years had filled out her formerly skinny body, as if the passing of time had acted as an air pump, rounding out her sharp corners and filling up what once looked like dead space.

She wore expensive clothes in the picture. A burgundy jacket with square shoulders and a white silk blouse with only a bit of a ruffle at the throat. A ring with a diamond the size of a lima bean glistened on her left hand, fourth finger.

From the floor, Snow rubbed up against her owner's legs, and the black eyes staring at the picture darted down to the cat. "Are you hungry, Snow?"

Snow meowed.

"In a minute."

The black eyes closed and remembered the interview with this woman. Not that it had been included in the article. No, that would have offered a too-obvious clue. But the interview had gone so well. The preacher's wife had preened and postured for the camera and talked and talked into the tape recorder. She had spilled out the story of her husband's life, highlighting his accomplishments, praising him as one man who could make a real difference in his world, as one man who deserved all the adulation the people gave him.

In a trancelike tone that sounded almost hypnotized, the preacher's wife had detailed her husband's latest success. He had impregnated her after all these years of barrenness. Yes, a new fertility drug had helped, but she had quickly glossed over that fact to give credit to her husband. She glowingly painted him as the man who would make a perfect father.

"Not true, Snow," said a soft voice above the cat. "The wife of the preacher has completely ignored the truth. She has brushed it under the rug again, the crimes he committed so long ago. She has done what she always did, scrubbed the stains of his sin away under the cloak of her own unwillingness to see."

Snow arched her back against her owner's strong calves.

"Tonight this woman of the lie will die, Snow," continued the breathy voice. "She will die where all will see, where all will see. Where all will see and understand me. She will die where all will see and understand me."

At the feet of the killer, Snow licked her lips and meowed.

Chapter 62

At 8:15 A.M. Jackie Broadus met Derrick Role in his office at Peachtree. For the first time since she had met him, he looked less than immaculate. His hair sprigged out on the left side of his head, and his white shirt needed ironing. The right cuff link was missing, and he had the sleeve rolled up. For once, Jackie looked better than he did. Though tired from the all-night shift she had just finished, she had run by her apartment for a quick shower and a change of slacks and blouse.

Role pointed to the sofa, directing her to sit down. "Okay, let's go through it," he said, his voice weary. "Everything you've found since last night."

Jackie took a deep breath. She didn't have a lot to tell. Since McVaine had sent the pictures over with his autopsy report, she and Role and four other detectives had gone through everything they knew about the four murders. But, even armed with the stark evidence given by the photos of Lisa Voss, nothing new jumped out at them.

They all agreed on a serial killer now. Even Role. But Jackie knew he didn't know how to say that without losing everything he had ever worked for. And, she realized sitting across from him, she didn't know how to tell him their investigation had turned up empty.

"I'm waiting," Role said.

Jackie cleared her throat. Wished for a cigarette. "We're at a dead end," she said.

"A dead end?" He looked like he was about to explode out of his chair. "I have a meeting with the mayor and the governor's chief of staff in an hour, and you tell me we're at a dead end?"

Jackie felt the blood rising in her face. She didn't mind taking her share of responsibility, but a whole team of detectives, including Role as their director, had worked this case for four weeks and come up empty-handed. When she spoke, her voice took on a firm edge. "You know what we've got. We've got zip. No fingerprints, no blood or body fluids of any kind, no murder weapon, no witnesses, no trace on the body bag, no fibers on the four bodies, no skin under the fingernails. You name it, we don't have it. All we have are four dead women killed by a maniac using the wounds of Jesus as his signature."

"Burke Anderson's theory."

"Come back to haunt us."

Role pushed up and walked around his desk. Shaking his head, he perched on the corner of the desk and ground his teeth together. His left leg kicked out and back, out and back. "I can't believe he went on television with Voss last night. Made us all look like fools."

"Turned out he was right though," said Jackie.

"Doesn't matter. Point is, he didn't know he was right when he said it. Unless someone has given him something he shouldn't have, he still doesn't know if he's right or not." He stared at her, challenging her to contradict him on this point. She didn't. Role continued.

"It was a publicity stunt. He was grandstanding, pure and simple. Letting Voss use him to bump up the ratings."

"You think Voss is that cold, that he'd use his own wife's death that way? You think he did that interview for ratings points?"

"No question. Why else would he do it?"

Jackie stood from the sofa and walked past Role to the window. Snowflakes dropped like soft flour to the ground outside. She turned and faced Role. "Maybe he wanted the killer to see it."

Role's leg paused in midair. "Why would he do that?"

"Think about it. Voss wants the killer caught. Anderson feeds him his theory. A theory that says another celebrity's wife will die on Christmas. Voss and Anderson don't want that to happen. They decide to break an egg or two, see if they can create a reaction. If Anderson is right, then the killer might get spooked, do something beyond the plan, do something that gives us a chance to catch up."

"You think those guys are that smart?"

Jackie grunted. "I don't know about Voss, but I've been trying to tell you about Anderson. He's the brightest guy I've ever met, outside of Avery Mays, of—"

The phone buzzed and interrupted her. Role held up his hand and twisted to pick it up. "Yeah." He listened for a second, then turned to Jackie, the corners of his mouth turned down, registering his disapproval.

"It's Burke Anderson," he said. "Says he needs to talk to you."

Jackie nodded and Role grudgingly gave her the phone. "Yeah, Burke, what's up?" she asked.

"We know the connection," he said, his excitement pouring over the phone line. "The connection between the four men."

"I'm listening."

"They all have backgrounds in Christian ministry. Drexler's you already know. But listen to this. Staton spent a summer in his late teens as a youth worker at his home church. Benton preached for three years for a Pentecostal congregation in Dothan. And Voss went to an Episcopal seminary for almost two years."

Jackie squeezed the phone, and her wide eyes expanded. She gave Role a thumbs-up sign. He ground his teeth, walked past her, and left the room, slamming the door for good effect. She shrugged. "How'd you find that out?" she asked Burke.

"Hal Staton got them all together. We met this morning at my house, talked it all through. Quite a group of men, if you ask me."

"You know about Lisa Voss?" asked Jackie.

"Yeah, I've seen the photos."

She didn't bother to ask him his source. Her mind jumped ahead to the implications of the information he was giving her. If it played out as it had so far, then someone else would disappear today. The wife of a celebrity. The wife of a man who had once served in some capacity in the work of the church. She sighed heavily. "So what do we do with this information?" she asked.

She heard Burke inhale. "We've got to figure out who the target is."

"But that's a stab in the dark," she said. "No way to make that kind of guess."

"I know," he agreed. "And I've been trying to think through another way to get at it. If we can't determine who the target is, then we've got to determine where it will happen. Everything else has a connection, I think that does too."

"You think there's a link in the places of abduction?"

"Yeah, I do, though I have no idea how. This killer works in patterns, according to a particular form. The wounds with a connection, the men with a commonality, so why not the places?"

Jackie sat down on the edge of the desk and swung her legs off it. "If there is a connection, you think it'll have a religious meaning?"

"If there's a connection, then yes, I believe it will definitely have a religious meaning."

"This is a weird guy," said Jackie.

She heard Burke pause. "For sure," he said. "But weird for a reason. Someone hurt him bad a long time ago, someone in authority, some religious person with authority."

"A preacher maybe?"

"Sure, that's possible. But someone else is possible too. A bishop or priest. A nun, a deacon, or an elder. Could have been anybody who called himself a believer. Evil doesn't discriminate, and temptation knows no labels."

Jackie stopped swinging her feet, and her voice dropped a notch. "How does God fit into all of this, Burke?" she asked, her heart heavy.

He paused again. Jackie swung her leg, once, twice, three times. When Burke spoke, his voice was as soft as hers. "I have only one answer for that, Jackie."

"I'm open to your answer."

"It's not my answer," he said, "It's from the Bible."

"I'm open to an answer no matter where it comes from."

"Okay, here it is. Jesus said it to his disciples right before his death. He said, 'In the world you will have trouble. But take heart! I have overcome the world.'"

Burke's voice quivered as he continued. "You ask me how God fits into all of this. That's all I know to say. God said this world would bring troubles and trials, even suffering and death. But God has conquered the world. In the life, death, and resurrection of Jesus, God has defeated the sin and evil that so terribly plague us. God is with us in all this—offering us the same ability to overcome the pain. No, not physically, because we all suffer at one point or another. But spiritually God offers us victory. Through God's presence, we can overcome too.

"God walks with us when we move and God laughs with us when we rejoice and God cries with us when we hurt and God calls to us when we walk away into sin. That's the only answer I have for you. God offers us his power to overcome when we suffer."

A tear rolled onto the edge of Jackie's left cheek. She raised her hand and flicked it away. But another tear followed it and then so many fell onto her face that her hand wasn't fast enough to move them all away and so they washed down on her lips and she tasted the salt and she dropped the phone to the desktop and didn't try to stop the tears anymore.

Chapter 63

At 10:35 A.M. a group of five men and one woman swept by the desk officer at Peachtree Precinct and headed straight to Jackie Broadus's desk. She greeted them warmly but without fanfare, then ushered them out of sight into an interrogation room in the back of the offices. She hauled in a couple of extra chairs, then closed the door and spoke to Burke in a low whisper.

"Role doesn't want you here," she said. "He's had a tough day. We released Delaney about an hour ago, and Role's at the mayor's office now, trying to put Humpty Dumpty together again."

"That'll take a bit of work, won't it?" asked Burke.

"Maybe more than he can do," said Jackie. "So if he comes in and finds you, he may get rid of all of us at the same time. He doesn't much care for you, as you can well imagine. Nor me either. He knows I fed you information over the last four weeks, and he's holding it over my head. Figures if I hadn't told you anything, you wouldn't have figured so much out. So what say we work through what we can here and then scoot you on along before he returns. I expect your entourage has Christmas plans." She motioned toward the four widowers and Debbi.

Burke pivoted to the group. "Have a seat, guys," he said. "Detective Broadus is anxious to get started."

They each pulled out a chair and squeezed in around the one square table in the room. Jackie pointed to Debbi. "This is all off the record, you know," she said.

"For now," said Debbi. "But the day you arrest someone, it's fair game."

Jackie agreed, taking her seat at the head of the table. "I asked you here for one reason," she began. "Whoever killed your wives knew a good bit about you. Knew a lot of your history. I suspect the killer worked from a larger group, narrowing it down, searching for the one thing that you all have in common, your former work in the church."

Debbi held up her hand. "So the question is, who would know that much about each of you?"

"A lawyer," suggested Drexler. "A lawyer might have that kind of information. Who's your attorney?" He turned to Staton who sat on his left.

"Rex Stamps," said Hal. "He's my agent and my attorney."

"No go," piped in Benton. "My guy's a girl."

"So, it's not a lawyer," said Jackie. "Who else?"

"A psychologist or psychiatrist?"

They all turned to Voss who shrugged at Burke. "No offense, Burke, but you guys open up your clients like a can of caviar. I attended a few counseling sessions with Lisa. Not many secrets on a therapist's couch."

"Nor on a preacher's," offered Hal. "A minister could know someone's personal history pretty well."

"But I don't have a preacher," said Benton, a hint of sadness tingeing his voice.

"And I don't have a counselor," said Drexler.

Burke stirred in his chair. "So it's not a preacher or a psychologist. Other options."

The room became quiet. Chair legs scrunched along the floor. Staton leaned backward, balancing his seat against the back wall. Benton dropped his bulbous head into his hands. Drexler and Voss stayed still, seemingly impassive. Burke stood up and placed his hands on Debbi's shoulders. His head had started to throb, and the air in the room seemed to go stale all at once. Long seconds passed and still no one spoke. A palpable tension crept into the tiny space, and Burke knew these men wouldn't stay here much longer. They had anxious families waiting for them to get home. Benton had already canceled one flight to do this.

Burke sighed. He wanted to get home too. Home with Debbi by the Christmas tree. Home where they could put all this sadness behind them and get on with their lives. He dug his fingers into Debbi's shoulders.

"We've got to come up with something," he said, his voice rising. "We're running out of time. A killer is out there, and he's going to grab another woman, if he hasn't already. And when he does, she will die. Once he gets her, I don't think we'll find him. I think he'll disappear, disappear as suddenly as he appeared, like a, I don't know, like a Christmas light that burns out after one year and never lights up again. This guy is a one-year Advent wonder, a movement of hell into our world for this one season, and if we don't catch him this year, we never will, we never . . ." His voice trailed off, and he felt the tension fall out of his arms.

Debbi touched his forearm and twisted around to face him. He sighed and sat down beside her. "Let's take five," suggested Jackie. "I'll get us a soda." She stood and left the room. The four men whispered among themselves, trying to sort through the possibilities.

Debbi turned to Burke, her voice a whisper. "You really think this guy will stop after this year?"

His head lying on his arms on the table, Burke nodded. "I hadn't really thought about it until now, but I do. I think he'll stop after Christmas. He may start up again next year, but for some reason I don't think so. I think something jump-started him this year, something significant. Maybe a milestone in his life, like turning twenty-one or something, or maybe a parent died, or he's been in prison and just got out. But something happened to push him over the edge, and Christmas will culminate it. If we don't get him now, we may never—"

"Soda for everybody." Jackie stepped back into the cubicle, her arms loaded down with soft drinks. Everyone took one. They popped the tops and sucked down the cold liquid.

"Let's try this one more time," Jackie suggested. "If nothing jells, we'll just have to give it up and go home. Any new ideas?" She sipped from her soda and looked around the table, one face at a time.

Benton cleared his throat. "Somebody who works for one of them 'who's who' books," he said. "I had me one come about two years ago to do me up for the 'Who's Who in American Retailing.' I know it's pretty much a crock, but my ad man told me it didn't hurt. Cost me $79.95 for the book, but I got my name in there right along with Sam Walton's and that Gates guy who owns that computer company. Anybody else work with any of them?"

The other three shook their heads. Another dead end. "Anybody had their biography written yet?" asked Hal. "A sports writer for the *Cordele Gazette* asked me about one last year."

"They don't write biographies about car salesmen," said Benton, a slight grin on his wide face.

"They did Iacocca," teased Voss. "Maybe you've still got a chance."

For several seconds, silence fell again. The men swigged off their drinks. Debbi interrupted the quiet. "Okay, no biographies except Hal, but what about newspaper stories, magazine articles? All you guys have had stories written about you, I'm sure."

They nodded with one accord. "More than one in the past couple of years," said Staton.

"Me too," agreed Benton.

"Karl?" Debbi turned to Drexler.

"Certainly. Several smaller ones but one major deal in *Atlanta Life*. An article called 'Atlanta's Famous Faces: Keys to Their Success.' Published last summer. Fifty people listed there. Can't remember the gentlemen's name who wrote it, but I do recall he was a redheaded man. My woman would remember his name. If she were still breathing with us, she surely would."

"Hey, I was in that article too," interjected Voss. "A guy came out to the house. Spent about three hours with me. But he wasn't redheaded, he was gray. Silver gray, almost as silver as mine." He patted his hair. "I can't remember everything I told him, but I did give him a biographical sketch that included my educational stint at the seminary. But he didn't use any of the religious stuff in the article."

Debbi shifted her focus to Hal and Benton. Hal nodded. "I remember the article," he said. "But it wasn't a man who wrote the part on me. It was a woman. She talked to my agent, not to me. Rex told me he visited with her for several hours. I have no idea if he told her anything about my work in the church. It's possible though. Rex grew up with me in Cordele. He knew all about that time in my life."

All eyes turned to Benton. "I'm in the article," he nodded, his face turning red. "My ad man made sure of it. I'm on the back page of the spread. Not my first choice, but there I am, fat and sassy and pretty as you please. A man named Andrew something or other did my interview. Not a big man, if I recall. Sort of thin and well, rather girlylike, if you catch what I mean. But we talked about everything. Well, almost everything. I told him about my time as a preacher but not about, well, not about my backsliding and all. Didn't figure that needed to get sounded out in broad daylight."

Burke wiped his hands on the thighs of his pants. He leaned forward, his elbows on the table. "Something doesn't add up here," he said. "All of you were interviewed for one article. In the interview each of you, except Hal who doesn't know for sure what his agent said, talked about the one thing that ties you together. So the killer could have gotten the information from those interviews.

"It makes perfect sense. If a killer wanted to find a set of targets, a set of targets that matched a certain preconceived profile, a profile of ministry-connected people, then the job of a freelance writer fits perfectly. A writer could work for years picking out his victims. Could interview hundreds in the effort to find five—one for each Sunday of Advent, plus one for Christmas Day!"

"But someone different interviewed each of them," said Debbi.

"Yeah, that's the problem. Did different writers interview the rich and famous of Atlanta, then have someone else compile the facts into one story? That doesn't make any sense. Especially if it came out under one headline."

Burke paused, drummed his fingers on the table, and took a swallow of soda. The room felt warmer to him, and his head started to ache more and more. A band of tightness pressed in over his shoulders, and he closed his eyes for a few moments trying to stay calm. A thought hit him.

The last people seen with the dead women!

Leslie Staton, a gray-headed man. Rosey Benton, a blind man. Drexler—no one seen. Lisa Voss—a woman at the theater.

He jumped up from his chair. "Disguises," he exclaimed, pacing across the small space. "The killer used disguises. For the interviews and for the abductions. He—or she—used disguises. Changed hair color, clothes, you name it, changed appearances, made it seem like a different person each time. That way even if the cops figured out this angle, they couldn't get a handle on one person. We've got a master at work in this, someone with enough money and intelligence to plan it and carry it out over a long period of time." He stopped his pacing and faced Drexler. "You said it had fifty people in it."

"Yeah, more men than women if I recollect."

Burke turned to Jackie. "Can we check out the fifty?"

Jackie shook her head doubtfully. "We can try, but it's the day before Christmas. We're down to a slim crew around here. I doubt if we'll get too far."

"But you'll try?"

"I'll do my best." The room fell silent for a second. Then Burke spoke.

"Anybody remember the name of the byline on the article?" he asked.

"I do," said Benton. "Alex Herod."

"You mean Harold?" asked Burke, his voice a whisper.

"No, it was Herod. Believe me, a car salesman is good with names. It was Alex Herod."

Burke walked over to Debbi and stood beside her. He pressed the fingers of both hands into his temples. The ache in his head turned into a crunching throb, and the room seemed to swirl around on him. He wanted to turn and run, sprint out of the tiny cubicle that suddenly felt extremely hot, escape from the nightmare of death and grief that had reached out for him once again. For a moment, he thought about Debbi's safety. The phone call she had received at the newspaper was bad enough, but his appearance on television with Voss had brought him to the public's attention. Then the other phone call came to him.

Unwittingly, he and Debbi had apparently caught the killer's attention. As if cold, he involuntarily shivered.

A more comforting thought flashed through his mind. The killer had planned his moves out long in advance. He surely had his last victim already targeted. He and Debbi were safe.

Calmed, he turned back to the subject at hand. The writer who had interviewed each of the four men whose wives had died. Burke sucked in a draught of air and faced the group. "The name is Herod," he said simply, without fanfare. "That's the name of the king who tried to kill Jesus when he was a baby."

Chapter 64

Snow sat on the window ledge and stared out at the squirrels darting around on the ground below. A half-inch layer of white lay under the squirrels' feet. More white fell from the sky, the flakes the size of dimes. Snow lifted a paw and licked it.

"A white Christmas, Snow," said her owner, standing beside her at the window. "The desire of everyone's dreams." Snow licked her second paw and meowed as if approving the snow falling outside.

"I must get dressed."

Snow meowed again as her owner turned away from the window and stepped to the bed. A double-breasted houndstooth suit lay on the bed, and a pair of shining black shoes sat under it. Standing in front of the floor-length mirror by the bed in a pair of boxer shorts and a freshly starched white shirt, the slender frame shuddered slightly. Long hours had been spent thinking about this outfit, this disguise. Go as a man or as a woman?

No one would suspect a woman. But high heels might cause a problem if speed became necessary, and running in a skirt or dress was problematic too. It would have to be a man this time.

A well-dressed man as befit the occasion. A man dressed to fit in with everyone else in the ornate room. A man with dark black hair to match his striking black eyes.

Snow jumped up on the bed and stared up at her owner. The slender fingers touched the cat and rubbed it behind the ears. Right, time to get moving. In less than two hours, at the stroke of midnight, it would end if all went as planned.

The black eyes turned upward at the thought, and the thin lips crinkled into a smile. At the stroke of midnight—as Christmas Eve and Christmas Day merged. As everyone lit their silly candles and sang their silly traditional song. "Silent Night," they would sing, their voices lifted in noisy clamor.

Tonight the cowardly woman—the woman who knew but did nothing—would sing with the rest. But then she would fall silent, silent as the night.

All the plans were made. The weapon was already planted. Taped to the bottom of the outside aisle seat on the third row from the front. Taped there in advance in case the authorities played it safe and used metal detectors to check those who entered. They did that sometimes for famous people.

The thin lips grinned again. What a panic the four murders had created! Everyone was talking about them, and no one felt safe. No one, especially not the rich and famous.

It would make sense to screen the crowd that entered the building tonight. Scores of the glitterati would attend—women with pearls and emeralds around their throats and minks upon their shoulders and men with gold watches and rings that flashed diamonds. Business leaders, sports heroes, political figures—all would attend. See and be seen—that was the name of the game.

The slender fingers of the killer slipped the gold cuff links through the sleeves of the shirt and lifted the expensive jacket off the bed. After the jacket came the pants and shoes.

Finished with the pants and shoes, the black eyes stared into the mirror. Time for the last piece. "The cross, Snow. Time for the cross."

The slender fingers reached past the mirror to the black box lying on the bed. The box that held the silver cross. The fingers slipped the cross on. The cross the child had worn the day of entry into the preacher's house so long ago. The cross the child had ripped off the night the preacher visited and practiced his evil upon the bed.

Now it was time for the cross again. Time for the cross. The child would leave it lying across the body of the slain wife after the thrust of the knife. Yes, the thrust of the knife.

The plan called for arrival at least an hour early to guarantee getting the seat with the weapon under it. Then wait. Wait for the precise moment. The moment when the lights went down and the people lit their candles. In that moment the strike would come. A quick strike, as decisive as a cobra flash.

It should take no more than three seconds. Then flight. Strike then flight. Flight then finish. Finish back here. In the home of the best of the foster parents. Finish back here. Finish back here at the end of the Jesus Year.

Chapter 65

Kicking the wet snow off his shoes, Burke pushed open the door and led Debbi into the house. "I'll make coffee," said Debbi.

"Good, I'll get a fire going."

He flipped on the Christmas lights on the front of the house, then walked to the den. Within minutes, an orange blaze jumped up in the fireplace, and he sighed, turned on the lights to the Christmas tree, and settled down in his recliner. Weariness rolled through his bones, and he leaned the seat back. Goodness, what a day.

The meeting at Peachtree had broken up right after 11:30. Though none of them particularly wanted to do it, the group had no choice but to go their separate ways. Each of the men had a family demanding his presence, so the seven of them dispersed, each one heading to a different destination for Christmas.

Burke hated to see them leave. Without the four men and Jackie, he felt defeated, unable to do a thing about the death he was certain would come in the next few hours.

At Voss's request, he and Debbi had stayed with him through Lisa's funeral. Tons of people came, and Voss and all the rest moved like robots through it. What a day for a funeral. But no one wanted to postpone it until after Christmas. That was too long, too long to wait. Somehow, Voss and his family managed to survive the service. Afterward, they quickly left the graveside.

Staring into the fire, Burke breathed a heavy sigh. Jackie had had no luck with the other names from the magazine article. They had reached a dead end. He felt like crying. He hadn't known Lisa Voss, and he knew that she and Reginald had endured some hard times. But in spite of that, he had no doubt that Voss deeply grieved his wife's death.

And what about the other three? Over the next few days, they would sit by their Christmas fires and sing songs with their families and eat more than they should and try to appear happy. But inside their guts would twist into knots and their hearts would throb from squeezing back the pain and they would want to scream and tell the world to shut up the songs and stop the silly laughter. They would want the world to pause and suffer along with them.

But the men wouldn't scream out what they felt. They wouldn't because they wouldn't want to ruin everyone else's joy. So for the rest of their lives, the widowed four would live a lie, would push their way through tinsel and trees, would plaster a crooked smile on their faces, and would try not to spoil Christmas for the rest of the world.

But Christmas would forever be ruined for them.

"Here's your coffee."

Burke jerked out of his reverie then looked up at Debbi.

"Oh, yeah, thanks." He took the cup from her and sipped the hot liquid. "That's good," he said.

"Glad you approve. Sit and enjoy it a second. I'm going to change clothes, then be right back."

He nodded, slurped again, and leaned back, trying to relax. Resting the cup on the arm of the chair, he stared up toward the ceiling. His eyes wandered to his right, to the Christmas tree. For a brief second, he smiled.

His first tree with his own family. At home, his dad was probably doing exactly what he was doing—sitting by a fire, drinking coffee, and looking at the tree.

Burke's eyes scanned the tree from top to bottom. He and Debbi had picked it out and decorated it. He had wrestled to get it on the tree stand and keep it straight. At the moment, it seemed to lean slightly to the left.

He moved his eyes up the tree, one row of lights at a time. Several of the ornaments were new, given to him and Debbi as gifts to act as mementos of their first Christmas together. His eyes lingered over these special trinkets, thankful for the people who had remembered them this way.

He gazed upward on the tree, up to the top. His gaze landed on the star at the top. The family star. The star twinkled on and off, on and off, one blink, then two, then three. Burke's eyes felt heavy, sleepy. He felt the fingers on his coffee cup loosening. The star blinked again and again. His fingers loosened. The star blinked.

He jerked himself up, spilling coffee on the side of the chair. In a split second, his eyes jumped open and his mind moved into warp speed. The star!

Flipping down the footrest, he pulled out of the chair, set his coffee on the side table, and ran to the bedroom. "Debbi," he called. "Where's a scratch pad?"

"In here, I think, in the desk."

He hustled to the desk, sat down, and pulled the pad out of the drawer. Debbi moved beside him, placed her hands on his back, and peeped over his shoulder. "What's the deal?" she asked.

He held up a hand. "Hold on a second."

He placed four dots on the scratch pad. One in the southwest corner, one in the northwest corner, one directly opposite the second one, in the northeast corner, and the final one right down from the third one, in the southeast corner.

"The abduction sites?" asked Debbi.

"Exactly, the scenes where each of the women was last seen. Notice how they match each other, the northern ones directly across from each other and the same with the southern ones."

"Yeah, and the same with the west and east!" exclaimed Debbi. "They're like a big rectangular box! Why didn't we see that before?"

"Because the pattern didn't fit until we found Lisa's body. Since then I haven't really thought about it."

"Wonder if the cops have?"

"Don't know, but surely they've got them marked on a map somewhere."

"If they do, then they can see the pattern too. But what can they do with it? Knowing where the first four were taken doesn't tell them where the next one will disappear."

Burke held up an index finger. "Watch this," he said.

Beginning with the dot in the southwest corner, he drew a diagonal line across the page to the dot in the upper right of the paper. Next, he connected the other two in the same way.

"It's a big x," said Debbi. "But that's still not answering my question about the next one."

"One more step," said Burke, his voice low as if not wanting to divulge a secret. "Try this."

He placed a fifth dot on the paper. Drew it exactly in the middle of the two top dots, but above them—above them at the point where a triangle's top would intersect.

Moving the pen, he touched again the dot in the southwest corner. His hands trembling, he drew a line from the first dot to the one at the top, then down to the one on the bottom right, then up to the one in the top left, then across to the one on the top right, and finally down to the one on the bottom left again.

Finished, he stopped and stared at his work. For several long seconds, neither one spoke. Burke tapped the pen on the desk. Debbi reached for a strand of hair but dropped it to her cheek.

"What's your verdict?" asked Burke, his words barely audible.

"A star," mumbled Debbi, "A five-pointed star."

"This has to be it," said Burke, his voice rising with excitement. "It all fits. Christmas Eve. The fifth murder. The star of Bethlehem, the star that guided the wise men to the birthplace of Jesus."

"So the last abduction happens at the top of the star!"

"I'm sure of it. It's so plain when you finally see it. Everything else has fit a pattern. Deaths on a Sunday of Advent. The victims all wives of men with religious backgrounds. The wounds on the women matching the wounds of Jesus. The killer has it all mapped out for us."

"If we have eyes to see."

"Exactly, whoever this is has drawn it out for us. All we have to do is have wisdom enough to follow the star."

"At the top of the star we'll find the place of the next abduction. If we're not already too late."

Pushing out of his seat, Burke twisted to Debbi. "I'll get a map from the car, you get dressed." He headed toward the door, then paused and pivoted back to her. He took her by the hands. "Do you still have your gun?" he asked.

Debbi nodded gravely.

"You'd better get it."

He dropped her hands and ran from the room.

Chapter 66

A couple of sound and light technicians darted out and back across the platform in the front, checking their sound levels and light meters. A sea of red poinsettias sat in bunches up and down the steps and between the wing-backed chairs on the rostrum. High above the platform, up near the ceiling of the room, heavy green garlands decked the walls. Every ten feet a red ribbon brightened up the garlands.

Three rows in front of the stage area, a slender man in a gray houndstooth suit dropped into the aisle seat on the left-hand side of the auditorium. For a couple of seconds, the man leaned forward, reached under his seat and tugged hard. A tiny tearing sound broke the silence of the room, but the technicians didn't notice.

Rising up, the man shoved his hand into the inner pocket of his suit coat, then slipped it out, and patted his chest. Looking contented, he snuggled into his seat and stared down at the program in his lap. The service would start at eleven and conclude at midnight.

How wonderful. It would all end at midnight. The technicians would lower the lights, and the people would light their candles and lift their voices to sing their song. In that instant, he would strike.

He knew the woman would sit in the front row, in the second seat from the left, only two rows away from him. She sat there every time she came here with her husband. Their bodyguard, a woman, in this age of affirmative action, always sat in the row behind them.

The woman and her husband had come a long way from the white-stoned church in western North Carolina. He had dropped out of the ministry less than three years after he left the mountains. No one knew exactly why. Or if they knew, no one was telling.

Leaving the church hadn't diminished his gift for fancy words and smooth manners. Instead, over the years he polished those gifts, polished them until they glistened bright and beautiful. With those gifts as his best weapons, he had gone far in his chosen field, and many said they would carry him farther still.

The man with the black eyes smiled. He didn't think the woman's husband would go much further. Not after the diaries were read. The diaries kept so faithfully over the years. The diaries that detailed the transgressions of the man of fancy words and smooth manners. Those diaries would stop his march and destroy his reputation.

Within a week, the man would have a dead wife and a shattered life.

A dead wife and a shattered life. What a poet you are.

He quivered. His nose twitched. What anticipation! Within the hour it would happen. The quick strike and the rapid flight in the confusion that would follow.

Confusion would follow. He knew that for a fact. If the people of Atlanta thought the deaths of the first four women had created a stir, then they would go berserk at the death of the fifth one.

The man closed his black eyes and reveled in the feeling. It seemed as if a thousand ants crawled around on his arms and shoulders. What a wonderful sensation! So alive. More alive than ever since the night the innocence died.

Oh, what a feeling. The feeling of awaiting the final revenge. After all these years. The years of loneliness and quiet suffering. The years when it seemed that no one would ever avenge the degradation endured so long ago. But tonight the revenge would come.

The man's hand reached up to his coat pocket. He patted the weapon he carried there—the knife. A ten-inch, straight-edged blade bought in a shop in Jerusalem during a pilgrimage to the Holy Land three years ago.

That's when the plot first began to emerge. The year he turned thirty, on the trip to the Holy Land, on the pilgrimage to Bethlehem and Jerusalem, by the shores of the Jordan River, on the walk up the hill of Calvary.

Make them suffer—the women and the men who controlled them. Make God suffer. The God who supposedly created all of us and threw us into this cesspool of hatred and anger and death. The God who couldn't do anything to stop the death of Jesus and the God who couldn't do anything to stop the agony of an eleven-year-old in the arms of a fallen messenger.

The black eyes opened and stared up at the golden chandelier that hung suspended from the cathedral ceiling of the church.

Tonight God would stand by and watch the last woman die. Later, at home in his own bed, the killer would follow the woman in death and hope to ask God why.

Chapter 67

"Get off here!" yelled Debbi, snapping her eyes up from the map and pointing to the exit less than twenty feet away.

Instantly, Burke braked and whipped the Volvo across the empty lane on the right and up the exit ramp. For a moment, his wheels spun in the snow and the car fishtailed in the back. Almost three inches of the white powder lay on the highway.

"Turn left over the bridge," said Debbi. "We're almost there."

Making the turn, Burke craned his neck and stared into the falling flakes. It had taken them almost forty-five minutes to drive across town. They had tried to reach Jackie Broadus by car phone, but the dispatcher at Peachtree told them she wasn't there. Leaving a message for her to call back, they tried her apartment also but received no answer.

Burke glanced down at the clock on the dashboard. 11:25. "It's got to be the place," he said. "Don't you think?"

"If we're right about the star, then it has to be," agreed Debbi. "It's right in the center of the two dots, at the peak of the triangle. The intersection of Robertson and Quincy."

Burke gunned the engine and sped past two cars. A hundred yards up, he made a right. For almost a mile, he hit no more traffic. The street was deserted. At a red light, he made another right and saw a packed parking lot dead ahead.

"Looks like a big crowd," he said.

"I would expect so," said Debbi. "The midnight Christmas Eve Service at St. John's Cathedral always pulls them in."

Burke knew of the church—one of Atlanta's wealthiest. An interdenominational congregation primarily made up of the conservative suburban elite. Liturgical in worship style and ornate in decor. A congregation for the moneyed types of Atlanta.

A man in an orange vest suddenly appeared in the glare of the

Volvo's headlights. Burke slowed to a stop and rolled down the window.

"You here for the service?" the man asked, his voice chattering in the cold.

"Yeah," said Burke.

"You're late, you know."

The words hit Burke with a deeper meaning and he hung his head, feeling guilty and hoping the man was wrong. "Yes, sir," he said, "we know, but we couldn't get here any earlier. Where can we park?"

The attendant grunted, then pointed to his left. "Over there, a couple of empty spots by the dumpster."

Burke rolled up the window and darted into the lot. As he parked, the phone buzzed. He grabbed it quickly.

"Burke, it's Jackie."

"Yeah, thank goodness you called," he said, relieved to hear her voice. "I don't have time to explain it all now, but I'm at St. John's Cathedral at Robertson and Quincy. You need to get over here. I think the last abduction will happen here."

"It'll take me at least thirty minutes," said Jackie.

"Then get moving."

"Right, I'm on the way."

Thankful that Jackie hadn't badgered him for details, he locked the car doors and hustled with Debbi to church.

In the vestibule, a man in a navy blue suit with a red carnation in the lapel handed them a worship program and a white candle and whispered, "I think there's a couple of seats in the balcony. That's the best we can do."

Noting the man's calm demeanor, Burke exhaled the breath he'd been holding since leaving his house. Nothing seemed amiss in the church. "That'll be great," he said.

The usher led them upstairs, showing them to two seats by the left side exit, almost on the back row. Though far from the platform, they had a good view. Burke sighed, grateful he could see the whole sanctuary—above and below.

For a couple of minutes, he scanned the crowd, trying to see somebody he recognized, some celebrity who fit the MO the killer had targeted. But he didn't see one. Though everyone in the congregation appeared wealthy, no face jumped out at him as a public figure.

For a split second, he relaxed and turned to Debbi. "Maybe we're wrong," he said. "Maybe it's already run its course."

Debbi shrugged. "We'll know soon," she said.

Burke nodded and looked down at the front page of his program.

"Candles, Carols, and Communion," read the heading. On the rostrum a choir of at least a hundred voices began to sing. In spite of the tension that gripped his shoulders like steel cords, Burke found himself listening to their peaceful song.

"What child is this who laid to rest, on Mary's lap is sleeping, whom angels greet and shepherds keep . . ."

Hearing the song, Burke tried to settle himself down. As the choir continued to sing, a crew of men—all of them in navy suits and red carnations—moved to the altar of the cathedral. One by one the men lifted silver trays off the communion table and moved out into the congregation. To his left, Burke spotted two of the men move up the stairs toward him and Debbi.

He glanced at his watch. 11:35. They had missed the sermon. The sharing of Communion had begun.

The choir finished their anthem. A man in navy passed him a silver plate. He took a thin wafer from it and passed the plate to Debbi. She lifted a wafer from the tray and handed it down the aisle.

Within five minutes, everyone in the building had taken one of the wafers, and the men in navy had moved back to the front of the congregation and served each other. Now everyone held the bread in their hands as Burke did, waiting for a minister to cue them to eat it.

On the platform, a rotund man in a black robe stood and swished his way to the pulpit. In a formal voice, he intoned, "Jesus said, 'This is my body broken for you. In as much as you do this, do this in remembrance of me.'"

Burke lifted the wafer to his lips and laid it on his tongue. For a moment, he thought only of the Lord Jesus, of the price the Lord paid, of the life Jesus sacrificed for the sins of the world. Turning to Debbi, he grabbed her hand and squeezed it. Her green eyes sparkled under the soft lighting in the cathedral.

Another robed man moved to the microphone and began to read scripture. "'Surely he took up our infirmities and carried our sorrows, yet we considered him stricken by God, smitten by him and afflicted. But he was pierced for our transgressions, he was crushed for our iniquities; the punishment that brought us peace was upon him, and by his wounds we are healed. We all, like sheep . . .'"

As the minister read, the platoon of navy soldiers fanned out from the Communion table again, this time carrying silver trays filled with plastic vials. Red juice—the symbol of the shed blood of Jesus—filled the plastic vials.

Burke and Debbi each lifted a vial from the tray as it passed them. They held the vials silently as the servers walked back to the front and as the rector moved to the pulpit. With calm dignity the minister proclaimed, "Jesus said, 'This is my blood given for many for the remission of their sins. In as much as you do this, do it unto me.'"

The rector lifted his vial to his lips and the congregation followed suit. Burke savored the warm liquid, letting it sit on his tongue for a moment as he contemplated what it meant. The rector began to pray, but Burke didn't close his eyes. Instead, he swept them across the crowd, hoping against hope and praying from the bottom of his heart that he would see something to tip him off, something to give him some clue as to what to do next, who to try to protect.

From all he knew, a beast sat somewhere in this room—a beast who had slain four women. A beast as evil as anyone who had ever lived—as evil as Jack the Ripper or Adolf Hitler or Jeffrey Dahmer. A beast so evil that he cared nothing for life and nothing for God.

Burke gritted his teeth and looked down at his hands. They were clenched into fists. As he stared at his fists, the irony of it all suddenly hit him. There he sat, at the Lord's Table, the place of forgiveness, and he felt nothing but rage at the evil of the Advent killer.

He sighed and told himself to let his anger go. God could forgive the worst kind of evil. God could forgive anything so long as the person repented and cast himself into the merciful arms of Jesus.

A pair of tears crawled to the edge of Burke's eyes. He knew he wouldn't forgive such evil. If he had his way, he'd wreak the worst kind of vengeance upon people who murdered and maimed and raped. He'd show them no mercy, no grace, give them no chance of redemption. They should suffer as those they killed surely suffered.

He wiped away the tears and thought of the irony of it. He who had no right to judge and condemn wanted to do both. But God who had every right to judge and condemn wanted to give up that right. God wanted to forgive, God wanted to wash away the evil in an ocean of abundant grace.

The rector concluded his prayer and interrupted Burke's musings.

Debbi pointed to her watch. 11:56. They both leaned forward, searching the faces below them on the first floor. On the platform, the rotund rector moved to a large white candle that sat in the center of the Communion altar.

"The Christ Candle," whispered Burke. The minister stopped by the candle and faced the congregation.

"We are so fortunate to have members of our church who embrace the Christian faith and are leaders of our community," he began. "Men and women who aren't ashamed of the gospel of our Lord. Tonight, as we do each year, we want one of our own to light the Christ Candle, to show each of us an example of a Christian witness in a largely secular world."

The rector pivoted a quarter turn to his right. With an ease that showed his comfort in situations like this, a distinguished man with slightly graying hair stood from his seat on the front row, walked to the rector, shook his hand, and faced the congregation.

From his vantage point, Burke didn't recognize the man.

The rector said, "The good governor of the state of Georgia will now light the first candle."

The muscles in Burke's neck squeezed together. The governor! Edward Robert Stapleton! Of course—it had to be! Stunned by the realization and not sure what to do next, Burke froze for several seconds.

The governor lit his candle from the Christ Candle and moved to the navy-suited ushers who stood in a straight line across the front of the congregation. From overhead, the lights in the sanctuary began to dim.

"Christ is the light of the world," said the rector. The governor lit the candles of the ushers from his candle, and the men fanned out to the congregation, holding out their candles for the people to use to light theirs.

A woman in a robe the color of gold moved to a lectern on the side and motioned for the congregation to stand.

Following her instruction, Burke stood and turned to Debbi. The choir minister began to sing, "Away in a manger, no crib for a bed . . ." The congregation took its cue and joined in the chorus.

Burke grabbed Debbi by the hand. "His wife," he whispered. "Where's the governor's wife?"

The lights overhead dropped lower. More candles began to burn as the light moved in rows from one person to another.

Burke stared down to the front row of the church, to the seats around the governor, trying to pick out his wife.

He saw her—Mrs. Melissa Stapleton. The dark-headed woman in the front row dressed in a Christmas red maternity suit.

The choir minister changed the song. "O little town of Bethlehem . . ." The congregation sang along. The lights from the candles spread. The lights in the sanctuary dropped still lower.

The realization hit Burke like a meteor from heaven. The governor's wife was pregnant and due on Christmas Day!

Chapter 68

Three rows from the front, in the seat by the aisle, a slender hand reached inside a houndstooth double-breasted suit coat and pulled out a ten-inch, straight-edged knife. For a brief second, the bright silver blade flickered in the dimming lights.

Dropping the knife to his side and holding it close to his leg, the man eased from his seat and walked quietly but urgently down the aisle.

⁂

In the balcony above, Burke saw something flash in the glare of the falling lights. Quickly, he focused on the origin of the light, hoping something would seem out of place. All he could see were men moving through the aisles, lighting candles as they walked. In a panic he grabbed Debbi's arm. "Something's going to happen," he said breathlessly. "Down there."

Debbi's eyes moved with his. "I don't see anything," she said.

Burke watched the scene below. Nothing seemed amiss. A line of navy-suited men with red carnations in their lapels were moving through the cathedral, lighting candles as they walked. Nothing more wonderful and beautiful than that.

He stared down at the men, to the left side of the congregation, to the row where the light had flashed.

The music minister changed the congregation to a new song. "It came upon a midnight clear, that glorious song of . . ."

Burke saw it. A man walking to the front. A man in a gray suit, not a navy one. The man had no carnation in his lapel!

Immediately, he pointed to the man and whispered loudly to Debbi. "He's wrong!" he said. "He doesn't fit!"

He and Debbi moved simultaneously—rushing into the aisle and bounding down the steps two at a time. "Get to the car," he said to

Debbi, his voice loud with panic. "Call Jackie again. Tell her we can't wait on her. Get a local unit over here."

For an instant, Debbi opened her mouth as if to argue, but Burke raised his hand to stop her. "Do it, Debbi—two lives depend on it."

The man's jaw was set and his eyes were focused. Only one row stood between him and her—between him and the woman who knew but did nothing. The woman who couldn't have children for all these years, but who was now, thanks to the miracle of modern drugs, expecting. The woman who didn't deserve children, especially not a Christmas baby.

The man bit his lower lip, and a drop of blood broke out on it. If he acted quickly, the bodyguard wouldn't have time to act. One sharp thrust would do it.

The governor's wife would not bear the child she carried so proudly. She would not bring another child into the house of the man with the gift for fancy talk, would not get the opportunity to stand by and let that man abuse still one more young one.

The blade of the knife would see to that. One thrust would do it. A thrust like the spear thrust into the side of Jesus.

For the sake of the child, it had to be done.

The man stepped around the last row between him and the front and moved confidently toward the woman in the red maternity suit.

The music minister changed the song again. "Silent night, holy night, all is calm, all is bright . . ." The overhead lights were almost completely dark now, the sanctuary lit only by the flickering of the burning candles in the hands of the congregation. The candlelight danced in shifting shadows along the walls of the cathedral.

As one body, the people lifted their candles into the air above their heads, a sign of their desire to live as lights for Christ.

Two steps from the governor's wife, the man in the houndstooth suit lifted his knife up from his thigh.

Halfway down the aisle on the first floor, Burke spotted the man's hand as it raised the knife into the air. In the light of two thousand candles, the blade glinted—a bizarre symbol of evil slashing through the holy moment.

In a dead sprint to the front, Burke screamed. "Look out," he yelled, his voice notched as high as he could get it. To his chagrin, he realized he had surely yelled too late.

With the knife above his head, the man in the houndstooth suit heard the scream. He watched with glee as the governor's bodyguard twisted her head to see about the commotion.

Wonderful. A diversion would make it all even easier.

The man's black eyes focused on Mrs. Stapleton. He saw her blink in confusion as she heard the scream and then spotted the knife. For a second, her face froze in disbelief.

The ten-inch knife plunged downward, downward toward the woman who knew but did nothing.

In the beat of a heart, the woman reacted to avoid the knife. Wrapping her arms protectively around her waist, she threw herself off the pew and onto the floor. But she couldn't escape the knife.

The knife slipped through her arms and bit into the red material of her maternity suit as she fell. She shrieked in pain, and blood spurted from her side, instantly drenching her clothing near her left hip.

The man lifted the knife for another thrust.

Mrs. Stapleton's shriek pierced the air just as the congregation finished the last refrain of "Silent Night." In the split second of quiet at the end of the song, the unearthly sound of her scream carried like a mournful echo through the crowd, and the people reacted. As if one body with two thousand heads, the worshipers turned in all directions at once, around and around, trying to determine the origin of the sound and what, if anything, they should do. Many of them tried to keep singing, as if the words of a song would somehow put everything back into place.

From the back, a loud voice roared, "He's got a knife," and a score of people rushed toward the exits, a herd of stampeding humanity, getting themselves out of harm's way. The singing broke down completely, and an elderly woman in a black hat near the front passed out and collapsed to the floor. The line of people heading to the exits became a wave—a wave crashing again and again, one over another, with every person desperate to flee whatever it was that had disrupted their worship.

Ignoring the panic, Burke pushed his way to the front. In the surge of the crowd, he lost sight of Mrs. Stapleton. For an instant, he wondered if she had escaped already, if she had sprinted out of the carnage, out of danger. But he knew he couldn't take that chance, couldn't stop now, no matter what happened in the next few minutes.

Elbowing past one of the navy-suited ushers, he rushed to the first pew. The sound of the rector's voice, aided by the microphone, broke through the chaos, urging everyone to stay calm. No one listened. Burke jumped over a man who had fallen down in his flight to the exit.

At the front row now, he searched the pew, looking for Mrs. Stapleton. He saw the man in the houndstooth suit. A knife raised up in the man's hand. The man thrust it downward.

In a headlong leap, Burke threw himself at the knife. Halfway there, someone grabbed his legs from behind. He threw out his arm and blocked the knife on its downward path. The knife slashed into his wrist and raked a bloody swath across it. The man wielding the knife focused a black-eyed glare on Burke. Burke's skin crawled as he saw the black eyes staring at him.

A sharp blow cracked across his shoulders, and Burke pivoted quickly to face his attacker. A bulky woman stood behind him, her face contorted in anger, her fist raised to strike him a second time. Confused as to why the woman would strike him, Burke paused momentarily. In that instant of hesitation, the woman smashed her hand into his nose.

Rolling with the punch, Burke fell to the floor. *A bodyguard!* he thought. The woman who hit him had to be a bodyguard.

Knowing he didn't have time to explain who he was, he twisted away and crawled under the pew. On the ground, he saw a stream of blood and thought of his wrist. In a heartbeat, though, he knew the blood wasn't his. It was Mrs. Stapleton's. The blood trailed away from him like a twisting stream. With his eyes, he followed the trail as it snaked under the pew. At the end of the stream he saw Mrs. Stapleton lying in a pool of red.

Reacting on instinct, Burke threw his body over Mrs. Stapleton, trying to protect her from the knife thrust he expected at any moment.

Above him, the raucous sounds of a frenzied crowd rolled across the sanctuary. For a millisecond, he bunched the muscles in his back, waiting for the knife to strike. But it didn't. He turned away from Mrs. Stapleton and jerked his head out from under the pew, his eyes darting side to side, looking for the man in the houndstooth suit. He didn't see him. The man had disappeared.

Not more than two feet away, a brown high heel raised off the ground and kicked at him from the side. The governor's bodyguard again—protecting Mrs. Stapleton, thinking he was trying to hurt her.

Still unable to waste time explaining, Burke grabbed the bodyguard's foot and jerked it forward, throwing the heavy woman to the floor. Pouncing on top of her, he shouted in her face, "Call an ambulance. Now!"

Before she could respond, he pushed up, rushed to the exit by the right side of the sanctuary, and sprinted out. In the hallway, he took a deep breath and jumped onto a chair by the wall so he could see over the rushing crowd.

Craning his neck, he twisted in all directions, searching for the man, knowing the killer had only a few seconds' lead on him. Instinctively, Burke sensed that he had to catch him tonight or the man would disappear. He would run and run and run. He would run and run until he disappeared into the dark of a snowy Atlanta night. If he didn't stop the killer tonight, he might move to another city, start his work there, slay more and more women before anyone could stop him.

Not seeing him, Burke leaped from the chair and sprinted toward the door that led out of the building. Somewhere beyond that door, the killer was running.

Chapter 69

Dropping into step behind a troupe of dazed people, the man in the houndstooth suit buttoned his coat against the cold of the blowing snow, sucked in a deep breath, and slowed his pace to match everyone else's. *Mix in with the crowd,* he told himself. *Don't do anything to stand out. Slow it all down, walk to your car, and drive it home.*

He swallowed hard and thought back over the last few minutes. He knew for a fact he had stabbed her twice—two sharp thrusts into her heavy body.

The group in front of him turned away toward their cars. Not liking the isolation, he sped up his pace. Another hundred yards and he would reach his vehicle. He had deliberately parked on the outer edges of the crowd, so he wouldn't get caught up in traffic.

He touched the knife in his breast pocket. He didn't know if he'd killed her or not. He hadn't had enough time to make sure. The man who attacked him prevented him from delivering the final blow.

Breathing heavily, he bit his lower lip. He didn't know the man who had attacked him. But he knew from the moment they locked eyes that the man knew him.

Turning left past a street lamp, he moved toward the farthest parking lot. A parking attendant in an orange vest at the corner yelled to him. "What happened in there?"

Still moving, he called back. "Somebody attacked the governor's wife. Everybody panicked."

"She okay?"

"Don't know."

Leaving the attendant behind, he skipped ahead. Only fifty yards to his vehicle. Snowflakes fell on his head and he looked up to the sky. Who was that guy in the cathedral?

In a sudden dawning, he knew the answer. Burke Anderson! The guy from television. He remembered the face now. *So, he figured it out.* Quite remarkable—wondrous really.

He turned the corner and eased toward the dumpsters where he had parked his Jeep. Approaching from the back, he spotted a blonde-headed woman walking toward him with a portable phone in her hand.

⫸

Exiting the building, Burke could think of only one thing to do. Get to his car phone. With only one main road leading from the church to the interstate, he would call the police and tell them to set a road-block. The cops could check every car that passed. They could find the man before he faded back into the anonymity of a city of three million.

Hustling past a stream of animated people, Burke sprinted across the street and jumped across some hedges. If he had it figured correctly, the killer wouldn't move as fast as he did. The killer would try to blend in with the crowd, make his escape under the cover of normality, not draw attention to himself. If so, that gave him a chance to get to Debbi and the car, call the police, and cordon off the area before the killer disappeared.

⫸

A hundred yards away from Burke, Debbi lifted her eyes from the phone and saw a man approaching her. She nodded to him and started to speak. He raised a hand to wave. Staring at the man, she recognized the houndstooth suit.

Before she could stop herself, Debbi paused and lowered the phone to her side. She thought of the gun Burke had reminded her to bring. It lay under the seat of the car.

She saw the man's eyes widen. She wondered if he'd noticed her hesitation. She decided to bluff her way past him, go back toward the cathedral. He had no reason to bother with her. If he wanted to make his escape, he would surely leave her alone.

She walked straight up the sidewalk toward the man. She came parallel to him. Okay, a couple more steps and she could run. One step, two—

She never took the second step. The man pivoted like a gymnast and grabbed her by the throat.

Debbi felt a knife blade against her flesh. "Move quickly and quietly," said the man. "Do that and all will be well."

She screamed. The cry cut through the falling snow like a surgical laser beam through human flesh. The man behind her chopped her across the back of the throat, and Debbi crumpled into his arms.

>>>

Burke heard the scream and knew instantly it was Debbi. With the force of a thousand volts of electricity, he sprinted toward the Volvo. Pushing past a clump of stragglers, he slipped on the ice and fell down. Within a second, he jerked back to his feet.

It didn't take him long to reach the dumpster by his car. Glancing past it, he saw the Volvo still in place. He scanned the parking lot quickly, but saw no one. He heard a beeping sound and dropped his gaze to the snow under his feet. He saw a car phone and bent to pick it up.

From behind, he heard an engine start. He twisted toward the sound and saw a Jeep spin across the snow and into the street.

Rushing to the Volvo, he shoved the keys into the ignition, gunned the motor, backed up, and screeched out of the parking lot. Ahead he saw the taillights of the Jeep.

Peering through the falling snow, he saw the back of a man's head but couldn't tell what the man looked like and couldn't see if Debbi were in the vehicle or not. For all Burke knew, this might be any one of the two thousand spooked worshipers who had poured out of St. John's Cathedral.

The Jeep approached a stop sign, but the driver didn't slow down. Instead he leaned the car to the left, then swerved sharply to the right, the vehicle almost leaving the ground as it made the turn.

Behind him, Burke speeded up. That kind of driving meant he had followed the right man.

>>>

Ten miles away, Jackie Broadus punched her car phone and called the dispatcher at Peachtree Precinct. "Get me backup at St. John's Cathedral," she said. "I got a call a couple of minutes ago. The governor's in danger. I'm on my way."

Jackie plowed her foot against the accelerator. She'd planned to go to Albany tomorrow to see her mother for Christmas. That might have to wait.

>>>

Hurtling through a red light, Burke glanced at his speedometer. Eighty-five and climbing on an icy highway. He kept focused on the taillights of the Jeep ahead. No matter how fast he had to drive, he wouldn't let the man get away. Debbi was in that car, and if he had to follow the Jeep to hell and back, he would do it.

The Jeep dodged past a slow-moving pickup, and Burke followed suit. Sliding back into his lane, Burke felt a surge of anger, and he thought of Debbi's gun under the seat. Sweat broke out in the palm of his hands and a sense of resolve seized him.

The guy in the Jeep had gone far enough—four women already dead and one maybe dying at St. John's. A sixth one—Debbi—probably unconscious in the Jeep.

Gritting his teeth, Burke leaned forward and reached underneath the seat, grabbing for Debbi's gun. It was time for it all to end, and God help him, if he had to end it with a gun, he would.

He couldn't reach the gun. He tried again, pushing his hand as far back as he could along the floorboard. The Volvo hit a patch of ice and swerved sideways. Burke jerked the wheel to the right and straightened up in his seat.

Not wanting to take a chance on wrecking, he decided to leave the gun alone. When he needed it, he would get it.

Flooring the accelerator, he edged up closer to the Jeep. Only twenty yards separated the two vehicles now. Burke's breath came in quick gasps. Only another mile to the interstate.

He didn't want the chase to go that far. He had to stop the man here on this relatively quiet road before he got on a main thoroughfare. Too much danger of an accident there. An accident that would kill Debbi or himself or someone else. If not an accident, too much danger of an escape. Lots of cars on the loop, even on Christmas Eve. If the killer managed to get mixed in with those cars, it would open too many avenues for him to get lost.

To Burke's surprise, the taillights ahead suddenly blinked as the driver hit the brakes. What was he doing?

The brake lights blinked again, and the man swerved to the right, careening off the road and into a grocery store parking lot. Though momentarily confused, Burke twisted the wheel to follow. Speeding through the parking lot, the Jeep bounced over a speed bump and plowed over a curb.

Burke gave chase. Okay, the guy didn't want to get on the interstate. Maybe a smart choice. Too many cops on the interstate.

The taillights ahead of him jerked to the left, out of the parking lot and onto a residential street. Burke stayed in feverish pursuit. Out of the corner of his eye, he caught glimpses of decorated Christmas trees in the windows of the passing houses and bright lights blinking from the porches.

Suddenly, the Jeep braked and shot to the left. Burke darted his eyes to the right to see what caused the shift in direction. To his horror, he spotted a tiny child, a girl in a pink outfit standing on the edge of the street. The child had a snowball in her hand.

Burke also jerked his wheel to the left to miss the girl. The Volvo careened wildly, the tires on the right almost leaving the ground and the front of the car sliding out of control. The left front tire bounced against the curb and Burke's head pounded forward and popped into the windshield.

Momentarily stunned, he heard a crash and thought for a second he had wrecked. But then he saw his headlights straighten out and his tire scrape the curb.

The sound of another crash pulled his attention to the left. Braking for a split second, he spotted the taillights of the Jeep. The vehicle had jumped the curb, plowed through a row of garbage cans sitting on the sidewalk, and rolled into the yard of a nearby home.

Without blinking, Burke wheeled to his left, bounced the Volvo over the curb, and moved into the yard behind the Jeep.

He watched the Jeep run through the snow-covered grass for almost twenty feet and swerve violently to the right to miss a tree. The left wheels of the Jeep left the ground as it swerved, and the vehicle rolled onto its right side and skidded almost thirty more feet before it bumped one more time and came to a thudding halt right next to a two-story house.

Braking hard, Burke brought the Volvo to a screeching stop. Jumping from the car, he sprinted toward the Jeep. A stiff wind cut across his face, and snowflakes the size of quarters dropped onto his shoulders.

Standing by the overturned vehicle, he peered frantically through the windshield, searching for Debbi inside. He didn't see her. He moved to the back of the Jeep, his eyes darting left to right, hoping against hope that he would spot her any second. He didn't. Debbi wasn't in the Jeep.

Panic gripped at his throat, and the anger he'd tried to keep banked up inside his gut tore through him like a river flooded out of its banks. If Debbi were hurt, he would personally tear the heart out of the guy who harmed her.

He heard movement from the front of the car near the house. He stared toward the house, trying to see through the snow. A bright floodlight from the side of the building threw a glare into the swirling white and made vision impossible.

A breathy voice floated through the snow.

"Burke Anderson."

Burke froze in place. The voice sounded close, not more than fifteen feet away, just past the glare of the floodlight on the house. If he shot into the glare of the light—

It suddenly hit him—he had left the gun in the car. For a second he wanted to curse himself, but then he realized that wouldn't help anything. Breathing deeply to calm his emotions, he peered through the floodlight, trying to see the face of the Advent killer. Without a gun, Burke prayed a quick prayer, asking God to give him something to use, a word, a weapon—anything to stop this man who had his wife. His pounding heart slowed a beat or two, enabling him to think.

"I'm Burke Anderson," he said, struggling to control his fears.

"I'm here for you." The man stepped to the left, out of the worst of the floodlight's glare. In front of him stood Debbi. The man held his left hand around Debbi's throat. In the right hand, he held a knife.

For an instant, Burke almost charged the man, almost rushed him to tear the knife from his hands, to tear it away from the hands that threatened his wife. But then he came to his senses. The knife would cut through Debbi's throat long before he reached her.

"Are you okay?" Burke asked Debbi, his voice soft.

She meekly lifted her hand and waved it. "I'm okay," she said.

Burke turned his attention back to her abductor. He wasn't more than five nine or so. His features were delicate, his body slender. Burke remembered his disguises, the appearances as a woman. He wondered if it really were a man standing across from him, holding his wife in the middle of a falling snow.

The breathy voice interrupted his thoughts. "It's ironic, don't you think?"

Burke took a deep breath, trying to decide how to play this. "How so?" he asked.

"Well, look at this." The man gestured with his knife hand at the scene around them.

Burke glanced quickly around. Behind Debbi and her abductor, Burke spotted a toppled Madonna. To the left lay a broken Joseph—a wooden head snapped from the rest of the two-foot-high body. To his right, just past the car near the house, Burke saw a manger with a baby Jesus lying in it.

The Jeep had crashed into a nativity scene.

Burke nodded. "I see what you mean. Ironic indeed."

"So what do we do now?"

"You're the one with the knife. You tell me."

"I could kill your wife. She would make five, even if the good governor's wife doesn't die."

"What would that accomplish?" asked Burke, keeping his rage at bay, trying to buy time, hoping that someone was at home inside the house, hoping that they had already called the police.

The man laughed heartily. "Oh, it wouldn't accomplish anything, at least not what I wanted to accomplish."

"And what was that? What did you want to accomplish?"

"Surely you know."

"I have a theory."

"Tell me, please."

Burke rubbed his hands on the sides of his pants. He knew this was his only chance. He had to keep the killer talking, talking until someone reported the wild chase through the streets, until Jackie could find him here with the killer.

"In one sense, I think it's pretty simple. You're angry, angry at God, angry at something you think God did to you or at something you think God should have done but didn't. Your anger causes you to strike out, to punish, to cause others to feel the pain you've felt."

"You think I'm angry at God?"

"Aren't you? Isn't that what this is all about? The killings with the wounds of Jesus. The killing of Mrs. Stapleton, a woman expecting a child on Christmas day. By killing these women, by killing Mrs. Stapleton, you're trying to appease your own anger, alleviate your own pain."

"You think I've felt pain?"

"I have no doubt of it. You've suffered great pain."

The hand holding the knife began to quiver. Burke stepped closer to the man. "Hold it there," said the man. "Come no closer."

"You can get help for your pain," said Burke.

"I am my own help." The hand lifted the knife higher. "I alone can avenge the loss I've suffered." The wind picked up and the snow started to swirl heavier and the breathy voice rose higher over the wind. "I alone can do what God refused to do. I alone can punish the evil and stop the man who destroyed the child." The man was shrieking now, and the knife in his hand was poised over his head like a guillotine about to fall.

Watching him, Burke knew the time for talk had ended. No one was coming to bail him out of this. He had to do it himself, he had to stop the man from jerking the knife through the falling snow and plunging it into Debbi's soft flesh. He lifted his eyes to heaven and raised his arms against the snow and prayed that God almighty would deliver a weapon into his hands—that God would give him what he needed to slay this man who deserved nothing better than death.

"It is time!" yelled the breathy voice.

Burke dropped his eyes from the sky and scanned the ground frantically, looking for a weapon—

"The Advent has come!" yelled the man.

A stick, a rock—anything he could use against the killer.

"This is the Jesus Year!"

Burke dropped himself into a crouch and barreled across the ground toward the killer, praying with every step that he would cover the fifteen feet in time.

The man jerked the knife down through the night, and it swished through the snow, cutting it asunder.

Burke heard the snap of a pistol shot from off to his right, and he jerked his eyes in that direction for a millisecond to see what was happening. The glare of the floodlight washed out his vision. Avoiding the blinding light, he dropped his head and plunged forward again, grabbing the wooden figure of Jesus off the ground as he ran.

Another shot fired, and he heard a woman's scream. Burke jerked his head up just in time to see Debbi collapse to the ground.

The man had disappeared.

Burke roared his anger as he covered the last two feet separating himself from Debbi. His roar pierced the snow like a wounded lion, and he threw himself on the ground beside her.

Debbi raised her head. "Get him, Burke," she shouted. "I'm cut, but I'm okay. Don't let him escape."

Though he wanted to stay with her more than anything else he'd ever wanted in his life, Burke sprinted past Debbi and through the front yard. Passing the floodlight that had kept him so blinded, he stared down at the ground by the side of the house and spotted a heavy splotch of dark stain. Bending closer, he touched it. It felt warm. He held his finger up to the light. It was blood.

Following the path of blood, he rushed into the backyard and around a screened-in back porch. Twenty feet past the porch, he saw a detached garage. One of the garage doors was open. The blood led like a sticky arrow into the darkness of the opening.

For a moment, Burke considered waiting for help. But then the sight of Debbi lying on the ground flashed into his mind, and he ground his teeth together. The man in the houndstooth suit had hurt his wife! He wouldn't wait, wouldn't give him an opportunity to escape. He would bring this to an end now, this minute. He would wreak his own revenge on this murderer!

Throwing caution to the wind, he rushed to the garage. At the door, he paused briefly and peered inside. Seeing nothing, he pushed his way through the open door. Immediately, he felt something grab for him.

Burke twisted to his right. The man stood in the shadows behind the door. He held a knife in his hand. The man jerked the knife over his head and lunged toward Burke. Burke quickly stepped to the side, avoiding the sharp blade.

The man plunged forward, the fury of his knife thrust throwing him off balance. As he fell, Burke lifted the baby Jesus and—with every ounce of rage-fueled energy in his body—smashed it into the back of the man's skull.

The killer collapsed to the snow in a heap, and a spurt of blood spouted out of his neck and puddled like strawberry juice upon the glistening white that lay like a cold cushion under his face.

His whole body shaking with fury and fear, Burke crouched beside the fallen man. The body didn't move. Burke reached for a wrist, tested for a pulse. He felt a weak throb, but the killer was unconscious and offered no more threat.

From behind, he heard rushing footsteps. He turned quickly, brandishing the wooden statue of Jesus as a weapon. Jackie Broadus sprinted to his side, her gun drawn.

Burke held up his hand, palm outward, stopping her charge. "It's over," he said, his voice shaky.

Still holding her pistol, Jackie pulled a flashlight from her coat pocket, leaned over, and flashed the beam at the figure in the snow.

"Did I hit him?" she asked, her words pushed together quickly.

Staring at the gaping wound in the man's throat, Burke nodded. "That you did."

"I was on the way to the church," she said, her voice rushed with adrenaline. "The dispatcher called—said someone almost ran over a little girl. The family had called in—I knew it had to be you. I got here just as you charged him, as he raised the knife. I shot at him, missed the first time. He stabbed Debbi; I hit him with the second shot. That's when he—"

Burke heard footsteps again, and he and Jackie turned simultaneously and saw Debbi, holding her left arm to her body, walk around the house. He jumped up immediately and ran to her, his hands extended. She fell into his arms.

Though careful of the wound in her shoulder, he hugged her as if he would never let her go. A groan sliced through the snow. Burke pivoted back to Jackie.

"Burke, he's coming to!" yelled Jackie.

With Debbi in tow, Burke hustled to Jackie and squatted down over the killer. Jackie kept her gun and flashlight trained on him. His gray suit coat was open, pulled back from his body. Blood caked his neck and chest, a shadowy red under the glare of the flashlight. A silver cross lay on his throat.

Burke squeezed his fists together, and for a second, his anger surged out again. How dare this killer wear a cross?

Burke exhaled a mouthful of air, telling himself to calm down. To his surprise, an overwhelming curiosity suddenly overcame him. Why would the killer wear a cross?

The killer's lips quivered, opened, mumbled something. More and more intrigued, Burke looked at Jackie. "He's trying to say something," he said.

Jackie bent down to the supine man. He mumbled again. Jackie rose up and stared at Burke, confusion etched on her brow. "He wants you," she said.

Quickly Burke dropped both knees to the cold ground and lowered his ear to the man's face.

The killer's lips opened again.

"He is . . . faithful and . . ." The words trailed off—weak and faint.

Burke swallowed and pushed himself closer still, his hands resting on the killer's open coat. The warm breath of the bleeding man caressed his cheek.

"Yes," Burke said. "I'm here."

The killer jerked up suddenly, grabbing Burke by the front of his jacket. A pair of black eyes blinked open, then stared full into Burke's face. Jackie cocked her pistol, but Burke threw up his hand.

"Hold it," he shouted, peering into the black eyes. "He's not going anywhere."

For several seconds, Burke waited, his eyes glued into those that had a few minutes ago wanted to see him dead. To his amazement, the black eyes seemed to soften as he looked into them. Burke sensed something happening behind the eyes, something he couldn't explain or understand. The eyes widened, the lips of the killer moved again, and for a second, the words sounded out stronger. "If we confess . . . our sin . . . he is . . ." The words faltered again, and the man lay his head back on the ground.

A surge of confusion washed over Burke. He gripped the man's coat in his hands.

The man lifted his fingers to his neck and touched the bloody cross dangling from his throat. "If we confess . . ." he mumbled, his voice breathy.

With a sense of awe, Burke suddenly understood. The killer was quoting Scripture! First John 1:9. It all made sense. The killer had to know Scripture in order to do what he had done. If he knew Scripture then maybe, just maybe, somewhere along the line, he had believed the Scripture, accepted it, trusted it. Perhaps somewhere in his past, this man had sought to follow God, to live as a believer in Jesus Christ.

But tragedy had happened, tragedy had entered his life and wrecked his spirit, chewed it up, sent it spinning off into sin, evil, murder, death.

But now as he faced death himself, he was coming back to it, coming back to what he once believed and trusted.

Though not sure if his theory were correct, Burke took a deep breath and completed the words of the verse. "If we confess our sins, he is faithful and just and will forgive us our sins and purify us from all unrighteousness."

The killer nodded slightly, and Burke breathed a quick prayer, asking God for enough courage to do what he was about to do. He acknowledged to himself that he didn't really want to do it. Didn't want to do it because this man had killed—again and again and again. This man deserved death and the hell that would surely follow it. But Burke knew that was not what God wanted for this man.

Staring into the man's angular face, Burke knew that God wanted something else.

A sense of remorse suddenly overcame Burke. The man was a killer, yes, but he was also a human being, a human being for whom Jesus had given his life.

For a moment, Burke wondered what had happened in this man's life to create such hatred within his soul. He wondered how he would have reacted if the same things had happened to him.

A tug of tears pushed toward Burke's eyes as he recognized his own self-righteousness. All he had wanted was revenge! Revenge on this killer during the Advent season. He was no better than the killer. Within his heart crouched anger too—the anger that was the mother of murder.

His hands shaking, Burke swallowed hard. He knew what he had to do.

"Do you want to confess?" he asked, his voice quivering. "Do you want to confess your sins?"

The killer nodded, and the black eyes glistened. Burke's eyes watered, too, and his heart pounded through his chest. This poor creature deserved justice, yes, justice for the four people he had killed. But he also deserved pity, pity for the pain that had driven him to such desperate and evil deeds.

"Do you believe that God will forgive you?" whispered Burke.

The killer nodded and tears filled his eyes, running down his cheeks and dripping onto the snow. Watching the tears, Burke prayed for his own forgiveness—forgiveness for his desire for revenge—forgiveness because he had wanted death for the killer, death with no hope for redemption.

His voice cracking, Burke asked a final question.

"Do you believe in Jesus Christ as the forgiver of all sin?"

The killer closed his eyes and nodded a third time. His slender fingers lifted the bloody cross from his neck and touched it to his lips. The tears on his face were a river now, a river of release, flooding out of his soul. His body relaxed and he sagged away from Burke's grasp, the cross falling from his lips back onto his neck. The Advent killer was dead.

For several seconds, no one moved. Snow dropped on the man's still form, the whiteness blanketing the blood seeping into the ground.

Burke reached for the bloody cross lying across the man's neck. He touched it. For an instant he wondered if the killer's repentance were real. But then he concluded it wasn't up to him to judge. God would decide that.

Holding the cross in his hand now, Burke felt a surge of adrenaline pump through him. A truth he'd known since childhood, but one he'd never really tested until this moment, dawned on him.

The cross of Jesus was for everyone who would accept it—even the worst ones. The love that drove the cross into the ground knew no boundaries. The baby born to die on that cross offered a grace to everyone who would accept it. The power of that grace exceeded even the power of the most despicable evil. Where sin abounded, grace abounded all the more.

Wiping the tears off his face, Burke stood and turned to Debbi. Jackie bent down to the body.

"It's Christmas," Burke said, hugging Debbi close. "It's time to go home."

"Burke, you need to see this."

Startled, Burke twisted around to Jackie. Her mouth dropped open as she waved him over. Burke held out his hand to help her up. She pushed his hand away. Tears glistened on her cheeks.

"Are you okay, Jackie?" he asked, squatting down beside her.

She started to sob, her body shaking with grief. Debbi knelt down with Burke and Jackie and put her arms across her friend's back. "It's okay," soothed Debbi. "You had to do it. He gave you no choice but to shoot."

Jackie pointed her flashlight at the slain killer. "No, it's not that," she said. "It's . . ." her voice faltered as her crying overcame her.

Burke's eyes left Jackie and followed the beam of the flashlight. The light cut through the dark night, focusing on the chest of the dead man.

Burke's heart sank, and his pupils dilated as he stared below the cross lying at the base of the man's neck. He gripped Debbi's hand. Below the cross he saw what he'd missed in all the frenzy of the past few minutes. Below the cross he saw the slender but unmistakable swell of the figure of a woman.

Chapter 70

Monday, December 26

Throwing another log into the fireplace, Burke turned away from the blaze and faced the group crowded into his den. Hal Staton rested in the recliner, Bobbie Benton slouched on the sofa, Reginald Voss stood by the Christmas tree, and Karl Drexler had pulled up a kitchen chair next to him. Each of them held either a cup of coffee or a glass of tea.

Rubbing his hands on his thighs, Burke smiled at Debbi—she and Jackie Broadus sat in a pair of straight-backed rockers brought in from the porch. The fire behind him popped, and its heat scorched through the back of his jeans. He stepped one stride away from the fire.

"I'm glad we could get together this afternoon," he began. "Even though it is the day after Christmas."

"We needed this," said Hal, "or at least I needed it.'"

"I'm with you, buddy," chimed in Bobbie Benton. "The minute I heard what happened, I wanted to jump in the truck, round everybody up, and—I don't know—talk about it, talk about it together. I'm just sorry we couldn't do this yesterday."

"That's the way I felt too," said Hal, "but we all needed to be with our families."

Burke nodded. "That's what I thought," he said. "Besides, the extra day gave Jackie time to filter through a few things." He turned to her. "Jackie, why don't you bring us up to date?"

Stopping her rocking, Jackie cleared her throat. "First, you should know that the governor's wife and her baby are going to be okay. The knife missed the vital organs, and her doctor delivered a healthy baby girl about 1:00 Sunday morning."

Behind Burke, the fire cracked and a collective sigh swept through the group. "A Christmas baby," said Debbi, her voice soft.

Karl Drexler sighed and leaned forward in his chair. The blinking of the Christmas tree lights played gently on his smooth face. "I still can't believe it was a woman," he said. "A woman who did these awful killings."

Jackie rocked forward in her chair. "But it was, Karl. A woman named Alexandra Maria Forster. She was the adopted daughter—the only child by the way—of a wealthy Atlanta couple. When they died, she got their money. She used it to get ready for this, to pay for her revenge."

"She'd been abused?" It was Voss who spoke—his rich voice low.

"Yes," said Jackie. "Just like the media reported it. Her diaries described it pretty plainly. It happened when she was eleven, living as a foster child in a preacher's home in North Carolina. Three years ago, when she turned thirty, she went to the Holy Land. The diaries say that's when she started planning this. That's when she cracked—her psyche broke while she was in Jerusalem. Seeing the places where Jesus lived and taught drove her over the edge. She was a believer as a child, but the pain of the sexual abuse boiled over in Israel."

"The fact that she was abused don't give her no excuse," said Benton. "No excuse at all."

"I didn't say it did," said Jackie.

"But something snapped in her," interjected Voss. "I can understand how it might happen. If somebody abused one of my girls, I would want revenge on them, too, just like this woman did for herself."

"But would you kill somebody to get your revenge?" asked Jackie.

The whole group stared at Voss, awaiting his answer. He pushed his silver hair from his eyes.

"I can't say what I would do," he said. "I might kill. I might not. Who can know until they're in that situation."

"But we didn't hurt her," said Hal. "That's what gets me. Why did she have to do this to us? She didn't even know us!" He turned to Burke as if expecting him to explain it.

Burke shoved his hands into his pockets. "I can't tell you why, Hal, and I don't think it helps much to look for a rational explanation," he said. "When someone breaks, they don't act in normal patterns. Alexandra Forster broke; she flipped over the edge. She picked you because you represented God to her. As former workers in the church, you symbolized the God she hated. She picked you out because of that."

"But why our wives?" pleaded Benton. "Let her come after me, that's okay, but why'd she have to kill my Rosey?"

Jackie raised her hand. "She explained that in her diaries too. She blamed the wives as much as she did the husbands. Said the wife knew of the abuse but didn't stop it. She hated the one who stood by and did nothing."

"Which is why she hated God," said Burke.

"Exactly, just like her diaries said it."

"She hated God because God didn't stop the man who abused her."

For several moments, the group fell silent again. The lights on the Christmas tree blinked on and off.

"Any idea who that man was?" asked Voss.

Jackie hung her head. "I can't say," she said.

"You know but you can't say, or you don't know so you can't say?" pressed Voss.

Jackie held up her hand. "We have a name from her diaries, but we can't say who it is until we've had time to investigate," said Jackie. "Derrick Role would kill me if he knew I'd told you as much as I have. So don't ask me anything else."

Voss refused to back off. "So the man who abused her is still alive?" he asked.

"If her diary is right, then yes."

"What'll happen to him?"

"We'll investigate, see what we can find out. See if we can locate anyone else from this man's past who will come forward. But you've got to remember, it's been twenty-two years since this alleged abuse. And all we have as evidence is the written diary of a dead serial killer. That's not a lot to go on."

"So whoever did this might never get punished?" Hal asked the question this time.

Jackie sighed. "Actually, there's almost no chance he'll get punished."

For several moments the room fell silent. The fire crackled behind Burke. He shoved his hand into his pockets.

"I know who did it," said Burke. "I know who it was."

All eyes immediately turned and riveted on him.

"You know?" asked Jackie, her voice registering disbelief.

Burke nodded. "Yes, I know. It was the governor. Edward Robert Stapleton. He's the man who abused Alexandra Forster twenty-two years ago."

"What makes you say that?" asked Jackie, her surprise showing in her wide eyes.

Burke pulled his hands from his pockets and sighed. "It all makes sense. Everything Alexandra did showed a pattern. The final death had to fit that pattern. And it did. When I came home Christmas morning, I stayed up most of the night trying to piece it together.

"I knew the final killing would fit the pattern. It was, after all, the grand finale—the effort to kill the wife of the man who stood by and did nothing. I kept throwing it around. Why the governor's wife?

"It had to be because the governor fit the pattern—the religious pattern of serving in the church. I asked Debbi to help out, and she did. We spent most of last night and this morning at the newspaper sorting through the computer, pulling up everything we could find on the governor's background. What we found made it obvious.

"All of us know the governor and his wife couldn't have children all these years. The computer reminded Debbi and me that they did have adopted children. Three to be exact. The governor has pointed more than once to his generosity in taking in these poor children so long ago.

"His biography also revealed that he had graduated from a Baptist college in North Carolina—with a major in religion no less. The biography also noted, though I have to say only briefly, that the governor pastored a church in North Carolina almost twenty-three years ago.

"So it all fits with what Jackie has just told us. Alexandra Forster was taken into a foster home twenty-two years ago in North Carolina. The same year the governor pastored there. He's the one who abused her. I have no doubt about it."

"But you still can't prove he abused her," said Jackie. "Even if he were her foster parent, that's no evidence of sexual abuse. As much as I wish it were different, the diaries of a serial killer won't be enough. He's too popular, and the crime was too long ago."

"I just hope Alexandra was the only one," said Burke.

"And I hope and pray this new baby won't suffer a similar fate," said Debbi, voicing the fear they all held.

For several beats no one spoke. The Christmas tree lights blinked on and off, on and off. Finally Hal stood up from the recliner, his head bowed toward the floor.

"There's a lot of bad in this world, isn't there?" he asked.

Karl Drexler left his chair by the fireplace and stepped toward Hal. He put his arm around his shoulders. "Yes, there is, Hal. There's a lot of bad in this old world."

"And God doesn't prevent it?"

"Nope, God doesn't prevent it."

"Then what's our hope? If God don't prevent it, then what's our hope?"

Drexler didn't answer. The fire crackled. Drexler sighed. "I can't rightly answer that right now, Hal. I know what I should say, but right now I'm too broken up to speak it." Shaking his head, he moved away from Hal, back to his chair.

Burke sighed and looked from one face to another in the quiet room—to Bobbie Benton, Karl Drexler, Reginald Voss, Jackie Broadus, Debbi. Turning from them, he faced the fireplace mantel. With trembling fingers, he picked up the Bible that lay there and pivoted back to the group. They followed him with their eyes, watching his every move.

He held the Bible up in the air. "I know of only one hope to offer you," he said. They all kept silent.

He opened the Bible to Matthew 1. He took a deep breath and began to read, his voice a whisper.

> But after he had considered this, an angel of the Lord appeared to him in a dream and said, "Joseph son of David, do not be afraid to take Mary home as your wife, because what is conceived in her is from the Holy Spirit. She will give birth to a son, and you are to give him the name Jesus, because he will save his people from their sins."

Quietly, Burke closed the Bible, laid it back on the mantle and moved over to Debbi. She stood from her chair. Burke locked his arm around her waist. She turned to Jackie, who also stood. The two women clasped hands.

Bobbie Benton pulled himself from the sofa and Karl Drexler rose out of his kitchen chair. Now they were all standing.

Jackie offered a hand to Bobbie Benton. He took it and faced Reginald Voss. Voss grabbed Benton and then Drexler, and Hal joined the circle, too, each of them holding to another.

Burke stared again into the faces of the group. His words fell gently from his lips. "You heard what the Bible said. 'You are to give him the name Jesus, because he will save his people from their sins.' That's all the hope I can offer. If we'll believe it, Jesus will save us from the evil within us all."

To his left, Hal squeezed his hand. "That's enough hope for me," he said.

"That's enough hope for all of us," said Jackie.

Behind Burke, the fire crackled. Beside him, the lights on the Christmas tree blinked. Inside him, his spirit soared. Jackie was right. It was enough hope for everybody.

About the Author

Gary E. Parker, a Ph.D. graduate from Baylor University, is the senior minister of the First Baptist Church of Jefferson City, Missouri. His wife is Melody, and his two daughters are Ashley and Andrea. When he's not with his family or at work, Gary enjoys cycling, golfing, and reading. This is his seventh book and his third novel.

Also read Gary Parker's first book about Burke Anderson,

Beyond a Reasonable Doubt

Pastor Burke Anderson has a serious problem.

All the evidence in the Carol Reese murder is pointing to him—and he can't account for where he was when it happened.

Though Burke knows he is innocent, everyone else is ready to condemn him when his Bible is found at the scene of the scandalous murder. Suspicious minds in the church become judge and jury, and Burke's guilt is assumed by police and parishioners alike when he disappears right after the victim is discovered.

Running from the guilt of temptation and self-doubt, the betrayal of his church, and the letter of the law, Burke finds one person—a young female reporter—who believes he might be innocent. Together they begin a search that becomes more than they bargained for . . . it could cost them their lives.

A preview of Gary Parker's next book,

Suffer the Children

Bethany Chapman, a twenty-nine-year-old divorcée, goes to pick up Stacy, her twenty-month-old daughter, from her mother, who keeps the child during the day while Bethany works. To her horror, Bethany finds her mother's yard filled with police cars and her mother distraught with fear. Stacy is missing.

Already in counseling with Burke Anderson, a Christian psychologist, Bethany goes to him with her grief, anxiety, and anger. She suspects her ex-husband, a police detective with a hidden pattern of abusive behavior toward her, has taken Stacy. On numerous occasions, he threatened this very action. Knowing Anderson's previous history with criminal investigations, Bethany asks him to help her check out her husband.

Burke, though, refuses to get involved. He believes it isn't his place to interfere with police work. In the past, his interference has gotten him into trouble, and he doesn't want to face that again.

The police, protective of one of their own, point their suspicions about Stacy's disappearance at Bethany. Her history of mental struggle makes them wonder if she didn't perhaps harm her own child and then seek to place the blame on someone else.

As circumstances add up, it seems the cops are correct. They move to arrest Bethany for the murder of her own child. Aware of the closing noose around her neck, Bethany flees to Burke and Debbi Anderson and asks for their help.

That night, before the police find Bethany, a second child disappears. Within two weeks, two other children in and around Atlanta disappear from their homes. Each one comes from a divorced family. Each one disappears without a trace and with almost no clues as to the identity of the abductor. Of the four missing children, three are white and one is Hispanic. Each is from a low income family.

The police suggest a number of suspects: 1) one or the other of the parents of the children; 2) a suspected satanic cult using the children for some unknown but doubtless horrifying purpose; 3) a single serial killer.

Tragically, one of the children, the Hispanic boy, turns up dead.

Driven by fear for her own child and unhappy with police efforts to find Stacy, Bethany Chapman walks closer and closer to the abyss of insanity. Only Burke and Debbi Anderson stand between her and total collapse.

Out of concern for Bethany, Burke and Debbi begin to investigate a few things for themselves. Why are the children from divorced families? Why is the Hispanic child the one found dead? Why are all the children under two years of age?

Using information gathered from Debbi's newspaper connections, Burke begins to unravel the mystery.